THE GATHERING STORM

HIGHWAY TO HELL

BOOK THREE

J.D. TOEPFER

PROLOGUE

Melanie Hartwell, a recently engaged 28-year-old redhead, rubbed her hand several times across the fogged windshield of her white Chevy Volt, trying to get a clearer view.

"Damn it! I can't see a thing out there. I've never seen fog like this before in my life. Hell, this is worse than when I lived in San Francisco!"

Gripping the steering wheel tighter, the insurance underwriter chastised herself for not having the intelligence to get her car serviced and the defroster fixed before driving 400 miles from Hartford, Connecticut, to Charlottesville for Thanksgiving.

If I had worked late last night, I could have left after breakfast instead of lunchtime today and avoided this altogether.

"UGH!" She slammed her hand down on the steering wheel.

Wishing she had insisted that Robert, her fiancé, join her rather than letting him go home to Denver, she flipped the radio on for some company. Instead, a blast of static reverberated through the car. Melanie turned the volume down but did not turn the radio off, finding some comfort in the noise.

She thought about Robert's concerns about her driving alone. The fog intensified, and Melanie slowed down to avoid inadvertently running into the back of another vehicle or possibly hitting a deer. A strange tingling sensation ran down her spine, causing her to shudder. It instantly felt colder.

Melanie exhaled, and a cloud of water vapor condensed before her. She tried to adjust the heat, but only lukewarm air came out of the vent.

"I'm not sure this shortcut was such a good idea," she murmured.

Last night, a rerun of *Unsolved Mysteries*, one of her favorite shows, aired a story about the Route 29 Stalker. From 2009 to 2014, five young women disappeared without a trace while traveling between Manassas and Charlottesville, Virginia. After watching the segment and finding out that no arrests were made or bodies recovered, Melanie decided to take an alternate route and picked up Route 28 in Centreville instead. Unfortunately, the road was one stoplight after another, which slowed her progress to that of a snail.

Suddenly, Melanie was startled by a series of blinding flashes of light that appeared in the rearview mirror. Squinting, she shouted,

"C'mon, dude. Turn off the brights!"

Instead, rotating blue and red lights materialized, further illuminating the fog.

Feeling relieved at the sight of a police car, she wondered if her brake light was out again.

I thought Robert had fixed that.

Melanie carefully pulled onto the shoulder and parked the car, leaving the motor running. The fog seemed even thicker now. While the flashing lights were still visible, it was impossible to see anything else. She expected to see a policeman, but no one appeared. She tried to dial 911, but there was no signal, and her phone would not connect. Anxiously, ignoring her instincts telling her not to, Melanie pulled the handle to open the car door.

* * *

The door opened. An indicator that everything was going as planned. The shape crept forward like a wolf hunting prey while the vehicle's driver emerged. A towering figure, it could assume any form it chose, human or otherwise. Slowly stalking the occupant, using the fog as cover, its acute hearing affirmed the sound of a beating heart, quickening with each second. A sniff of the air confirmed it was a young woman—the preferred target.

* * *

Melanie leaned out but saw nothing. She had not seen another car since she left Manassas, and slowly, nervously, she exited the vehicle.

What the hell is happening? I don't like this. I don't like it at all.

Her nerves and the frosty air caused Melanie to shiver, and she strained to see someone or something through the dense fog. As she slowly stepped forward, she ran her finger along the side of the car to the trunk. Checking the brake lights, she found them in working order.

For a moment, the clouds parted, and the full moon cast a ray of light, faintly illuminating the silent night. She saw what she thought was the outline of a figure.

"Is there someone there?" The murkiness absorbed her voice.

* * *

The thirst pushed the shape closer. A hunger that was never satisfied. An acquired taste for humans that was unquenchable. Moving in for the kill, all it heard was her heavy breathing. All it felt was her body heat. Only steps away, she could do nothing. The shape ruled the night and the darkness.

Suddenly, the flashing lights vanished, and the moonlight disappeared behind the clouds. Two bright yellow eyes with intense red pupils were before her, gazing down at Melanie. She backpedaled at first. Then she stopped, mesmerized by the hypnotic stare. A peaceful feeling gripped Melanie, and a strong desire for sleep overwhelmed her.

She felt herself slumping to the ground, but a pair of muscular arms scooped her up before she fell. Soon, no trace of Melanie Hartwell remained except for a single shoe on the shoulder next to the open car door. The only noise was a voice from the radio of the idling vehicle.

"It's nearly Thanksgiving, and this is open mic Tuesday on the Mark Grant show. That means you, the listeners, determine what we talk about tonight. To kick things off, let's go to the suburbs. Tim from Manassas, you're on the Mark Grant show?"

"Thanks for taking my call, Mark."

"Certainly, Tim. What's on your mind?"

"Mark, I want to talk about the Route 28 Phantom."

"Go ahead."

"I have a theory on the Phantom; I think it's something paranormal..."

CHAPTER 1

> 65 Million Years Ago
> Kingdom of Hiti on the Continent of Mu, Now Lost
> Under the Present-Day South Pacific Ocean

The outstretched wings of a pterodactyl acted like a sail as it rode the updraft, almost touching the cotton-white clouds moving across the sapphire-blue sky. From the lush green jungle surrounding the walled city, an angry roar of a reptilian monster reverberated throughout Tuvalu, the capital of the Kingdom of Hiti. King Pohnpei, followed by his council of advisors and military commanders, entered the enormous courtyard to greet a visitor, an unexpected and unwelcome guest.

The refreshing ocean breeze could not dry the bead of sweat that fell from the king's tanned forehead. Despite decades of living under the hot sun and the pressure of being king, Pohnpei retained his youthful appearance and had no wrinkles on his forehead. He rubbed his wiry red beard as he moved across the ornate marble floor and stood before his black, alabaster throne. The rare stone, shipped to Hiti long ago, symbolized Pohnpei's regal origins. Those surrounding the king were kneeling with their heads lowered, but the visitor stood arrogantly.

The polished armor of the royal guards reflected the sun. With their swords unsheathed, they approached a gruesome figure basking in the oppressive heat. It stood nearly eight feet tall with bony reptilian skin like black leather, pointed ears akin to a dog, and large fangs protruding from its jaws. The hooded black robe it wore with a gold belt around the waist could not conceal the hulking, muscular physique underneath.

"Kneel before the King!" the commander of the guards demanded!

Lucius Rofocale, the demonic messenger of Satan, squinted at the guards with his piercing red eyes afire. Snapping his elongated, clawed fingers, he immolated the commander, whose screams echoed through the courtyard. Lucius thundered,

"It seems that another lesson in obedience is in order! The slaughter of your brothers in arms during my previous visit does not appear to have had the impact I desired."

King Pohnpei, dressed in a purple robe, the color of royalty, raised his hand.

"Enough of this!"

Never taking their eyes off Lucius, the guards retreated.

"I was not expecting you." The king glanced at the smoldering remains of the captain of the guards and, stepping down from the throne, stood in front of Lucius.

Pohnpei towered over the demon envoy. At fourteen feet tall, he was nearly double Lucius's size and attempted to use his height to intimidate his adversary.

"If I knew you were coming, I might have been better prepared."

Lucius smirked, amused at the king's bluster, and locked eyes with the monarch. He sensed a change in Pohnpei. During their last meeting, he saw fear in the king's face, but this time, he detected confidence and assertiveness on the borderline of defiance. Satan's henchman eyeballed the king unpleasantly.

"No doubt it would have been a warmer welcome."

Then, there was silence. It was a seemingly endless moment as each tried to make the other stand down. The smell of sulfur emanating from Lucius's pores and the stench of burnt flesh engulfed them. It forced King Pohnpei to cough and break their test of wills.

Turning toward the onlookers, Lucius bellowed, "I am here to fulfill Lucifer's edict! The men will board the boats moored in the harbor. Women and children will assemble here in the piazza for processing."

"You mean extermination, do you not?" the king angrily countered. "We know what happened to the wives, sons, and daughters of the Quinametzin tribe."

Lucius's piercing eyes narrowed as he sneered, "Do you? Well, euthanasia is far more merciful in comparison to your fate."

The sovereign ruler of the Hiti flexed his massive muscles, nearly bursting the seams of his regal robe, and asserted boldly, "I think not, Lucius. It is time for a new agreement."

In a show of force and solidarity, leaders of dozens of other tribes, steely-eyed and determined as Pohnpei, emerged from buildings bordering the courtyard. They surrounded Lucius.

"Do you think we are negotiating?" Lucius scoffed as he surveyed the growing crowd of allies. "I assure you that I do not bargain. Failure to comply will cause my demon legions to destroy your city."

The oil from Lucius's slick, jet-black hair began to smolder as his anger swelled. Through his clenched teeth, he seethed, "You will watch me butcher your women and children without mercy before I slowly pull the skin from your bodies."

Suddenly, a powerful voice emanated from the crowd. It was a voice that Lucius knew well.

"Whose demon legions, Lucius?"

"Kazimir," Lucius muttered, then angrily asked, "What are you doing here?"

A figure appeared, similar in height to Lucius, with a patch over his right eye and long, blond hair tied back in a ponytail. Charismatic and brutally handsome, he was as powerful as Lucius but also held the allegiance of the demon legions. Kazimir had earned their loyalty through his exploits in battle, having lost his eye at the hands of Saint Michael himself.

Surveying the crowd, Kazimir remarked, "Getting you out of trouble, it appears, brother."

Lucius preferred to rule the legions through terror, believing it better to be feared than loved. He despised his brother and felt inferior to him in many ways. Most of all, he feared Kazimir's power and influence with Lucifer.

"Your assistance, I do not need," Lucius growled.

Kazimir looked over his shoulder at the mob. "Brother, you are viewing all of this incorrectly."

Lucius stormed, "I am following Lucifer's wishes!"

Circling Kazimir, eyeing him warily, Lucius demanded, "You even present yourself as one of them. If you love these humans so much, why did you not stop me from killing the commander?"

"These humans are indeed inferior," Kazimir countered. "But they can be a useful resource and should not be discarded like trash. Besides," Kazimir went on. "To subdue an enemy, it is sometimes easier to look like them."

"Enemy, Kazimir?" Lucius scoffed. "That would imply they are my equal." Lucius screamed, "They are vermin and need to be exterminated!"

The mob, incensed by Lucius's statements and growing more unruly by the second, began closing in on him. Lucius started to remove his robe, preparing to do battle.

Kazimir put up his hands to stop his brother. "Wait. Look."

Pointing toward the harbor, Kazimir showed Lucius that the legions had returned to their ships.

"Go home, Lucius," Kazimir advised. "I will handle these humans."

Enraged and humiliated, Lucius glared at King Pohnpei. "This is far from over." Sarcastically, he finished his sentence, "Your Highness." Turning to Kazimir, Lucius threatened, "Revenge will be mine! You can count on that, brother!"

*　*　*

> *Several Days Later*
> *The throne room at Pergamon, Satan's Earthly Residence*
> *in the Present-Day Republic of Turkiye*

Perched on a mesa of volcanic rock, the white columns of the acropolis stood like a spire over the valley. The sides of the summit at Pergamon fell away on the north, west, and east, with the citadel's entrance facing south, forever absorbing the sun's intense heat. A fuming Lucifer paced around the pentagram of black basalt embedded in the throne room floor as steam from the active volcano below filled the oven-like chamber.

"I sent for both of you!" Lucifer roared. "Where is that brother of yours, Lucius?"

"I do not know, my Lord." Lucius hesitated, then continued, "Am I my brother's keeper?"

Lucifer shot Lucius a look. To most, it would have felt like a dagger. "Not amusing, Lucius. If I were you, I would keep your jokes to yourself."

Having been rebuked, Lucius responded sheepishly, "Yes, my Lord."

Each second that passed caused Satan's anger to build, his leather-like skin becoming an extreme hue of red until it appeared as if he were on fire.

Finally, Kazimir appeared in the room. His skin was like Lucius's, but the color of cobalt blue. A blond mohawk bisected his ears, which were smaller with a less pronounced point. His dark red lips hid rows of sharp, piranha-like teeth, and coal-black pupils were at the center of his yellow eyes.

"Do you realize how long you have kept me waiting?" Lucifer screamed.

"I am truly sorry, my Lord." Kazimir squinted furiously at Lucius, realizing his brother had purposely told him the wrong time for their gathering.

Lucifer clenched his jaw.

"What could be more important than meeting with me, Kazimir?"

"Cleaning up a mess—"

Lucifer interrupted, "A mess you created!"

Kazimir stuttered, "But, but my Lord—"

"My orders for dealing with humans were unambiguous," Lucifer yelled. "They are to be exterminated!"

Usually cocky and self-assured, Kazimir was apologetic. "I am sorry, my Lord, I merely thought—"

"You thought what, Kazimir?" Lucifer challenged in a voice filled with cynicism.

"He views these humans as useful, as if they are an asset," Lucius interjected mockingly. Lucius twisted the knife further, "I also much prefer how you appear now, Kazimir, than when you paraded around like one of them."

Staring at Lucius, Kazimir scowled, and the lines on his forehead tightened. Ignoring Lucius's insult, he defended his actions, "If we eliminate the human race, who will build our temples and monuments?"

"You mean my temples and monuments," Lucifer abruptly corrected him.

"Yes, my Lord," Kazimir agreed. "Your temples and monuments." Kazimir continued to drive home his argument, "Forced labor is necessary for building our new society here on Earth."

Lucifer rubbed his clawed hand across his chin as he considered Kazimir's rationale.

"Would it not be a greater insult to your Father, my Lord, to turn these humans away from God?" Kazimir asserted. "Make them the rebels and convince them that they created themselves. This corruption of humankind would demonstrate your greatness!"

Lucius smiled unpleasantly and sprung the trap he had set for Kazimir. Lucius did not want Kazimir gone; he wanted him dead.

"This is not the first time he has interfered with your edicts, Master. Perhaps Kazimir can explain why, instead of eliminating the Cuauhtemoc, Tenexuche, and Xeliluna tribes, he used them to build a temple in a place called the Yucatan. A monolithic pyramid that glorifies himself!"

Kazimir immediately defended himself, "Master, I meant no disrespect, and I do not intend to be critical of your proclamations. I only wanted to show you the value of keeping humans alive."

Eyeing Lucius, Kazimir declared, "As to who the temple glorifies, come see for yourself."

"Instead of planning revenge on my Father..." Lucifer closed his eyes. "I spend more time preventing another civil war between the two of you."

Staring at Kazimir and then at Lucius, Satan continued, "That Grand Canyon in the northern continent bears witness to the destruction of which you are both capable."

Steam rose from his body as Lucifer sat down on his diamond-encrusted throne.

"My greatness, Kazimir, would best be demonstrated by turning humans and their world to ashes!"

A long, uncomfortable silence came over the chamber before Lucifer finally broke it.

"Kazimir, you will return to this pyramid in the Yucatan until I call upon you." Lucifer eyeballed Kazimir suspiciously. "Consider yourself in exile. Under no circumstances are you to interfere with your brother's orders. Are we clear on this point?"

"Yes, Master. I hear and obey." A subdued Kazimir bowed and disappeared.

Lucifer scowled and turned to Lucius. "Keep a close eye on your brother."

Lucius bowed, hiding his gloating. "As you wish, my Lord."

* * *

> **Later That Same Day**
> **Lucius Rofocale's Chambers at Pergamon**

"Agares, let us go through the plan one last time," Lucius insisted.

"You will return to Kazimir's fortress and, using your ability to manipulate the sand, create an artificial legion army. Then, march that army toward the sea as if it were going to war."

Agares placed his clawed fingers on his mentor's shoulder.

"Trust me, Lucius. My loyalty to you is equal to yours to Lucifer. I will not fail you."

"I know, my friend. Your covert work in Kazimir's lair has been invaluable."

Tapping his lips with his bony, elongated fingers, Lucius silently reviewed their plan. It was true that Kazimir had the loyalty of the legions. Still, Lucius, using his control over the bureaucracy, had slowly constructed his power base, and now he was ready to strike.

Looking at Agares, Lucius smiled menacingly. "Lucifer will do more than clip Kazimir's wings by banishing him. He will remove this thorn in my side for good this time."

Lucius continued, rubbing the leather-like skin on his chin with his black fingernails, "Humans are a virus, and we must stop the spread. Lucifer's views on humans mirror our own. We only need to show him Kazimir's disloyalty. With their advocate out of the way, we will be free to exterminate humanity once and for all."

* * *

Kazimir's Palace in Present-Day Yucatan Peninsula, Mexico

Kazimir slowly ascended the 666 steps of the face of the pyramid. As he climbed, Kazimir admired hieroglyphs of Satan's battle against Saint Michael, each painstakingly chiseled into the structure's stone. Reaching the flat summit of his citadel, he paused to take in the panoramic vista. A giant moon, bathed in the color of blood, dominated the pitch-black sky and illuminated the desert floor below. The sounds of the creatures of the darkness, including a lonely howl in the distance, echoed through the night. Reflecting on his meeting with Lucifer and his brother, Kazimir empathized with the animal, seemingly crying out for company.

"My Lord, welcome home," a familiar voice greeted Kazimir.

"Grigori." Kazimir smiled weakly. "It is good to be back."

Reading Kazimir's face, Grigori knew the meeting had not gone well.

The duo reached an elaborate rectangular portico shaped out of the acid-bleached bones of angels slain by Kazimir and started down a corridor. The pyramid, constructed of gray granite and black rock from the volcanic bowels of the Earth, had nine concentric circles with frescos and murals glorifying the deadly sins.

The passageways wound down through the massive monolith, ending in a great hall adorned with Kazimir's weapons of war and a throne fastened from the rocks of the heavens that sometimes struck the planet. A throne dedicated to Lucifer's glory and on which only the King of Hell could sit.

Kazimir remained quiet the entire journey from the surface and threw himself into a chair in frustration. Finally, he broke the silence.

"Grigori, I failed to convince Lucifer to stop the extermination of humans. My powers of persuasion and rational arguments were futile. He and Lucius are united in their contempt and intense hatred of this race."

"A short-sighted vision on their part, my Lord," Grigori declared.

Recalling his nearly treasonous challenge to Lucifer's policies, Kazimir warned, "Be careful who you share that belief with, Grigori. Lucius has infiltrated our ranks, and such a statement is punishable by death."

"But I don't understand, Kazimir," Grigori persisted. "You bravely fought, side by side, with Lucifer and even lost your eye to Saint Michael. It seems to carry no weight with the Master."

"I fear Lucius has convinced Lucifer that I am a threat to him, Grigori. I am banished here until Lucifer calls upon me."

"Lucius," Grigori growled. "He is the real serpent."

Kazimir leaned back in his chair and closed his eyes.

"Grigori, Lucius loves Lucifer, as I do. The problem is that he loves power and intrigue almost as much as the Master."

Slamming his fist on the table, Grigori declared, "The legions are behind you, Kazimir!"

An angry Kazimir yelled, "Grigori! You are my most loyal aide, but I cannot tolerate such talk. It is treason!"

"Please forgive me, Kazimir," Grigori apologized. "I didn't mean to—"

Interrupting Grigori, Kazimir shook his head and waved his hand. "No, forgive me, my friend. I am as frustrated as you. Lucifer pits my brother and me against one another. Our animosity runs deep, and Lucifer uses that to keep us at one another's throats. He pretends to be annoyed by having to arbitrate our differences, but he is testing us and our loyalty to him."

Grigori sighed. "So what do we do, Kazimir?"

Kazimir ran his fingers through his long blond locks. "I am not sure, Grigori, but we must prepare ourselves. Lucius is up to something; I can feel it."

* * *

Several Days Later
Lucifer's Chambers at Pergamon

"Here you go again, on and on about still another new plan to attack Heaven." Lucifer squeezed his lower lip between his claws. "Lucius, I am tired of your talk. Your incessant scheming gives me a headache."

"I apologize, my Lord," Lucius pleaded. "I am eager to watch Heaven fall, but..."

"But what?" Satan frowned, rolling his eyes.

"We must harvest a significant number of pained and tormented souls to ensure a sufficient—"

Agares entered the chamber and prostrated himself on the floor at Lucifer's feet.

"Please pardon my intrusion, Master. There is an urgent message for you."

"Get up," Lucifer ordered. "What is it?"

Glancing at Lucius, Agares gulped and nervously answered, "It—it's Kazimir, my Lord."

Lucifer's eyes narrowed, and he stared icily at Agares. "Go on."

"Large groups of demon legions are marching toward ships anchored in the harbor a short distance from Kazimir's headquarters."

Satan ground his yellow teeth angrily. "Are they?"

With a bejeweled, golden chalice in his hand, Lucius stepped next to Agares.

"Shall we see for ourselves, Master?" Lucius questioned.

Agares's eyes opened wide with shock when Lucius's serrated fingernail quickly rushed across his throat. Agares gurgled and gasped for air while his thick, blue blood flowed into Lucius's cup, held steadily under the lethal wound. Agares dropped to the ground, and Lucius stirred the blood with his bony index finger. A picture slowly emerged in the viscous contents of the chalice. An image of thousands of soldiers marching in step with one another came into view.

"Come with me, Lucius," Lucifer insisted, as his steely tone could not hide his escalating rage.

Satan angrily threw open the heavy wooden doors to the room where his demon courtiers were gathering, leaving nothing but splinters on the hinges. The mirrors and artwork shook on the hall's walls, and the evil nobility stepped back, fearing the King of Hell's wrath.

Standing in the middle of the room, Satan thundered, "Let this be a lesson for those who would perpetuate treason against me!"

Startled, demons throughout the hall stood agape, glancing at one another, attempting to identify the traitor in their midst.

"I exiled Kazimir for defying my order to eradicate humans." Whispers filled the room as Lucifer continued, "Now legions loyal to Kazimir are on the march."

Steam emanated from every pore of Satan's crimson, leather-like skin. His eyes blazed with a deep, fire-red glow. He screamed,

"Now, bear witness to the price of Kazimir's defiance and treachery! Scribes will erase Kazimir's name from every demon history book! From every document and memorandum! Stone masons will expunge his likeness from every monument! I will not hear his name again!"

A palpable feeling of terror gripped the hall, along with an eerie silence. No one spoke, and some even held their breath. Every face was open-mouthed, with one exception. Lucius Rofocale stood arrogantly with a grotesque smirk on his face.

"Do it," Lucius whispered to himself with anticipation. "Do it, now."

Still seething, Satan made one final declaration.

"The meaning of the name Kazimir is 'he who destroys the world.'"

Reaching toward the heavens, Lucifer cried, "SO BE IT!"

* * *

A ten-mile-across spherical body, floating in the asteroid belt between Mars and Jupiter, suddenly alters its infinite orbit around the sun and heads toward Earth. Composed primarily of iron and nickel, it is as hard as any object in existence and the size of a city. Billions of years old, it is one of the millions of space rocks left over from God's creation of the universe, but it has no immunity against the influence of evil.

Like a beacon, the Earth grows closer and closer, and the velocity of the meteor accelerates. Friction causes the solid mass to become enveloped in flames as it speeds through the atmosphere. Kazimir's supposed legions, once heading to the harbor, suddenly disappear back into the sand from which they arose. Right before impact, a deafening explosion rips through the Yucatan Peninsula, and a massive, mushroom-shaped cloud rises from the desert floor.

CHAPTER 2

September 1973, Labor Day Weekend
Jack & George Aitken's Childhood Home, Long Island, New York

The buzz of the window air conditioning unit sounded like a hive of angry bees, but it managed to keep the room cool. Still wearing shorts due to a late summer heatwave, and despite the comfortable temperature in his father's den, seven-year-old George Aitken found his bare legs sticking to the brown leather couch. He nervously shifted, trying to get comfortable, but it was impossible when he knew his father wanted to speak to him... alone. The heavy golden oak door closed, and the child stuttered with trepidation, "Did I—did I do something wrong, Dad?"

George Aitken Sr. towered over his son, looking like the Incredible Hulk in his green polyester slacks and matching collared golf shirt. He pulled up a chair and then sat in front of the boy. His large hand, big enough to crush a person's skull, at least as far as the young boy was concerned, tousled George's sweaty, light brown hair. Then, the usually stern man cracked a smile as he answered, "No, son. You're not in any trouble. But there is something I want to talk to you about. It concerns your brother, Jack."

Realizing he was not about to be destroyed, George relaxed a little. He innocently asked, "What about Jack? Did he do something wrong?"

George's father maintained his cheerful demeanor, saying, "No. Jack isn't in trouble either."

The youngster shrugged, unsure of what they were really talking about. Seemingly on cue, the din of the air conditioner ceased as it cycled off, and the smile on his father's face receded. The room grew quiet, and the second hand on the clock, hanging on the wall behind George, clicked several times before the elder Aitken spoke again.

"Did Jack have a lot of friends in kindergarten?"

Shaking his head from side to side, George answered, "No. My friends became his friends."

"That's right, and now you are both going into first grade. I'm worried Jack might have problems making friends again."

George squirmed and cast his eyes downward. He wasn't sure if he should tell his father Jack's secret. Sensing his son had something he needed to say, George Sr. placed his meaty index finger under the youngster's chin and raised it.

"Is there something you're not telling me?"

The boy's eyes darted in all directions before finally confessing, "Jack got beat up a lot. He asked me not to tell anyone."

"Is that why you got sent to the principal's office for fighting last year? You were protecting your brother?"

George just nodded. He leaned backward, avoiding eye contact, preparing for the storm he saw brewing in his father's hazel-green eyes. He anticipated the yelling to start at any moment. Instead, his father held out his hand. Apprehensively, George reciprocated until his hand disappeared inside his father's.

"That's exactly what I expect you to do for your brother."

* * *

Thursday, November 21st
Bradford House, Culpeper, Virginia
10:00 p.m.

George Aitken turned the handle, and cold water gushed from the rust-encrusted spigot jutting out from the stone wall above him. Exhausted from his massacre of the bikers, he slowly yanked the mildewed curtain across the opening to allow the water to get warmer and began removing the dirty rags he called clothes. George reveled in memories like his father telling him his responsibility was to protect his brother. He recalled the incident filled him with pride as his father congratulated him for doing so. It was one of the few things about his past that he could remember.

Stepping into the shower, simply a hole in the wall, seemed like entering a claustrophobically small closet. George closed his eyes and immersed himself in the torrent of lukewarm water flooding from the pipe. It was a tight squeeze, but he managed to turn around, feeling the water splatter across his sore shoulders. Opening his eyes, he examined the palm of his hand, which an hour earlier had held the beating heart he had ripped from the body of another human being.

The dried blood now fell like drops of rain from his fingertips. It collected at his feet, and the crimson water bubbled as the screen in the floor attempted to drain it away. What was it that Lucius had asked him?

Do you feel any remorse?

The question echoed in his ears.

Any conflicted emotions?

About killing the biker gang?

Turning the water off, he had to admit, there were none. What should have repulsed him, he found to be exhilarating. Water droplets fell from his matted, lumberjack-like beard and plunged into the still-draining water below. He grabbed a tattered gray cloth that had once been a towel and stopped to study his hand once more. The truth was he liked the power he felt over life and death. He liked it a lot.

Moving in front of a mirror, the rag wrapped around his waist, George admired his washboard abs. He ran his fingers across his rock-hard stomach and up to his tight pectoral muscles, stopping at a large scar on the nape of his neck. He inspected it and remarked, "How and where did I get this bite? Looks like an animal bite, but I just can't remember how or where I got it."

Shoving his foot into the pants leg of a new pair of blue jeans he found on a hook, George soon found himself lost in another childhood memory.

* * *

Late September 1973
The school Bus Stop Across from the Aitken Home

"You did a great job building that Lego castle!"

George Aitken ran his finger across the corner guard tower, admiring his twin brother's handiwork, and added, "I think Dad is going to like it too!"

"Cool!" Jack responded excitedly.

Sitting across from George, Jack carefully balanced the plastic fortress in his lap, protecting it from the bumpy bus ride home from school. Beaming with pride, he could not wait to show it to his parents. The brakes squeaked as the banana-yellow bus slowed down, approaching their stop.

"Big deal," a sarcastic voice from the seat behind them interrupted the brother's conversation. "Anyone could make that."

Jack's eyes dropped as Tommy Messina, the neighborhood bully, appeared above the back of the seat and weighed in on his building skills. Messina wore his hair short, buzzcut like a marine, and to the neighborhood kids, he acted like one. He was a head taller, bigger than all of them, and loved to push and order everyone around, Jack in particular. George eyed him warily as the bus stopped at the corner near their house.

Slowly walking down the aisle, his Lego masterpiece securely in his hands, Jack did not see Tommy push his way in front of George. As he exited the bus, Jack saw his mother standing on the stoop in front of their yellow house. He took a few steps and began to check both ways before crossing when someone slammed the Lego structure from his hands, sending it to the ground and shattering it. The sneak attack left Jack in disbelief, staring at the Lego pieces littering the street.

Halfway down the block, Tommy Messina laughed. Turning to taunt Jack some more, he instantly found himself flat on his back. Like an angry linebacker chasing down a running back in a football game, George flew through the air, tackled the bully, and began to wail at him.

"Leave my brother alone!" George shouted, punching their tormentor in the face. Sitting on the bully's chest, he continued to assault him until his mother, after a slow and deliberate walk across Wentworth Avenue, told her son, "Okay, George. That's enough."

George gave Tommy one last shot in the nose and stood over his stunned and bloodied adversary.

"Pick on us again, and I'll beat you up some more!"

* * *

Slipping his sock on, George felt a sense of satisfaction and muttered, "Tommy Messina never bothered anybody after that."

George found he was not alone when he exited the bathroom with a coal-black dress shirt hanging around his neck.

Tatiana quickly turned away.

"I'm sorry, Mr. Aitken. I did not realize you were still dressing."

Blushing, she continued, "Master Lucius indicated it is time for you to get cleaned up. He sent me to give you a haircut."

George slipped an arm into the sleeve. "It's fine. I'll take a seat over by the table."

George heard the rapid snips of the razor-sharp, stainless-steel scissors and watched clumps of salt-and-pepper-colored hair fall to the floor.

"I still can't believe I took on that gang," George remarked, making conversation. "I've never felt stronger."

Still thinking about his childhood reminiscences, as Tatiana shaved the back of his neck, George declared, "It will help me protect my family."

Standing behind George, Tatiana smirked. "I'm sure it will, Mr. Aitken."

After cleaning up, Tatiana pointed to a cup on the table filled with an olive-green liquid.

"Master Lucius instructed me to bring you this tonic. After this evening's contest, he thought you might be slightly amped up and need it to help you sleep."

George finished buttoning his shirt, which stretched tightly across his chest. He held up the glass and gently shook it, but the contents were as thick as a milkshake. Downing it in a few gulps and wiping his chin with his sleeve, his eyes watered, and he turned his nose up.

"That's horrible! What's in this? It tastes so bitter!"

Ignoring his question, Tatiana answered reassuringly, "Good medicine often tastes bad."

She took the empty glass and headed for the door.

"I will check back later to see if you require anything else."

George called out, "Tatiana, wait."

Tatiana stopped and turned. "Is there something else, Mr. Aitken?"

"I know I owe a debt of gratitude to Lucius for all his help these past few months," George admitted, taking several steps toward her, "but I don't know that I ever properly thanked you for bringing me here."

George gently kissed Tatiana on the cheek.

"If you had not found me wandering around on the shoulder of that highway and offered me a ride, well, I don't know where I would be."

Momentarily caught off guard by his expression of gratitude, Tatiana replied, "No—no thanks are necessary, Mr. Aitken."

Quickly regaining her composure, she turned back to the door. George could not see the Cheshire Cat grin on her face as she added, "Try to get some sleep. I think you are going to need it."

* * *

Friday, November 22nd
Bradford House, Lucius Rofocale's Chambers
3:15 a.m.

A red light, like the color of a fire truck, filled the room. It was a good omen, a sign that the spirits of the netherworld were present. Lucius Rofocale sat at a wooden table in his room. The piece of furniture appeared simply made, but it was no ordinary item. Constructed of blackthorn, the witch's tree, Lucius covered it in a purple cloth embroidered with pentagrams and Wiccan symbols representing the elements of air, water, earth, and most of all, fire. It all served as a sign of respect, a tribute to the Wiccan spirits who long ago passed down the rites that Lucius was about to perform.

The Prime Minister of Hell diligently observed the clock as he held his wrist over a ceremonial bronze bowl. The inside of the vessel was stained a deep shade of red, as if filled with burgundy wine for several months. He readied a bejeweled dagger to draw his blood for the second time that night, precisely at 3:15 a.m., the witching hour.

Earlier, he had mixed his dark, black demon blood into George Aitken's drink. Now, his blood mixed with George's hair would enable Lucius to enter a sleeping George Aitken's subconscious and finish exorcising what remained of his human soul. Lucius never took his eyes away from the timepiece.

While transforming Jack Aitken into my disciple might have been far sweeter, his brother will do quite nicely.

The licorice-like smell of smoldering wormwood filled the air. Mixed with sandalwood, it enhanced Lucius's psychic powers and helped raise the spirits of the dead.

After what I discovered deep in his psyche, George Aitken will be a far more deadly instrument than his brother.

A singular chime from the clock echoed through the room. The time had come, and Lucius ran the razor-sharp blade slowly across his vein. The blood oozed into the vessel and instantly began to thicken.

He took the lock of George's hair between the talons of his clawed fingers and sprinkled it into the tar-like substance. The hair caused the mixture to bubble like Alka-Seltzer added to a glass of water. Smoke rose from the container, and the now flashing red light in the room signaled the spirits were ready.

Raising the bowl over his head, Lucius began to chant.

"Prince of darkness. Lord of the underworld. I invoke your dark power. Expel the soul of my slave so that I may replace it with a purer, more worthy life force."

* * *

"NOOOO!"

Screaming in the night, George Aitken shot straight up in bed. Panic overwhelmed him as his eyes shifted wildly, searching the darkness, fearing what he might find there. The bed sheets were taut, gripped tightly in his hands, and his skin painfully tingled, like when, as a child, George had ignorantly stuck his finger in an electrical outlet. The hair on his arms and back of his neck stood straight up, and the sweat oozing from his pores caused the shirt he was wearing to stick to him like glue.

George flung himself back down on the bed, his eyes riveted on the ceiling. Fighting to stay awake, he begged, "Please, God. No more. No more..."

* * *

> *November 1978, Just Before Thanksgiving*
> *Basketball Court, John D. Caemmerer Park*
> *(FKA Albertson Park), Albertson, New York*
> *3:00 p.m.*

"You jackass!" George yelled. "I told you not to do it!"

Standing at half-court, Jack cringed at his brother's rebuke.

"I thought I could make the shot," Jack shouted as he slowly walked back toward the foul line.

Jack's attempt had hit the back of the rim but ricocheted over the backboard.

"You made it, alright." George grabbed Jack's blue thermal sweatshirt and shoved his brother across the basketball court. "You dick! Now the ball is down in the pit!"

Albertson Park stood on what had been a trash dump. Now, the town had reclaimed most of the land, and the pit was all that remained. Forsythia bushes, whose yellow flowers signaled the arrival of spring, wild honeysuckle vines, and invasive sumac trees lined the steep slopes of the deep cavity surrounded by a chain-link fence topped with barbed wire. It was late fall, and the naked branches of the scrub brush and trees made the pit more menacing than usual.

It seemed that whenever they were in the park, the pit was a topic of conversation. Some of their friends told the brothers stories about kids going into the pit and never coming back. Everyone dared someone else to go down to the bottom. Offers of money were often made, but no one ever took the bet.

Exasperated, George asked, "Now, what the hell do we do?"

"I'll just go down and get it," Jack declared defiantly and started exploring for the best place to climb the fence.

"You know we can't go in there," George cautioned. "Dad will kick our ass if he finds out."

Jack found a spot where someone had bent the barbed wire, creating a gap, and rattled the fence to ensure it could take his weight. Satisfied, he pointed to the opening.

"See, someone already has gone through here."

"I don't like this idea." George nervously looked around. "What if someone catches us?"

"You chicken shit!" Jack mocked him. "Stay here. I'll go."

As Jack dug the toe of his sneaker into an opening in the fence, a cold wind swept across the open fields of the park. The sky had turned a gloomy gray, like it always seemed to in November, and daylight was already disappearing. The birds weren't even chirping. It was quiet—too quiet.

Jack managed to get to the top of the fence and shimmied under the barbed wire. He landed with a thud on the ground. A perfect landing!

"See! No problem!" Jack announced triumphantly.

"Wait... J-A-C—" But before George could finish his sentence, Jack had found a gully that appeared to lead to the bottom and disappeared.

* * *

George paced back and forth in front of where Jack had entered the pit. He stopped and scrutinized his watch. Running about fifty yards down the fence line to get a different view, the nervous feeling that he had instantly transformed into fear. Jack had been gone for forty-five minutes, and it was nearly twilight. George searched the shadows, which crept across the side of the pit, for a sign of his brother. He began climbing the fence.

"I've got to get down there. Something's wrong."

Squirming his way into the enclosure, George studied where Jack had disappeared but saw nothing. He placed his hands around his mouth and shouted for his brother. There was no answer, only the echo of his question. He started down the fissure, and the ground gave way under his sneaker, causing him to grab tightly to the truck of a tree rooted into the hillside.

"That's not good." George apprehensively gulped but continued his descent. He was about halfway down, and the light was fading fast, but he saw a glow below him. Then, the smell of smoke. He heard voices and called out once more for Jack. Still no response. Unlike the loose dirt he found all the way down the hill, George sensed something solid under his feet. Reaching down, he grabbed a cold, rough-edged, rectangular object.

"Feels like it is made of metal," He picked it up and swept the dirt off. Holding it close, it read, "KEEP OUT! DANGER!"

Flinging it over his shoulder in frustration, George commented, "Yeah, no kidding."

Finally arriving at the bottom, George noticed to his left a pond, which was more like a cesspool, with a shopping cart and other debris immersed in it. A dirt path through the brush, obviously made by regular foot traffic, was directly in front of him. It led toward the light of the fire he had seen earlier, and he swiftly made his way in that direction. He knew that Jack had no matches to light a fire.

"Must be somebody else. Maybe they can help me search for him..."

His voice trailed off as three figures in denim jackets emerged from a stand of tall grass and surrounded him. Their jeans had rips and tears in the knees and several other places that suggested they were put there intentionally.

"Burnouts," George mumbled. They were a group of older kids he heard smoked pot in the school bathrooms. Rumors suggested they did harder drugs, too.

They grabbed George and shoved him forward. Someone with slicked-back hair tied into a ponytail, most likely the group leader, bathed in the firelight. Wearing a leather vest, he tossed a basketball up and down in his hand, then stopped.

"Searching for this?" Pointing to his left, he asked, "Or are you searching for him?"

Two boys George did not recognize, their lips turned upward with menacing leers, stood next to Jack, who was on his knees. A filthy red bandana in his mouth prevented him from screaming. George could not help but notice Jack's wide-eyed look of terror. A bead of sweat ran down George's temple, and he felt his stomach tighten with dread.

'Protect your brother...' George heard his father's commandment echo through his head.

"Have to do something," George whispered. "Think. Think."

Suddenly, George bolted toward Jack's captors, knocking them to the ground.

"JACKKKK! RUNNN!" George yelled at the top of his lungs.

Freed by his brother, Jack ripped the bandana from his mouth and took off into the darkness that had settled over the pit.

"Forget him!" the leader yelled. Pointing at George, he ordered, "Get this one!"

One against five were odds that George could not overcome, and after a short struggle, they quickly subdued him. Now, he was in Jack's place, on his knees, surrounded by the gang.

SWAT!

The leader slapped George across the face. Tears welled in George's eyes and rolled down his cheeks.

"I like the feisty ones better," the leader declared. He unfastened his belt and slowly unzipped his fly.

"You're gonna do what your brother was gonna do," he added, pointing at the gang members with eager grins on their faces, "to all of us."

CHAPTER 3

Friday, November 22nd
Prince William Orthopaedics, Manassas, Virginia
10:00 a.m.

"C'mon, Jack. Push yourself! Give me two more!"

Jack Aitken clenched his teeth while trying to fulfill the demand of his occupational therapist, Taylor Davis. Wearing a blue sweatsuit, Taylor was in her mid-thirties, a marathon runner in her free time, and the best therapist in the practice. Jack jokingly referred to her as "The Tyrant." Lifting the one-pound weight tied to his injured right hand off the gym mat was as pleasant as seventeenth-century dental work, but Jack got through it.

"Nice job, Jack, way to push through the pain." Taylor pumped her fist enthusiastically. "Take five, and we will finish up with some stretching!"

Jack wiped his sweaty brow with the sleeve of his gray sweatshirt; it read Ocean Isle Beach on the front. Since being discharged by his surgeon, he had worked with Taylor several days a week, but as hopeful as Jack was about regaining some use of his severely damaged hand, progress was slow. The logo on his chest and the nearly constant throbbing pain in his fingers were uncomfortable reminders of what had happened in Coastal North Carolina at the hands of Lucius Rofocale and the Strigoi months earlier.

Just then, Jack's phone vibrated, and he wrestled it from his pocket. It was a text about a breaking news video, and as a self-admitted news junkie, he quickly swiped the screen.

"I couldn't do that last week." Jack beamed, glancing at his index finger. He slowly bent it up and down to convince himself that what had happened was real.

A woman with shoulder-length, dark black hair in a bright red dress was on the screen. What she uttered next got his attention immediately.

"This is investigative reporter Jenny Phillips. I am standing outside the Brunswick County Medical Center in Bolivia, North Carolina, with an exclusive American Press Service (APS) Newsflash. While the deaths of media magnate Constantin Antonescu and his wife, as well as their daughter Maricela's disappearance, remain an open investigation, other new and potentially alarming developments have come to light in this three-month-old case.

"An unnamed source revealed that upon arriving at the Antonescu compound in Lake Waccamaw, police officers shot several private security personnel dead. The guards were foaming at the mouth and later tested positive for a pathogen identified as a previously unknown strain of rabies. When questioned, Brunswick County Public Health officials refused to confirm the potentially lethal variant's existence and denied any reason for the public to be concerned.

"Please stay tuned for more details about this story. At 6:00 p.m., The Connor Crew will debate what is behind the sudden spike in bomb scares in the U.S..."

Jack turned off the phone and groaned. His tired blue eyes dropped as he struggled to put the phone back in his pocket.

"Something wrong, Jack?" Taylor asked as she sat down on the mat across from him.

Jack held his hand out, and Taylor began to stretch his fingers.

"I was watching a newsflash from Jenny Phillips. Do you know her? She is that investigative reporter for the APS."

Taylor nodded. "I get those updates, too. I just got the one about a possible new strain of rabies."

Jack thought about his brother, George. *It's not a possible strain. Unfortunately, it is all too real.*

"Yeah, I just finished reading it too." Taylor palpated Jack's index finger, causing him to flinch.

"Brunswick County is where my friend, Anne, is working," Jack continued. "She's the Interim Police Chief there. This story probably means she won't be here for Thanksgiving."

"I am sorry to hear that." A loud crack caused Jack to wince, and his eyes opened and shut several times, causing them to water. "Sorry! I am just trying to break up adhesions. That's it for today. Remember, ice and Advil tonight."

Taylor got up from the mat and patted him on the shoulder. "Try to have a nice Thanksgiving!"

"You do the same, Taylor." Jack flexed his hand, which was aching. "See you in December."

Jack pulled on his jacket, probably faster than he should have with his injury, and grimaced. He had some calls to make tonight.

* * *

Later That Night

Ring, Ring, Ring

The phone connected, and Jack heard,

RUFF! RUFF!

"Hi, Daphne," Jack yelled into the phone. "Do you miss us?"

Anne Bishop's smiling face appeared on the screen. "I'm sure she does." Reaching into the kitchen cabinet and taking down a bottle of Tylenol, she added, "And so do I."

Tapping the container on its side caused two tablets to fall on the countertop. "What a day I had, Jack."

"Based on that news report, I can only imagine."

Anne took the pills and drifted into the living room. "Everywhere I turned, there was a microphone or a camera in my face."

"Any idea who may have leaked the rabies information to APS?" Jack asked.

Falling onto the couch, Anne answered, "None. I guess it could have been one of the hospital employees, but everyone denies they had anything to do with it."

The ginger-colored cocker spaniel jumped into Anne's lap and made herself comfortable. Anne gently scratched the dog's ears. The friends made small talk for several minutes before Jack inquired,

"I guess, um..." Jack stumbled over his words. "I guess that means you won't make Thanksgiving dinner?"

"It doesn't look good." Anne's voice trailed off. "I don't think I can get away right now."

Jack sounded cheerful, but she heard the disappointment hidden beneath his lighthearted tone. "I understand. The boys will miss you."

Anne smiled. It was a sad one. "Call me over the weekend. Okay?"

"Sure," Jack replied. "Talk to you soon."

* * *

Jack hung up the phone and immediately began the mental version of whack-a-mole that he seemingly played after each call with Anne. He tapped the wedding ring on his finger, and a wave of guilt washed over him. Jack heard a loud purr and watched their new cat, Poppy, rubbing her head on his leg. He gently pulled the cat's raccoon-ringed tail.

"Okay, girl. Time for your dinner."

Opening the cat food can, Jack debated with himself. He felt increasingly drawn to Anne with each call but also wrestled with his conscience and questioned if he was dishonoring his late wife Amanda's memory by getting this close.

The cat dove into her dinner enthusiastically. Jack emptied the dishwasher and muttered, "Why didn't I tell her I would miss her? Jesus Christ! I'm acting like I'm back in high school."

"Dad, can we watch a movie?" Louis asked as he rocked back and forth in the den.

"And make some popcorn?" David added, running into the kitchen, dressed in his New York Giants pajamas.

The smell of popcorn filled the air as Jack placed the bowl on the table.

"What movie are we watching?" Jack asked as he slumped into a chair with a bunch of popcorn in his hand.

"*Without a Clue.*" Declared Louis. Poppy jumped into Louis's lap and laid down for a nap.

"It's a funny movie, Dad," David spoke into the remote as he called up Netflix and got comfortable in the corner of the couch.

Jack crunched on his popcorn.

This is appropriate. Just like me, without a clue.

The boys roared with laughter at Michael Caine's antics, but Jack was too distracted to enjoy the movie. One question, something running through his mind for the past three months, taunted him again: *Did Anne say, "I love you" while they were in the catacombs under the Antonescu house, or was he just delirious from the beating he was taking?*

* * *

Ocean Isle Beach, North Carolina
11:00 p.m.

Jack told Anne on the phone that it had gotten colder in Virginia, but it seemed like summer was not ready to relinquish its hold on Ocean Isle Beach. Despite the late hour, it was steamy, and the usual ocean breeze was absent. Anne's sweat caused her lightweight black slacks and loose-fitting blouse to stick to her back like rubber cement. Notwithstanding the heat and her fur coat, Daphne appeared determined to take a long walk. If she were being honest, Anne needed the time to sort through her feelings one more time.

Anne focused on the stars, sparkling like diamonds in the moonlight, as Daphne sniffed the ground and pulled her along.

"Lord, this is uncharted territory for me," Anne pleaded.

Blithely kicking a stone on the road, she recalled meeting Jack at Giuseppe's restaurant in Haymarket after his acquittal by the Grand Jury investigating Amanda's death. At that time, he told her that he would never be able to fall in love again.

"I feel that something between us caused that to change. I don't want to pressure Jack, Lord, but why does he keep so much emotion inside? Why won't he say that he needs me? He always tells me how important I am to the boys, but I know he needs me, too. He has tremendous challenges but doesn't need to face them alone."

Daphne stopped and looked up as if Anne had been talking to her.

Anne knelt and peered into Daphne's teddy bear-like brown eyes. "It's okay, girl. I know you need me."

A warm, damp, red tongue ran up and down Anne's cheek, then Daphne began pulling on the leash again.

"Anne, you've got to take the bull by the horns!"

Anne chuckled at suddenly hearing Ross Martin's words ringing in her ears. As her former partner on the Prince William County police force, whenever Anne was in a quandary about a case, Ross always used this phrase to encourage her to stop thinking about what action to take and to do something.

They turned the corner toward home. How could she tell Jack that she understood he might feel conflicted, even guilty, over Amanda? Maybe he was scared he was doing something wrong. *I'm not trying to replace her; I could never do that.* But she wanted to reassure him that loving her would not be a mistake or an assault on Amanda's memory.

Dropping Daphne's leash, Anne grabbed the mail. The streetlamp's light was sufficient for her to scan the contents, and as she did so, she considered Ross's advice.

What I should be asking Jack is, did he hear me say "I love you" in the catacombs?

Suddenly, Daphne growled, but Anne could not see her.

"Where are you, Daphne?"

The growl became a bark, and Anne followed it around the corner of the garage. Daphne was sniffing the ground around the red brick foundation of the house.

"What is it, girl?"

Anne bent over and saw the ordinarily damp, mottled gray soil next to the foundation had been disturbed. Even in the dark, there was more of a blueish tint, but only Daphne's superior sense of smell noticed the hint of sulfur in the air.

Odd. Anne picked up Daphne's leash and pulled her back. *Something has been digging there.*

Daphne barked, then growled again.

Pulling on the leash again, Anne dragged Daphne backward, making a mental note to call a pest control company.

"Come on, Daphne. Time to go in."

Begrudgingly, Daphne followed Anne, but before rounding the corner, she turned and gave a more prolonged stare into the darkness.

* * *

> Wednesday, November 27th
> Aitken Family Home Bristow, Virginia
> 5:30 p.m.

Jack's sister Emma finished setting the table. Recently retired, Emma's hair was still golden brown, like a stalk of wheat, despite being five years older than her brother, whose hair was virtually white. New York was once home to the entire family, but Emma was now the last Aitken living on Long Island. Previously married to her job, she was figuring out the next phase of her life. Emma had a heart of gold, and having lived with his family during most of David's illness, she and Jack were particularly close. Emma was the sister and aunt everyone would want to have.

Emma handed her sister, Michelle, a worn piece of paper whose date read July 27th, 1984.

"I was searching for a pen upstairs and found it in one of the desk drawers. I didn't want Jack to think I was snooping, so I waited for him to leave before I showed it to you."

Michelle Brandt was Jack's middle sister. Her braided blonde hair had streaks of gray, but she retained her youthful appearance and could otherwise have passed for someone in their forties rather than her early sixties. When her ex-husband demanded an open marriage, Michelle told him to go to Hell and moved to Santa Monica, California, to start her own business. She was confident, assertive, and a computer genius, the owner of an e-commerce company, and nobody's fool.

Michelle rubbed her lip as she examined what Emma handed her, then remarked, "A ticket stub from Great Adventure. I wonder if that amusement park is even still operating?"

"It is," Emma answered as Michelle returned the ticket to her. "I saw a billboard on the New Jersey Turnpike."

"Why don't you want Jack to see it, Em? You know he isn't going to care where you found it."

"Well, that's the thing, Michelle," Emma whispered. "It was Amanda's desk."

"Oh." Michelle nodded. "Gotcha. But it isn't unusual to save something like this. You know how sentimental both he and Amanda always were. Amanda might have kept it for him."

"I agree, but that was not a good day." Emma's eyebrows drew closer together. Her tone became serious. "Frankly, what happened there is something anyone would want to forget, particularly Amanda."

Michelle took a sip of water, then asked curiously, "What happened?"

Emma paused, running her fingers through her hair.

"We went there to celebrate George and Jack's birthday. Jack had started dating Amanda a little over six months earlier, and George was dating that girl, Missy. Do you remember her?"

Michelle scowled. "Yeah. She was very bossy. I never liked her."

"Things were not going well between Jack and George," Emma continued. "George hadn't been very kind to Amanda."

Michelle crossed her arms. "I only heard a few years ago what George told Jack back then, that everyone was saying Amanda was sleeping around. They fought, and Jack broke his ribs. It's one instance where you could argue that George deserved what he got."

"I agree, Michelle," Emma groaned. "What George did was unconscionable, but this day was an attempt to mend fences, and it went okay until George and Missy insisted on going on Lightning Loops."

"I think I remember that ride. An upside-down roller coaster? Right?" Michelle asked.

"Not only did it go upside down, but it went backward too. Amanda and Jack did not want to go on the ride. Missy and George pressured them into going. George was especially persistent. They eventually relented, and the forward loop went fine, but the backward loop stopped in the middle."

"They were hanging upside down?"

"That's right, Michelle," Emma replied. "But it got worse. The harness failed in the car in front of Jack and Amanda, and someone almost fell out. That unfortunate rider was hanging in mid-air with someone holding onto them with one hand."

Michelle's eyes bulged, and she covered her mouth.

"Then, Amanda's restraint began to fail, and Jack had to hold it in place for nearly half an hour before the ride operator could get the cars to move again."

"My God, Em. Why didn't I hear about this before?"

"Amanda was traumatized by the whole thing. For many years, she kept reliving it. Jack asked everyone never to speak about it."

Suddenly, David shot up the stairs from the basement. Emma glanced at Michelle and got up from the table. She buried the tattered ticket deep in the garbage pail.

* * *

"Dad's home!" Louis shouted from the family room as he heard the car pull in.

David threw open the kitchen door into the garage for his father. Jack entered the house. "Thanks, kiddo. Here, take this and put it on the table."

Chinese food on the night before Thanksgiving had become an Aitken family tradition that everyone eagerly anticipated, except for the boys. But all of them were feeling George's absence. His disappearance hung over the house like a cloud, dampening their usual enthusiasm.

While Emma ladled won ton soup into bowls, Michelle asked, "Did you get duck sauce for the spring rolls, Jack?"

Jack replied, "Try the island drawer."

Michelle was about to bite into a spring roll when Louis stopped her.

"Wait, Michelle; we have to say grace first."

Michelle was passionate about her nephews not calling her aunt, so they always addressed her by her first name.

Louis led them in prayer, with the family saying in unison, "Amen."

CRUNCH. Jack bit into a golden-brown spring roll. "These are always so good! Hey, Louis, do you want to try it?"

Louis leaned over his plate, ensuring no one could take it. "No way. I'll stick with my macaroni and cheese."

Emma joked, "You have eaten that virtually every day for the past eighteen years. Don't you think it is time to try something new?"

David announced impatiently, "You're teasing him, Aunt Emma."

Emma replied, "You know I'm only kidding."

"Jack, you might find this interesting." Michelle finished sipping her soup and continued, "Do you remember the Savannah River Bridge? The one we used to go over on our trips to see Nanny and Poppy in Florida?"

"How could I forget it?" Jack playfully groaned. "You got me so worked up about it that I was hiding in the back of the station wagon, scared out of my mind. What about it?"

"There was an accident on the bridge today involving a truck hauling logs," Michelle stated. "The truck's cab broke through the guardrail and was dangling over the river."

"Geez. Is the driver okay?" Jack asked, his voice filled with concern.

"They were able to rescue him," Michelle replied. "But the bridge was closed for hours."

"I remember that bridge, too," Emma earnestly added. "It makes me nervous just talking about it."

"I've never recovered, Em." Jack pretended to hyperventilate. "To this day, I hate going over bridges. The longer I go without driving on one, the more anxious I get when I finally do."

Tensely tapping his fingers on the table, Jack told Michelle, "See what you've done to me?"

David chewed his chicken nugget and interjected, "What was so bad about that bridge?"

"It only had one lane in each direction." Michelle's brown eyes peeked up as she pointed to the ceiling. "It went straight up and then straight down."

"Yeah," Jack chimed in. "It was a drawbridge with a traffic light to stop cars when the bridge opened for a ship. We got stuck at that light once, waiting for a boat to pass through. It seemed like an eternity."

Jack grabbed his chest and joked, "Even now, I can feel my heart beating out of my chest!" Everyone laughed as Jack playfully fell out of his chair and hammed it up as he rolled on the floor.

* * *

The boys helped clear the dinner dishes and went downstairs to play video games. Emma stood at the counter, waiting for the water to boil for a cup of tea.

Sitting back down at the table, Michelle asked, "Since when did Louis and David get so religious, Jack? They never insisted on saying grace before."

Michelle joked, "I think Louis wanted to slap my hand."

Jack hesitated.

Haven't I told you? Your nephews are prophets of God.

Then he answered, "It started after Amanda died."

That's not a total lie, Jack reasoned to himself.

Ring! Ring! The kitchen phone rang loudly.

Jack picked up the phone, grateful to be saved by the proverbial bell.

"Hello, Thanksgiving Central," Jack joked.

A familiar voice came on the line. "Hi, Jack, it's Lynne."

Lynne was the eldest of the five Aitken siblings and twelve years older than Jack. Married to her husband, Bob, for over forty years, she was the mother of two girls and a boy, who made her a grandmother four times. Her hair was gray, but she was always health conscious and had maintained her athletic physique. Lynne and Bob lived in coastal Delaware but frequently enjoyed visiting with their children and grandchildren.

"Lynne, let me be the first to wish you a happy Thanksgiving. I'll put you on speaker."

Jack pressed a button, and Michelle asked, "Are you hosting again this year?"

"We'll have a full house tomorrow, Michelle. Em, are you there too?"

"Yup. Hi, Lynne. I got here this morning."

Lynne went on, "Great! I thought I would call tonight. Tomorrow will likely be a little busy. Jack, how is your ear?"

Jack closed the door to the basement. He glanced at both of his sisters and then answered, "I just wanted to close the door so the boys didn't hear. I got the biopsy result earlier this week. The roughness on the rim of my ear is skin cancer, but not the malignant type. I've got an appointment the last week of December to have it removed."

The kitchen got quiet. The only noise for a few moments was a drip from the faucet in the sink.

Jack raised his hands before his chest. "I promise I will take care of this."

"This is your big sister talking, Jack." Lynne's voice filled the room. "You better. Don't make us worry about you like we worry about..." Her voice trailed off. "*George.*"

Emma somberly interjected, "It's going to be different not having George and his family here tomorrow."

As a tear slowly rolled down her cheek, Jack put his arm around Emma's shoulder.

Michelle touched Emma's hand. "Don't give up hope. George is strong. If anyone can make his way home, it is him."

Jack's head dropped, and his shoulders slumped. "I wish I had better news, but there still hasn't been any sign of him anywhere."

In the background was a voice: "Mony. Mony. Where are you, Mony?"

Mony was what Lynne's grandsons called her.

"I'll be there in a minute, sweetie," Lynne told her grandson.

"Have a great day tomorrow, Lynne," Michelle shouted into the speaker.

"We love you all!" Emma, Jack, and Michelle yelled in unison.

"Hugs and kisses," Lynne responded. "Love you lots!"

Click. The line went dead, and Jack hung up the phone, thinking, *Where are you, George?*

* * *

Jack blew on his coffee cup, hoping to cool it off before he sipped it. Michelle placed a cup of tea before Emma and sat across from Jack.

"So, Jack," Michelle smiled coyly. "What's up with this friend of yours? Anne? Is she coming tomorrow?"

"Unfortunately, no," Jack answered regretfully. "She is tied up with a case that will keep her in Ocean Isle Beach."

"Stop it, Michelle," Emma reprimanded her sister. "Don't tease him."

With a mischievous look, Michelle retorted, "I'm watching out for our little brother."

"Thanks, Em," Jack laughed. "You always protect me."

"Are you in need of protection, Jack?" Michelle giggled and continued teasing her brother. "From Anne or me?"

"Anne is my friend, and that's all she is, Michelle."

Michelle went on, "Methinks our brother doth protest too much. What do you think, Em?"

Emma winked at Jack, "Well, maybe a little."

Jack pretended to be upset. "Now you two are ganging up on me. I need one of these."

Jack grabbed a fortune cookie from the middle of the table and broke it open. He ate a piece of the cookie and started reading the message. The joy on his face vanished as his forehead wrinkled, and a perplexed expression appeared.

"What does it say, Jack?" Michelle inquired with a tone of concern.

"Read it out loud," insisted Emma.

Jack hesitated, then spoke slowly.

"Irony is dying in the living room?"

CHAPTER 4

> Wednesday November 27th
> A Necropolis in Hell
> Just Before Midnight

Nee-naw! Nee-naw! Nee-naw!

The screaming sound of the sirens echoed through the vast network of caverns, briefly drowning out the anguished wails of the damned. This signal, announcing the arrival of those newly condemned to Hell, even penetrated the deep necropolis where the Angel of the Abyss resided. Apollyon's existence was deeply complex, serving as the chief guardian at the underworld's gates as well as God's Biblical instrument of retribution.

Strapping on his armor, Apollyon rose to register the unfortunate souls in the Book of the Dead before they entered a realm beyond their worst nightmares. The angel was perplexed to arrive at the gate and find it unattended and eerily quiet. There were no cries of grief nor the ceaseless lamenting of those pleading for mercy from their torment. Something was different, so hearing a voice pierce the silence was less than a surprise to Hell's gatekeeper.

"Greetings to you, angel of the abyss."

"Where are you?" Apollyon barked out, straining to see into the darkness of the chamber.

The gate to Hell stood at the crossroads of countless corridors leading to the planet's far corners. The blazing fire of the pit would glow in shades of yellow, orange, and red, dancing like shadows on the stone walls of the passages. But now, the ordinarily fiery furnace was cool, and the only illumination was a beam of white light that grew wider as it drew closer. It stopped, but it was still floating in mid-air, materializing and hovering above Apollyon; it was shaped like the outline of a being seated on a white stallion, holding a lantern in its right hand.

After a few moments, the entity spoke, "I bid you greetings once more."

The tone of the visitor's voice told Apollyon he presented no threat, so he raised the faceguard from his helmet and commanded, "Identify yourself!"

"I am Cassiel, servant to the Arch Angel Gabriel, the messenger of God."

Skeptical, Apollyon's eyes narrowed, and his demand echoed loudly through the chamber, "What is your business here? We do not receive many visits from angels."

The horse snorted, and Cassiel pulled back the reins on his steed to steady the animal, then replied, "I bring you a message from the Father."

"Father?" Apollyon questioned. "Do you mean God?"

Cassiel nodded affirmatively.

The angel of destruction's eyes shifted quickly from left to right and back again. Still suspicious of the authenticity of the being he saw before him, he scoffed dismissively, "So this is a vision, then? Why does Gabriel not deliver the message himself?"

"Gabriel is attending to other matters," Cassiel quickly replied.

Apollyon challenged the messenger, "Prove it! Show me something that confirms your divinity!"

The horse's eyes turned black, and smoke poured from its nose in a sign of growing frustration. Cassiel patted the animal's neck and snapped his fingers. Instantly, the fires of Hell ignited beyond the gate behind Apollyon, and Cassiel bluntly asked, "Satisfied?"

Apollyon peeked over his shoulder at the inferno. Convinced, he replied, "What is your message?"

"It is simply this," Cassiel answered. "Stand down."

"Stand down?" The Destroyer scowled. Then, he began to laugh in a vocal sound as loud as thunder.

"This is not a request. It is an order!" the floating angel responded harshly. "The Father no longer requires your services. Is that clear enough?"

"You forget that my existence goes back almost as far as God's. Do you think such a request has not been made of me before?" Apollyon's sarcasm dripped like drops of water from the stalactites on the cavern's ceiling. "He has changed his mind in the past."

"Not this time! You would do well to heed me!" Cassiel declared angrily as his horse circled several times.

Apollyon folded his arms in defiance. "And why should I listen to you? Let God tell me himself!"

"Beware! Yours is not to reason why! Yours is to obey!" Cassiel shouted as he and the stallion disappeared.

Hell's furnace was instantly cold again, and Apollyon stood alone in the darkness. The word "obey" cascaded through his head.

* * *

> *Thanksgiving Morning*
> *Bristow, Virginia*
> *Before Sunrise*

Jack sat on the edge of the bed with a brown blanket draped across his legs. Rubbing his eyes, he declared, "I sure don't sleep like I used to, do I?"

He ran his tongue across his teeth to hydrate his dry mouth and wondered when he had become such a light sleeper. He used to be able to sleep through fire alarms and earthquakes. *Hell, one night, someone got shot on the corner of our street, and George could not believe I slept through that.*

George.

The thought of his brother never strayed far from Jack's mind. He closed his eyes, but before he could reminisce further, the beeping of the clock radio brought him back to the present. Shutting it off, he yawned and shuffled toward the bathroom. Glancing at the bedroom door, he shook his head.

That creaking noise kept waking me up. It sounded as if someone was walking around the house, but every time I checked, everyone in the house was asleep... except for me.

Jack passed his fingers through his thinning gray hair while looking in the mirror and joked,

"You aren't getting any younger, kid."

A slight smile came to his face when he thought of George's obsession with his hair when they were in high school. His brother would sleep on his chin to avoid combing his hair in the morning.

Dressed in a black sweatsuit with a white stripe down the legs, he carefully descended the stairs, only to be met at the landing by the cat, loudly meowing. Jack held his finger in front of his lips.

"Shh... You'll wake everyone up."

Poppy rolled around on the floor, tugging at his shoelaces and rubbing her back on Jack's sneakers.

The cat raced Jack to the family room and stood on the coffee table like a statue.

"Okay, girl. I'll pull back the curtain from the window so you can watch your bird friends."

Jack grabbed his phone from the charger in the kitchen and felt a vibration. Turning it on, he saw a headline on the APS news feed.

"Scientists Baffled! A mysterious undersea volcano in the waters off Barbados has erupted! There is no evidence of tectonic activity in this geographic region in recorded history!"

"Hmm... that's interesting." Jack put the phone in his pocket.

With a basketball under his arm, Jack left his family asleep and slipped quietly out the front door. The frost hugged the grass like a light blanket of snow, and the brown leaves, only recently dropped from the now barren trees, crunched under his feet. Jack's condensed breath hung in the air like a cloud of smoke as he crossed Linton Hall Road and headed for the basketball court. Each bounce of the ball on the pavement echoed through the peaceful morning, but when he stood at the foul line, preparing to shoot, all Jack could hear was a rising wind blowing in his ear.

The blue sky was adorned with stunning hues of orange and red, creating a spectacular sunrise. Jack could not appreciate it. Shooting hoops usually helped quiet Jack's mind, but his thoughts were anything but calm. Cradling the basketball in his hands reminded him of unpleasant things. George gave him the ball during David's illness to help him manage his stress. It was not working. Another equally troubling memory tried to pry its way into the present, but Jack managed to chase the thought away. Preparing to shoot a free throw, Jack vented out loud.

"So, let's sum up where we are right now. Because of me, George is some half-dead zombie who has vanished without a trace. Anne can't make it for Thanksgiving dinner, and I can't figure out if we are friends or something more than that. My sons are God's prophets, and oh, by the way, their destiny is to be murdered. Finally, an unfortunate young girl is pregnant with some demon spawn who, if you believe the Book of Revelation, is supposed to bring about the apocalypse."

Jack shot the orange ball, which clanged off the back of the rim and over the backboard.

"Well, happy fucking Thanksgiving to me."

* * *

> **Thanksgiving Day**
> 10:00 a.m.

"Hurry up, Louis!" Michelle called upstairs. "You too, David. We must leave now to ensure we're at the starting line when the race starts."

"Why don't you come with us?" Emma pressed Jack as she put on a shamrock-green windbreaker. "It'll be fun."

Jack yawned, "Thanks, but I thought I would go for a quick visit to the cemetery before it is time to cook."

Michelle pulled on a pink shoelace and tied a tight knot. She turned toward Jack as she stretched her legs. "It's no wonder you're yawning. I heard you walking around last night."

Jack lowered his eyes. "I'm sorry. I heard a creaking noise."

Michelle interrupted and retorted, "Heard a creaking noise? You were the creaking noise! I saw you in the hallway, and then you went down to the basement."

"Basement?" Jack questioned. "I didn't go in the basement last night."

"Yes, you did!" Michelle put her hands on her hips and groaned. "You think you can scare me like when we were kids? You and George were always jumping out at us from behind doors and stuff like that."

"I can't fool you anymore, Michelle." Jack tried to laugh off what she had seen.

Emma interjected, "If we get back from the turkey trot before you get home, we'll put 'Thor' in the oven."

Jack asked Emma with raised eyebrows, "Thor?"

"Yes," Emma answered with a grin. "That's what David named the turkey."

"Okay," Jack giggled as he hit the button that opened the garage door. "Thor is in the refrigerator...."

Jack's voice trailed off. "In the basement."

Jack warily eyed the basement door as the boys dashed past him and raced to Emma's car.

In unison, they shouted, "Bye, Dad! Say hi to Nan and Pop."

"Sure, guys." Jack managed to smile at their comment. "See you in a little while."

* * *

> *Thanksgiving Day*
> *Route 619 Toward Quantico National Cemetery*
> *10:00 a.m.*

Say hi to Nan and Pop....

Jack veered right at a sign pointing toward Quantico National Cemetery. He knew his sons' request to say hello to their deceased grandparents was more than a tender notion. It reflected their innocence. To Jack, it was also at the core of why God had chosen them to be his prophets. In their own way, the boys believed Jack was going to the cemetery to do exactly what they suggested. This truth left him deeply troubled.

Over the past several months, Louis and David had asked him several questions, for which he struggled to provide a coherent answer.

Why do prophets die?

"How do I answer that question?" Jack murmured, shifting the car into its next gear.

What does it feel like when you die?

Jack stared out the windshield. *They have no concept of what death means.*

The inability to articulate a logical response they could understand left Jack frustrated. He questioned God's motives and wondered why the Almighty would exploit his sons' naïvete. Twice, Jack had rejected offers from Lucius Rofocale, the demon Prime Minster of Hell, that would have saved his sons from their destiny, their date with death. A deal with Lucius was as good as a pact with the Devil himself, and Jack was fully aware of the ramifications of such a contract.

Yet, he could not help but ask, "Why them? Why our family? Haven't we lost enough? Is this some sort of test, like Abraham to Isaac, to see if I will sacrifice Louis and David for the greater good?"

* * *

Passing the Independent Hill Special Education School, Route 619 snaked through a densely wooded area. The first time Jack visited Quantico National Cemetery, he noticed a historical marker for "The Lost Community of Kopp, Virginia" along the road. For some reason, Jack could never put his finger on it; every time he passed the sign, it made him think of the movie *The Town That Dreaded Sundown.*

Jack remembered reading that not long after being founded in 1901, the citizens of Kopp abandoned the town. By the early 1940s, what was left was absorbed into the Quantico Marine Base, and the only evidence that Kopp existed was the Belle Haven Cemetery. Rumors were that the villagers fled the village due to a disease outbreak, but no one could quite confirm what caused them to abandon it. Jack often thought there was more to the story, but having sworn off being an author, he had given up on the idea.

Seeing the sign for Kopp let Jack know the entrance to the cemetery was coming up on the right. Pulling through the front gate, he noticed the grounds still decorated for Veterans Day, with American flags in front of every grave marker.

"Dad and Mom would love to see this display," Jack uttered as he turned left.

Glancing skyward, he acknowledged, "I know you both are thrilled to be interred here."

Approaching Thomas Jefferson Road and the columbarium containing his parents' remains, Jack saw several vehicles with flashing lights.

What's going on? Thanksgiving seems like an unusual day for a burial ceremony.

Parking his car on the shoulder, Jack pulled on the stubble of his beard, wondering what was happening, then opened the car door. As he got out, he heard a voice.

"Sir, we have an investigation in progress." A young, clean-shaven Marine moved toward him. "I must ask you to get back in your vehicle."

Jack saw the structure where his parents' ashes were stored, wrapped in yellow crime scene tape. Pointing at the columbarium, Jack asked the officer, "What happened? My parents are in that row."

"What is their name, sir?"

"Aitken. George and Louise Aitken."

Jack waited anxiously. Several Marines with white dress hats under their arms, wearing blue uniforms with red trim and gold buttons glistening in the sun, talked amongst themselves. Finally, one of the officers came over to Jack.

"Mr. Aitken, I am Major Brian Armstrong. I am sorry to be the one to tell you this, but your parents' remains are missing."

Jack was incredulous. "What? Missing? How?"

Major Armstrong continued, "Someone removed the stone marker bolted to the wall."

"The one inscribed with their names?" Jack asked hesitantly.

"Yes," Major Armstrong confirmed. "He or she took the urn inside it."

"Took the urn?" Jack's eyes opened wide in disbelief at what the officer told him.

"Yes, sir. The inscribed stone and the urn are both missing," the young Marine stated solemnly.

Jack inspected the area. Major Armstrong anticipated the question. "We've already checked the security cameras, sir."

"And what did you find, Major?" queried Jack, with more than a bit of foreboding in his mind.

"There was a single perpetrator, but none of the angles show a face." Major Armstrong straightened his belt. "Highly unusual. But we'll get them, sir."

As he leaned on the hood of his car, Jack rubbed his forehead, trying to process what was happening.

"Major, do you need me to file a report?"

"Yes, Mr. Aitken." Major Armstrong gestured to one of the officers. "Corporal Righetti will take you to the information center to complete the forms."

Jack opened the car door. "Okay. I'll keep this to myself until you confirm that all the families know what happened to their loved ones."

Corporal Righetti glanced at Major Armstrong.

The Corporal asked, "Sir, do you know anyone who might have a grudge against your family?"

Well, there is this demon from Hell....

Jack drove the thought from his brain. "No one I can think of, but I can ask my sisters and bro—"

Catching himself, Jack continued, "My other family members."

Major Armstrong added, "I apologize for the questions, Mr. Aitken, but your parents' receptacle is the only damaged one. None of the other remains have been disturbed."

Jack completed the necessary forms and drove home in complete silence. Usually, he would have had Christmas music on the radio. He wasn't feeling it. All Jack could think about was how to tell his family what had happened. Maybe more importantly, he could not shake a nagging feeling that the incident at the cemetery, the creaking noises he heard last night, and whatever Michelle had seen going down in the basement might be connected.

CHAPTER 5

> *Thanksgiving Day*
> *Aitken Family Home, Bristow, Virginia*
> *Noon*

The realization that the turkey needed to get into the oven took Jack's mind off the unsettling events of the last twelve hours. Despite it being lunchtime already, so few loved ones around the table this year meant that the small turkey would only take three to four hours to cook. A sense of relief came over him when he saw no sign of Emma's car. Jack pushed the button on the remote to open the garage door, aware that he had to check the basement before they came home.

Tentatively, he went downstairs to the cellar, which he jokingly called Louis's "man cave" as he spent so much time there. The green glow from a clock radio was the only light cutting through the pitch-black darkness. Jack flipped every switch, turned on each lamp, and cautiously checked every blind spot and possible hiding place for someone or something. He found only the bird in the refrigerator. After putting it in the oven, Jack decided to finish setting the dining room table. Smiling, he opted for the good china, knowing Amanda would have liked that.

Entering the dining room, he flipped the light switch and immediately stumbled backward into a corner. His mouth agape and eyes wide open, he viewed with horror the emerald-green, cobweb-covered marble container in the middle of the table. A gray granite marker leaned against it with the names George and Louise Aitken chiseled into the stone. Jack slowly moved toward the table.

"What the hell…"

Leaning over the table, Jack fought his emotions as he read the gold inscription: *"George Aitken 1930–2019. Louise Aitken 1929–2021."* Tentatively, he ran his fingers on top of the urn. Suddenly, Jack heard the slam of a car door.

"Oh, God," Jack gasped. "I need to get this out of here!"

He grabbed the stone marker and gently placed it on top of the urn. Due to his injured hand, he struggled to pick both items up. "Jesus, how much does this weigh?"

As the garage door opened, Jack labored to get the urn upstairs. At the top step, he saw Poppy playfully waiting to pounce on him.

"NOT NOW, POP!" he shouted, and the cat dashed down the hallway.

Emma's voice echoed through the house. "Jack, are you home?"

Sweat pouring down his brow, Jack managed to kick the bedroom door open. Someone was coming up the stairs. He frantically lowered the "care package" to the floor near his bed.

"Dad, are you up here?" Louis called out.

As Louis entered the room, Jack pushed the urn under his bed. He greeted his son cheerfully, "Hi, Louis, how was the turkey trot?"

"It was okay." Louis questioned Jack, "What are you doing?"

He quickly pulled a leaf for the dining room table from under the bed and answered, "We need to make the table bigger," pushing the leaf toward his son. "Please take this downstairs for me."

"Alright," Louis huffed with apprehension. Picking it up, he complained, "This is heavy."

You don't know what heavy is, kid! Try running upstairs with an urn full of ashes!

Jack encouraged Louis, "You can handle it. Just be careful."

After Louis was out of sight, Jack went to the bathroom and splashed cool water on his face. Drying himself with a towel, he caught a glimpse of his bed and knew he had to find a better hiding place later. There was no way he could sleep with the urn under there.

Making his way downstairs and stepping into the hall, he checked the front door and found it locked. Staring out the door's inset oval window, he murmured, "So, how in God's name did someone get in the house with that urn?"

* * *

> *Thanksgiving Day*
> *Jack Aitken's Bedroom*
> *3:00 p.m.*

"Jack, all I am saying is let's not jump to conclusions," Anne cautioned. "I am not minimizing what happened, but it doesn't mean George did it. Remember what I told you previously? Never underestimate JESU. It could have been them, too."

"Yeah, or Lucius. How about some teens out for kicks or the boogeyman?" An animated Jack tried not to raise his voice.

Before Anne could respond, he added, "I'm sorry, Anne. I didn't mean to be so sarcastic, but I am worried."

"And with good reason," Anne replied reassuringly. "I am not saying you are wrong. Let's just not get ahead of ourselves. You confirmed the cat hasn't been acting strangely, nor have the boys told you anything. If something truly paranormal were happening, they should react to it."

Anne paused, then said, "Tell you what. I will check with several of my former colleagues at JESU and see if anything is happening. Try to enjoy Thanksgiving with your family. I will tell you what I find out."

Knock. Knock. Knock.

"Are you in there, Jack?" Emma asked. "I think the turkey is ready."

"I'll be right there," Jack answered, covering the mouthpiece not to yell in Anne's ear.

"Anne, I've got to go," Jack admitted. "I really wish you were here."

Anne beamed at Jack's sentiment. "Me too, Jack. I will text you if I find out anything important."

* * *

At the bottom of the stairs, he fought to paint a smile on his face. Not wanting to worry or alarm anyone, he was determined to make this Thanksgiving as happy as possible.

"Did you take Thor out of the oven, Em?" Jack shouted from the hallway.

Emma met Jack in the kitchen and pointed at the island countertop. "He is right there resting."

"I didn't realize he was so tired," Jack joked.

Michelle rolled her eyes. "Your sense of humor is so warped, Jack."

Before carving the turkey, the trio prepared the stuffing and other favorite sides.

"You missed an interesting program, Jack," Emma announced while pressing the buttons on the microwave. "It was our kind of show."

"Oh yeah. Ouch!" Jack kissed his finger after touching a steaming bowl of creamed spinach. "What was it about?"

"Lost civilizations. Archeologists are searching for a lost continent under the Pacific Ocean?"

"Really?" Jack stopped what he was doing, intrigued by his sister's statement.

"Mainstream science dismisses the research, but there is an ongoing hunt for bones and artifacts in Fiji. They mentioned legends of giants over ten feet tall with red hair."

Emma followed Jack into the dining room with mashed potatoes in a serving dish in one hand and peas in the other.

"They refer to it as the lost continent of Mu," she continued. "It is supposed to be the Atlantis of the Pacific."

"You're right; it sounds like our kind of show." Jack stopped and shouted, "Louis. David. Time for dinner! Thor is waiting!"

CHAPTER 6

Thanksgiving Day, Late

"That was delicious!" Jack pushed his chair away from the table. "I'm stuffed!"

While the meal had been tasty, Jack still struggled to feel thankful. Three years ago, the table extended into the living room to accommodate everyone. Today, the table was smaller, with too many empty chairs. Amanda and his parents were dead. George was missing, and his family, grieving and shattered, stayed in South Carolina. Finally, there was Anne, who was in Ocean Isle Beach. He understood more than ever why his father loved being surrounded by family and put so much value on these relationships.

Jack peered into the living room and saw the Christmas tree box. Despite his melancholy, it triggered a joyful memory. Amanda had instilled a love of the holiday season in all of them. It was no surprise that the boys had brought up the decorations. The day after Thanksgiving was the beginning of "decorating weekend," which usually filled Jack with joy. He normally reveled in everything about Christmas, from decorating the house to the music and Christmas movies. But Jack worried he would be fighting a mood tomorrow, which would mirror the term "Black Friday." He knew it would be a struggle to find the hope he typically had and desperately wanted to feel again.

Jack's musing was interrupted when his sons returned to the dining room. The boys were stone-faced as Louis asked, "Aunt Emma and Michelle, can we talk to Dad alone?"

Michelle and Emma glanced at one another, concerned by the serious expressions on their nephews' faces. Emma answered, "Sure. Michelle, let's get the coffee and dessert."

Pulling at his lower lip, Jack tried to read their faces. He asked, "Why so serious, guys?"

David elbowed Louis, whose eyes could have bored a hole through the floor. "Louis, you tell him."

"Tell me what?" Jack leaned forward and strained to hear as Louis, his brown eyes wide open in fear, whispered, "She's here, Dad."

* * *

> **Thanksgiving Day**
> **The Basement of Bradford House, Culpeper, Virginia**

"You need to try to eat something."

Lucius Rofocale's faithful demon aide, Tatiana, picked up the tray of uneaten food. Opening the door, she peered back at the miserable human lying on the bed in a white cotton gown. If Tatiana were capable of any form of compassion or empathy, it would be for this poor soul. Knowing any expressions of sympathy for humans would almost surely lead to her destruction, she kept such thoughts to herself. Quietly, she closed the door.

A catatonic eighteen-year-old girl lay in a bed, wide-eyed and staring at the stone wall. Since giving birth, Maricela Antonescu had barely moved a muscle. The protracted delivery proved exhausting. The news of the murder of her parents and boyfriend at the hands of her abductor destroyed whatever hope she had left. Above all, knowing her infant, conceived in a vile violation of her body by a savage beast, was the spawn of the Devil was more than she could take.

"Ah-Ooh-Ah."

Noises emanated from the infant in the bassinet at the foot of Maricela's bed. The crib bounced as the baby kicked her feet. Despite her despair, Maricela could hear the rapid pace of the child's breathing.

It was a sound that she listened to endlessly. It had become familiar and, in some way, soothing. Then, it stopped. Maricela heard nothing but the silence of the room.

Maricela's baby blue eyes fluttered, and she waited to hear the sound again. Finally, a noise broke the silence, but it wasn't the sound she usually heard. It was panting, like someone trying to catch their breath. Instinctively, she sat up, and her bare feet touched the cold tile floor, causing a shiver to run down her back. Maricela noticed her toenails were still painted red and then got up for the first time since giving birth. Steadying herself, she stepped toward the bassinet with some apprehension, unsure exactly what she might see. Surprisingly, a feeling of happiness came over her.

Staring up at Maricela was a beautiful baby with big green eyes and black hair, cooing and grabbing its toes. She gently stroked the baby's head and felt the soft skin of her cheek. The child's mouth turned down, Maricela's motherly intuition kicked in, and she picked her baby up right before the infant started to cry. She cradled the newborn in her arms and sat in a rocking chair, the only other piece of furniture in the sparsely furnished room.

"Shh. That's right, sweetie," Maricela whispered. "Don't cry."

Rocking back and forth in the chair, Maricela suddenly felt a painful, throbbing pressure in her chest. She loosened the top of her nightgown, exposing her firm, swollen breast, engorged with milk. Maricela held her child sideways and guided the baby's mouth to her hard nipple. Mother and daughter struggled initially. Eventually, the baby latched on, and Maricela felt calm and relieved. The baby met Maricela's gaze and reached up toward her mother.

Suddenly, Maricela's back arched in a spasm of pain, and she attempted to push the infant away. With barbs on each tip, the baby's forked tongue clamped on, digging into Maricela's breast, and started nursing furiously. Maricela's arms and legs flailed as she fought her daughter, but the resistance soon subsided, and Maricela's appearance changed. Her youthful skin, now wrinkled, took on a dull, chalky white color and began to flake. Dark circles appeared under her eyes as they sank into her skull. Her rosy, pink lips retreated, exposing her gums, which turned black.

The desiccated remains of Maricela Antonescu slowly slid back into the chair. Retracting its forked tongue between its black lips, a full-grown demon woman with red, serpent-like skin and small, bony horns protruding from above her eyes stood next to the body. Her shiny black hair containing blood-red highlights covered the middle of her back. Her emerald-green eyes surveyed the room.

Snapping her fingers, which had black fingernails, caused her to become instantly clothed in a tight red skirt that flattered her hourglass figure and a black, strapless bustier that held back her ample breasts and accentuated her fire-red skin.

Standing over her dead mother, she hissed, "There really is nothing like a mother's milk, is there?"

The door opened, and a contingent of demons preceded by their leader, Lucius Rofocale, entered. They immediately knelt and lowered their heads.

"I am Prosperine, daughter of Lucifer and Princess of Hell."

His head still bowed, Lucius spoke, "Majesty, I am at your service."

"You are just as my father described you," Prosperine replied. Staring at Lucius, she commanded, "Rise. There is much to do, and time is of the essence."

* * *

Thanksgiving Night
Jack Aitken's Bedroom
9:00 p.m.

"They told me her name is Prosperine," Jack revealed to Anne as he viciously tapped an app on the screen in frustration.

Why can't I get this video to work? Damn it, I hate technology!

Speaking quietly into the phone he held in the palm of his right hand, he paced around the room.

"I am not sure how they know that."

Looking toward the ceiling, he stated skeptically, "Maybe it was a message from Heaven."

Jack kicked a cat toy across the rug. His tone grew frantic. "It means 'Princess of Hell.' I Googled it. Louis was biting his nails, and I could see the concern all over his face. David went to bed early without saying a word. Fortunately, they didn't tell Emma or Michelle. The last thing I need right now is to have to try to explain something like this to them."

"Now is the time to maintain your composure," Anne advised. "I know it is difficult to think straight. Your sisters must have noticed the change in their nephews' demeanor."

Jack exhaled. "I know you're right. If they ask, I'll tell them it was something scary from Louis's video game. Michelle and Emma will be out Christmas shopping most of the day tomorrow. They are both going home on Saturday. Hopefully, I can keep a lid on things until then."

"That sounds like the right plan," Anne spoke reassuringly.

Jack pushed a pile of laundry to the rear of a chair and sat on the edge. He closed his eyes and anxiously rubbed his pounding temple with his left hand. "What do you think happened to Maricela Antonescu?"

The silence between them seemed interminable. Finally, Anne broke it. "I wish I could say that Lucius would let her go, but there will be no fairy tale ending here. Once she is no longer needed, Lucius will kill her."

Jack grimaced. "Just like that?" His shoulders slumped.

Anne did not sugarcoat her response. "Probably quite painfully. Mercy is not in Lucius's playbook. You know that."

"She's still a child," he mused. "Nearly the same age as David."

Jack lamented, "Why does God allow these things to happen?"

"I don't know, Jack," Anne replied sympathetically. "I wish I had the answer for you."

She caught her breath, then added, "There isn't anything we can do for Maricela now. We must protect the boys. Never lose sight of that, Jack."

"Anne, do you think Prosperine is the false prophet or the antichrist?" Jack asked, his trepidation building.

"Lucius let slip something about going off the script," Anne reminded Jack. "I'm not sure what that means, but being a princess could mean something much more dangerous."

"At least Prosperine is a baby," Jack groaned, getting up from the chair.

Surprised at Jack's assertion, Anne's tired eyes opened wide as she questioned, "What do you mean?"

"Come on, Anne," Jack countered cynically. "How much damage can she do? She's still an infant. Even in *The Omen,* Damian was a toddler before he had any power."

Jack cradled the phone with his neck and knelt beside the bed. Pulling his parents' urn from under it, he inquired, "Did you hear anything about George from your former colleagues?"

"Nothing yet," she answered, but Jack failed to hear the troubled tone in her voice.

"Thanks for calming me down, Anne." Jack pushed the urn between his dresser and the wall and covered it with a blanket. "I am feeling better. I'll call you tomorrow."

"Good night, Jack." Anne slowly hung up the phone and murmured, "I hope you're right about Prosperine. I sure hope you're right."

* * *

Thanksgiving Night
Former Town of Kopp, VA/Present-Day
Quantico Marine Base Midnight

The trapdoor in the floor creaked as it slowly opened. A large, long-haired creature with a chiseled physique emerged. Water dripped from holes in the roof. The abandoned concrete building constructed over what remained of a post office provided an ideal home. A cold, damp night such as this would have typically driven a person to seek shelter and the warmth of a fire. But Melanie Hartwell no longer felt the cold.

While the surrounding structures differed, the location was familiar to the beast. More than 100 years earlier, it terrorized the small town that once stood here. It killed livestock and threatened the residents until the only inhabitants left were in the cemetery. Along with the citizens, the food supply disappeared, and the monster moved south, searching for prey. The deserted buildings eventually fell into disrepair and were torn down when the Marine Corps absorbed the land and converted it into an urban combat training center.

Having outlived its usefulness, the Marines never visited the site, leaving the structures to decay slowly. Nature reclaimed parts of the property, now barely visible from the dirt road connecting it to the rest of the base. Only the neglected cemetery hinted at its origins. A light mist surrounded the moon, creating an eerie yellow shade, and small animals rustling through the wispy brown grass avoided the entity trudging through the brush. An earlier downpour caused the small creeks and streams to overflow their banks, turning the dirt road into a sea of mud. Each step by the creature, bearing Melanie Hartwell's corpse in its arms, caused deep imprints in the muck. It methodically slogged toward an even more remote part of the base—a place known as the "Killing Field."

The former training ground once included anti-tank traps, barbed wire, and machine gun nests, simulating defensive fortifications to prepare troops for assaults on seemingly unassailable positions. When the Marines shifted this training to a different base, the location sat vacant until a year ago, when the state of Virginia leased it for a research study. Lying on the ground, attached to a piece of chain-link fencing, a sign read, "Experimental Composting Facility. Keep Out!"

The brute stopped, raised its nose, and took several sniffs. Its superior sense of smell detected an earthy, putrid odor, the smell of decay and decomposition. It caused the creature to shake its nose several times to clear the scent before entering the complex.

CRACK!

A loud snap echoed through the night as the Route 28 Phantom stepped on the warning sign, obliterating it. A light rain began to fall, and a dense ground fog crawled over the sandy soil, hiding the uneven terrain littered with gullies and craters. Ordinarily hazardous, the topography was no obstacle to the beast, who had been here several times in the past few months. Arriving at a long trench, the beast placed Melanie Hartwell's body in the ditch on top of its prior victims and dozens of other bodies in various states of decomposition. The experimental human composting complex on the base proved to be the perfect place to dispose of the dead.

Stepping back from the trench, the killer gawked at the woman. Drops of rain bounced off Melanie's forehead, and traces of blood still ran from the puncture wound in her neck. She lay on her back, mouth agape and eyes wide open. For some unknown reason, the beast knelt and ran its furry, clawed fingers down Melanie's face, closing her eyes. As the shower became a steady downpour, the beast saw a tarp lying on the ground and, grabbing it, covered Melanie, protecting her from the weather. Then, it just stood in the torrential rain, scrutinizing the remains. The water dripping off its matted gray fur began to puddle at its feet before the creature finally turned and began the trek back to its lair.

CHAPTER 7

> Monday, December 1st
> Dr. Kathleen Colby's Office
> 1:00 p.m.

Jack brought his fingertip to his lips, lightly licked it, and then turned the magazine's page. Since Thanksgiving, his sons appeared calmer, almost back to normal, which Jack accepted as confirmation that Prosperine was not an immediate threat. The family's annual Christmas competition was in full swing. They drove around each night admiring the Christmas lights and trying to see who could find the most Grinch blow-ups. However, Jack was still troubled by other matters, despite the more relaxed atmosphere at home.

"Come in, Jack. It is good to see you." Dr. Colby, wearing a colorful sweater with a red-nosed reindeer, stood in the doorway and ushered Jack into her office. "I see your sling is gone. Your hand is feeling better?"

Jack held his right hand up and flexed his fingers. "Yes, but it is a little sore. I had physical therapy this morning. I'm noticing increased dexterity in my fingers, but I still have problems grasping things. There isn't much strength there."

"I'm happy to see you're making progress." She motioned for Jack to sit on the couch.

"So, what's with the sweater, Doc?" Jack's mouth turned upward in a large grin as he sat down.

Dr. Colby glanced down, tugging at the front of her shirt. "Office Christmas party. It's an ugly sweater contest."

Shrugging and gritting her teeth gently, she asked, "What do you think? Any chance I could win?"

Jack chuckled. "I think you'll be in the running."

Dr. Colby sat down and picked up her pencil and pad. "So, how are Louis and David? Getting ready for Christmas?"

"It's their favorite time of the year," Jack replied. "Always has been."

"And you, Jack? How has the season been for you so far?"

"Normally, it is as joyful for me as it is for them." Jack absentmindedly scratched his head. "But thus far, it feels like I am just going through the motions."

Jack edged forward in his chair. "Maybe hanging the outdoor lights the other day in a cold rain didn't help. The gutter fasteners kept breaking, and when I got to the end, the light strands didn't work, and I had to replace some of them."

Dr. Colby sat silently, taking notes, then put down her pencil. "Please go on, Jack."

He hesitated before resuming, "Doing all the decorating is hard. Every ornament reminds me of Amanda. Decorating was always something we did together."

The events of the past several months flashed through Jack's head. George's disappearance, his injured hand, trying to define the nature of his relationship with Anne and the responsibilities placed on his son's shoulders. All these things weighed heavily on him.

Jack exhaled deeply. "I know I should be thankful for David's recovery and other things, but I am finding it difficult to feel gratitude. I can't seem to find the Christmas spirit."

Dr. Colby shifted in her chair and stated, "The holidays can be challenging, Jack. It is often a stressful time of the year for many people."

A bird chirped outside the window, causing Jack to peer over his shoulder and remark, "Such a pretty song." Jack smiled unconvincingly and continued. "Anyway, I'm not sure that stress is my issue. I don't know... it just feels like something is missing. While setting up the train set over the weekend, I came across a Lego railroad station that David had built years ago. I remember being impressed as he did it all with one hand."

Jack closed his eyes and rubbed his forehead. "But now, it's in ten pieces, and the directions he used to build it are missing. I don't know if we have all the right pieces to put it back together. I can't help but see the symbolism in that train station. It is like I can't put my own life back together."

Dr. Colby bounced the pencil eraser on her lips, deep in thought. She put her notepad in her lap and asked, "So what do you think is missing? Something?" She gave Jack a sideways glance. "Or someone?"

"Well played, Doc." Jack nodded. "I feel very mixed up. As I acknowledged during our last appointment, I have feelings for Anne but worry that I am dishonoring Amanda."

"Jack, the author John Green wrote, 'grief doesn't change you. It just reveals who you are.' Your feelings are admirable, yet, at the same time, quite normal. The bond with Amanda started when you were teenagers."

Dr. Colby leaned forward. "Closing a chapter in your life doesn't mean you disregard or forget it. Your feelings for Amanda will always be intense, but what you miss might be the love of another person in the here and now."

The doctor placed her hand over Jack's, emphasizing, "After everything you and your boys have been through, you all deserve happiness. I think it is what Amanda would want. Don't you?"

"I want to believe that, Doc," Jack whispered, his voice choked with emotion. "There is one problem. I don't know if Anne feels the same way... I don't want to lose her friendship over this."

"Love and the risk of losing something go hand in hand. One thing is for sure." Dr. Colby's eyes locked with Jack's. "You will never know unless you take that first step."

* * *

> Tuesday, December 2nd
> Bradford House, Culpeper, Virginia
> 3:00 p.m.

The ornately furnished study had elegant furniture, and the walls were lined from floor to ceiling with bookshelves. In its center, an enormous red mahogany table with four legs as thick as tree trunks dominated the room. Around the table, a demon strike force, personally assembled by George Aitken, reviewed a series of maps. Since slaughtering the biker gang, George had been busy. He was diligently planning a campaign whose outcome would demonstrate his complete loyalty to his new master, Lucius Rofocale.

"What is happening here?" George pointed to one of the diagrams on the table. "When will all the equipment be in place, Barbas?"

Barbas, a demon known for being particularly vicious, glanced anxiously at his peers around the table. Rumors of George's brutality in killing the biker gang spread quickly, and his now prominent position at Lucius's side struck fear in even the most ruthless members of the legions.

"All is going as planned, Lord Aitken. The last items will arrive early next week, and my team has been meticulously training to fulfill their mission flawlessly."

George scratched the razor stubble under his chin while locking eyes with Barbas. "I expect nothing less. Is that understood?"

Glancing at the other lieutenants in the room, he slammed his fist on the table and repeated loudly, "Is that understood!"

Each demon team leader stood at attention and declared, "Yes, Lord Aitken!"

"Very good, my executioner," proclaimed Lucius Rofocale as he stood in the doorway, slowly clapping his hands. "I am pleased."

The entire room knelt at the sound of Lucius's voice.

"Thank you, my Master," George uttered, with his head bowed. "I have disposed of the bodies of the bikers as you suggested, and the preparations for my plan are nearly complete. We are already rehearsing. The results are nearly perfect."

"Well done."

In an almost paternal gesture, Lucius placed his clawed hand on George's head.

"And you will soon tie up those loose ends we discussed?"

George nodded. "And exorcise my demons once and for all."

"Now rise." Lucius beckoned. "Come with me! We are meeting with Lucifer."

* * *

"So, this is the uncle of the prophets?" Prosperine asked, having assumed the appearance of Maricela Antonescu. She leered at George, who stood at attention.

"Yes, Princess," Lucius proudly replied. "He is *our* disciple now."

"Is he?" Prosperine purred, then whispered in Lucius's large, pointed, canine-like ear, "He is handsome... for a human."

Prosperine circled George, running the long black fingernails of her right hand up and down the skin-tight black shirt covering his chiseled abs. She questioned, "So, you will obey all my commands?"

George knelt, kissed the blood-red nails on the fingertips of Prosperine's other hand, and lost himself in her hypnotic green eyes. "You need only command me, Princess."

Turning toward Lucius, she leered wickedly. "Ooh... I think I will like him."

Suddenly, Lucifer's image stood in the center of the room. His projection even reeked of brimstone, and smoke rose from his crimson body. Lucius and Prosperine immediately joined George on their knees.

"Hello, Father," Prosperine greeted Satan. "It is a privilege to see you."

"I am sure it is, daughter," the Devil retorted indifferently. "Tell me, why do you appear to me as a human? You know that I detest them."

Prosperine explained, "Forgive me, but it makes feeding easier. The hunger is still insatiable."

"Very well." Lucifer's nose turned up dismissively. Turning to Lucius, he demanded, "Is our package nearly ready for delivery?"

Lucius quickly answered, "Yes, Master. I am finished and anticipate delivery will be timely. All that remains is to secure our deliverer, which is nearly complete."

"It better be, Lucius," Lucifer threatened in a thundering voice. "Everything is riding on it!"

"I understand, Master. I will not fail you."

"See to it that you don't." Satan viewed George Aitken contemptuously and challenged, "What is this human doing here?"

Lucius stepped forward and replied, "He is my acolyte, Master,"

Prosperine added mockingly, "The uncle of *Grandfather's* prophets, Father."

The Devil raised his lips in a scowl and asked George, "Why should I trust someone who would betray his own kind?"

Still kneeling, head bowed, not daring even to glimpse the Lord of Darkness, George responded, "I have no love for humanity, Master. I will prove that to the three of you."

Steam rising from his superheated body, Lucifer snapped, "We will see."

Flying into a rage, Lucifer screamed, "I want to emphasize one thing! I want humanity to suffer! When they feel they have suffered enough and cry out to God, my Father, for deliverance, I want them to suffer some more. The extermination of humanity will not be quick. It is to be agonizingly slow and painful."

Prosperine affirmed, "I will see to it personally. Father, shall we move operations to Pergamon?"

"Yes," Satan answered bluntly. Turning to Lucius with a steely glare, he menacingly snapped, "Make sure you do not fail me!"

Lucius gulped. "Yes, Master. I understand."

* * *

Lucifer disappeared, but his evil presence still filled the room. It took several moments before Prosperine, Lucius, and George dared to stand up. Lucius shouted for his assistant, "Tatiana, come in here!"

The latch turned, and clawed hands slowly pushed the door open. Terrified that Lucifer might still be present, Tatiana fearfully peered around the door. Quickly surveying the room and finding no trace of Satan, she shut the door and knelt at Lucius's feet.

Tatiana stared at the floor with only the rough purple skin of her head visible. "Yes, Master. What are your commands?"

"So obedient. Just like Aitken." Prosperine pointed at George, hissing through her forked tongue. "I see why my Father relies on you, Lucius."

Lucius bowed, "Thank you, Majesty. Tatiana has served me well. Most of her predecessors were, shall we say, ineffective."

Glancing back at Tatiana, Lucius commanded, "We are moving to Pergamon immediately. Be ready to leave tonight."

"I hear and obey, Master!" Tatiana shouted.

Lucius glared icily at his aide. His black lips curled around his jagged teeth and razor-sharp canines. "There is an older trunk among my possessions. I suggest you take particular care with it. Understood?"

Prosperine's index finger slowly lifted Tatiana's head, and she locked eyes with her. "I also have a command for you."

Tatiana stuttered, "Ye—Yes, your Majesty. How may I serve you?"

Prosperine's lips turned down in an exaggerated pout. "While Father wants humans exterminated, for the time being, they serve a purpose. When we get to Pergamon, I want a herd of them waiting for me. I like variety, so a mix of men and women of all races, ethnicities, and faiths, but they must be the strongest among them."

Prosperine's eyes closed, and a shiver ran down her spine, thinking about her next taste. She let out a moan in ecstasy.

Turning to Lucius, she playfully pouted. "I have a job for George, too. May I make use of him?"

"Of course, Princess," Lucius agreed. "I would be honored."

Instantaneously, George dove to Prosperine's feet. "Your wish will be my command, Highness."

She ran her fingers through the salt-and-pepper hair on George's head. "I know that Lucius has instructed you to kill your nephews, but I want you to bring them to me... alive."

Biting one of her red fingernails, she cooed, "I want to taste prophet."

* * *

Later the Same Evening
Lucius Rofocale's Chambers
Bradford House, Culpeper, Virginia

Tatiana scrambled feverishly to gather up Lucius's possessions. Assuring that Prosperine's human smorgasbord would be ready had taken up far more time than she anticipated, but failing to have her master's belongings prepared for transport would result in, at best, a fierce rebuke. Assuming her human form helped her pick up the pace.

As much as she hated to admit it, her human hands gave her improved dexterity over claws. Tatiana blew her blonde hair from in front of her face and grunted as she wrestled with the last of Lucius's things. She realized why Lucius told her to be careful with the chest. It weighed a ton, and as the sweat dripped from her brow to the floor, she saw it appeared ready to fall apart.

In addition to being damned heavy, the chest had solid gold rivets holding it together and leather straps on both ends to help carry it. The elaborately designed brass lock, a replica of Lucifer's face, hinted this was no ordinary case and held something of considerable importance. Finally, two thick metal straps wrapped around the trunk, further securing it. Suddenly, her ankle buckled.

"SHIT!"

She yelled as she stumbled, dropping the chest to the floor. Alarmed, Tatiana frantically inspected it and, to her horror, found several gold rivets had come loose, and something was on the floor. Tatiana tried to reassure herself she could fix the chest as she checked the rivets to see if they were damaged. Then Tatiana carefully checked if the wooden pieces they secured would go back in place. Finally, she picked up the item on the floor and identified it as a book.

"I can't believe the worn human skin leather, and tattered ends on the pages," Tatiana remarked in amazement as her eyes opened wide. She gently opened the cover. "This is old. I mean, really old." Daring to read the first page, she recognized the title.

L'Histoire Du Demon (The History of the Demon)

"It's our demon textbook, but I've never seen one like this," Tatiana murmured, growing even more curious. She glanced at the doorway, knowing there wasn't much time before Lucius checked her progress. Flipping through the first few pages, she immediately saw something was different.

"Kazimir lost an eye fighting by our Master Lucifer's side."

"Who's Kazimir? I've never heard that name before…"

"The brothers, Lucius and Kazimir."

"Lucius has a brother?" Tatiana's jaw dropped as she read on in astonishment.

"Fought one another. Lucius ended Kazimir's treachery."

"I guess I should say he had a brother," Tatiana whispered.

Shaking her head, she knew something was not right. Lucius would want everyone to know about this. It was the kind of glory he would bask in, but Tatiana knew if she hadn't heard about it, no one else had either.

Tatiana sat on the floor and swept her sweaty hair back as she tried to remember any monument, memorial, or celebration honoring Lucius for this act of bravery. Nothing came to mind.

Suddenly, Tatiana heard footsteps in the hall, and her eyes fixed on the heavy wooden door to Lucius's chamber. Instantly unnerved, she quickly repaired the chest.

Good as new!

She examined the book in her hands, knowing it meant her instant disintegration if Lucius caught her with it. But her need to know more was too strong, and she slipped it into the rear waistband of her jeans and positioned her loose-fitting shirt to hide it.

CHAPTER 8

> *Wednesday, December 3rd*
> *Sulphur Springs, Near the Gate to Hell*

In the aftermath of the visit from Cassiel, Apollyon grew progressively more unnerved. Through the millennia, he compelled penitence from humans, but now, at least for the time being, the use of force and violence was, at best, on hold and possibly over. Unlike in the past, there was still no explanation from God for this shift in strategy. As a result, Apollyon struggled to understand the rationale for the change, let alone accept it. However, the angel's message was unambiguous; Apollyon would no longer be the instrument of God's wrath and judgment.

Staring Apollyon in the face was another fact he could not deny; questioning God forthrightly or demonstrating disobedience was not an option. Therefore, he threw himself into his work, hoping God would come to his senses, remember Apollyon's dependability, and reinstate him to his rightful role in the looming apocalypse. He took solace in the fact that the two prophets had only recently begun their ministry, leaving time for the Lord to change his mind.

Perhaps due to his renewed dedication to his duties or his intensified efforts to divert his attention from God's silence, Apollyon had noticed someone moving in the shadows and began to track the potential intruder. He watched the figure disappear through a fissure in the cavern wall.

"That leads to the Sulphur Springs," Apollyon grumbled. "I will circle around and use the main entrance to confront them."

***

The noxious smell of rotten eggs permeated the large chamber carved in the belly of the Earth millions of years earlier. Banana-yellow, crystallized minerals encrusted the rocks on the lake's shoreline. At the same time, the viscous liquid that filled each crater bubbled up in various shades and colors like cherry red, goldfish orange, and lemon yellow. A lone figure, immersed up to their chin, basked in the sulfuric pool. Apollyon, gripping his battleaxe tightly, stealthily approached the bather.

"Listen to me carefully," Apollyon's voice echoed and boomed through the space. "Get out of the pool, slowly."

A familiar voice responded, "It is I, Lucius."

Lucius exited the lake and approached Apollyon, who loosened the grip on his weapon.

"My old friend, I do apologize," The last droplets of liquid sulfur slid from Lucius's lizard-like skin to the cave floor. "I should have made my presence known. I was performing my detoxing ritual."

Apollyon hooked his battle axe to his armor and replied, "It is alright, Lucius. I was just being vigilant."

Lucius touched the angel of destruction's shoulder. "As you always are, Apollyon. There are no better guardians than you."

Peering through the faceguard of Apollyon's helmet, Lucius saw deep, dark circles under the angel's eyes and asked, "Is something wrong? You seem less than rested."

Lucius apologized before the angel could respond, "Forgive me if I am overstepping. That is a private matter."

Apollyon reacted by removing his helmet and saying, "I wish everyone shared your sentiments."

Lucius tapped his front lip. "Lucifer has not expressed any displeasure with your efforts." But Apollyon did not react.

Intrigued by Apollyon's silence, Lucius's face scrunched in a surprised expression, and he asked, "Are you suggesting that *God* is unhappy with you?"

Apollyon stared down at the cave floor.

"Are you sure you are not imagining things, my friend?" Lucius questioned. "After all your years of loyal service, it seems implausible."

"I am not imagining it, Lucius," Apollyon insisted in a steely tone.

Lucius expressed his sympathy to Apollyon, "I recognize that the duality of your responsibilities to God and Lucifer makes things complicated for you. I also will not insult your intelligence by emphasizing the differences between God and Lucifer or attempting to convince you that God does not understand or care about you. After all, I have my own bias in these matters."

Putting his helmet back on, Apollyon told Lucius, "I must get back to the main gate. Please stay as long as you wish."

"Thank you, Apollyon," Lucius replied. "While I have my prejudices toward God, for your sake, I hope things will improve."

Apollyon walked toward the entrance to the chamber and then stopped. Turning back to Lucius, he sounded uncharacteristically grateful. "Thank you for listening and for your supportive statements. I appreciate it."

Lucius waded back into the sulfur pool. "I will immerse myself once more and then be on my way."

* * *

Friday, December 5th
Brunswick County Sheriff's Office, Bolivia, NC
7:30 a.m.

Anne leaned back in her chair, stretched her hands toward the ceiling, and yawned. She had been experiencing a lot of sleepless nights and was hoping to get some rest over the weekend. The interview process for Sheriff Hill's replacement felt like it might never end, but Anne had narrowed it down to several candidates.

Initially, Anne instantly thought of Ross when asked for her opinion about who should succeed her. His background and experience were perfect for the job. Having worked together for so long, they could almost read one another's thoughts and anticipate each other's every move. In fact, to say she trusted Ross with her life was an understatement.

She called and tried to convince him that he should consider applying for the position, but he reminded her that he was only a few years away from becoming vested in his pension. Anne rolled her eyes, thinking about his other excuse. Ross told her he had a thing for the medical examiner and was going to ask her out.

Regardless, Anne hoped that the hiring committee would decide soon as she was anxious to get her affairs in Ocean Isle Beach tied up so she could join Jack and his sons in Virginia. Anne's phone began to vibrate; it was the call she had been waiting for.

"Hello, Schlomo." Anne pulled her hair back and tied it into a ponytail. "Thanks for returning my call. So, what were you able to find out?"

"Are you somewhere private?" Rabbi Schlomo Tannenbaum asked. "I have a confidential video that I want to send you."

"Send it to this address, Schlomo," Anne texted an e-mail account. "This is a secure platform."

She waited anxiously for the video to come through. "Okay, got it."

"Anne, this is footage from a drone flying over Route 666 outside Culpeper early yesterday afternoon."

Anne opened the link and cringed at the mention of Route 666. She stated, "I thought it was familiar."

"We're coming up to three minutes on the timer in the lower right part of the video. Anne, please inspect what I will freeze on the screen closely."

"Sweet Jesus." Anne's jaw dropped.

"I don't think it is a coincidence. You called asking about any news on George Aitken, and the name George shows up carved into the brush."

"There is no coincidence when it comes to this location either." Anne's voice trailed off.

"I know this is a shock, but we haven't noticed any demon presence in this sector for some time." The rabbi pressed his friend, "Do you know anything about this? It seems ominous, Anne."

What do I tell him? I must say something, but I don't want to risk Jack or the boys' lives further.

"Okay, Schlomo. I'm going to level with you...."

* * *

Friday, December 5th
Aitken Family Home, Bristow, VA
8:00 a.m.

Jack poured the canned tomatoes into the pot and increased the heat on the stove. He pulled a few leaves off the basil plant in the window above the sink and added them to the sauce. The landline phone rang, and Jack picked it up. Before he could speak, Anne's voice came on the line. She sounded strangely anxious.

"Jack, I sent you a video you need to see."

"Anne, what's wrong?"

"Get your cell phone," Anne begged. "Do you have it yet?"

He pressed the speaker on the kitchen phone and searched for his cell phone. "I'm searching for it. What happened?"

"One of my friends at JESU sent me footage that a drone captured early this morning."

"Got it!" Jack declared as he frantically entered the security code and opened his e-mail. "Okay, Anne. What am I looking for here? There are just a lot of trees."

"It's footage from Route 666 in Culpeper," Anne answered nervously. Jack froze for a moment before he heard Anne's voice again. "Can you forward it to the three-minute mark?"

"Culpeper?" Jack questioned. "Route 666?" A surge of fear swept over him like a tidal wave. Studying the screen again, the pavement of Route 666 was still visible despite the weeds and brush growing in the cracks. What Jack read was instantly recognizable: G-E-O-R-G-E.

"Do you see it?" Anne asked pleadingly. "Jack, are you there? Jack!"

* * *

Friday, December 5th
Route 666, Culpeper, VA
11:00 a.m.

The smell of decaying flesh invaded Jack's nose, an odor that made him drop to his knees and gag. While racing down Route 29 to Culpeper, Jack had turned the ringer on his cell phone to vibrate, but that had not stopped it from going off incessantly. The phone vibrated again; this time, Jack answered it, knowing who was on the line.

"Anne," Jack gasped for air.

"Jack, thank God!"

"Body parts," Jack whispered.

"What was that, Jack?" Anne asked. "I can't hear you."

"It's all body parts. Arms, legs." Jack got up and staggered away from the carnage. "His name is made out of body parts."

Realizing where he was, Jack beelined toward the two large rocks that marked the entrance in the woods leading to the Bradford House.

"Jack, go home," Anne begged. "Please don't go there."

"Anne, it's my brother. He could need my help. I called Amanda's parents and asked them to pick up Louis and David. I promise I will call you later."

Anne's head dropped as the call ended. "What have I done?"

* * *

> Friday, December 5th
> Bradford House, Woods Outside Culpeper, VA
> 3:30 p.m.

Remembering what Anne had taught him, Jack stopped in the tree line, just in sight of the Bradford House, then watched and listened. The trail through the woods to get here was so familiar he could have walked it blindfolded. As before, every step Jack took felt like a thousand eyes were watching him, staring from the woods, behind the rocks, everywhere. Having been here more times than he could count, the same creepy feeling each time was unmistakable.

Acutely aware there were no bird songs or squirrels digging through the dead leaves, Jack surveyed the canopy for a sign of life. It was quiet. Too quiet.

"Why does it always have to be so damn quiet around here?"

Of course, Jack knew the answer. It was simple: "Evil lives here." Despite the cold, he wiped the sweat from his neck with the sleeve of his gray sweatshirt and noticed the blood. "Those thorns on the wild roses get me every time."

Jack felt for the phone in his rear pants pocket. Unable to find a signal, it had stopped vibrating hours ago. As it always did when he came here. He was totally and utterly alone. Or so it appeared. Jack crept forward, and after carefully checking his blind spots—another tip from Anne—he made it to the front porch. Peering through a window of the house, it appeared deserted.

Guessing that if Lucius held George captive, he would have him in the basement, he first checked the main floor for demons. *Of course, it could be a trap....* Jack knew that possibility existed, but after everything George had done for him, he would not stand idly by, even if there were only the slimmest chances of finding him.

Turning the knob, Jack gently pushed the front door in and quietly closed it behind him. Going from room to room, he found no one, so Jack headed for the basement. Pressing his body against the wall, he cautiously peered around the corner and down the stairs. It was dim but not completely dark, and Jack snuck down the carpeted stairs. He thought his heart would beat out of his chest as he methodically checked each room, including the cell where Amanda and the boys had been held captive. There was no trace of George anywhere.

Well, one last room.

Jack put his ear against the door but heard nothing. The door creaked as he opened it, making him cringe and murmur, "Jesus, if they haven't heard me before, they know I am here now."

Although it was in the basement, this room had a window. The last rays of daylight shined through it. Jack saw a figure in a chair beside an unmade bed.

Someone's here.

Then Jack quietly asked the person in the chair, "Hello, can you hear me? George, it's Jack; I'm here to help you?"

The figure did not move nor acknowledge his presence. Jack inched nearer and touched the sleeve resting on the chair's armrest. Jack's eyes bulged, and he instinctively covered his mouth to muffle a scream as the arm fell to the floor in a cloud of dust. Recovering from his shock, Jack crept to the front of the chair. Seeing the nightgown worn by the figure and the crib beside the bed, Jack recognized what he was looking at.

"Oh, God. It's Maricela." He gaped. "What the hell did they do to you?" Realizing George was not there, Jack sat on the floor. Tears began rolling down his cheeks as he buried his face in his hands and cried mournfully. After a few minutes, Jack composed himself, gently gathered Maricela's remains, and started for the door. He saw something written on the wall above the bed as he left the room. Still stunned by the condition of Maricela's body, he had to read the sentence several times to memorize it.

Darkness had fallen, and Jack made another all-too-familiar trek to the graveyard where he had buried so many of Mark Desmond's friends, massacred by Lucius. Delicately laying Maricela Antonescu's remains on the ground, Jack dropped to his knees and began digging.

* * *

Friday, December 5th
Route 29 North, Heading Away from Culpeper,
VA Nearly Midnight

It took Jack several attempts to dial Anne's phone number. The cramping in his left hand and the wet dirt and grass under his fingernails made it challenging to press the numbers accurately. His right hand was useless. Jack had dug a grave for Maricela with only his left hand and a rock he located nearby.

Recognizing Jack's number, Anne answered with great relief, "Jack, thank Christ, it's you! I have been so worried!" Anne knew the lecture about Jack's rash actions would wait until another time.

Jack tiredly interrupted, "He wasn't there, Anne."

Anne's heart ached for Jack. "I'm so sorry."

"Lucius knew I would come, Anne." Jack inhaled and hit a button in the car to open the window for fresh air. "He left Maricela Antonescu's body for me to find, desiccated as if someone or something had literally sucked the life from her."

"That poor girl." Anne wiped a tear from her eye, both grateful that Jack was okay but saddened by Maricela's fate. She added, "Maricela did not deserve this."

The glare of headlights from a car coming in the opposite direction caused Jack to squint. He glanced at the passenger seat, afraid Lucius Rofocale would be next to him, as had happened previously on this stretch of road. Thankfully, there was no one there.

"There's more." Jack gulped, wishing he had a water bottle to soothe his parched throat. He spoke hoarsely, "Lucius left me a message on the wall above Maricela's bed."

"What did it say?" Anne asked, unsure if she wanted to know.

Jack closed his eyes for a second to remember, then repeated the phrase Lucius had left for him. "Is this the end of the beginning or the beginning of the end?"

Anne and Jack continued discussing the message's meaning until Jack's throat no longer allowed it. They agreed that Jack would call when he got back to the house. He flipped the radio for the company of a voice. Jack no longer felt like talking. He was exhausted, physically and mentally spent. His thoughts drifted to an incident when he and George were at Boy Scout Camp. They were preparing to fight off several other kids in their troop, planning on a humiliating initiation.

He remembered how, in that moment and throughout their childhood, George appeared to relish the opportunity to face "danger." He never seemed afraid of anything. Jack always felt safe when George was around, but George wasn't there, and Jack was frightened. As his mind raced on, a voice came over the radio. Lost in thought, it was a voice he did not hear.

"In other news, Melanie Hartwell, a twenty-eight-year-old from Hartford, Connecticut, traveling to Charlottesville, is missing, never making it home for Thanksgiving. A motorist found her abandoned car still running on Route 28 South. The only evidence left at the scene was a shoe on the ground near the driver's side door. Based on the vehicle's location, police fear she may have fallen victim to the Route 28 Phantom. Authorities believe this unknown perpetrator is responsible for the disappearance of at least five women since

September. Police are asking for any witnesses to step forward. A picture of Melanie Hartwell is on the Virginia State Police Facebook page. The State Police Superintendent encouraged the public to contact them at the following phone number if they think they have seen Melanie..."

CHAPTER 9

> Saturday, December 6th
> Grand Council Chamber Justice Ecumenical Society United (JESU)
> World HQ Vatican City
> 9:00 a.m.

"Order! Order!" Father Maximus Popovic, a leader in the Eastern Orthodox Church and current Chairman of the JESU Grand Council, slammed his gavel several times on the dais to quell the murmuring and sidebar conversations. Once he restored order, Father Popovic showed video footage from a drone flyover in Culpeper, Virginia.

When the video ended, he proclaimed, "This confirms beyond any doubt that, once again, demons are occupying the Bradford property as a base of operations."

Rampant speculation about how this had gone undetected and the significance of the name "George" imprinted into the ground on the road formerly known as Route 666 was taking hold of the chamber. Father Popovic was determined to end it.

"We will have order!" Chairman Popovic shouted once again, and the room finally fell silent.

"Now, can we all agree that the first question is how demons could have returned to the Bradford House without our knowing?"

The Council members raised their hands in agreement.

"Good. The chairman recognizes Rabbi Tannenbaum."

Rabbi Schlomo Tannenbaum, a long-time member of the Council, stood up and adjusted his gartel, a belt worn by Hasidic Jews. Before he spoke, he placed the back of his hand in front of his mouth and cleared his throat. "The unfortunate reality is that modern technology has its limitations. There is no substitute for boots on the ground; sadly, our numbers have fallen to levels limiting our effectiveness. But I am afraid we may have a much bigger problem."

The Council members studied each other's faces but remained silent, waiting for the rabbi to continue. "I believe I know the 'George' referenced in the video. Last week, I received a call from Anne Bishop." Whispers echoed through the room at the mention of Anne's name. "She was asking if I had any news about the disappearance of George Aitken. Jack Aitken's brother."

Whispers gave way to an intensifying buzz after Jack Aitken became part of the conversation.

Chairman Popovic glared at the Council members, whose chatter immediately ended. He put his open hands in front of his body and shrugged. "We have no intelligence about any George Aitken that I am aware of, rabbi."

"I told Anne that." The rabbi leaned on the dais, preparing to reveal a bombshell. "I am very aware of this Council's frustration at Anne's departure from our organization. Throughout her tenure, she always brought us reliable intelligence. Therefore, I hope we can all keep an open mind about the disappearance of Jack Aitken's brother and what is on that video."

"What are you hinting at, Schlomo?" one of the Council members asked suspiciously.

"I shared the video with Anne!" the rabbi declared.

The hall erupted, and only the clattering of the chairman's gavel restored order.

"Schlomo, what possessed you to do this?" another delegate questioned.

Defiant, Tannenbaum demanded, "Hear me out before you condemn it!"

"Go on," replied a nearly breathless Maximus Popovic.

The rabbi adjusted his rimmed glasses. "After Anne viewed the drone footage, she was profoundly upset and highly concerned that Jack Aitken would react rashly to the contents of the recording if he saw it. What she shared with me next, if true…" He paused. "Well, it could be cataclysmic. I still don't believe it myself."

Alarmed, the chairman pleaded, "What is it, Schlomo?"

* * *

A half-hour later, every Council representative sat in their chair, speechless. There were no more sidebar conversations or heated rants.

"I don't recall anything about a Princess of Hell in the archives," Popovic stated emphatically.

Dressed in an orange robe with gold tassels, Buddhist Master Kelsang Gyatso asked, "Chairman, I know this topic is taboo, but don't we still have access to Mark Desmond's library? While his reputation is that he fell from grace, his research skills were unparalleled. Perhaps there is something in his journals or ancient texts that could shed more light on this matter?"

Removing from his head the red biretta that confirmed his clerical rank, Cardinal Francesco Borghese rubbed his forehead nervously and then exhaled. "Unfortunately, that will not be possible, Brother Gyatso. Six months ago, all the Desmond documents went up in flames. A fire at the Lawrence, Kansas, facility destroyed it all."

"A fire still under investigation due to its unknown and suspicious origin, I might add," Rabbi Tannenbaum interjected.

Imam Kamil Mufti addressed the group, "While our ranks have thinned, front-line reconnaissance is our best source of information. I suggest we send a message to our operatives in the field and see what they may be able to find out. Perhaps a few demon interrogations might confirm the validity of this assertion."

Chairman Popovic nodded in agreement. "Whatever our differences, Anne Bishop was never disloyal to our order and has kept our secrets. As incredible as her claims appear, we must take them seriously."

Turning to his aide, the chairman ordered, "Send word to the entire field organization. We need information, and we need it urgently! Emphasize they are to use any means necessary to obtain it."

* * *

> Sunday, December 7th
> Louis and David Aitken's Bedroom, Bristow, VA
> 9:00 a.m.

David and Louis sat in the middle of their room, their eyes closed in silent meditation, but their teacher's voice for the last several months echoed in their ears.

"Your studies are complete. It is time for your ministry to begin."

"I am nervous," Louis whispered.

"Your nerves are normal, but you have worked diligently and prepared well."

"What if they won't listen to us?" David asked.

Remember, while you share the good news of God's return to live among humanity, there will be doubters, and others will seek to persecute you, but God's message will flow through both of you. Do not be afraid; all of Heaven is with you.

Louis opened his eyes and asked his brother, "Are you ready?"

David nodded his head up and down. Closing their eyes again, they locked hands and, in unison, called out, "God, our Father, open a portal for your servants...."

* * *

> Sunday, December 7th
> Wentworth United Methodist Church, New Hyde Park, NY
> 9:00 a.m.

The Reverend Charles Young was an imposing figure dressed in a black robe, a purple stole trimmed in fringes, and a gold cross worn prominently around his neck. The former Marine stood six foot four, and his shoes were always so well polished they could cast a reflection. Despite his graying temples, he commanded respect wherever he went. Founded in the 1940s, Wentworth United Methodist Church was once a thriving congregation. As a minister for the past forty years, twenty of them at Wentworth, Reverend Young had watched the flock shrink. Now, only fifty people routinely attended services. Regardless, as the Lord's loyal servant, his devotion never wavered. He ministered to the faithful with all the passion he could muster.

Standing in the pulpit, the Reverend glanced over his shoulder at the large cross anchored in the weathered brick wall, then up at the thick rafters of cherrywood, and prepared to deliver a sermon on judging others. As he began to speak, two figures materialized to his right. They floated in the air, surrounded by a green aura. Noticing the startled faces of the congregation, Reverend Young realized they also saw them.

Wearing a navy blue sweatshirt, Louis Aitken concentrated on what he should say. "Peace be with you," he pleasantly greeted the congregation and pointed at his brother. "This is my brother, David, and I am Louis."

Reverend Young searched for a beam of light from a projector or another source for the images but found none. Outraged, he shouted, "Is this supposed to be some joke? This sanctuary is God's house! How dare you ridicule it in this way!"

"This is my father's house, too," David declared.

"Are you saying God is your father?" The Reverend scoffed angrily.

"No, silly," David answered matter of factly. "My dad went to church here when he was a kid."

Afraid of what they were witnessing, members of the congregation were unsure if they should react.

Then Louis interjected, "We are sorry to interrupt, Reverend. Please go on with your sermon. I believe it is about judging others."

Charles Young's bewildered eyes narrowed, and he ran his fingers across the skin of his closely shaven chin. "How did you know that? No one knows what my sermon is about until I give it. I don't even tell my wife what I intend to preach about."

Louis responded, "I know. It is like the combat medals you won for valor that you never told anyone about and keep in a locked trunk in your basement."

Members of the congregation whispered amongst themselves as a shocked Reverend Young asked the boys, "Who are you? This ruse isn't amusing."

David replied, "Like the ruse God has perpetuated about Jesus?"

Louis floated down the middle aisle of the sanctuary and, spreading his arms wide, proclaimed, "Former President Reagan, referring to Jesus, in a letter to his dying atheist father-in-law, wrote, 'either he was who he said he was, or he was the greatest faker and charlatan who ever lived.'"

Joining Louis, David added, "President Reagan took his argument one step further: 'But would a liar and faker suffer the death he did when all he had to do to save himself was admit he'd been lying?'"

Reverend Young nearly stumbled down the stairs from the altar and steadied himself by holding the communion rail. Members of the congregation slowly slid away from the boys toward the opposite ends of the pews.

"Don't be afraid," Louis pleaded.

Quoting scripture, David revealed, "We are not here to abolish but to fulfill."

"Fulfill what?" Reverend Young questioned.

"I'm surprised you don't remember this one, Reverend," David teased. "Revelation 11: 'And I will appoint my two witnesses, and they will prophesy for 1,260 days.'"

Regaining some of his composure, Reverend Young challenged, "You two? Prophets?"

"Wasn't your sermon today to be about judging others?" Louis asked. "Is it our appearance?" He pointed at his brother and asserted, "Maybe his New York Giants jersey? Is it our youth that makes you question your senses?"

"Maybe it is our autism," David interrupted.

Reverend Young turned his head to the side and asked quizzically, "Autism?"

"Second Corinthians Chapter 12, Verse 9." Observing the congregation, Louis asserted, "My power is made perfect in weakness."

One of the congregants exclaimed, "My cousin has an autistic child, and he says his son can't lie."

Louis smiled. "That is not entirely true. We can develop the ability to lie, but we're terrible at it."

David shrugged and acknowledged, "Dad always knows when I lie."

This time, the congregation, less fearful than before, laughed quietly.

A voice shouted from the rear of the church, "How do we know you are not false prophets like the Book of Revelation tells us?"

Suddenly, the doors to the sanctuary flew open. A young woman stood in the doorway, bent over with her hands on her thighs, catching her breath.

The noise immediately drew the congregation's attention, and their jaws instantly dropped. They slowly turned back, looking at Reverend Young, whose face was ashen white, as if he saw a ghost.

"Jessica?" he muttered. "It can't be."

"Grandfather!" Jessica yelled as she ran down the aisle and fell into his arms. He hugged her tightly, making sure it was all real. Stunned, the Reverend found the boys still floating in the center aisle. Jessica had been mute and spent most of the past ten years of her life in a wheelchair.

"Isn't this the time of year we celebrate the birth of one who performed many miracles?" Louis reminded the spectators. Turning to Reverend Young, he affirmed, "It is your faith that has made her whole."

As the boy's images faded, their voices echoed through the chamber. "We will all see one another again very soon."

* * *

> *The Same Day, Just Before Dark*
> *Main Street, Downtown Warrenton, VA*

Old Town Warrenton was a twenty-five-minute drive from Bristow. Jack had planned to do his Christmas shopping online, but when his in-laws suggested they take his sons for the afternoon, he thought the change in scenery might do him good. After finding no sign of George at the Bradford House, he was in a dark place mentally.

Turning toward Main Street, a policeman bundled against the cold wearing a ski hat greeted him.

"Good afternoon, sir. Here for some holiday shopping?" the policeman asked; water vapor from his mouth condensed like a puffy white cloud in front of his face.

"Yes, officer. My first time here," Jack replied. "Could you direct me to the parking lot?"

The officer leaned next to the open car window and, pointing to the right, stated, "The south lot has no spots left. Try the one two blocks over."

"Thank you."

As Jack pulled away, the officer added, "Merry Christmas."

Finding a space in the lot, Jack exited the car and turned up the collar of his jacket against the rising wind. The rapidly falling temperatures were already causing a thin layer of ice to form on puddles near the storm drains, and Jack browsed the icy windowpanes of the shops along First Street as he headed toward the center of town. Despite his melancholy mood, even he had to admit the holiday decorations were beautiful.

Entering a park in the village square, Jack saw Santa and Mrs. Claus, dressed in red suits with white fur trim and black boots and wearing broad grins. They were holding court in a gazebo. Children struggled to behave while they waited in line, in the cold, for their turn to tell Santa what they wanted for Christmas. Jack recalled that the boys loved Santa, but only from a distance. A cautious wave of their hand was the closest either got to his lap.

An open-air pavilion with white pillars wrapped in silver and gold garland covered a skating rink, from which joyous shouts and screams echoed throughout the square. The sweet smell of hot chocolate filled the air, but nothing could top the dazzling white lights on an immense spruce tree. It was adorned with red bows on every bough and topped with a translucent blue star.

A vendor selling chestnuts yelled, "Hot chestnuts. Four dollars a dozen." He filled a paper bag and handed it to a customer who seemed just as interested in using it as a hand warmer as they were in eating the nuts.

"Bratwurst, sausage, here!" another seller cried.

I wish Dad were here; he would love the bratwurst.

However, one thing appeared out of place in this joyful pre-Christmas setting—a scene ripped from a Currier and Ives print or a Dickens novel. A towering presence wearing a brown robe strolled across the commons, throwing handfuls of shimmering water in the air, which fell to the ground as flurries of snow. The figure followed Jack across the park, and neither Jack nor any other shoppers noticed its existence.

* * *

Entering Warrenton's Main Street was like stepping back in time. Christmas wreaths fashioned from sprigs of holly leaves or Douglas fir limbs hung from every lamp post, and brick buildings constructed in the 19th century lined both sides of the cobblestone road. Thousands of white lights, strung from the rooftops, created a bright umbrella over the shoppers who delighted in the splendor of the unexpected snow flurries. They continued to hurry from store to store in search of the perfect gift.

Masquerading as an elf dressed in a red plush hat with a jingle bell on the tip, a young lady approached Jack. Her chapped lips drew back, revealing pearly white teeth.

"Would you like a map of the town?" she asked cheerfully.

"Thank you," Jack answered, cracking a slight smile as she handed him a diagram with a list of the retailers.

He briefly studied the map, tucked it in his coat pocket, and wandered the increasingly windy winter streets. There seemed to be an endless stream of out-of-tune Christmas carols played by a sidewalk band. Jack stopped before The Open Book, a quaint, independent bookstore whose window display featured many holiday titles. There was Dr. Seuss's *The Grinch Who Stole Christmas* and a leather-bound first edition of Jack's favorite, *A Christmas Carol*. It was the type of store he, Amanda, and Josephine would have had to drag George out of any day of the year, let alone at Christmas. With a deep, sad exhale, Jack wondered if he would ever see his brother again. Jack moved on, still unaware of the figure that shadowed him as he walked through the town.

* * *

Clutching a steaming hot cup of coffee from the Deja Brew Café, Jack strolled further down Main Street and came across the Warrenton Hobby Shoppe. Long icicles hung from the eaves of the overhang, and strings of colored lights glowed from inside. He blew away the steam rising from the hot beverage and, after a brief debate, decided to go in. A bell jingled as he opened the door, and a rush of cold air swept in behind him, causing a chill to run down his spine.

A young male voice called from one of the aisles, "Hello! My name is Max. I'm restocking the shelves, but if there is anything I can help with, give me a shout."

Jack's gloved finger rubbed his lip as he saw a sign for board games. A thought popped into his head, "Do you have any vintage Monopoly games?"

The top of Max's head appeared. "We sure do!"

A tall teenager with acne and wavy black hair, wearing jeans and red Converse high-top sneakers, stepped out and signaled Jack. "Over here." Max pointed at a shelf in the back of the store and asked, "Looking for anything in particular?"

"The 2004 NFL Collector's Edition," Jack answered. "My son loves to play so much we have worn out the board."

While David was fighting cancer, the one thing he would get out of bed to do was to play Monopoly. David, Jack, and Aunt Emma played for nearly a year at lunch and after dinner. Max's blue eyes carefully scanned the shelves, and he moved boxes around, searching for the game. "I don't see it here, mister, but let me check in the back."

Max disappeared behind a curtain and left Jack standing in the aisle. Watching out the store window, Jack saw that the snow flurries had become larger flakes.

"I guess the weather forecaster missed this one," he murmured. Jack surveyed the curtain, hoping Max would return soon so he could go back to the car and head home. He overheard groans and sounds like something scraping across the floor, and then Max emerged cheerfully and handed a box to Jack.

"I found it! It was on the top shelf. I could swear there was nothing up there when I straightened up the backroom after closing last night."

The weight of the endless anxieties on Jack's shoulders shifted briefly, and he felt a small rush of excitement for the first time in days. "David is going to love it!" Jack exclaimed. "Thank you for taking the time to find this! You have made this trip worthwhile."

Jack paid for the game and, reaching into his wallet, handed Max a ten-dollar bill saying, "Merry Christmas."

Max waved his hands. "I can't accept that. I'm only doing my job."

Jack pressed the money into the palm of the teen's hand and whispered, "Don't hurt an old man's feelings. I insist."

Locking eyes with Max, Jack repeated, "A Merry Christmas to you."

* * *

The intensity of the snowfall was picking up, thinning the crowds as Jack backtracked along Main Street toward the parking lot. From the corner of his eye, across the street, he noticed a family with two small children pointing through a wrought-iron fence at a nativity scene. The white spotlight, directed at baby Jesus, illuminated the entire display. Jack finally realized what the children had been pointing at; unusually tall figurines. They were life-size. As the family departed, Jack crossed the street and took their place.

A sign identifying the building as the Warrenton Presbyterian Church stood near the sidewalk by an arched entrance topped with stained glass and dominated by two heavy wooden doors. Like the rest of the town, the red brick structure appeared old but immaculately maintained. The exterior was also far more ornate than the town's other structures, with extensive architectural cornices around the roofline and a majestic steeple stretching skyward, topped with a large cross that stood out even in the falling snow.

Placing the plastic bag with David's gift between his sneakers, Jack grabbed the fence with both hands and peered through it at the display. A temporary wooden structure lined with a thatch roof served as a replica of a stable, topped with a bright silver star. Straw covered the ground, but snow piled up where the grass met it. Mary, her hands clasped in prayer and her head covered with a light blue scarf, with Joseph standing by her side, knelt at the manger, staring adoringly at her child.

Jack fixated on Mary and Joseph, thinking... *Did they know? Was their child's destiny communicated to them like—*

"*Like your sons, Jack?*" a voice answered.

CHAPTER 10

> Outside Warrenton Presbyterian Church
> Warrenton, VA

Jack gripped the black iron fence tightly, unsure if what he heard was just his imagination. With a certain trepidation, he turned his head to the right. His eyes widened as his mouth dropped open. Beside him was a man dressed like a monk in a brown robe. Jack raised his hand to shield his eyes from the blinding light radiating from under the figure's hood.

"Perhaps you'll get to ask that question to someone who truly knows," the same voice calmly suggested, then added, "You need not fear me. I will not harm you."

Still in shock, Jack noticed that the snow had let up; in fact, the flakes hung around him, suspended in mid-air, and melted away when he touched them. Across the street, it was as if time stood still. Patrons leaving restaurants froze in place with the doors wide open. People along the road halted mid-step, one foot on the ground and the other dangling in the air. A father, scolding his child, had his mouth open, and his smoky breath hung in the air as his index finger, which was part of the lecture, did not move.

"Wh-what's going on?" Jack stuttered, trying to get the words out.

The stranger began pulling down its hood, and Jack backed away in fear, expecting the worst. However, it revealed a human face with rosy cheeks and sandy blond hair instead. He began to speak. "I thought this form would reassure you. I am Gabriel." He pointed his index finger at the nativity scene and continued, "I have something you need to see."

Jack watched in wonder as the iron fence disappeared and the star rose from the roof of the exhibit. As it climbed into the sky toward the heavens, it grew more prominent, and the light radiating from it was magnificent beyond words. A strong smell of animals penetrated Jack's nasal passages as the once-inanimate lamb stirred and snuggled up to its mother. A donkey brayed as it ate the straw, and Jesus, lying in the manger, kicked and cooed. Jack's eyes welled up, overcome by its simple beauty and the seeming peace of it all.

Wiping a tear running down his cheek and forgetting Gabriel's presence for a moment, he whispered, "What a privilege."

"Indeed, it is, Jack," Gabriel stated firmly. "A privilege no human ever received, until now."

Jack, shaking with emotion, asked, "This is real? Do you mean I am witnessing the birth of Christ?"

Gabriel placed his hand on Jack's shoulder to steady him and answered, "These are shadows of what has been, but you are seeing it as it happened."

Before Jack could ask his next question, Gabriel responded, "Yes, I am the angel who told Mary God would favor her." Locking eyes with Jack, he added, "I know you have questions." The angel paused, then continued, "And doubts."

Jack's eyes dropped, and he responded, "And who am I to question God, right?"

Surprisingly, Gabriel answered gently, "Our Father understands your reservations. But there is more you need to know. Look again."

He had not noticed it previously, but Jack saw two glowing, fiery red eyes staring from the darkness of a corner of the stable. Slowly, a figure dressed in black, unseen by Mary or Joseph, emerged and moved toward the manger. Large fangs protruded from its mouth, and steam filled the air around its head when it removed its hood. Not wanting to see, Jack turned his head away, but he recognized the figure as Satan.

As the Devil approached the family, a thundering voice asked, "What are you doing here, brother?"

"Michael, my so-called brother." Satan curled his lip defiantly. *"I have come to see this abomination our Father has created for myself."*

The Arch Angel Michael, his shiny armor reflecting the starlight and his hand tightly gripped on his sword's hilt, floated in on a cloud. *"You don't belong here!"*

Satan mocked his brother, *"Ever the dutiful son. Tell me, Michael, why would you, with all your power and might, bow low to these humans?"*

"You silver-tongued serpent!" Michael declared. *"You are the prince of deception and lies! I am unlike those of your demon minions, who you can easily manipulate and control. You can never mislead me into betraying our Father!"*

"We will see," Satan snarled as he gnashed his teeth. Enraged, he glared at the manger and vowed, *"God's so-called son will not live to sit on his throne! I swear it!"* As Satan disappeared, his voice echoed, *"His death is inevitable and coming much sooner than you think. He will never fulfill his prophecy!"*

* * *

Turning to Gabriel, Jack pleaded, "Why does God allow Satan to exist? To do the things he does to humanity?" Boldly, Jack added, "Why does he not destroy this evil?"

Gabriel closed his eyes. "It is humanity that allows evil to endure, not God."

Jack scratched his head. "I don't understand."

"Humans are not robots," Gabriel explained. "You have the choice to obey or disobey God's laws. The price for Adam and Eve's expulsion from Eden requires that humanity choose a path, not just accept the one our Father provides. One of those choices includes wandering in darkness. This challenge allows evil to endure."

An awkward silence gripped the two of them. Then, like deep channels, grooves appeared on the angel's forehead as his expression grew more serious. "Lucifer is my brother. You have a brother, too, Jack. Tell me, would you kill him if he were a murderer? Would you put his head in the noose? Would you give the order to pull the trigger or flip the switch yourself?"

Jack retreated like a dog with his tail tucked between his legs, but still, the angel persisted, "Are all the souls that demons harvest good people whom they have corrupted? Perhaps these demons serve as instruments of punishment for those beyond redemption?"

Softening his tone slightly, Gabriel continued, "You may find this difficult to accept, but our Father wrestles with similar concerns. Lucifer is God's son, as Louis and David are to you. Besides, a campaign to eliminate Lucifer could destroy the world! God promised Noah he would never again lay waste to the planet, a covenant our Father intends to keep. Even if humans do everything they possibly can to destroy it."

Jack exhaled deeply and questioned, "If all of this is as set in stone as it appears, why do you show me these visions? Is it right to give me hope when none really exists?"

"War is the ultimate test of wills," Gabriel answered cautiously. "Victory is never a foregone conclusion. War always produces two different perspectives. Do you choose to understand the battle from only one point of view? Sometimes, there is a deeper message than just who wins or loses."

Sheepishly, Jack asked, "What did Satan mean when he declared that death was coming much sooner than Michael thought? According to the Bible, Jesus started his ministry as an adult."

The angel hesitated. "I am not sure you want to know, Jack."

Despite Gabriel's warning, for some reason that he could not explain, Jack insisted, "Please, I need to know."

Slowly waving his hand from left to right, the angel called out, "One shadow more."

* * *

Shortly After Christ's Birth in Bethlehem
Royal Chambers of King Herod the Great in Judea

"BETRAYED!" King Herod screamed. "They have betrayed me!"

Herod paced the room, seething with anger. Members of the court stood back, trying to avoid being the target of Herod's wrath.

Frothing at the mouth, he thundered, "Kill them! I want these three self-styled kings hunted down and brought before me!"

Wiping the saliva from his beard with the sleeve of his robe, Herod yelled, "Find the child, this so-called Messiah. Kill him!"

A figure standing next to the king's throne stepped forward and whispered in the king's ear, "Sire, may I have a word?"

* * *

"Lucius!" Jack cried, pointing at the advisor. Turning to Gabriel, Jack exclaimed, "That's Lucius Rofocale!"

Gabriel acknowledged, "Evil never sleeps; it is always there. Like ignorance and fanaticism, it needs feeding."

As he saw Lucius whispering in Herod's ear, Jack questioned, "Is Lucius behind the massacre of the innocents?"

"Watch, Jack," the angel responded.

* * *

"Yes, Lucius, you are right!" Herod declared. "Guards!"

A contingent of Roman centurions dressed in blood-red sagum garments entered the chamber.

"Marcus, I want you and your legions to leave for Bethlehem immediately. You will visit the surrounding areas as well. Leave no stone unturned."

"Yes, Prefect," the Roman Captain responded.

Lucius stepped forward, a particularly vicious grin on his face. "You will put to the sword every child, in every village, under the age of two."

Turning toward Lucius, the Captain replied, "I will see to it personally, my Lord."

* * *

Jack fell to his knees, his face buried in his hands. "It isn't possible."

Tugging on Gabriel's robe, Jack begged, "Tell me it isn't so. That Roman Captain resembled me!"

CHAPTER 11

Still Outside Warrenton Presbyterian Church
Warrenton, VA

An unfamiliar voice answered, "Sir, are you alright?"

Jack found himself kneeling in the snow, grabbing a man's coat.

Helping Jack to his feet, the man asked, "How long have you been here?"

Suddenly, feeling the cold, Jack shivered.

The man grabbed Jack's hands and suggested, "You might have frostbite. I'm Pastor Adam Graves." Pointing at the Presbyterian Church, he insisted, "Why don't you come inside to warm up, and perhaps we can talk? You seem to be troubled."

Dusting the snow from his pants, Jack tried to collect himself and answered, "That is kind of you, Pastor, but I need to get home."

"Are you sure you are okay to drive?" Pastor Graves eyed Jack skeptically. "You haven't been drinking, have you?"

Jack checked his pocket for his car keys, still trying to understand what he had experienced, and replied, "Really, I am fine. But thank you for your concern."

Flexing his fingers in his gloves to keep them warm and shaking his head, Pastor Graves watched Jack walk to the end of the block and turn the corner.

Jack found the car, and as he headed home, the growing realization of what it meant to be God's prophet was getting to him. Despite Christmas's message of hope, no matter how hard Jack tried, he could not embrace Louis and David's fate. While considering the boys' destiny, he could not help but contemplate his own. Viewing the face of the Roman soldier was like looking at his reflection, and it chilled him to the bone.

* * *

> *Simultaneously with Jack's Vision*
> *George and Josephine Aitken's Home,*
> *North Myrtle Beach, South Carolina*

Her glasses perched on the end of her nose, Josephine Aitken absentmindedly twirled her blonde hair while studying the computer screen on the desk before her. Then, she once again began furiously pounding the keyboard. Her cybersecurity skills were in great demand, and the opportunities to work were seemingly endless. Despite the intensity of the job, she was thankful for the distraction it provided. Her husband's disappearance weighed heavily on her mind.

Josephine took a long sip from her aluminum water bottle, then pushed up the sleeves of her black and gold Towson University sweatshirt to her elbows. Leaning back in the chair, she flexed her fingers and reached toward the ceiling for a long stretch. Bringing her arms down, Josephine caught a scent on the sweatshirt and inhaled deeply. Her lips turned up sadly, and then she spoke to no one in particular.

"Are you there, George?" Josephine yearned for her husband. "I can't explain it, but I can sense your presence for some reason. It feels like you are nearby."

What happened to George remained a mystery. Josephine pulled up a video on her computer, watched her husband walk across the hospital parking lot, and then vanish. She had watched it nearly a thousand times, searching for some clue to explain how he appeared in a video after being declared dead. There were no answers, which mirrored the explanation from the doctors on how George survived a strain of rabies that had never existed before. None of this made any sense.

"Time to take a break," Josephine announced.

Getting up from her chair, she went to the kitchen and grabbed dinner from the freezer. A few minutes later, she returned to the office with a plate of pasta. Entering the room, she froze and dropped her plate to the hardwood floor, shattering it.

"Oh, God." Josephine gaped and took a step backward. "It can't be."

Somehow, George was standing in front of her. She felt faint but stayed upright by throwing herself at him and burying her face in his chest. Wrapping her arms around George's back, Josephine squeezed him tightly, and the tears poured from her eyes like rain. Overcome with emotion at seeing him, she failed to notice the tangible changes in his appearance. His body was tightly sinewed and thinner than she would have remembered. His hair had lightened in color, and he had a tapered buzz cut, showing the veins on his skull as they pumped. His clothes were like nothing she had seen him wear before. They were dull, drab, and reeked of an odor she could not place. She held George as if she would never let him go, but his smell repelled her enough to take a step backward.

Sobbing, she managed to ask, "Where have you been?"

There was no response, but looking into his eyes for a moment, Josephine thought she caught a glimpse of her husband. But then, his typically light blue eyes darkened, turning almost black. The eyelids were so far back in their sockets that they were not visible, and he never blinked. George's lips curled in an unnerving way. It was not a face filled with joy… it was an appearance of insanity.

Josephine's moment of happiness instantly transformed into fear. She loosened her grip and backed away. The transformation in George's appearance was more readily apparent as she did.

"What's wrong, George?" she asked, uneasily. "You don't seem like you are feeling well."

Josephine pleaded, "Say something. Won't you speak to me?"

George broke the silence between them, not with his voice but by raising his hand, causing the door to slam behind Josephine. An ominous click echoed a second later, locking them in the room.

"Where is the zip drive with the program you developed to tap encrypted communications?" George demanded in a monotone voice that filled the room. "I want it."

Josephine's eyes darted around the room, but she knew there was no way to escape. Beads of sweat rolled down the back of her neck.

"Wh-why?" she stammered.

George rolled his lower lip down. It was his way of saying he was sorry. She called it his "boo-boo" face. Typically, she would return the gesture, but George grabbed her throat with his right hand before she could respond and started choking her. Her feet were dangling as her husband raised her slowly from the ground.

"Don't make me hurt them." Holding his phone in Josephine's face, he impatiently declared, "I won't ask you again."

The picture of her children caused Josephine to stop struggling. Horrified, she frantically pointed to a desk drawer. Without releasing his grip on Josephine, he opened the drawer and quickly found a zip drive. Holding it in front of his wife, he asked,

"Is this it?"

Josephine nodded anxiously. Shaking the disc in front of her, George threatened, "It better be. If it isn't, I will kill them... and you."

Releasing Josephine, he pocketed the drive. Still gasping for air, she begged, "Please don't hurt our children."

Revealing his true intentions, the same look of madness appeared on George's face as he grabbed Josephine's throat again.

CHAPTER 12

> Monday, December 8th
> American Press Service (APS) Studio, Washington, DC
> 6:00 p.m.

"One minute to show time," the floor manager shouted as she darted around the studio, making last-minute adjustments to the set. Maria Connor, the moderator of the highly successful cable show *The Connor Crew,* made her way to the chair at the center of the stage. Another crew member clipped a microphone to the lapel of Maria's black jacket. A hairstylist gave Maria's platinum-blonde hair one last squirt of hairspray before swiftly exiting the set.

"Three, two, one," the camera operator counted down and pointed to the red light on his equipment, showing Maria and her guests that they were on the air.

Maria sat up straight, drew back her shoulders, and smiled directly into the camera. "Good evening, I am Maria Connor. Welcome to *The Connor Crew.* On tonight's show, we will go where many people fear to tread these days and seek answers to the question: Is religion in decline?"

The camera angle broadened, bringing two figures sitting on a couch into view. Turning to her right, Maria continued, "Our guests tonight are Constance Wright, Executive Director of the World Atheist Forum, an international organization that has seen its membership increase sharply in the past few years."

Sitting on the edge of her cushion, wearing a blue blazer with matching slacks and a white blouse, Constance spoke confidently, having been on television many times. "Thank you for having me, Maria."

"And Doctor Bartholomew O'Brien," Maria added, "Dean of the School of Theology at Saint Ignatius University and one of the world's leading theologians."

Dressed in a three-piece, gray, pinstripe suit, Doctor O'Brien leaned back in his seat and crossed his legs. "Yes, Maria. I also thank you for the opportunity to be here."

Maria Connor said, "Constance, let's start with you. Tell me, what do you think about the status of religion today?"

Constance watched Maria, and the camera moved to the right so both women could share the screen. "Statistically, organized religion and its closely linked beliefs are on the decline. Since 2007, nearly 90% of industrialized countries, representing roughly 60% of the world's population, have seen decreased numbers of people identifying as religious."

Maria's eyebrows raised, surprised by the numbers. "What about in the United States? What are the trends here?" she asked.

"Interestingly enough," Constance answered, shifting in her seat, "of all of the countries surveyed, the most significant drop was in the United States."

The corners of Maria's lips fell downward, and an appearance of concern came across her face. "I see." Turning to her other guest, she inquired, "What are your thoughts on this, Doctor O'Brien?"

Doctor O'Brien leaned forward and replied, "For the devout among us, Ms. Wright's facts are cause for concern, but I would not be dancing on the grave of organized religion just yet."

Maria motioned with her hands as she encouraged her guest, "Please explain, Doctor?"

Adjusting the gold-rimmed glasses on the end of his nose, Doctor O'Brien expanded on his answer. "What I mean is the history of the world's great religions is one of evolution. As the so-called flock's attitudes and ethics change, religious leaders often find the need to change along with them."

"That is an interesting perspective," Maria declared. "After this commercial break, I will get my guests to comment on an extraordinary event—or, I might say, events—that occurred yesterday and whose impact is sweeping the globe."

* * *

"We're back," Maria Connor announced. "I want to show a brief clip of just one of many videos that went viral yesterday, and then I will ask my guests to share their thoughts. This video is from the Wentworth United Methodist Church in New Hyde Park, New York."

"Grandfather!"

A voice cried out, and a teenage girl running down a church aisle flashed across the screen. She entered the minister's embrace, and the camera turned to the left, revealing an empty wheelchair in the doorway leading to the church sanctuary.

A woman's voice heard off camera shouted, *"It's a miracle!"*

The video ended, and Maria quickly turned to her guests, anticipating their responses. "So, what do you make of the video you just saw?"

Constance scoffed dismissively. "I don't see anything miraculous about it. It strikes me as a hoax."

Doctor O'Brien added, "I'm afraid this is one time I have to agree with Constance."

Maria pointed toward a screen across from the panelists, already showing the image of a person wearing a clerical collar, and stated, "Joining us now is Reverend Charles Young, Minister at the Wentworth United Methodist Church. One of the members of his congregation shot and posted this video. Reverend Young, thank you for appearing on *The Connor Crew*."

THE GATHERING STORM

Reverend Young replied, "It is my pleasure, Ms. Connor."

Maria asked concisely, "So, tell us about your relationship with the young lady in the video we just saw."

"That beautiful young lady is my granddaughter. Until yesterday, she had lived most of her life in that wheelchair."

As Maria glanced in their direction, Constance and Doctor O'Brien sat uncomfortably.

She continued, "Reverend, what explanation do you have for what occurred in your church yesterday?"

"An earthly one?" the Reverend responded. "I have none. Pure and simple, this is a miracle from God."

"That is preposterous!" Doctor O'Brien blurted out.

"You are misleading the public!" Constance Wright shouted.

Calmly, Reverend Young replied, "With all due respect to your guests, they were not present in my church. If they wish to call me a liar, they can do so. But if you investigate my background, you will find that my integrity is not in question. Particularly considering the other visitations that occurred yesterday."

"I wanted to get to that next. What do you know about these visitations?" Maria asked eagerly.

Reverend Young was stone-faced, the intense focus of a former Marine. "I know how this sounds, Ms. Connor, but two young men, calling each other Louis and David, appeared in our sanctuary. They emerged out of thin air in front of the whole congregation."

"Is this a serious show, Ms. Connor, or a circus? That is ridiculous and impossible!" Constance decried, sweat pouring down her forehead. "It is a fake, and you know it!"

Reverend Young countered firmly, "Hoax? Fake? More than 100,000 people from all over the world have posted videos of similar occurrences. Even if I assume that 99% of these people are frauds, how many would be real? Who could pull this deception off without any leaks to the press or general public?"

"Where are these two prophets?" Doctor O'Brien asked skeptically. "I don't see them on the video."

"Unfortunately, I have no answer to that question," Reverend Young admitted while he shook his head. "Their voices are audible, but their images do not appear in any videos."

"Isn't that convenient?" Constance rebuked the Reverend.

"It is decidedly inconvenient," retorted Reverend Young as he stood his ground. "But only to those such as yourself, who need to see and touch things before you can accept their reality. Those of us who have faith know the truth."

Maria Connor interrupted, "I am sorry to end this intriguing debate, but our time is up. I want to thank my guests but, most of all, my viewers. We will be back tomorrow, but today's topic might be difficult to top!"

* * *

> Tuesday, December 9th
> Cubicle at Etna Casualty Insurance Company, Chantilly, VA
> 9 a.m.

Jack clicked the mouse and pulled up the next file in his electronic underwriting queue. Cloverleaf Construction was an unfamiliar account, so he popped a spearmint Life Saver into his mouth and prepared to get into the details. Since his gardening was over with for the winter, and the boys worked full time, Jack took a part-time position with Etna Casualty Insurance just to keep busy.

Despite his doubts about his sons being prophets, Jack could not help but be proud of what they had accomplished two days ago. However, he would have preferred they had told him about it first. Nonetheless, their debut was a success, and in some respects, getting on with this journey carried with it a slight sense of relief.

A binging noise came through his headset, signaling he had a Skype call.

"Good morning, this is Jack Aitken."

"Jack, it's Anne."

Anne's face appeared on Jack's screen after clicking a prompt at the bottom of the box.

"I've been trying to get you, Anne. I was beginning to get concerned."

Anne rubbed her tired eyes. "I'm sorry about that. Between this situation at the hospital surrounding the rabies virus and the search for my successor, I have been burning the midnight oil."

"You seem exhausted."

Giving the thumbs-up sign, she reassured Jack, "I'll take a nap."

Anne grabbed a bottle and had a long drink.

Jack immediately recognized the brand and kidded her, "Classic Coke, the morning coffee drink of the South."

"I need the caffeine this morning. While there is a break in the action here, I wanted to catch up with you about Louis and David."

Anne's facial expression changed, and she beamed.

"Jack, they were extraordinary!" Anne gushed as if Louis and David were her children. "It was astonishing to hear their command of the Bible and how they challenged and sparred with religious leaders who have been studying liturgy all their adult life."

"That's high praise coming from someone with your background in religious studies, Anne. What impressed you the most?"

She exclaimed, "Their answer to a rabbi's question about identifying God's prophets! Louis spoke fearlessly, without compromise; his answers focused on God's word and the mission he and David were undertaking."

Anne's glowing assessment of their effectiveness rivaled his pride in their accomplishment. Jack added, "Personally, I liked David tackling modern concerns, specifically the use of social media."

"That was another high point, Jack." Anne continued, "He challenged people by asking how they could attend church on Sunday and listen to sermons about not bearing false witness against their neighbor, only to hide behind an anonymous handle or e-mail address the rest of the week."

Jack replied, "I know what you mean. He confronted that one young lady about bullying her peers and taking some perverse pleasure in the misery of others. It was powerful stuff."

"Even I learned something, Jack," Anne admitted. "While my JESU training emphasized respect for those who worship differently, the concept of redemption, even for those who lead good lives but profess not to believe in God, was illuminating."

"Whoever did their training figured out the boy's capabilities and how to leverage them," Jack acknowledged. "I'm also grateful that their identities remain secret, at least for now."

"While I know how the story goes . . ." Anne paused, with the tone of her voice growing serious. "It was sobering to hear them talking about what lies ahead. Humanity is heading for a reckoning that most are unprepared for and thus will not survive."

"I know, Anne, it is a tough pill to swallow." Hesitating, Jack searched around to ensure none of his colleagues could hear him. He added despondently, "Sort of like seeing your face on a Roman soldier sent to butcher newborns, including the Messiah."

Anne cautioned, "Private visions are challenging to interpret, Jack. While not universally accepted, most religious philosophy suggests they are a gift, not a curse."

"I can't stop thinking about what I saw," Jack replied, then dug for a bottle of Tylenol in his computer-carrying case. "It is giving me a headache."

"It's easy for me to say, but you must be patient. Eventually, God will reveal the meaning of what you saw."

Despite the weight of the worries on his shoulders, Jack snickered at Anne's advice and apologized, "Sorry, I am not laughing at you. What you shared reminded me of something my Scottish grandmother would tell us."

Intrigued, Anne asked, "What was that?"

"Nanny had a saying for everything," Jack answered. "She would say something like, 'Patience is a virtue; catch it if you can. Sometimes in a woman, but never in a man.'"

Anne smiled in agreement. "A smart woman, Jack."

Reflectively, Jack agreed. "Between you and my grandmother, maybe I just received my answer."

* * *

> *Tuesday, December 9th*
> *Jack Aitken's Home, Bristow, VA*
> *10:00 p.m.*

POP! POP! POP!

Jack drew the screen back and tossed another small log on the fire, causing it to hiss and crackle. As the wood ignited, he picked up the book he had been reading and sat in a green upholstered chair next to the fireplace. A steady wind pounded against the siding and sped down the fireplace flue, causing the flames to dance. Jack cozied up in the chair with his New York Rangers blanket, a gift from George last Christmas, and appreciated the warmth of the fire on such a cold night.

Trying to pick up where he had left off, Jack let out a long yawn. He placed the book back in his lap and stretched his arms toward the ceiling. After Louis had gotten home from a movie and gone to bed, the seemingly endless news stories speculating about the beginning of the boys' ministry became monotonous. Jack had turned off the television and picked up a book, hoping it would tire him out. It seemed to be having the desired effect.

Gazing at the poinsettia on top of the entertainment center reminded Jack what time of year it was. He closed his eyes and reflected on the events of the past forty-eight hours. So much seemed to happen quickly, from Gabriel's appearance and the visions he had shared with Anne to the boys becoming a worldwide news sensation.

Jack giggled, saying aloud, "What would the world think if they found out that God's prophet just finished watching the animated movie *Puss in Boots?*"

POP!

The sound startled Jack. A spark flew through the fireplace screen onto the white marble hearth. Jack watched it quickly burn out and thought about the roller coaster ride of the angel's visitation. Goosebumps appeared on the skin of his arm, and he felt once more the joy of witnessing Jesus's birth. At the same time, a chill ran down his spine, recalling the attempts by Satan and Lucius to kill the Messiah so soon after his birth.

Shaking his head, Jack wanted to understand the reason for the script and all of the rules. Sunday school taught him that God protected Jesus initially, only to allow his crucifixion later.

Does that imply he is watching over my sons now, only to allow their slaughter later? Or are they at risk, even now?

Jack shuddered at the thought of Lucius and the bloodlust in his eyes as he convinced Herod to sacrifice not just Christ but all the innocent infants and toddlers in Bethlehem and its vicinity. His look reminded Jack of a vampire, fangs bared, ready to drain its victim. It was the same one he was sure Lucius would have at the opportunity to slay Louis and David.

Staring into the flames, Jack once again found his conscience raising the one thing he had constantly been trying to avoid. The face—his face on the Roman soldier sent to slaughter children. A flurry of questions ran through his head.

Am I his descendant?

What happened to him?

Is his destiny tied to my own?

Another wave of anguish washed over Jack, like at the nativity scene, but then the voice of Mark Desmond suddenly rang through his head.

"It is one thing to reflect on all this, but it is another to regret it. Regret is useless, Jack."

Jack opened his book and decided to read it a little longer.

* * *

Wednesday, December 10th
Louis Aitken's Bedroom, Bristow, VA
Midnight

"Not again," a tired Louis Aitken muttered as he sat up, rubbed his eyes, and then focused on the figure sitting on the end of his bed. "Uncle George, why do you keep waking me up?"

"I miss you, Louis." The darkness in the room masked George's sadistic grin. The tone of his voice feigned an ache in his heart. "Visiting like this helps me remain close to you."

"I'm tired." In frustration, Louis laid back down and pulled the covers over his shoulders. "I have to go to work tomorrow."

Uncle George grabbed Louis's ankle tightly and insisted, "No! You need to get up and come with me. There is something you must see."

"Ouch!" Louis cried. "You're hurting me! Okay! Okay!"

His uncle released his grip, and Louis got up.

"Why don't you wake up David?" Louis questioned. "Shouldn't he see this too?"

George replied bluntly, "He is more unpredictable than you are. I have other plans for him."

Standing beside his bed, Louis glanced down and saw his body under the covers, fast asleep.

"I'm dreaming again?" Louis asked, turning to his uncle.

George's ordinarily blue eyes were now a fiery red and pierced the blackness of the night. He stared menacingly at his nephew. "Yes. Let's go downstairs."

"I don't like how you look at me, Uncle George," Louis asserted. "It's scary."

The color of George's eyes quickly dimmed, and he asked, "Is that better?"

Louis watched the bedroom door open on its own. They seemed to glide rather than walk down the stairs. The house was quiet, except for blips and beeps that Louis instantly recognized. On the landing of the stairs, Uncle George pointed toward the living room, but Louis refused to move.

"Please, Uncle George." A tear fell from Louis's eye as he begged. "Don't make me go in there. I don't want to see Mom like that again."

George's left hand was on the back of Louis's pajama top, while his right index finger made an audible *POP* as it, once more, insistently directed Louis forward. Feeling his uncle pushing him, Louis reluctantly advanced.

"Louis, unlike our other outings," George whispered, "this one, you will remember vividly."

A force that Louis could not resist compelled him to enter the room. The lights were dim, and even though he knew his mother was in a coma, she rested serenely; her eyes were closed, and a look of peace was on her face.

"Hi, Mom," Louis mumbled. "I love you."

Maybe seeing her like this isn't so bad.

Then, Louis heard footsteps in the hall. Stepping back, he watched his father enter the room and begin to check the machines that kept his mother alive. George stood behind Louis with his hands on his nephew's shoulders. Louis could not see the viciousness in his uncle's face. George's eyes did not blink. He was relishing each moment that passed.

Jack leaned over Amanda and kissed her. Louis heard him say, "Amanda, you are the love of my life. You have always been my heart, my soul, and my world. I promise I will do whatever is necessary for you and the boys."

Click! Click! Click!

His autism precluded Louis from recognizing the compassionate tone of his father's voice as he whispered, "Amanda, I will love you always and forever."

Louis heard the noise of each switch as he watched his father turn off the machines that kept his mother alive. Jack stepped back as the display on the heart monitor turned into a straight line.

Louis put his hands in front of his eyes and screamed, "NO MORE! I DON'T WANT TO SEE ANY MORE!"

"I will come soon and take you and David away," George promised. He pretended to reassure his nephew as he glared. "I will keep you safe from your father."

* * *

Louis sat up like a lightning bolt in his bed. The room was silent, and the only light emanated from his clock radio. Louis wept, remembering the nightmare that he had witnessed minutes earlier. He placed his head back on the pillow and tried to go back to sleep. Louis wanted to forget this dream, like all the others that Uncle George had been showing him the past few weeks. But he tossed and turned uncomfortably, trying to drive away the thought echoing in his brain.

Dad killed Mom.

CHAPTER 13

> *Thursday, December 11th*
> *Satan's Earthly Headquarters at Pergamon*
> *9:00 p.m.*

George Aitken waited impatiently as one of his demon crewmembers, wearing a headset, quietly deciphered a communication to JESU headquarters. The demon's black eyes opened wide, and his lips turned wickedly upward. Hitting a button on the keyboard before him generated a printout of what he had just heard. Ripping it from the machine, he handed it to George, who grabbed and read it anxiously.

"There is no news to report on the identity of George in Culpeper. Demon interrogations are continuing. More to follow."

George gritted his teeth and pumped his fists, crushing the paper in his hand. "Yes! We have done it!"

The demon operator shouted, "You did it, Master! Now we can monitor every communication coming in and going to JESU headquarters!"

"It's much more than that," George announced. "We can trace those communications back to their source. For the first time, we can build a map showing every JESU operative's location anywhere in the world. In time, we will even triangulate the position of their secret headquarters in the Vatican!"

Basking in George's success, the sycophant boasted, "Lord Rofocale will be most pleased."

Almost on cue, Lucius appeared. George knelt. "Master, I have accomplished what you asked me to do."

"Have you?" Lucius asked curiously. "We can access every JESU communication?"

A machine, printing furiously, spit out message after message until the floor was no longer visible under the pile of paper.

George waved his hand to show the ever-increasing number of printed documents and replied, "Master Lucius, every one of these messages references the name 'George' on Route 666. JESU took the bait just as you suggested they would."

Steam rose from Lucius's black, reptilian skin, and a sulfur smell filled the room. His bloodshot eyes opened widely, and he questioned, "What about the content of those messages?"

George's lips drew up in a satisfied grin. "They all say the same thing. No news to report."

Lucius pounded his clawed hand into the other. "Excellent! Keeping our plans a secret ensured that when captured and interrogated, our spies gave up nothing because they knew nothing!"

"It gets better, Master," George revealed proudly. "Thanks to my wife's tracking software program, we know where the messages go and where they originate."

"You have outdone yourself, Lord Aitken," Lucius complimented his protegee. "I am impressed by your resourcefulness and desire to succeed where others have failed me. Well done."

Lucius hesitated, then inquired, "Speaking of your wife, was there any difficulty obtaining what you needed?"

"No, Master," George snarled. "Once properly persuaded, she was very cooperative. She will be another loose end I must tie up eventually. However, she may be valuable regarding our encryption initiative, so I have her in my custody."

"Very good." Lucius beamed. "You must share the details with me later."

George's tone grew more cautious. "The cellphone encryption, on the other hand, will be more of a challenge, Master."

Lucius's demeanor changed. Now concerned, he asked, "What is the issue?"

"Thus far, the few phones we captured had different encryption software," George explained. "No two phones have the same program, and no universal software exists. It is in development, but until it is available, we need to crack each phone individually."

"I see." Lucius struck a surprisingly supportive tone. "I understand these matters take time. I expect you will succeed very soon."

"Your confidence in me is humbling," George acknowledged. "It will not be misplaced. I have my top people working on it. I am leaving now to pick up the Princess's *packages*, and I will update you upon my return."

"See that you do," Lucius replied caustically. "By the way, if you see him, give Jack my regards."

* * *

Friday December 12th
David Aitken's Bedroom
6:00 a.m.

David Aitken lay on his pillow with his fingers laced behind his head, staring at the ceiling. He never needed an alarm; his internal clock roused him at 6 a.m. every morning. This morning seemed like any other, but it wasn't. He did not have a nightmare or hear a noise, but something had disturbed his sleep, and he had been in the same position since 3:15 a.m. He hadn't moved a muscle. A sliver of daylight illuminated his room, and he had never been so happy to see the sun.

Putting his work uniform on, he could not shake a sensation in the pit of his stomach. Something was wrong; he could feel it but lacked the vocabulary to explain his emotions. David went to the kitchen and sat on a stool at the island as he did each morning. His iPad was in front of him, but he did not turn it on. Several minutes later, his father came down the stairs.

"Good morning, buddy," his father chirped. "How did you sleep?"

David did not answer; he just sat in silence.

Concerned, Jack asked, "Do you feel okay?"

"Yes," he softly replied. "I'm okay. I'm just hungry. Can I have a bagel?"

"Sure." Jack observed his son guardedly and asked again, "You're sure you are okay?"

David nodded and turned on his iPad.

* * *

> *Friday December 12th*
> *Walgreens, Bristow, VA*
> *11:00 a.m.*

"It's the most wonderful time of the year."

David sang along with the Muzak playing in the background as he checked the expiration dates on the stock and removed the expired items from the shelves. The job would be incredibly tedious for many people, but he reveled in it. Something about the repetition associated with the task was soothing. After arriving at work, he felt better. Moving to the seasonal aisle in the middle of the store made David happy. There were inflatable Christmas characters: the Grinch, Rudolph the Red-Nosed Reindeer, and his favorite, the Abominable Snow Monster.

The store manager, Deniece, called out to him, "David, we need to replenish the holiday movie DVDs. Please get them from the storeroom."

"Okey dokey," he replied and headed to the rear of the store.

Passing the pharmacy, David suddenly was overwhelmed by the same feeling that had kept him up last night. Slowly pushing in the swinging doors, he walked past the time clock and peeked into the break room. No one was there. A large opening in the wall led to the unfinished part of the store, and he went through it. Storage racks packed with stock and inventory from the floor to the ceiling surrounded the room.

"Hello, David," a familiar voice greeted him. "I am happy to see you again."

Standing by the overhead delivery door was Uncle George, flanked by two men dressed in black from head to toe. David instinctively stepped back, but a third man emerged from the bathroom, leaving him surrounded. They all instantly gave him the creeps, and he uncomfortably asked,

"Uncle George, where have you been?"

"Missed me, have you?" George smiled, rather unpleasantly. "How touching."

David sensed something was wrong with his uncle. The voice was recognizable, but George spoke deliberately, with no warmth. He appeared different. Usually parted in the middle, his hair was slicked back and seemed much shorter than he remembered; it revealed deep creases in his forehead. His beard was now a pointy goatee. Most disturbing, however, was the icy stare of his bloodshot, bluish-black eyes, which raised the hairs on the back of his neck.

"You sound like Uncle George, but you don't look or act like him," David stated flatly.

George moved forward, the veins in his neck pulsing as his muscles tensed like a predator, ready to pounce. "Come now," his uncle beckoned. "We will go pick up Louis and be on our way. Don't you want to play some golf with me? I know a few golf courses that are 'hot' and will challenge your game."

"Do not be afraid."

A voice echoed in David's head, but he still found himself trembling.

"I'm not going," he insisted. "My friends are telling me to say that."

"Your friends—I am intrigued. Where are they? Your father always told me that it was just the four of you. I forgot that after your mother died . . . really . . . It is just the three of you. Did your father tell you how that happened?"

David stood his ground. "If you try to take me, they say they will hurt you."

One of the henchmen snickered, "I don't see anyone here. Whoever your friends are, they have left you standing alone."

George signaled to the figure behind his nephew, silently instructing him to grab David. The demon moved forward, but a golden hue encircled the boy, and a burst of energy radiating from his body struck the subordinate, sending him head-first into a cinder block wall.

The remaining aides immediately retreated. George folded his arms, then rubbed his lips and hairy chin with his open hand. He studied his nephew for a moment before he spoke.

"Interesting, but no matter. I will figure out another way."

George approached him slowly and clapped his hands in mock approval of his nephew's response to the demon who tried to abduct him. "Well done. Obviously, you have proven I cannot compel you to come with me, at least for now. I will not try to force you. We can plan something exciting for later when I take you and your brother to a real house of fun."

George moved closer and stopped, just out of range of the lethal energy field still radiating around David.

"While I am thinking about it, I would like you to ask your father something." George leaned in and whispered, "Ask him why . . ."

* * *

Friday December 12th
Tool Shed, Outside of Hell's Gate
11:00 p.m.

Entering his shop in a shed just outside Hell's gate, Apollyon removed his heavy black helmet, placing it on a workbench, revealing the u-shaped hairline on his massive, block-like skull. Golden yellow streaks were still visible in his light white shoulder-length hair, which curled on the ends. Heavy beads of sweat fell from his broad forehead, and a walrus-like, horseshoe mustache dominated his bony jawline and cheekbones. His intense, dark blue eyes examined the weapon he held before him.

Apollyon twirled the massive battleaxe, admiring the ornate images carved in the gopher wood handle. He made it himself from timber harvested from the same forest used to build Noah's Ark. One side of the handle depicted fire and brimstone raining down on Sodom and Gomorrah. The other commemorated Apollyon's role in leveling the walls of Jericho. Two blades, forged from the purest steel and anchored at the top of the handle, gave it the appearance of a massive bat spreading its wings.

Each side of the blade honored more of his handiwork. On one side was the toppled Tower of Babel, and on the reverse, an image of the firstborn dead of Egypt. A rare smile, revealing tombstone-like front teeth, gradually emerged as he reminisced about his historical exploits.

He ran his finger along the edge of the blade. It was sharp, as always, but Apollyon pumped the pedal of the grinding table, setting the granite wheel in motion, and meticulously moved the axe blade next to the wheel, causing sparks to fly. A few minutes later, he took his foot off the pedal, and drops of blood emerged from the slit on this finger that opened as he tested the sharpness of his weapon again.

"Better. Yes, much better."

He carefully leaned the weapon against the workbench and searched for his helmet when something in the corner of the shed caught his eye. He lowered his enormous hand.

What is this?

Through the doorway, the light from Hell's fires reflected off a triangular object. It twinkled like a star, and despite the hard callouses on his fingers, Apollyon felt the smooth cuts and bumps on it. Holding it in front of his face, he recognized it as a crystal decanter with a large cursive letter "H" etched into the side. As he shook the container, the amber-colored liquid inside the bottle danced like waves on the ocean.

Apollyon pulled the pentagon-shaped stopper, held it to his nose, and inhaled deeply. His eyes opened wide as he recognized the delightful aroma from the bottle.

"Hitian Vodka! I haven't had this in more than 1,000 years! I was certain I drank the last bottle long ago."

Glancing back at the corner of the shed where he found the bottle, he scratched his cheek and wondered how he had missed it. Holding the magnificent decanter high, it didn't really matter how it got there. He would truly enjoy it later!

* * *

Later That Evening

The reflected light of the torches lining the cavern hallway guided Apollyon to his chamber, a space carved out of the rock and simply furnished, from the cold stone slab upon which he slept to the long table on the back wall where he placed his polished armor and helmet. His treasured battleaxe hung on a hook in the corner. His only other possessions were the empty bottles of Hitian vodka he had consumed over the millennia. Each container had a unique shape, but the distinctive letter "H" was prominent in each design.

He admired his collection as he poured another glass of his favorite libation. The kings of Hiti had paid Apollyon in vodka for his protection from other tribes. It enabled Hiti to become a world power. Still, he could not protect them from what occurred 65 million years earlier.

Apollyon displayed the decanters in order, from the first one he had consumed to what he thought was the last. Holding the bottle he discovered today, he considered saving one final drink for another time but decided the vodka was too good to keep. The glass shook in his quaking hand as he poured the last drop. He held it up in a drunken toast.

"To Hitians. Y-o-u, you may be extinct, but there are no finer brewers in history."

Downing the last swallow, Apollyon fumbled with the stopper. Failing to insert it in the decanter, he left the empty bottle on the table and staggered to his bed. Sitting on the edge of the stone slab, he recalled that while Hitian vodka came in a small bottle, it packed a punch! Apollyon's eyelids slowly fell, and he collapsed on the bed, instantly asleep.

*　*　*

A Few Hours Later...

H-U-F-F. Apollyon's chiseled chest rose as he inhaled deeply. His respiration ceased momentarily. *P-U-F-F.* A soft whistle followed as the air rushed out of his nose. His rhythmic breathing was the only sound that broke the silence in the room. The Destroyer slept as if he were dead to the world.

The last drop of Hitian vodka hung, suspended on the end of the stopper, and seemingly in concert with one another, a smoky mist formed in the empty decanter as soon as the final drop hit the table. The vapor spilled out from the top of the bottle, like a convict crawling to freedom from a prison cell. Slowly, the gas gathered into a compact cloud, which in an instant disappeared, leaving a hooded figure standing in its place. Its black robe blended with the darkness, but the raging fires burning in each eye socket lit up the room. The Reaper moved toward Apollyon.

Standing over the sleeping sentry of Hell, the collector of souls, clutching a scythe in its bony, skeletal fingers, raised his weapon, then waited for the last grains of sand in the hourglass he held in his other hand to fall. The Reaper's jaws, devoid of flesh, opened, and he began chanting, preparing to sever Apollyon's head from his body and gather the Destroyer's soul.

"To everything, there is a season and a time for every purpose unto Heaven."

The scythe began its downward arc toward Apollyon's thick neck as the Reaper averred, "A time to be born—a time to die."

The firelight from the Reaper's eyes reflected off the sharp blade as the soul harvester continued his chant, "A time to plant." Inches from its target, the assassin finished his song, "A time to reap...."

Woosh!

Apollyon's eyes popped open, and he instinctively rolled away as he heard the blade pass over him and trim some of the hair from his head, which fell to the floor.

Woosh!

The Reaper took another swing with the scythe. Apollyon stepped back, but the scythe tip ran across his stomach, leaving a gash that began to bleed. The fog of the vodka lifted as adrenaline coursed through the Destroyer's veins. He grabbed the scythe and began wrestling with the Reaper for it. Using his size and strength to his advantage, Apollyon drove the Reaper into the rock wall and jarred the weapon from the slayer's fleshless fingers.

His mouth wide open, gasping for air, Apollyon stood over his attacker and demanded, "Who sent you?"

His jawbones popping and teeth grinding, the Reaper answered, "The one who reaps us all."

Apollyon frowned and, in disbelief, asked, "God?"

The Reaper's bones clicked as it nodded affirmatively.

Enraged and without thinking, Apollyon raised the scythe and swung it at the reaper. It tore through the thick robe and hit its mark, severing the skull from the body. Apollyon watched it dance across the stone floor until it came to rest next to his bed. A sickening feeling overcame him as he leaned on the scythe for support.

"I have killed a reaper," Apollyon murmured. "The only punishment for that is death."

Hours later, Apollyon gathered the Reaper's remains from behind a rock outcropping, cautiously approaching the pit. Peering around one last time to ensure he was alone, he dropped the bones in, instantly vaporizing them along with the scythe in the hellfire below. The gurgles and pops of the liquid rock sounded like stomach acids digesting a meal as Apollyon stood over the pit wondering, "What do I do now?"

CHAPTER 14

Saturday December 13th
National Earthquake Information Center, Boulder, Colorado
7:00 a.m. MDT

Veteran geologist Doctor Pamela Grey stomped her feet, removing snow from her boots as she entered the fortress-like building that housed the National Earthquake Information Center. It was customary to navigate the maze of cinder block hallways and never see another person, so it was a surprise when she entered the lab and found her graduate research assistant already there.

"Marty, what are you doing here so early on a Saturday?"

Martin Pearson, Marty for short, was in his mid-twenties and a self-described "rockhound." The stereotypical graduate student, Marty, had curly brown hair, a scruffy beard, and was as thin as a rail, looking like he had not eaten a good meal in months. Spinning around in his chair, he waved. "Hi, Doctor Grey. I'm doing some research for my thesis. I also wanted to beat the snowstorm."

Shedding her insulated Patagonia vest, she used a paper towel to dry the melting snow from her graying black hair. "It's starting to snow pretty heavily." She plugged in her laptop and asked, "Do you have the overnight seismic readings?"

Marty chewed on the pencil in his mouth as he searched through the mess of papers on his desk.

"I know they're here somewhere," he muttered. "I was just looking at them an hour ago."

Doctor Grey smiled, looking at the picture of her husband hanging on the sterile white walls of the lab. They were on their honeymoon, posing in front of a river of molten lava in Volcanoes National Park in Hawaii. Doctor Grey entered her password and pulled up the past month's historical data, which finally had become available. She scanned the information, and her smile turned into a worried frown.

Rubbing the back of her neck anxiously, she asked, "Hey, Marty, are these figures accurate? They don't make any sense."

Marty handed Doctor Grey the printout she had requested earlier. "Here are the overnight figures. I thought the same thing. I looked it up, and that seismograph became active last month but, before that, did not register any measurable activity in the past ten years."

Pam's eyes never left the computer screen. "I'm even more concerned about what seems to be happening right now."

Pam's chapped lips puckered as if she were going to whistle, but all she did was exhale. "Here, look." She pointed to some numbers on the screen. "This is for a different location. I know the equipment is sensitive, and until recently, it picked up one or maybe two small earthquakes a month. But now, the same seismograph has picked up over thirty in the last few days alone."

"There's more." Marty pulled a piece of graph paper from the pile and pointed to a cluster of dots. "Historically, quakes occur in the desert area of the Western zone, but this concentration is in the Eastern zone."

Marty locked eyes with Doctor Grey. "That area has no historical record of earthquake activity. It also has a higher population density and significant infrastructure."

Doctor Grey's eyes opened wide. "My God. They would be unprepared for even a small event, let alone a major earthquake."

Marty nodded. "Yes, and this increase in activity suggests that it is a real risk and possibly imminent."

"Great work, Marty. I'll share this with the Executive Director immediately." Scratching her cheek, she added, "And if my theory about predicting earthquakes is correct, all of this is a precursor to a massive event, but with such a large geographic footprint, there is no way to pinpoint exactly where."

*　*　*

> Saturday December 13th
> The Gates of Hell
> Around Midnight

Apollyon lifted the face mask on his helmet and stared at the stalagmites rising from both sides of the cavern floor. As far back as he could recall, he never paid them any mind, but today, he thought they resembled curved, elongated fingers ready to grab anyone who might pass by. Apollyon grew increasingly distracted from his duties since his deadly confrontation with the Reaper twenty-four hours earlier. At any minute, he feared that the moment of reckoning for his unspeakable act could arrive.

Hot steam, the vaporized sweat from his body, rose like smoke escaping around the seam of a city manhole. Turning back to the gate, two gargoyles carved from the blood-red mineral cinnabar sat atop pillars that supported heavy gates forged from an unknown metal. They stood as silent sentries along with himself, protecting what lay beyond the entrance—a bottomless crevasse whose raging inferno ran deep into the planet's bowels.

Having finished processing the daily delivery of the newly damned, Apollyon reached down to re-attach the gate key to a chain on his waist. Something made him stop and hold it in his hand; he studied it. He pondered how this simple key, so small and almost insignificant, could open the gate to a kingdom of misery and everlasting torment. Only when he turned the key in the lock, and the gates opened to admit those poor souls condemned for eternity did it loom large. Then, you could hear a pin drop until he locked the gate, the desperate screaming started, and the cries of intense agony echoed through the chamber.

Apollyon protected it all, but as Hell's caretaker lowered the face guard on his helmet, the vertical lines of the bars gave him a feeling of being a prisoner, too. A hostage to a destiny already in doubt before yesterday and now dangling on a precarious thread. Seeing a figure in the shadows caught him by surprise and caused the nervous jailer of the dead to shout uneasily, "Who goes there? Identify yourself!"

The figure raised his hand to reassure him and answered, "It is Lucius. I am here for the soul harvest." In his increasingly panicky state, Apollyon had forgotten about Lucius and his routine pick-up.

"I have them here in the guardhouse." The usually organized gatekeeper shuffled feverishly through the mess in the shed, looking for a container. Nearly in a frenzy, Apollyon called out, "One moment." After finally locating the package, he exhaled in relief, met Lucius at the gate, and handed it to him.

Lucius accepted the delivery and noted Apollyon's disheveled appearance. "Are you alright?"

Trying to regain his composure, Apollyon replied tersely, "I am fine. Why would you ask?"

"I meant no offense, but I could not help but notice that your armor is not polished. I have never seen it like this." Glancing into the guardhouse, Lucius added, "You seem preoccupied, like you did not expect to see me today."

"I had a little too much to drink last night."

Holding the container of souls tightly in one hand, Lucius slapped Apollyon on the back with the other. "I see. Well, I will not keep you then."

Lucius turned away, but then an audible fizz, like the bursting of a series of gas bubbles, emanated from the pit where Apollyon had disposed of the Reaper. It sounded like a belch, as if the Reaper were a meal still being digested. Apollyon glanced over his shoulder, and the weight of his sin grew too great for him to bear alone.

"Lucius, wait."

Lucius finished sweeping the dust off his clothes. "Yes, what is it?"

Apollyon blurted out, "I killed a Reaper last night!"

Lucius was not stunned by Apollyon's assertion. He was amused and laughed, "Oh, come now. Do you honestly expect me to believe that? No one has ever killed a Reaper."

Pointing to the smoldering pit, the Destroyer confessed, "I got rid of the body in there."

"Apollyon, you said yourself that you were drinking last night. I am sure it is just your mind playing tricks on you."

Reaching into a gap behind his armor, Apollyon pulled out the Reaper's hourglass. "Then how did I get this?"

Handing the timer to Lucius, the Angel of the Abyss lamented, "I cannot destroy it. It won't break, nor will it burn."

Lucius's jaw dropped. Holding the sacred object, he locked eyes with Apollyon and asked, "Have you told anyone else about this?"

Apollyon shook his head. "Not a soul."

"I do not have to tell you the punishment for killing a Reaper, do I?" Anxiously, Lucius glanced around the cavern. "If God or Lucifer finds out, you will wish for death!"

Realizing the ramifications of what he had just asserted, Lucius chastised Apollyon, "By telling me and showing me this, you have now involved me in your predicament! If Lucifer discovers I know anything about it, my neck will be on the block, too!"

"I am sorry! I had no idea!" Apollyon could not look at Lucius. "But I need your help. I don't know what to do."

Lucius handed him back the hourglass. "It is unsafe for us to discuss this in the open. Quickly, we must go somewhere private and think carefully about what to do next."

* * *

Lucius tensely paced around Apollyon's room. "Just so I am clear, this angel told you unequivocally that God wanted you to stand down?"

"Yes, the emissary indicated God no longer required my services."

Despite his fears about the ramifications of killing the Reaper, it still stung Apollyon to repeat what the angel had told him.

"His covenants with humankind will take precedence. My role as the destroyer is over."

"That is the influence of his son, the Christ," Lucius seethed. Hot smoke, reeking of sulfur, rose from his body. Looking up at the giant guard, whose size dwarfed him, he added, "Now you, too, know what it is like to be pushed aside for these humans."

Rubbing his temple with his black fingernail, Lucius then asked another question. "And the Reaper confirmed that God had sent him to gather your soul?"

Apollyon affirmed. "Yes, I asked him that question specifically."

Contemptuously, Lucius crossed his arms. "This makes no sense. Humankind is a cesspool of crime and corruption. Like wildfire maintains a healthy ecosystem on Earth, God knows you are needed to bring order to his creation. This type of purge is both natural and necessary."

"You don't need to convince me, Lucius. At God's command, I delivered the flood that covered the Earth. I rained fire and brimstone down on Sodom and Gomorrah. I destroyed the firstborn of Egypt and parted the Red Sea. The weeding out of non-believers is all I know. This role is all I have. What is there for me?"

"Your identity swept away instantly," Lucius commiserated. "And you are powerless to stop it."

"Yes, God is all-powerful," Apollyon admitted in frustration.

Seeing the container of souls on the table caused the wheels to turn in Lucius's brain. He tapped his lips several times, then muttered, "But not invulnerable."

"What do you mean, Lucius?" Apollyon leaned back and crossed his arms. "I already have a death sentence on my head, so what good can come from confronting God?"

"You misunderstand me, my friend." Lucius placed his hand on Apollyon's shoulder. "I meant to imply even God is not immune to a little flattery."

Before Apollyon could respond, Lucius held his hand up. "Let me finish. As much as Lucifer wants to condemn souls, God, perhaps even more so, wishes to save them."

Lucius pointed at the container. "An offering of souls in need of redemption might be just the proper tribute to gain the Lord's favor and get you back in his good graces."

The giant unfolded his arms, but holding up the hourglass, swinging back and forth on its leather string, he asked, "What do I do with this?"

Lucius took the hourglass from Apollyon and stuck it inside his robe. "I, too, cannot destroy it, but I can make it disappear."

"I am grateful, Lucius." A great weight lifted from the Destroyer's shoulders. Grateful for Lucius's assistance, he placed his hand over his heart. "How can I repay you?"

Waving his hand, the Prime Minister of Hell replied, "No payment is necessary, but we will need many more souls for a suitable gift."

"Consider it done! I will stoke all the fires of Hell to produce them!" Apollyon jumped to his feet. "But these souls are tormented and damned. How can they be an appropriate gift for the Lord?"

"Leave that to me, Apollyon. I will refine them, personally."

Lucius placed his clawed fingers on Apollyon's shoulder. "I even have the perfect receptacle to place them in for your delivery to God."

* * *

> Sunday December 14th
> Jack Aitken's House, Bristow, Virginia
> 7:00 a.m.

Jack adjusted the belt on his black fleece bathrobe and yawned as he stared out of the French doors that led to the patio. He had been up for nearly an hour and still found himself rubbing the sleep from his eyes. Shades of red and orange spread across a pale blue sky, the start of a beautiful sunrise. Ordinarily, he would have stepped outside to enjoy the solitude of the morning, but it was chilly, a little above freezing. Only a few degrees colder than the mood of his sons. David had not spoken one word to him on Saturday, and after picking Louis up from work that same evening, he wasn't talking to Jack either. It had been a long, sleepless night.

The creaking staircase caught Jack's attention. "Good morning, David," Jack greeted his son, who sat down, turned on his iPad, and began watching videos, ignoring his father.

"Still nothing to say?" Jack stood motionless, unsure of what to do next. "Okay, have it your way. I'm ready to talk when you are."

* * *

> Later the Same Day
> Kitchen of the Aitken Household, Bristow, Virginia

David had always been the quieter of the two brothers, so Jack was not surprised that he had maintained his silence the entire day. Louis, on the other hand, despite his autism, had never been able to keep his mouth shut. He confessed his "crimes" before anyone even knew about them. It was how Jack and Amanda learned their son was incapable of lying. But Louis had been avoiding him all day, and, to

Jack's surprise, he had managed to keep quiet about whatever was bothering him.

Jack heard the basement door creak as it opened, and Louis appeared in the doorway. He stopped chopping vegetables on the kitchen counter and pointed at a plate on the table. "Your dinner is over there, Louis."

Louis remained silent and began shoveling the macaroni and cheese into his mouth. Despite eating the same thing for dinner every day for the past twenty-plus years, he consumed it with gusto. He scraped the leftover cheese sauce from the plate and licked his fork.

"Maybe now that you finished dinner"—Jack poured Italian dressing on his salad—"you can tell me what is wrong?"

Still sitting at the table, Louis avoided eye contact.

Jack pulled up a chair beside his son. "Please, Louis. Talk to me. I can't help you"—he glanced over his shoulder at David, sitting at the island—"or your brother if you don't."

David ran out of the kitchen and dashed upstairs; a door slam shook the house. Jack looked up at the ceiling, concerned that his son might have broken the door. It had happened before. He chose to refocus his attention on Louis.

The young man sat on the couch and fiddled with the television remote in the family room. All at once, he blurted out, "Uncle George visits me in my dreams!"

"What?" Jack's jaw dropped open.

Dumbfounded, flashbacks sped through Jack's mind—scenes from their childhood. Then, Wallace's attack in Anne's garage and his vicious bite on George's shoulder. He saw his brother lying in a hospital bed, deteriorating, as the rabies virus raced through his veins. The feeling of hopeful anticipation when he poured the River Styx water down George's throat and the agony of finding out it did not work. Then, finally, the shock of watching the video where George got up from the slab in the morgue and walked out of the hospital.

Jack knelt, gently grabbed Louis's arm, and asked, for the first time in months, with a sliver of hope, "Did he tell you anything?"

Louis's eyes dropped to the floor. Jack gently grabbed his son's chin, looked him in the eye, and pleaded, "What is it? What did he say? Please, Louis."

Fidgeting in the chair, Louis nervously chewed on his cuticles. He stuttered, "Un-Uncle George...."

Jack leaned forward, urging his son to speak, "Go ahead, Louis. Just say it."

Raising his voice, something he rarely did, Louis shouted, "I SAW YOU KILLING MOM!"

Jack froze. His eyes fixed straight ahead, but he could not focus. Everything was a blur. He was speechless, but this time, the flashbacks were of his wife comatose in a hospital bed. Amanda's voice echoed in his head. *"You have to let me go, Jack."*

Louis sniffled, tears running down his cheeks. Trying to soothe his anxiety, he intensely rocked back and forth and repeated softly, "He said he needed to take David and me away from you to keep us safe."

Jack felt a phantom pain in his abdomen, like a knife tearing through his soul. He unconsciously reached for his stomach as if he expected to push back in the intestines spilling out of his body cavity. He pulled Louis close, trying to hug and console him, but his son could not sit still long enough to be comforted. Jack stood up from the couch and wandered around the room, unsure of what to do next.

BAM! BAM!

Jack felt a blunt force strike him from behind and an intense pain radiating through the side of his head. It drove him to his knees. Instinctively, he raised his hands, but a similar punch hit the top of his head, sending Jack tumbling to the floor. David stood over his father, eyes wide open with rage, battering him with both fists like a gorilla would attack a potential threat. In blind fury, David raised his arm, preparing to deliver a knockout blow.

A loud, stern voice, not Jack's, echoed through the home. "DAVID, STOP!"

Jack moaned and rolled onto his stomach, trying to avoid the shot he was sure was coming. David had stopped but was now punching his own head instead. Breathing heavily, he glanced around, retreated, and fled back up the stairs to his room. Louis wailed, kneeling next to Jack with his hand on his father's shoulder, repeating the same sentence, "I'm sorry, Dad. I'm sorry, Dad...."

* * *

> **Tuesday, December 16th**
> **Jack Aitken's House, Bristow, Virginia**
> **9:00 p.m.**

Standing in the garage, Jack's mother-in-law rolled down the car window.

"Thanks again for having us. I only wish David would have allowed us to sing 'Happy Birthday' to him."

Jack leaned in and kissed her goodbye. "I know, Mom. For some reason, I don't think David even understands why, he never liked the song."

She gently touched the bruise on Jack's cheek.

"That looks so painful. Are you sure there are no broken bones?"

"Thankfully, no. The X-rays were all negative. Be careful going home."

Jack shivered as he waved goodbye to his in-laws. Locking the door, he turned off the lights and sat alone in the family room with the boys asleep. The glow from the Christmas village on top of the entertainment center gave the room a cozy feeling. It was one Jack recalled he and Amanda often enjoyed together.

Wincing, Jack's lips quivered as he slipped his damaged hand out of the sling around his neck. During his son's outburst the day before,

Jack had landed on it. Worried that he had injured it further, he had gone for X-rays earlier in the day. Luckily, the doctor confirmed it would only result in a minor setback in his rehabilitation.

Earlier in the evening, true to form, Louis told his grandparents that David had struck Jack. Gingerly touching the bump on his head, he marveled that the beating had not resulted in a concussion.

"At least I didn't have to lie about what happened."

David was never one to apologize, but he was tiptoeing around Jack, which was a sign that he had remorse for the assault. On the other hand, Louis always shook these things off quickly and returned to his routine as if nothing had happened. Just shifting in the chair caused Jack discomfort, but not as much as acknowledging that what happened yesterday would live forever.

"The two of them remember everything. They bring up stuff I did when they were three years old."

Jack checked his phone for messages, but there was nothing from Anne. He rubbed his forehead, desperately hoping he would hear back from her. Jack felt himself slipping toward a dark place. A room in the mansion of his mind that he thought he had locked securely, but his personal demons were tempting him with the key. He needed to discuss what had happened between the boys and himself, but even more, he wanted to talk about the proverbial sword of Damocles hanging over all their heads.

"This prophet business is the sword, and it's only a matter of time before someone cuts the string."

CHAPTER 15

> *December 16th, Near Midnight*
> *Family Room in the Aitken Household,*
> *Bristow, Virginia*

Having pushed himself to the edge and stared into the abyss, Jack had somehow pulled himself back. It had taken that part of himself that was still a kid at heart to do it. Jack was confident that most adults would think him silly for watching a Rankin-Bass Christmas show. They were simplistic, even naïve. He could never be sure if it was a desire to cling to a sliver of his childhood or the uplifting endings, but he looked forward to seeing them every year. He and George had always enjoyed it, even if George had taken to psychoanalyzing Rudolph and making fun of the characters. They always boosted his Christmas spirit, and tonight was no exception. One line of dialogue had stood out to him.

How can they talk about Santa Claus when there is so much unhappiness in the world?

He had sat in the dark for quite some time, contemplating this statement, before heading to the hall bathroom. Staring at himself in the mirror, the dark circle under his right eye almost matched the bruise caused by David's fist around his left one. Even Jack was surprised at his appearance and hoped the melatonin he had taken hours earlier would help him sleep through the night. The haggard look on his face reiterated that he desperately needed it.

"Stille Nacht, Heillege Nacht"

Jack tried cleaning his ears by inserting an index finger in each canal and twirling them several times.

"I must be hearing things. It sounds like a chorus of voices singing in different languages."

"All is calm. All is bright."

Jack slowly opened the bathroom door. Turning his head to the side, he put his hand to his ear, listening.

"Must be a group of late-night, very drunk carolers."

However, he quickly realized the singing was coming from inside his home. Jack was not so much afraid but intrigued as he returned to the family room.

"Vierge Ronde Yon, Mere Et Enfant"

The television screen showed what Jack recognized as a war zone. He carefully sat on the coffee table, reached for the remote, and mumbled, "I turned the television off. I know I did."

The scene was dark, but the moonlight revealed deep trenches, like those dug by a grave digger. These scars in the earth ran in many directions, the length of which disappeared deep into the night. Protecting these trenches were large, brown, earthen mounds topped with razor-sharp barbed wire. The land in front of the earthworks, littered with craters, broken tree limbs, and other debris, stretched as far as the eye could see.

"Holy infant, so tender and mild."

The singing grew louder as voices from around the battlefield sang in unison. It was a moving scene, but Jack was tired and ready for the movie to be over. He hit the button to shut off the television; nothing happened. Jack tried changing the channel, but the show was on every station.

Pressing the guide button on the remote, Jack asked, "What is the name of this movie?"

A forceful voice, easily heard over the singing, answered him, *"It is not a movie, Mr. Aitken. I am afraid it is all too real."*

"Who said that?"

THE GATHERING STORM

Jack searched the room for the voice's source. It was eloquent and eerily familiar.

The singing continued as the voice persisted, *"The date is December 24th, 1914, a little less than five months after World War I started. A war that will continue for another four years, a conflict many of these young men will not survive. The 'war to end all wars.' How ignorant were we?"*

In an instant, the room was quiet. The singing stopped. The television screen was now black.

"That accent. It's British. I know I've heard it before."

Suddenly, a feeling of warmth touched Jack's face. Turning to the left, he noticed flames in the fireplace where there had been none before. A decorated Christmas tree, including wrapped gifts underneath, appeared in the corner. Something out of place hung on each bough.

"Tinsel?" Jack had only seen decorations like this in photographs from a Christmas long in the past.

The flooring under Jack's feet transformed from dark green wall-to-wall carpeting to a circular, light blue area rug embroidered with winter scenes. Three young children burst into the room, almost knocking Jack over, and dove to the floor next to the tree. They appeared to be entirely unaware of his presence. The two girls wore plain green dresses, and their brother's navy blue shorts resembled knickers. Their clothing was not modern.

Jack sat on a table that moved backward, making him a spectator of the unfolding event. A bespectacled man in a wheelchair with a gray blanket covering his legs pushed himself into the room. He jauntily held a long holder with a lighted cigarette between his teeth. A woman wearing a dark green skirt with a white blouse, her hair in a bun, quickly entered the room.

Clapping her hands, she chastised her children, *"Astrid! Harald! Ragnhild! Children, where are your manners?"*

"*Your Highness,*" the man began to speak. Glancing at the woman, he smiled and corrected himself, saying softly, "*Martha.*" The woman smiled, confirming her approval. "*Christmas is a time for joy.*"

Grinning from ear to ear, he asked the children, "*Isn't it?*"

The brother and sisters looked at one another gleefully and said in unison, "*Yes, Uncle—*"

"President," Jack shouted, finishing their sentence. "It's President Roosevelt!"

ARF! ARF!

A jet-black puppy, possibly a cocker spaniel, ran into the arms of the children, licking their faces. The scene froze like someone had hit a pause button. The same powerful voice spoke once more.

"*Like a gathering storm, Nazism grew in Germany, and by December 1940, a black cloud descended upon Norway and the whole of Europe. It was a bleak time for the Queen of Norway and her children. They were living in exile.*"

"Winston Churchill!" Jack blurted the name out. "That voice! It's Churchill!"

"*Uncertainty, Mister Aitken, is an unfortunate part of the human condition. Still, through these shadows of the past, I've shown you proof that happiness is found even in the world's darkest moments. Look at the faces of those children. You cannot deny their joy.*"

The word joy echoed in Jack's ears as he once again found himself alone in the dark. He only heard the clock ticking as he sat quietly, reflecting on the message of the images he had just seen. Beyond tired, Jack slowly climbed the stairs, conceding that the night of unbroken rest he so desperately needed would be out of reach.

* * *

Wednesday, December 17ᵗʰ
Odell Williamson Auditorium, Bolivia, NC
11:00 a.m.

The digital sign on the façade of the Odell Williamson Auditorium announced that the Sea Notes, a local choral group, were performing a free holiday concert at 7:00 p.m. that evening. A tall state trooper dressed in a gray uniform and wearing body armor exited the building with a German shepherd on a leash. He reached for the walkie-talkie on his belt and pushed the button on the side.

"This is Sergeant Wall. The sweep of the building has come back negative. We can stand down."

Walking past Anne Bishop, several other team members, all accompanied by dogs, headed toward their cars.

"All clear, Jerry?" Anne asked.

Jerry Wall nodded his head affirmatively. "That's right, Captain. We searched every inch of the building. None of the dogs found anything. Another fake bomb scare, I'm afraid."

Holding her hand for the dog to sniff, Anne frowned. "That's the third one in the past two months."

"It's not just us," Jerry added, scratching his dog's head. "This is going on in several places around the country. Mostly here on the East Coast, but in California too."

Anne's cell phone rang; it was Jack.

"Jerry, I have to take this call."

"I'll leave my report on your desk," Jerry replied, heading toward the parking lot. As he settled the dog down, Jerry glanced back at the building and shook his head, lamenting, "I just don't know about people today."

* * *

An all-clear siren blew, and Anne put a finger in her ear to drown out the noise. She apologized, saying, "Jack, can you hear me? I'm sorry I didn't call last night. I hope David had a good birthday."

"No problem, Anne. You told me the committee had not yet agreed on a permanent replacement. I figured you were tied up with that or something like it. I just texted you a picture."

Pulling up the text, Anne cringed at the picture. "Jesus, Jack. That looks very painful! What the hell happened?"

Jack exhaled. "David hammered me, but good. I never saw it coming."

Concerned, Anne asked, "I don't understand. Why would he do that?"

"Ordinarily, this is where I would say something like, 'You won't believe this,'" Jack answered.

"But..." Anne added.

"They both received a visit from George." Jack paused, then continued before Anne could respond. "Louis while he slept, and George confronted David at work."

Anne let Jack's words sink in, then stated, "Confronted suggests something negative happened."

"George went to see David and tried to abduct him."

Incredulous, Anne opened and closed her eyes several times in disbelief before saying, "What?"

"Whoever, or maybe I should say whatever, came back after I poured that water down his throat isn't my brother. David said George showed up with three demons in tow, and when one of those demons tried to grab him, something intervened and threw the demon against the wall, killing it."

Anne's eyebrows narrowed, and she held her phone closer. "David is protected, Jack. Louis is, too. The Book of Revelation says the Antichrist can't harm the two witnesses for 1,260 days."

She paused, then cautioned, "I can't say there is a consensus about whether or not a day to the Lord means twenty-four hours. Unfortunately, that remains a mystery."

"I guess there is some comfort in that. I think," Jack acknowledged skeptically. "It turns out that George realized they were protected too and did what he always did when we were kids."

"What's that?" Anne asked uneasily.

Jack retorted, "He went for the jugular. He always knew how to cut my feelings to the bone."

A long moment of silence passed, then Jack added, "He told them that I killed their mother."

"Oh God." Anne's hand instinctively covered her mouth. She quickly tried to console Jack, "Talk about tormenting the three of you on so many levels. It must feel like you are reliving it all over again."

Anne leaned back in the car seat and closed her eyes. Honoring Sheriff Hill's memory was the right thing to do, but knowing what Jack and the boys were going through was more than she could take. She resolved to pressure the committee to conclude their deliberations about the candidate to replace her.

Anne's tone was resolute as she buckled her seat belt. "I'm going to give the committee an ultimatum, Jack. They need to conclude their search this week."

Jamming the key in the ignition, she added emphatically, "I promise I will be there for Christmas."

"Thanks, Anne. We've got a lot to talk about."

* * *

> *Thursday, December 18th*
> *Lucius Rofocale's Chamber at Pergamon,*
> *Satan's Earthly Residence in the Present-Day*
> *Republic of Turkiye*
> *Midnight*

Reaching the entrance to Lucius's inner sanctum, a nervous Tatiana hesitated, then slammed her clenched claw against the heavy stone door.

Knock! Knock! Knock!

Lucius's powerful voice easily penetrated the monolithic barrier. "Come!"

She leaned her shoulder into the door and pushed with every ounce of her strength to move the stone. The muscles inside her purple skin flexed, and the razor-sharp nails on her toes dug into the floor as the door slowly opened. The vessels surrounding the room held blazing fires that reflected like a mirrored disco ball off the flakes of mica in the granite walls.

She dove to her knees immediately and bowed. "Forgive me for disturbing you, my Lord, but I fulfilled Princess Prosperine's request."

Glancing up at the princess, Tatiana added, "And it is waiting in her chamber."

Prosperine purred, "MMM." As her barbed, forked tongue slid over her lips in anticipation, she cooed, "Lucius, are we almost done? I am starving."

"Leave us." Lucius signaled to Tatiana, who rushed out. With a wave of his finger, he closed the door behind her.

"Yes, Princess. We are nearly finished. Lord Aitken, please finish your update." Glancing at Prosperine, he added, "Quickly."

"Master, I apologize to both you and the Princess." George Aitken lay prostrate at Lucius's feet. "I was unable to capture my nephews.

An energy field protects them. One of my team got too close, and the force tossed him across the warehouse into a wall, breaking his neck."

Haughtily tapping her six-inch talons on the glass-like, black obsidian table, the princess disclosed, "I seem to recollect reading about this somewhere. I guess it should not be a surprise that they have a shield protecting them. For now."

George continued, "Since I could not abduct them, I thrust a different dagger into my brother's heart."

Instantly interested, Prosperine leaned forward and entreated, "Do tell. Do not keep me in suspense."

George rose and pulled at the closely shaved, triangular goatee on his chin. His eyebrows drew downward menacingly as he answered, "I told both of my nephews about how their father, my brother, killed their mother."

Lucius clapped his hands, and a deep, sinister laugh rose from his throat. He glowed pridefully and crowed, "Well done! You truly are my disciple!"

Prosperine chimed in, "His transformation is nearly complete, Lucius!"

"If only I could see the look on your brother's pitiful face when those two brats ask him about what happened," Lucius gloried in George's revelation. Then, he pivoted to a different subject. "And what of Anne Bishop?"

"The committee members are deadlocked and will remain so," George responded. "Despite the progressive nature of human society today, greed and sexual transgressions still do not resonate well, making blackmail an effective tactic. Also, Bishop's sense of duty won't allow her to leave before they choose a successor to Captain Hill. She isn't going anywhere."

"Excellent!" Lucius cried. "Everything is going as planned, but I want to keep your brother and Anne Bishop separated. Remember, divide and conquer."

* * *

> *Friday, December 19th*
> *Woods Surrounding the Bradford House*
> *on the Outskirts of Culpeper, VA*
> *After Dark*

The strike of a match echoed through the quiet forest as the team leader, Gaap, once again tried to light the cigar he was smoking. A rare kind of demon, Gaap always presented as a human male but with bat wings concealed in his shoulder blades. These traits made him ideal for guard duty. His ability to fly allowed him to secure large forest areas, and he easily scared off human trespassers without drawing too much attention to himself. He shook the ashes from the cigar, never taking his eye off the surrounding trees.

"I don't see anything, Raum," Gaap whispered. Like Gaap, Raum presented as a human but could transform into a crow.

"Of course not," Raum scoffed. "There isn't anything out there. Nothing has happened here since the Princess, Lucius, and the entourage left for Pergamon."

"I know I heard something moving around," Gaap insisted. "Something doesn't feel right."

"I think you smoke too many of those death sticks," Raum joked. "They make you paranoid!"

Chewing on the cigar, Gaap laughed, "At least tobacco won't kill me like it does these humans."

Shouldering their guns, the duo laughed as they continued walking the perimeter of the Bradford property—water vapor condensed like a cloud of smoke in the cold air with every breath they took.

"When do you think we'll get transferred from this chicken shit assignment?" Raum asked. "While I love your company, I'm bored out of my skull."

Gaap saw something out of the corner of his eye, but it was too late... *BAM!*

Out of nowhere, a fast-moving object slammed into Gaap and Raum, launching them violently into the air. Gaap flew thirty feet, landing in a patch of wild raspberries, but Raum, hurtling sideways, struck a thick oak tree, breaking his spine. Gaap winced as the thorns from the raspberry canes tore at the flesh on his arms and face. Looking around the tree line, he saw nothing but Raum lying motionless. Still groggy from the assault, he stumbled over to his friend.

"Can you hear me?" Gaap asked as he grabbed Raum's shoulder. "Are you alright?"

Raum moaned, "I can't feel anything. I think I broke my back."

Attending to his friend's injuries, Gaap heard the crack of a branch and noticed a large shadow approaching. He slowly turned around, and a hulking figure covered in matted gray hair with elongated canine teeth protruding from its jaws stood over them. A thin ring of fire-engine-red pigment encircled the bright yellow eyes. Gaap instantly knew it was not a typical animal.

"*Strig—Strigoi,*" he stuttered, barely able to get words out.

* * *

"Where's Lucius?" the Strigoi demanded.

Gaap was unsure which terrified him more: the fact that he stood face to face with a mythical monster, thought to be a demon legend, or that it could speak.

"No... Not here," he whispered.

Gnashing its teeth, the Strigoi grew angrier and more impatient by the second. "WHERE?"

"Pergamon," Gaap added.

Realizing his enemy was gone, the Strigoi yelled, "NO!" The roar boomed through the forest.

Unable to roll over, Raum begged Gaap to answer. "Please, Gaap. What the hell is happening?"

Turning its attention back to the demon pair, the Strigoi breathed heavily and grabbed Gaap by the shirt. Gaap's black eyes opened wide, and his lips quivered. He struggled to flap his bat wings, but they were not powerful enough to break the grip of the Strigoi. A large paw with sharp, bony claws roughly pushed his head to the side.

"*What is it doing?*" Gaap thought to himself. "*A Strigoi doesn't drink demon blood.*"

The thought barely finished; the Strigoi plunged its canine teeth into the soft skin around Gaap's jugular vein. Gaap felt the sting of the canines pierce his skin, but he could not scream. A loud sucking sound echoed through the trees as Gaap's dark, black demon blood flowed from his veins into the Strigoi's mouth.

* * *

"Who's there?" Raum screamed several times, but there was no answer, just the words reverberating through the woods.

Within minutes, but what must have seemed like an eternity to Raum, Gaap hung limply in the Strigoi's hand. With a thud, it dropped Gaap's lifeless corpse and knelt by Raum. Raum's eyes darted back and forth, trying to see who or what was there, but they quickly rolled back when the Strigoi plunged its teeth so deeply into Raum's neck that it nearly decapitated him. After a short time, its urge for blood satisfied, the Strigoi headed toward the Bradford House.

The house came into view, but the Strigoi stopped in its tracks. It smelled the residual presence of his former master, Lucius, and many other demons, but one odor was more potent than the rest and irritated the Strigoi's nasal passages. Snorting to remove it, the Strigoi rubbed its nose and shook its head violently.

It identified the unpleasant scent as female, but there was also a corresponding energy imprint, a powerful force that the Strigoi had never felt before but recognized as completely malevolent. Too intense, even for an ancient titan like himself, the Strigoi turned away and, listening to a thought, an instinct that had been in its subconscious for weeks, headed south.

* * *

> Friday, December 19th
> Route 17 South Near Ocean Isle Beach, NC
> 10:00 p.m.

Sitting at a stop light, Anne pushed her hair back. Making a left turn into Brick Landing Plantation, she grabbed the steering wheel so tightly that the veins in her hands and arms were visible through her skin. Passing through the security checkpoint, she headed home, but her blood was still boiling. The meeting to choose her successor droned on for hours, but the committee seemed no closer to deciding.

Anne turned into the driveway, and as soon as she hit the button to open the garage door, Daphne started barking. Anne stopped the car before pulling into the garage and just sat there. She had lost her temper and was frustrated with herself as much as the process. There were several qualified candidates, but a few committee members seemed unable or unwilling to decide. Anne sighed deeply and reached to turn the radio off when she heard a breaking news update.

Australia is known for many things, but volcanoes are not one of them. The last volcanic eruption on the Australian mainland is estimated to have occurred more than 5,000 years ago. With no tectonic plate boundaries, what happened today is considered nearly impossible. However, the Tweed Volcano in New South Wales on Australia's East Coast has erupted for the first time in 23 million years....

CHAPTER 16

> Saturday, December 20th
> Anne Bishop's Home, Ocean Isle Beach, NC
> 4:30 p.m.

Keith Gordon exited his truck and brushed the dried mud from the last job off his worn overalls. Grabbing a coal miner's headlamp, he placed it on his hat and adjusted it. The calendar indicated that tomorrow was the winter solstice, the shortest day of the year, but it was nearly dark already. Anne Bishop had contacted him almost a month ago about something digging around her foundation, but it had taken several weeks for him to fit this job into the schedule. Keith had been an exterminator for over twenty years in coastal North Carolina and had never seen a fall quite like this.

The heightened levels of critter activity were so unusual that despite his years of experience, Keith could not explain why he was still so busy. As he made his way around the side of the house, he continued the same debate with himself that had been raging for weeks.

"I don't think it has been warmer than normal," Keith mumbled, following the light from his headlamp around the side of the house. "It hasn't been drier or rainier either."

Searching for the activity area along the foundation that Ms. Bishop had described, he just shook his head. "I don't understand it, but I'm not complaining." Keith whistled as he worked. "It will make for a merrier Christmas for the family."

Raising his filthy hands to his mouth, Keith blew into them. Pulling gloves from his back pocket, he slipped them on and muttered, "As soon as that sun went down, it got chilly. I'm glad this is the last job of the day."

Feeling the ground for the disturbed area, he asked, "Where are you?"

A few minutes later, he hit paydirt. Turning his headlamp to the right, Keith leaned down. Running his gloved fingers through the dirt and glancing at the adjacent undeveloped lot, he grumbled, "It could be squirrels, mice, or, based on the density of the brush, even rats."

Returning his attention to the foundation, he studied the ground intensely, hunting for additional clues. An area of disturbed soil caught his attention, and he followed a trail with the light from his headlamp. Perplexed, Keith bit the inside of his cheek.

It's too late in the year for moles or voles, but it looks like a collapsed trench.

Kneeling on the sandy dirt, Keith pushed his finger into the loose ground, which quickly gave way. Creating a small hole, he felt something solid.

Crack!

A loud noise, the snap of a branch, startled Keith and raised the hairs on the back of his neck. He searched the woods with his headlamp and saw nothing.

"Must have been a squirrel," Keith reasoned. He put his finger around the object and started to lift it. The ground gave way in all directions. The experienced exterminator expected to see a tree root but held an insulated black wire in his hand instead. Instinctively, he glanced upward, but no television or phone cables led into the house.

CRACK!

It was the same sound but much louder, as if it were right behind him. Spooked, Keith turned quickly. A figure emerged from the darkness, but his features were indistinguishable; it was just a black mass. It raised its hand, and Keith's eyebrows promptly elevated.

Alarmed, he stammered, "Who—who the hell are you?"

The light on the headlamp began to flicker, and then Keith grabbed the side of his head in agony. Electrical impulses from the battery shot through his brain, and Keith Gordon collapsed like a demolished building.

In disgust, the figure dropped its hand and commanded, "Get this piece of shit out of here. Bury the cable properly this time and dispose of the truck before Bishop comes home. Get moving!"

"Right away, Barbas!" The demon crew flew into action.

As the truck turned over and Keith Gordon's lifeless body slid along the ground, disappearing into the woods, Barbas's blazing red eyes stared into the darkness.

* * *

The Same Night
Amberleigh Station Subdivision, Bristow, VA
10:00 p.m.

As Jack studied the stars, the sky seemed like a warrior fighting itself. Unambiguous and powerful, the black night poured from the heavens like an invincible army. Yet a cool, electric blue hue hung on the horizon, still trying to resist the inevitable transition from day to night. Wispy strands of the snow-white cotton clouds, all that remained of the daylight hours, struggled and failed to stem the tide of the stars that flooded the darkness like lighthouse beacons. Bundled against the biting cold, Jack leaned into the cold winter wind howling through the oak tree branches as he plodded up a steep hill.

Adjusting the scarf around his neck, Jack questioned the wisdom of taking this walk, but the exercise helped him sleep, and the festive holiday decorations also raised his spirits. Jack's sisters were returning this week to spend the holidays, which also made him smile. But the grin quickly disappeared, and he flinched as the cold breeze hit his sensitive teeth. Jack turned the corner so the wind would be at his back and, walking faster, tried to warm up.

Memories of Christmas long past raced through his mind—like singing hymns on Christmas Eve at Wentworth United Methodist Church. The *First Noel* was his favorite, and he began humming it. He recalled the Christmas mornings that his sister, Emma, coaxed him into peeking at the presents under the tree before their parents were awake. The one when Jack got his first bicycle was a particular favorite. Jack saw a hockey net on a driveway, and it reminded him of one just like it that he and George received one Christmas.

"George." Jack exhaled a cloud of condensed water vapor. "What am I going to do about you? I was trying to save you as you always did for me, but I cannot deny the...."

Jack hesitated before finishing his sentence. "The evil that now runs through your veins."

Another arctic blast slapped Jack in the face, returning him to the present.

"This reminds me of my first Christmas with Amanda." Jack shivered as he walked but could not help but feel the warmth from the recollection. "It was cold, just like this, and Dad, thinking I was already home, had locked me out of the house. I had to climb on the roof to get in through my bedroom window."

As Jack walked up and down the streets, it was noticeably quiet. No barking dogs or cars pulling into driveways. He only heard the wind blowing in his ear and saw no one. Turning for home, a piece of paper, driven by a gust, tumbled along the ground, stopping at Jack's feet. Leaning over, he picked it up and silently read it.

1-2-4-5-4 Sapphire Ridge

Jack examined the object; it was a Christmas card that had fallen out of a mailbox or gone undelivered. The address was up the road, in the direction he was heading, and he decided to return it. Walking again, he clutched it tightly. Christmas cards were always something

Jack looked forward to receiving. He enjoyed reading them and relished his emotional connection with the sender, even if only once a year. Jack taped them on the back of the door to the garage, but the years when the door was full were long gone. More and more people were sending electronic cards or not sending any cards at all. Once it was gone entirely, Jack knew he would miss the fading tradition.

Slamming the door to the mailbox, ensuring this card would reach its recipient, Jack found himself standing at the top of the hill he had climbed earlier. This vantage point gave him a perfect view of his house, and he almost always stopped there to admire his Christmas lights. This year, he particularly enjoyed the newest addition to the display, a set of white solar lights that brightly outlined a garden arch.

Jack suddenly felt the sensation of a familiar hand slip into his as he stood in the frigid air. His lips drew up in a joyful smile, and he shed a tear that rolled down his cheek. Softly, Jack asked,

"Is that you, Amanda?"

An angelic voice answered, but Jack never heard it.

The best years I ever knew were the ones I spent with you.

Jack sighed, "I would give anything to have you back again."

You must cease to grieve for me, Jack.

Wiping the tear from his eye, Jack added, "I never wanted to take you for granted. So many things I left unsaid."

Being imprisoned in your past will ultimately rob you of your future.

Jack's head lowered. "Maybe if I had done things differently."

You constantly challenge yourself and your actions but find a way to move forward.

"Your quiet strength showed the way." Jack breathed deeply and exhaled. "You always put the needs of everyone else before your own."

You do not realize the many things you have done that touched and changed lives. How your support of Louis and David will change the world.

Jack closed his eyes and whispered, "You taught me how to love. Nobody else can understand the part of me that can't let you go."

But you must learn to love again.

The sound of bells jolted Jack back to reality. It was not the jingle of Christmas bells but those from a dog collar.

A warm feeling surrounded him despite the bitter cold, like being hugged. Jack waved to the dogwalker and slowly headed for home. He felt comforted by his experience. Anne's smiling face popped into his head. Jack realized something had changed as he turned the key to the front door.

That's the first time I thought of Anne without feeling a pang of guilt about Amanda.

Hanging up his coat in the hall closet, Jack wondered, *Maybe this is what Dr. Colby meant by a first step.*

* * *

> Sunday, December 21ˢᵗ
> Garden of Gehenna at Pergamon
> in the Present-Day Republic of Turkiye
> 10:00 a.m.

The first official day of winter was sunny and warm, very unusual for southern Turkiye at this time of year. In need of a break from his relentless scheming and planning, George Aitken sought refuge in a garden on the plateau above the acropolis at Pergamon. Encircled by a black, wrought-iron fence, the Garden of Gehenna was just what George needed to clear his head before the extraordinary events of the coming days unfolded.

The skull and crossbones on the heavy gate guarding the entrance hinted at what was inside. Gehenna was no ordinary garden. Lucius had it planted, making a mockery of Eden and Gethsemane. Tunnels of poison ivy, whose once green leaves were now a brilliant yellow, boldly contrasted with the black volcanic stone of the walkways.

Lucius filled the pentagram-shaped planting areas with Earth's most toxic and poisonous plants. The only rival to the stunning colors of the flowers were the attributes of their fruits, sap, and fragrance. Each made everything in the garden inherently lethal.

George strolled, the sun warm upon his face, admiring the fire-red leaves and flowers of the castor plant, whose beans contained the deadly biological agent, ricin. Not far away, the giant hogweed stood nearly fourteen feet tall, and its white, umbrella-shaped flowers could be as large as five feet across. George peered up at the blossoms that towered over him and ran his hands up and down the stems, admiring their strength. The sap of the giant hogweed caused severe blisters and burns to humans, but George's hands suffered no such effect.

The garden was small but contained nearly one hundred deadly plant species. When George finished his visit, he felt refreshed and energized. Tatiana lowered her head respectfully, greeted him at the entrance, and handed him a bottle, saying, "This is your daily elixir, sir."

Taking the container filled with River Styx water and other mysterious minerals, George gulped down the bitter-tasting liquid. He handed the bottle back to Tatiana.

"One of your aides is here. Shall I send her away?" she asked.

"No," George replied bluntly. "Send her here."

Tatiana left, and another demon carefully navigated the steep slope leading to the garden.

Kneeling, the assistant said, "I have an update for you, Lord Aitken."

"What is it, Maya?" George asked curtly.

"Regretfully, the encryption team is still not getting very far. Progress is slow. I know that Master Lucius wants constant updates."

George folded his arms in frustration and wondered what the next steps should be. Pacing and scratching the back of his neck, he realized....

"Why search the Dark Web to find an expert in AES-256 algorithms when I have one at my disposal? Bring our *guests* to my chambers. Ask Princess Prosperine to join us."

"I will see to it immediately, my Lord," Maya quickly replied, then added, "I also want to show you these."

Maya handed George a deck of cards, which he carefully began to examine. On one side was an image of a graveyard. The outline of a leafless tree was on the right, and in the forefront was a tombstone, crookedly leaning to the left with the letters R-I-P prominently engraved toward the top. A figure wearing a tattered black robe and holding a tall scythe stood behind the gravestone—a Reaper, collector of the dead.

George nodded with an unpleasant smile. "Yes, these are good. Very good."

Turning the cards over, he flipped through the pictures. Each was a facial photo. He paused briefly, glancing at a card with an image of Anne Bishop. The following cards bore the likenesses of his nephews, but George stopped and stared menacingly at the last card—the picture of his brother.

"Print copies of these right away," George ordered. "I will present them to the team later."

As Maya left, George strolled back into the garden and announced, "Jack, my so-called brother, we have unfinished business to settle. Gehenna means misery or agony. You should prepare to experience both."

* * *

> An Hour Later
> Solitary Cell Deep Below the Halls of Pergamon
> in the Present-Day Republic of Turkiye

The small slot in the door allowed a narrow ray of light into the room. Without it, the underground cell, about the size of a storage closet, would have been pitch black. To the occupant, it felt more like a crypt. Being shackled in the claustrophobic compartment only stressed the ominous nature of the situation. A key turned over in the lock's tumbler, and as the heavy iron door slowly opened with a loud creak, Josephine Aitken cowered in a cobweb-filled corner, trembling with fear.

"Get up, you filthy human!" a female guard demanded as she yanked the chains around Josephine's wrists and ankles. Josephine offered little resistance as the hulking demon dragged her across the floor. "Lord Aitken wants to see you."

Josephine had not been out of the cell since she arrived. She had no idea how long she had been a prisoner. Her ankles were shackled, so she shuffled her feet across the floor. While the hallway, more like a cave passage, was not brightly lit, spending so much time in her dark cell left Josephine sensitive to the light. She raised her handcuffed hands to shield her eyes. It was oppressively hot, and sweat from her forehead fell to the floor like rain. The dark-colored prison garb she wore stuck to her body like glue.

Josephine screamed as her arm touched the rock wall lining the hallway. The guard merely laughed and roughly pushed her forward. The smell of sulfur invaded Josephine's nostrils; it was everywhere.

Reaching the entrance to a room in a nearby corridor, the guard pushed open the wooden door and forcefully shoved Josephine into the chamber. Her husband, George, was with a strange and provocatively dressed woman. At least it was George in some semblance, but it was harder to know it was him every time she blinked. He looked so aggressive and diabolical.

Josephine noticed a trembling and seemingly terrified young girl was also there. The sparsely furnished apartment and sterile white paint suggested the room would be suitable for an institution of the criminally insane. Exactly the place where she believed her "husband" belonged.

"Come in, Josephine," George suggested as if she had any alternative. "I have something I wish to speak to you about."

* * *

The sight of her husband incensed Josephine, and she lunged at him like a tiger. The guard pulled back on the restraints, stopping Josephine just short of her target. She looked at George with eyes like daggers and gnashed her teeth in frustration at her inability to scratch his eyes out.

"I'm happy to see you too," George laughed at the sight of his wife. Then, he taunted her, "Your hair is a little askew, and you look rather disheveled, but that hunter-green jumpsuit is quite flattering. I also love that new tattoo on your neck."

George's snarky comment about a tattoo reminded Josephine of the near-constant burning sensation in her throat since her capture.

"I don't have a tattoo, you bastard," Josephine seethed. "What did you do to me?"

"I left you my brand, Josephine. What you are feeling is the seared image of my fingers around your throat."

"How long have I been here?" Josephine demanded.

"Two weeks, my dear," George answered cheekily.

"Some people here would like to make your acquaintance." Pointing to his right, George introduced his first guest. "This is Prosperine, the Princess of Hell."

Josephine eyed the woman standing next to her husband. She was tall, wearing a skin-tight, one-piece, blood-red dress that hugged every curve of her body. Her long, shiny black hair was the same color as her stiletto heels. She had hypnotic green eyes.

"Princess of Hell, you say?" Josephine's lip curled upward in disgust. "I wouldn't be the least surprised. Is she your new wife?" Josephine's veins pulsed in her temple. Locking eyes with Prosperine, she yelled, "You can have him, you bitch!"

"She's charming, Lord Aitken." Prosperine yawned, then said caustically, "I can certainly see why you stayed with her all these years."

Prosperine sniffed the air and turned her nose up in disgust. "Next time, make sure she showers before entering my presence."

George moved toward his spouse. His eyes were narrow slits, and he stared menacingly at her.

"I would watch my tone if I were you," George warned as he slowly squeezed his fingers into a fist, causing Josephine to choke. Her eyes bulged as she sunk to the floor, trying to catch a breath. Just before she passed out, George released his grip, opening her airway. Josephine coughed and gasped for air.

He knelt beside her. "I trust we will have no such disrespectful language from you moving forward. I hope we understand each other."

George looked at the door and shouted, "Bring them in!"

* * *

The door opened, and a different guard escorted two women into the room. A third figure, a male, wrestled with his jailers before being forcibly thrown to the white and gray marble floor. Seeing Josephine gasping and struggling to breathe caused all three individuals to dive to the ground beside her.

"Mom! Are you alright?" her son James asked. Then, with dark blue eyes, the color of a raging storm at sea, he turned and glared at his father.

Her eldest daughter, Kate, helped Josephine stand up. The youngest child, Erin, her eyes darting around the room fearfully, asked, "What is happening, Mom?"

Unsure of what to do next, Erin ran to George and threw her arms around him. She received no reciprocation. Through her sobs, she questioned, "Daddy, why are you doing this?"

"Erin." George grabbed her arms and pushed her away. "The man you loved as your father is gone." Looking at what once was his family, he added, "It will be best for all of you to accept this."

"They look positively delicious," Prosperine cooed, as her snake-like tongue licked her lips. She sharpened her claw-like fingernails by running them down the stone wall. It gave off a shrill noise, like nails on a chalkboard. George cringed in response, but unfazed, Prosperine suggested, "Let's get down to business, shall we?"

The hair on the back of his neck still standing, George lowered his head in deference to the princess. He announced, "I have a proposition for your mother, but it also involves the three of you."

Making eye contact with his wife, George explained, "My technicians cannot develop software that will bypass all forms of encryption."

His hands laced behind his back, George paced back and forth, then stopped and stared at James, Erin, and Kate. "In exchange for your mother's assistance, upon completing the project, I will allow her to choose which of the three of you will live. That child will be allowed to leave unharmed."

George paused, allowing his proposal to sink in, then continued, "The remaining family members, including you, Josephine, will be given merciful deaths."

"I will never help you!" Defiantly, Josephine shook her head and insisted. "I will see you in Hell first!"

Standing before his wife, George pressed his lips together tightly. After a few seconds, he replied, "Your defiance is admirable but pointless."

Turning away, he added, "Besides, that isn't much of a threat." George began to laugh and quickly turned and faced his family again. He told them, his eyes bulging from his skull, "I've been to Hell, and it is my kind of place!"

Kate interjected, "You're insane! Mad! You've taken total leave of your senses!"

"On the contrary," George whispered, malevolently. "I've come to them."

Erin wept and tasted her own tears, saying, "Daddy, please don't do this. You don't have to do this."

"There is no time for tears," George scolded Erin, wagging his finger in her face. "Moreover, desire is irrelevant. Only the mission for my Master matters now."

* * *

Watching his father continue to pontificate about his mission, James Aitken stood silently, stewing in his juices. Each hand clamped tightly, like a vise, waiting for an opportunity to attack. Sensing this, George baited him,

"Go ahead, James. Take a swing. I can see it in your eyes and feel your rage. Rage is a good thing if you know how to use it. It makes us powerful and willing to do anything for revenge! You have always wanted to, so why not throw a punch?"

George stood before his son with his chin out. "I will let you take a free shot."

His face flushed in anger; James Aitken tried to restrain himself. Meanwhile, his father began to insult him.

"Gutless. Pathetic. Fucking weakling!"

James could take it no longer and reared back, throwing a vicious right cross. George's hand grabbed his son's fist in mid-air, and he began to squeeze. James's face turned from anger to agony, and he struggled to free his hand from his father's vise-like grip.

"Would you like to know how your Uncle Jack's hand feels?"

George raised James in the air, never relinquishing his hold on his son. The boy flailed around like a trout on a hook. Josephine rushed forward, but the guard holding her chains restrained her. She clasped her hands together as if she were praying and pleaded,

"George, stop it! Please! I'll do whatever you want."

Immediately, George dropped James to the floor, who clutched his injured hand to his body in anguish.

George motioned to one of the guards, who pulled a girl the same age as George's daughters into the middle of the room. Her eyes were wide open, her jaw slack. Tears ran down her cheeks as she trembled. Prosperine approached the young lady, who began shaking her head and begging,

"No. No. Please don't do this to me."

"Watch the fate that awaits you all if your mother double-crosses me or fails to achieve our objective," George locked eyes with Josephine and asserted. "I will make you watch this happen to each child, one after the other."

Prosperine put her index finger before her lips, and as the guard held the terrified young woman by the shoulders, she whispered to her, "Shh..."

The Princess of Hell leaned in as if to kiss the girl. Instead, her snake-like tongue emerged from her mouth. Each fork of her tongue crawled slowly across the youthful, milky white complexion of the victim's face, then pried open her mouth. Josephine and her children tried to look away, but the guards held their heads tightly and forced them to watch what was unfolding. Kate screamed.

The barbs on Prosperine's tongue sank into the now hysterical victim's mouth; instantly, her body became rigid. She fell to the floor within seconds, a desiccated pile of leather-like skin and bones. Erin leaned over, trying to vomit, but only dry heaved. Josephine stroked her daughter's hair, trying to comfort the child.

Prosperine licked her lips and leaned over to whisper in Erin's ear, "I think you will taste best of all. MMM... so sweet."

George grabbed Josephine tightly by the chin and pulled her closer until they were nose to nose. Then he announced, "You can give up any fantasy you might have about rescue. No Fluke Starbuck, Dodo, Yo-Yo, or whatever other hobbits you admire are coming for you. You will obey me! Are we clear on that, Jo-Jo?"

Josephine sighed and rolled her eyes at the word obey. When the minister who married them suggested it as part of their wedding vows, they intensely argued after she insisted upon its removal. Josephine knew he had used it now, on purpose. Equally irritating was being called Jo-Jo, which she despised. Responding through her gritted teeth, Josephine seethed, "You know I hate when you call me that."

George's lips drew up in a wicked grin, "Yes… I know."

CHAPTER 17

> *Later That Same Evening*
> *The Halls of Pergamon in the*
> *Present-Day Republic of Turkiye*
> *11:00 p.m.*

Tatiana peered around the corner of the hallway leading to Lucius Rofocale's chambers. Tucked under her arm, along with the daily reports, was the true legacy of her kind. Not the alternate universe described by Lucius and Lucifer. The last three weeks were the most exhilarating yet frightening of her life.

Reading Lucius's book enabled Tatiana to understand the truth of demon history, but having it in her possession meant certain death. She reflected on several passages that impacted her greatly.

Fought one another. Lucius ended Kazimir's treachery.

It was no surprise to Tatiana that Lucius orchestrated his brother Kazimir's death. She had a front-row seat, witnessing Lucius's gift for survival and mastery of palace intrigue. Tatiana admired Lucius's genius, but her respect for him lessened after reading about Kazimir's bravery. It was this discovery that caused her to make a dangerous decision. She made a copy of Lucius's book.

Painstakingly, word by word, she wrote it all down. Tatiana even went as far as to find and use the same ancient paper. She also studied and duplicated every detail down to the cover made from human skin. While on a mission for Lucius several years ago, before being captured and killed by JESU, Tatiana's sister, Nadia, told her about breaking into Mark Desmond's apartment and discovering books on demon liturgy hidden among JESU texts. Tatiana copied the tactic of Lucius's most despised adversary. She hid her copy in plain sight by mingling it with the other books she kept. The most challenging part was what she was doing now: placing Lucius's demon Bible back in his room.

Several demon guards passed, and Tatiana knew this might be her opportunity. For the past few evenings, she had carried the book with her when she dropped off the briefings that Lucius always read in his private chamber. Unfortunately, Lucius had been meeting in his conference space, and while he had her put the documents in his room, there was no time to access the trunk and replace the book.

KNOCK! KNOCK! KNOCK!

Tatiana pounded on the door, expecting to hear Lucius's voice, but there was no answer. She needed to be sure, so she knocked again.

KNOCK! KNOCK! KNOCK!

Realizing this was her chance, Tatiana quickly transformed into her human form, which gave her more dexterity. Despite having no soul, she felt anxious, and her fingers shook. She pushed on the heavy stone door. It moved slowly but opened enough for her to enter the conference area. Scanning the room, Tatiana saw a map on the table that had not been there days earlier.

"*No one's here,*" Tatiana thought to herself. Her heart would have been beating out of her chest if she had one.

Tatiana carefully tried to move across the room, but nervously dropped the reports on the floor. She quickly picked them up and stood trembling before Lucius's inner chamber door. Glancing behind her again, assured she was alone, Tatiana turned the knob and entered. Her eyes darted around the space and found the chest in the far corner. She dropped the reports on a table and hurried to the trunk.

"Damn it!" Tatiana muttered fearfully. "The lock is different. Lucius changed it!"

Recalling the repairs she had made previously, Tatiana carefully began removing the gold nails on the side of the chest.

Struggling to remove the wooden pieces, Tatiana moaned, "This is taking too long." She was getting uneasy. "I have to get this done."

Finally, prying off the last piece, she slid the book back into place.

"Whew." Tatiana exhaled, wiping the sweat from her brow as she quickly began repairing the chest again. As she began tapping the last nails in place, she felt a vibration through the floor. Tatiana hesitated and heard the door to the conference room start to open. She struck the final nail, and it fell onto the floor.

Tatiana panicked. "Nooo...." She frantically felt around on the floor for the nail. "If he finds me here, I am dead!"

* * *

Lucius entered the conference room, finding his aide, Tatiana, standing in front of the door to his private chamber. Instantly suspicious, his steely glance locked on Tatiana as she dove to his feet.

"What are you doing in here, Tatiana?" Lucius demanded, like a lawyer interrogating a witness.

Still kneeling, Tatiana raised her hand above her head, clutching papers, and answered, "The nightly reports."

Lucius continued probing for answers, not sold on her explanation. "What about them?"

Tatiana never looked up and replied, "I was placing them in your private room for security purposes."

Rubbing his chin with a clawed fingernail, unconvinced, Lucius grabbed Tatiana's hair and dragged her into his chamber, shouting, "What are you up to, Tatiana?" Tatiana struggled but did not cry out.

Pulling her hair tightly, he scanned the room, but everything looked the same. Lucius hauled her from corner to corner, sure she was not being truthful, before stopping in front of the chest containing his personal papers.

"What are you hiding?" Lucius tightened his grip, stretching Tatiana's hair until it almost tore away from her scalp. Like a fish on a pier, she flopped around on the floor as he examined the chest from every angle. He found nothing out of place.

Lucius sneered at Tatiana but was secretly impressed that she neither called out nor begged for her life. With more critical matters on his mind, he released her. With one shrug of his head toward the door, Lucius said curtly, "I have too many other important things going on now. Go. Get out. Before I change my mind."

"Yes, my Lord," Tatiana said as Lucius unleashed her from his painful grip. She bowed and hurried out of the room.

* * *

> Monday, December 22nd
> American Press Service HQ, Washington, DC
> 10:00 a.m.

The day had started quietly, but now the newsroom was abuzz about a breaking story. Maria Connor dashed to her seat behind the news desk and nervously checked her makeup in a mirror.

"One minute to airtime," a camera operator shouted. An engineer from the control room whispered to Maria through an earpiece, "There is a lot of interference, and the connection with Jenny is not good. You have thirty seconds until we go live."

Maria nodded. "I hear you loud and clear, Mitch. I'll handle any gaps in the interview."

The producer held up her hand and, having Maria's attention, counted down with his fingers, "3-2-1." She pointed to the news anchor, who stared directly into the camera and announced, "Good morning, Washington. I am Maria Connor with a breaking APS exclusive. Several weeks ago, an underwater volcano off the coast of Barbados in the Caribbean erupted. Until recently, volcanic activity was not a concern in the region. This unexpected incident has continued to evolve, and via a deteriorating satellite connection, we are speaking to our reporter, Jenny Phillips, who is live in the capital of Bridgetown."

A technician flipped a switch, and a loud burst of static echoed through the newsroom. A weak signal caused the video feed to cut in and out.

"Jenny, can you hear me?" Maria asked. There was no response, just intermittent bursts of interference.

Concerned, Maria shouted, "Are you there, Jenny?"

Another short pause and a response came through the open line. "I'm here, Maria. It isn't easy to hear you. The situation in Bridgetown is chaotic. Overnight, 800 soldiers from the Barbados defense forces took up positions around the city to maintain order, but there are reports of looting in some neighborhoods. I don't think it is an exaggeration to use the word panic. British authorities have been consulted and offered to fly in emergency troops if requested. They are also coordinating relief efforts with international agencies."

Maria followed up on Jenny's response, "What brought on this unrest?"

Like nails down a chalkboard, a shrill sound came over the line, causing Maria to flinch and adjust the volume on her earpiece.

Jenny's voice came back online. "When I arrived here a few days ago, the anxiety levels of the people I interviewed were already quite high. Since the initial eruption, constant smoke from the volcano has impacted the air quality, caused eye irritation, and required citizens to wear masks. The smell of sulfur is everywhere. Yesterday...."

More interference came through the line, and the video feed was lost.

"Jenny, we've lost the video." Maria tried to remain calm, but Jenny was her friend, and she was growing worried.

"I'm still here," Jenny continued as Maria visibly sighed with relief. "We are broadcasting from a former prison, and the infrastructure is interfering with the signal. Saturday night, an ash cloud rose from the volcano, affecting the island's television signal. Tensions increased yesterday after a video surfaced showing the waters around Barbados boiling, and there are unsubstantiated reports of a small tsunami in the northern coastal areas."

BOOM!

A loud, audible explosion came across the line, which went dead. There was no static or interference; a hush fell over the newsroom, and the employees were stunned.

"Jenny, what happened?" Maria asked desperately, breaking the silence.

The connection resumed, but there was only the sound of an open line. A minute, which seemed like an eternity, passed before Jenny's voice, in broken phrases, returned. "Mushroom cloud. Screams. My God! A wall of fire—"

The line went dead.

CHAPTER 18

> Tuesday, December 23rd
> Jack Aitken's Home, Bristow, VA
> 6:30 a.m.

Jack yawned as he grabbed the rail and walked downstairs, carefully avoiding the pile of laundry Louis had left on the stairs.

Reaching the landing, Jack saw that the kitchen light was on, which usually signaled that one of the boys was awake, but it was uncharacteristically quiet. There were no whistles or the sounds of train cars running over tracks, which ordinarily emanated from David's favorite videos. Instead, Jack found his child lying on the couch, sobbing into a pillow.

"David, what's the matter?" Jack sat on the edge of the couch and gently grabbed his son's shoulder. Since the beating David administered to his father, they had barely spoken.

Pulling his face from the pillow, he answered, "I had a bad dream."

"Do you want to tell me about it?" Jack asked, patting him on the back.

The young man shook his head back and forth, indicating he didn't want to answer.

Jack sighed. *"This shouldn't be this way. It shouldn't be so hard for him, for Louis... for me."*

Through his tears, the boy suddenly said, "You died."

"What?" Jack leaned closer, not sure he heard what his son said.

Rolling toward Jack, David's watery eyes met his father's. Then he wrapped his arms around Jack and hugged him.

Instinctively, Jack met his child's embrace, but he was stunned. It was the first time his son ever sought comfort from him. "You can't go away like Mom."

"Shhh." Jack closed his eyes and held him tighter. "Everything I do is for you and Louis, to keep the two of you safe."

Jack brushed away a tear rolling down David's cheek with his shoulder and added, "I'm not going anywhere. I'll always be here whenever you need me."

"Why did all those people die?" His son sniffled, abruptly changing the subject.

"David..." Jack hesitated, unsure how to answer the question.

"Louis and I tried to deliver the message we were supposed to yesterday, but people kept asking why God allowed the volcano to erupt and kill all those people."

Jack gulped nervously. "And what did you say?"

* * *

The Same Day
7:00 p.m.

The boys played video games in the basement while Jack leaned his head on his hand and picked at the spaghetti on his plate. Then his cell phone, on the table next to him, vibrated. It was a text from Anne.

Shifting in his chair, Jack typed, *"A crisis of conscience."*

"About what?" Was the quick response Jack received.

Jack stared down the hallway as he collected his thoughts and answered, *"Raising children in general, let alone autistic children, should come with an owner's manual."*

Jack put the phone down and ate another forkful of pasta. The phone bounced on the table. This time it was a call. Jack saw Anne's name on the screen. He answered and heard a chuckle before he could greet her.

"I'm sure you are not alone in that thought."

Jack said, "Sometimes breakthroughs arise out of the worst circumstances."

"I'm not following you, Jack."

"For example, before Louis could speak, we used a picture book to help him communicate. Amanda had to go to an out-of-town funeral, and I took care of Louis for the weekend alone. By Sunday, I was exasperated, trying to figure him out, and yelled at him. He went over to the book, grabbed one of the picture slides, and handed it to me."

"What picture was it?" Anne asked curiously.

"It was the picture showing someone looking angry."

Jack moaned, "I still feel a pang of guilt over my lack of patience."

"I think I understand, Jack. What happened today?"

"David had a dream where I died, and he hugged me. It was the first time he ever sought comfort from me."

The excitement in Anne's voice was unmistakable. "Jack, that is a breakthrough moment if I have ever heard one!"

"It is a moment I won't forget, but there's more, Anne. He asked me why the people in Barbados died."

"He was expressing concern about others?" Anne interjected. "I guess, in his own way, it was empathetic. Compassionate."

"Right," Jack agreed, "but he never expressed that before. Then he told me about questions he and Louis got during their sermon yesterday."

Jack paused, then resumed, "Anne, you would not believe how they answered the question. What happened in Barbados is a tragedy of epic proportions, and I don't know that I accept the answer the boys gave. But I am blown away by how they answered it."

"Go on, Jack," Anne pleaded. "Don't keep me in suspense."

"Louis spoke first. I wrote it down. I have to get the piece of paper from my pocket."

"'All ten of Job's children died when a windstorm destroyed his home. When confronted with this tragedy, Job accepted that the Lord could give and take away, but he blessed the name of the Lord anyway. Job shows we can worship God even if we don't understand why bad things happen.'"

Anne gushed, "A Biblical scholar would be hard-pressed to give any better answer."

Soberly, Jack added, "Then David told them, 'When Adam and Eve fell from grace, they took the natural order of things down with them. As a result, the destructive force of volcanoes is as essential to the formation of our planet as the terrible role it played in the events in Barbados.'"

"Jack, from my JESU training, I recall three criteria used to identify a prophet."

Jack gripped the phone tightly and held it closer to his ear.

"First, there are supernatural signs or events that coincide with their appearance, and I think the ability to project their image all over the planet yet remain invisible on video qualifies."

Anne paused, then continued, "Second, they engage in an ongoing conversation. It is not just a one-time occurrence."

"We can check that box, too," Jack added.

"Agreed," Anne responded. "Finally, they must demonstrate divine wisdom. I think I am well versed enough in religious doctrine to say they just proved that point."

While he allowed Anne's assessment to sink in, Jack had another thought he needed to share. "It seems wrong to feel happiness after such tragedy, but I do. For the first time, I feel like Louis and David might understand what they are preaching and not just saying it. Does that make sense?"

Anne suggested, "Jack, it seems to me that your emotions are not unlike a person feeling fortunate that they are not one of the 290,000 people who perished yesterday. Sort of like survivor's guilt, in a way."

"I hadn't thought of it that way until you said it."

Shaking his head in disbelief, Jack acknowledged, "What happened yesterday is incomprehensible. There are no words to describe it. I watched that poor woman, the reporter, die on camera."

Jack hesitated. "Anne, do you think…"

"You're wondering if Lucius and this Prosperine had something to do with what happened in Barbados. I thought about it, too."

There was a long moment of silence between the two before Jack spoke. "Let's hope not because I don't want to think about what might happen next."

*　*　*

Later That Night
10:00 p.m.

Plop!

Jack dropped the pile of paid bills on the hall table so they would go out in the mail in the morning and tiredly made his way upstairs. After showering, he lay beside a stack of his parents' forwarded mail on the bed. It never ceased to amaze Jack that so much mail continued to show up despite his parents being deceased for several years. He reached into his bathrobe pocket, grabbed his glasses, and started reading. Forty-five minutes later, he reached the bottom of the stack.

Thankful to be finished with the pile, Jack picked up the last envelope and examined it. The white envelope was very yellowed.

Jack pulled at his lower lip, uncertain about the piece of mail, and flipped it over to read the front. His uncertainty turned to shock.

Wentworth Avenue?

He removed his glasses and held the envelope closer to read it better.

"How can that be? None of us have lived there for more than thirty years. And wait a minute, what's with this five-cent stamp?"

Jack ran his finger across the postage. It was red with hands clasped in prayer, surrounded by a white aura and a Christmas star in the left corner—the words "Christmas Noel" imprinted on the bottom. "Return to sender" was stamped on the envelope in several places. While the date was faded, Jack could make out the year 1966.

Jack's eyes nearly popped out of his head at the Florida address on the label in the left corner of the envelope. His curiosity beyond piqued, Jack carefully lifted an edge of the envelope and slid his finger to open it. He pulled out a card with an imprint of the nativity on the front and the words "Merry Christmas" in large letters on the bottom. Opening it, he read the message.

Dear Louise and family,

With every good wish for a merry Christmas and a very happy New Year.

Love,

Mom & Dad

Jack's eyes twinkled in amazement. It felt like he was holding a piece of family history. He turned the card and studied it from every angle, wondering what Christmas in 1966 had been like for his family. Jack opened the card to reread it when he noticed something else written at the bottom.

Take nothing for granted. In the blink of an eye, everything can change.

Putting the card on the bed, Jack leaned back on a pillow and scratched his chin.

Jack gathered the remnants of the mail, got up, and threw them in a wastebasket in the bathroom. He put the Christmas card from his grandparents in his nightstand drawer. Turning off the lights, he pulled up the covers.

Why did my grandparents write that to my mother? And what does it mean?

* * *

> Tuesday, December 23rd
> Lucius Rofocale's Chamber at Pergamon
> 11:30 p.m.

A ball of blinding white light suddenly appeared in the corner of the room and floated to the head of the table. In an instant, it morphed into a being of enormous stature. Apollyon stood at attention, and his beautifully polished armor reflected the light from the torches in Lucius's chamber. He removed his helmet, placing the shiny silver headgear on the black obsidian table.

"Welcome to Pergamon, Apollyon," Lucius greeted the Destroyer. "You look well, my friend. Better than the last time we met."

Apollyon bowed slightly and replied, "Thank you, Lucius. All is going as you have foreseen, restoring my optimism."

Apollyon pointed at an opulent urn in Lucius's hands and asked, "Are those the souls?"

Lucius nodded and ran his hands across the bronze container. It had an etched leaf design encircling the vessel's base and top just below the lid.

"I forged it personally. Do you think it is lavish enough?"

"It is extraordinary! May I hold it?" Apollyon asked. Lucius handed him the urn, and the Destroyer carefully examined it.

"It is exceptional craftsmanship. I expected something larger. Are there sufficient numbers?"

"It will be enough," Lucius responded politely, but cautioned, "I have packed the canister beyond capacity to maximize the value of its contents. As a result, the reduced volume increases the pressure inside, making the souls volatile. I do suggest you handle it delicately."

"Understood," Apollyon acknowledged Lucius's instructions, then added, "Producing the additional souls required me to ignite all of Hell's furnaces, which resulted in the activation of volcanic activity on the Earth's surface."

Striking a cautionary tone, Apollyon continued, "This activity did not go unnoticed, and I received word that I am to appear in Heaven early in the morning on December 25th."

"Do not be concerned," Lucius reassured Apollyon. "I have foreseen this. It is a modest reminder of the power at your disposal; after all, you also work for Lucifer. In reaction to your efforts, this audience allows you to personally deliver your tribute to God."

Calmed by Lucius's explanation, Apollyon put his helmet back on and declared, "I will send word to confirm when our plan has succeeded."

Lucius replied, "I will look toward Heaven for a sign. I am certain it will be unmistakable."

Instantly, Apollyon disappeared.

CHAPTER 19

> Wednesday, December 24th
> Quantico National Cemetery, Quantico, VA
> 8:00 a.m.

Whirr, Whirr, Whirr, Whirr

The rhythmic sound of a drill echoed through the quiet graveyard as Jack watched four screws securing George and Louise Aitken's nameplate inserted in quick succession. He turned the collar up on his charcoal gray, woolen coat against the breeze that always swept through the fields of headstones regardless of the time of year. After a moment of meditation, a young marine in dress blues with bright white pants raised his bugle and softly began to blow *Taps*.

Jack would have been satisfied to have his parents' remains reinterred without making a fuss, but the Marine Corps would have none of it. *Duty. Honor. Country.* These hallowed words were what the respectful Major quoted to him, and who was Jack to disagree? The morning sun reflected off the bugle and the buttons on the young Marine's jacket, almost blinding Jack. But, once the bugler finished playing, Jack stood alone, keeping a silent vigil at his parents' grave.

Placing his hand on the marble nameplate, he ran his fingers across the etched letters and numbers, then stepped back and proclaimed, "Mission accomplished. I got you back where you belong before Em, Michelle, Lynne, and Geo..."

Jack caught himself, gulped, and finished his sentence. "Show up."

His shoulders slumped, and he hung his head, saying, "I don't know what else to do about George. I am open to suggestions if you're up there and listening."

A chill ran down Jack's spine as a wind gust blew directly in his face. "It sure feels like snow, Mom. They say it is going to get bitterly cold. We might even have a white Christmas. Not your kind of weather, either of you, but I sure wish you both were here right now."

Jack reached into his coat pocket, pulled out two cookies, and laid them on the ground. Smiling, he stated, "One for each of you. Chocolate chip for Pop and your favorite, Mom, oatmeal."

Checking his watch, Jack sighed. "I've got to get home; Em and Michelle will be waiting. Merry Christmas. I love you, both."

Jack ran his fingers across the nameplate again, put on his gloves, and started toward the parking lot.

*　*　*

> Wednesday, December 24th
> Bradford House, Culpeper, VA
> 8:00 a.m.

"Yes, Lord Aitken. While on patrol last night, we found the guards' bodies," the demon sentry reported but hesitated before adding, "They were both exsanguinated."

George studied the lines on the palm of his hand, lost in thought, before pronouncing, "It seems we have a vampire on the loose. Are there any other desecrations of the bodies?"

Shaking his head, the patrol leader replied, "None. All that we have found is a trail of footprints leaving the area. They start out like those of an animal, with pronounced claws, walking on all fours."

His right eyebrow raised, George probed further, "Intriguing. What else did you see?"

"My Lord, the tracks morph into the feet of a bipedal entity with five toes on each foot."

George removed his glasses, blew on the lenses, causing them to fog up, and began to wipe them clean.

"I will inform Master Lucius." George waved his hand, demanding, "Send in the team leaders."

Three weeks earlier, he had met with his demon strike force in the same room. Now, they spread out around the table in the middle of the space, awaiting their final orders. George pushed small packages across the table to each squad member. They opened the envelopes and studied the contents as their evil master spoke.

"Each of you is receiving a deck of cards. They have pictures of high-value targets. Our primary campaign objective is to neutralize these individuals. With few exceptions, we want dead bodies only."

George shouted, "Barbas!"

The demon snapped to attention. "Yes, Lord Aitken!"

Scowling, George commanded, "You will capture Anne Bishop alive. Is that clear?"

"I will see to it personally, Master!"

"You will transport her to Pergamon." George looked around the table and continued, "I will remain here in Northern Virginia and deal with my so-called brother and God's prophets."

George grabbed the edges of the massive mahogany table with both hands and leaned forward. Through his gritted teeth, he announced, "Training is over. It is time to execute our plan, and I expect precision. Do we understand one another?"

In unison, the demons said, "Yes, Lord Aitken!"

"Good. Now, go do your jobs! And do not forget that I am always watching."

As the team leaders exited the room, George sat behind a desk and thumbed through his deck of cards. Grabbing the picture of his brother, he threw it down on the blotter. His lips rose into an evil grin.

"Nothing can stop me now." Glancing at his watch, he proclaimed, "Here I come, Jack. Ready or not!"

* * *

> *Wednesday, December 24th*
> *Jack Aitken's Home, Bristow, VA*
> *9:30 a.m.*

"Looks like I beat them home," Jack muttered as he parked his silver Ford Focus in front of the house. Hitting the garage door opener, he added, "I'll let Michelle and Emma park in the garage."

Jack exited his car, and as he stepped onto the concrete driveway, a young girl ran over from the house next door and shouted, "Hi, Jack! Merry Christmas!"

"The same to you, Zinnia," Jack responded. "I like your glasses."

Zinnia smiled. "They're sunglasses but don't have lenses." She pulled the plastic-framed glasses off and showed them to Jack. "I like to wear them…"

"Because pink is your favorite color!" Jack interrupted.

"You remembered!"

Zinnia was eight years old and in the second grade, but going on thirty. She had long brown hair, and quite a few teeth were missing when she grinned. From March through December, Zinnia was Jack's gardening buddy. Mostly, she talked, and Jack listened, but he knew she paid attention to what he told her as she had memorized the names of most of Jack's flowers. Zinnia and her older brother, Liam, were well-mannered, and Jack adored them. In some respects, he thought of them as the grandchildren he knew he would never have.

"Are you and Liam ready for Christmas?" Arching his eyebrows, Jack asked, "Have you been good?"

"Well, most of the time," Zinnia admitted, scraping her shoes across the ground. "I need to tell you something."

"Okay, what is it?" Jack knelt so he could see her eye to eye.

She placed her hands on her hips, and a serious look came over her face. She told Jack with more than a hint of annoyance in her tone, "I saw someone looking around the outside of your house."

"You did?" Jack tried to match her serious expression. "Who was it?"

"He said he was a termite inspector, but I told him he should not snoop around without you being home!"

Jack rubbed the razor stubble on his chin. "Thank you for looking out for me! You are a great friend!"

Honk! Honk! Honk!

Jack heard three noisy sounds in quick succession. He turned to look, and it was Emma pulling into the driveway.

"My sisters are here, Zinnia. Are you and your family going to be home later?"

"We're going to church but should be home after that."

"Good," Jack replied. His lips drew up in a broad grin. "I want to drop something off for you, Liam, and your mom and dad. I will see you later, okay?"

"Okay, Jack." Zinnia dashed away and shouted, "See you later!"

Jack watched her shut the front door but then glanced curiously down the side of the house. Tapping his lip with his finger, he wondered,

It's an unusual time of the year to look for termites. I'll have to check it out myself in the next few days. I thought Amanda canceled the termite service years ago.

* * *

> **Wednesday, December 24th**
> **Jack Aitken's Home, Bristow, VA**
> **11:00 a.m.**

Michelle grabbed a clipboard hanging off the edge of the countertop and, holding it up, asked, "What's this, Jack?"

"That, sister of mine, is evidence of my victory." Jack chuckled. "Last night was the end of our annual Christmas competition. I saw the most Grinch blow-ups. It was close for a while, but in the end, I pulled away and won for the eighth year in a row."

Michelle rolled her eyes. "You have always been too competitive. I hope it was at least fun."

"We had a great time! We always do," Jack responded boastfully, then teased, "At least I know I do. You'll have to ask my sons how they feel losing to their old man again."

Jack continued to set the kitchen table, putting the plates down on the red tablecloth imprinted with green holly leaves. Handing Michelle a fork, he questioned, "I did not get a chance to ask, but how was your flight?"

"It was fine, Jack, but the volcanic debris from what happened in Barbados reached so far into the atmosphere that they had to divert the plane to Philadelphia."

Emma chimed in, "It's good they didn't send you to a different airport. At least Philadelphia was on the way here."

Michelle nodded in agreement and groaned, "All those poor people that died. It is terrible that it happened, let alone at this time of year."

"You are so right," Emma agreed, her eyes lowered in sympathy. "I just don't understand it, but things seem to happen on a bigger scale these days, and they seem to come in bunches."

Jack grabbed a carrot from the salad bowl, and Emma slapped his hand. "Stop picking at the salad! What are we going to do with you?"

Biting the raw vegetable, Jack flinched and grabbed his cheek. "You both probably won't believe this, but I think I may have my first cavity. Every time I bite something on a tooth in the back of my mouth, I get this uncomfortable twinge."

"Sounds like it." Emma wagged her finger playfully. "That's what happens when you pick at the food on the table!"

"You better get to the dentist." Michelle yawned and covered her mouth. "Sorry, these red-eye flights are killers. Em, you may be right about these natural disasters. However, it was an incredible sunrise. The sky was a brilliant shade of scarlet red."

"That reminds me of something I remember from Boy Scouts," Jack interjected. "Red sky at night, sailor's delight." He paused and continued, "Red sky at morn, sailors be warned."

* * *

> Wednesday, December 24th
> Lucius Rofocale's Meeting Room at Pergamon in
> the Present-Day Republic of Turkiye

Lucius finished reading the last daily dispatch from the demon legions and tossed them into the fiery container beside him. Tapping his claws on the arm of his stone throne, he watched the papers go up in smoke. In his mind, Lucius ran through the plans for the next twenty-four hours. Barring something unforeseen, he anticipated an even more significant victory than the elimination of his brother Kazimir millions of years ago.

Tatiana's voice, barely audible through the heavy stone door to his chamber, jolted him from his reverie. "Master Lucius, Lord Aitken wishes to speak with you. He did suggest that the matter was important."

Lucius snapped his fingers, and the door opened. Tatiana entered, carrying a bejeweled gold bowl of steaming, cherry-red blood.

"Leave us," Lucius tersely dismissed her. She placed the ornate container on a table in front of Lucius and dashed out the door.

Placing his finger in the bowl, Lucius began mixing the coagulated liquid in a circle until George Aitken's face appeared.

"Greetings, Master." George closed his eyes and bowed his head. "Forgive my intrusion, but I have information on an incident I thought you should know about."

"Proceed," Lucius replied bluntly.

"Last night, during a routine sweep of the area, a patrol came across two dead sentries." His image faded briefly but reformed, and George paused, then resumed speaking, "Master, they were devoid of any blood."

Lucius shot up straight in his chair, and there was an awkward silence before he responded.

"Devoid of blood," Lucius repeated his acolyte's disclosure. "Anything else?"

"Yes, Master. At first, when we tracked the entity, it presented as an animal walking on all fours. But further down the trail, it must have transformed as the footprints became humanlike."

"I see." Lucius's eyes narrowed, and he scratched his temple with his clawed finger. "And there is no other sign of this being, correct?"

"None. The entire area, including the town of Culpeper and its surrounding subdivisions, has been searched with nothing else to report."

Lucius was quiet once more, and George asked, "Master, is there anything about this news that is cause for concern?"

"No," Lucius answered abruptly and redirected the conversation. "Are your preparations complete?"

"Yes, Master. Everything is ready."

"Excellent. Send me confirmation of our triumph." Lucius brusquely cut their connection.

The update over, Lucius stood up and paced around the room.

"I anticipated you were going into hibernation again," Lucius muttered. "But even you cannot stop what will happen."

Lucius scratched the alligator-like skin on the back of his neck; he commanded the chamber door to open and shouted, "Tatiana! Come in here!"

"Yes, Master," Tatiana quickly entered the room and dove to Lucius's feet.

"I want you to double the guards on the surface entrance. They are to report any unusual activity to me directly."

"I will take care of it immediately, Master!" Tatiana sprang to her feet and fled the room.

CRACK! Lucius's joints popped as he sat back down. Lucius rolled his shoulders and neck. He forced himself to think only of tomorrow's events and drove any concerns about the Strigoi from his mind.

* * *

Wednesday, December 24th
Jack Aitken's Home, Bristow, VA
5:00 p.m.

Earlier in the afternoon, Jack watched *It's a Wonderful Life* for the first time in several years, then subjected his sisters to the 1951 version of *A Christmas Carol*. There was something about this Dickens classic that always got to him. It did not matter how many different film versions of the story he watched or that he read the book every holiday season; Jack reveled in the story of redemption.

He brushed off the tear running down his cheek and declared, "That is still the best version of the story to me," as he turned off the television. "I always save the best for last."

"It's my favorite, too," Emma agreed. "But it must be in black and white. The colorized version does nothing for me."

Michelle joined in, "That makes it unanimous! Alastair Sim's performance as Scrooge is the best as far as I am concerned."

Looking at Jack, Michelle teased, "Nice try, but I see that tear in your eye. You are so sappy!"

Raising his hand, Jack admitted, "Guilty as charged. It doesn't matter how often I see it; I always tear up at the end."

Emma got up from the chair and asked her brother, "What is it about the story that moves you so much?"

Jack quickly responded, "Hope. The message for me is that it is never too late to change the trajectory of your life. I believe we all have a little Scrooge in us. Both the good and not-so-good."

Looking to his left, Jack noticed the light in his fish tank was off. Sidestepping a chair, he clicked the light on, and the colorful Guppies dashed to the surface. Jack chastised himself, "Ugh! I forgot to feed the fish this morning."

As he watched the fish eat, the words hope and redemption echoed in his brain. Jack had to admit that his brother had been on his mind throughout the movie. No matter what George had become, he wanted to believe there was still a way back for him. Somewhere, maybe deep in a small corner of his soul, a small part of his brother remained. Like Scrooge, George was not beyond saving.

Jack saw Michelle reach for her luggage, and he intercepted her. "Your bellhop is here. I will take your bag to the guest room. Emma's, too. Have a seat and relax."

Heading to the hall, Jack joked, "I hear the service in this hotel is good!"

* * *

Making his way upstairs, Jack could hear what he believed to be the tail end of Louis and David's Christmas Eve sermon. While being a gentleman had been ingrained in Jack from as far back as he could remember, he undeniably grabbed his sisters' bags to ensure the boys had finished proselytizing.

"The fewer questions Michelle and Emma ask, the better," Jack whispered to himself.

He knew that keeping this secret from his sisters was impossible. Sooner or later, he would have to discuss it, but he wasn't ready. Jack sat at the top of the stairs and listened to his sons.

"Judging others—we all do it," David proclaimed. "In doing so, we play God, but not the God we profess to worship each Sunday. When we learn to love and not judge each other, we will really be children of God."

Then, he heard Louis speak. "Remember, the birth of our Messiah is the fulfillment of God's covenants with us. He promised Noah never to destroy the Earth again. He pledged to Abraham to make him a great nation and strengthened Moses to lead his people from bondage while writing his laws on their hearts. King David's descendants, as God promised, sat on the throne of Israel. But most of all, Jesus succeeded where humans failed. Through him, we receive forgiveness and can live righteously with God."

Listening to his sons, Jack was proud, but he also felt a pang of guilt. He conceded that he had allowed himself to believe that Christmas and Easter were only great stories, like fairy tales. His sons' humble faith made him feel ashamed of his disbelief, and he conceded,

"I guess, in some respects, I've made *A Christmas Carol* my Bible."

*　*　*

After an enjoyable dinner, Jack sipped his coffee and stared out the rear window into the darkness. A distant sound caught his attention and slowly got louder.

Wee-oww! Wee-oww! Wee-oww!

Suddenly, the basement door flew open, and David shouted, "Santa!" He dashed out the front door into the stinging cold without shoes or a jacket. As Jack followed his son out, he saw a bright red fire truck coming down the road, followed by other emergency vehicles.

Jack handed David a pair of sneakers and a coat, insisting, "Put this on before you catch a cold."

Strings of multi-colored lights adorned the vehicle, and a red and green wreath, spinning in a circle, was attached to the front grill. It slowly made its way down toward the cul-de-sac, and the man of the moment, Santa Claus, stood in a white spotlight. His contingent of elves threw candy canes to the children lining the block, and Santa repeatedly shouted, "Merry Christmas!"

Michelle and Emma had joined them and stood shivering in the cold.

"Now I know why I live in California," complained Michelle. Emma jumped up and down, trying to keep warm. The whole scene amused Jack.

The prophet of God, who is nearly twenty years old and still believes in Santa Claus.

"May I have a candy cane?" Louis asked his brother. David handed one to him but never took his eye off Santa.

"Louis, you left the front door open." Jack dashed to close it before the cat got out of the house.

Standing on the front stoop, he wished he could stop the hands of time and remember his sons just as they were at that moment. The enthusiasm on David's face and his absolute joy were palpable. Even Louis, who was nearly five years older, beamed at the sight of Santa. Michelle elbowed Emma and, smiling broadly, pointed at her nephews.

A few minutes later, the fire truck left the subdivision, and the noise from the sirens slowly disappeared. Jack stood in the living room doorway, admiring their Christmas tree. He walked over to it and flipped the sign on an ornament that read naughty to the word nice. At the top of the tree was a ceramic angel holding two candles. He and Amanda had bought it for their first tree after getting married.

Watching the lights of the candles flicker, he thought about Louis and David.

"I understand why God wants you both to be his prophets," Jack reflected. "Your innocence is priceless. Just like Clarence in *It's a Wonderful Life,* you both have the faith of a child."

* * *

> Wednesday, December 24th
> Riverside Trail, Roanoke Rapids, NC
> 9:30 p.m.

"Turn the heat on, Brian!" Crystal Lee Parker shouted. "My feet are freezing!"

"Okay, Crystal, just hold on!" Brian Kinleigh, her boyfriend, retorted in a southern drawl as he turned the ignition key in his black Ford F-150. The truck roared to life, and he pressed a button, turning the heat up full blast.

Reaching his arm around Crystal's shoulder, he exclaimed, "Just give it a few minutes now, honey!"

Brian cozied up to his girlfriend with a sly grin and added, "I'll warm you up in the meantime."

"Oh no, you will not!" she declared, pushing him away and evading his advances. "Whose idea was it to go parking when it is so cold outside?"

Sufficiently chastised, Brian slid away. Attempting to lighten the mood, he pointed out the windshield, saying, "Look at all those stars, darling, and how the moon reflects off the water."

The leaves still left on the oak tree they parked under rustled in the wind, and the steady *swoosh* pounded on the windows.

"Those are some gusts!" Brian checked the window to make sure it was fully closed. "I bet whitecaps are forming on the Roanoke River tonight! If it were summer, I would do some night skiing."

Turning toward Crystal, he teased, "I'd even let you drive the boat!"

Crystal rolled her eyes, and a reluctant smile appeared. "I don't know how I let you talk me into coming out here, but I just can't stay angry with you!" Leaning over, she kissed Brian. "You make me laugh!"

CRASH!

Shards of glass from Brian's driver-side window flew around the truck's cab, and some pieces became entangled in Crystal's long brown hair. A figure dressed in a dark jacket quickly dragged Brian through the opening. Despite being six feet tall and a tackle on the varsity football team, the assailant manhandled the young man.

"AARH!"

The teen struggled to free himself, but the attacker drove his boot into Brian's neck, pinning him to the ground. The moonlight flashed on the blade of the machete wielded by the figure, and he forcefully opened the car door, telling Crystal, "Get out of the car, now!"

Still subduing Brian, he roughly pulled Crystal from the truck and pushed her to the ground beside her boyfriend. The wind howled, whipping around the long hair of the attacker. He knelt, pulled a roll of shiny gray duct tape from his jacket, and roughly bound Brian and Crystal with it. Then, he rolled them over on their backs.

"I don't care if you see my face." His black eyes pierced the veil of the night. "I'm the last thing you're going to see!"

"Please don't hurt us," Crystal sobbed and pleaded.

"I'm a demon, bitch! I don't give a damn about you, human scum!"

CRACK!

The noise of a snapping branch got the demon's attention. An imposing figure whose head nearly hit the tree limb overarching the truck's cab stood silhouetted by the light of a harvest moon.

"After I do them, you're next!" the demon yelled, pointing his machete at the individual.

The giant shook its head and replied in a deep, monotone voice, "I do not think so."

While the demon attacker was distracted, Brian tried to loosen the duct tape and free himself. Then, he heard a bone-chilling scream that cut through the gale-force gusts. Quickly, he glanced at Crystal, whose mouth was so wide open that her chin nearly hit her chest. She was bug-eyed. The only word that came to Brian's mind was terrified.

Turning his head to look in the same direction as Crystal's gape, Brian understood her fear. The giant had transformed into a hairy beast. Holding the throat of Crystal and Brian's attacker in its jaws, it sucked furiously while the demon's limbs twitched and spasmed.

"Crystal!" Brian whispered, trying to get her attention. "Crystal!"

Finally, she turned to look at Brian, her mascara running down both cheeks.

"I'm so scared, Brian," she muttered.

"Me too." He kicked his feet and said, "But I think I might be able to get out of…."

Brian stopped moving. A large shadow slowly covered the couple. Certain that this was the end, Brian and Crystal closed their eyes and awaited their fate. The few moments seemed like an eternity until Brian felt his legs pulled upward and heard the tape tearing away from his jeans. Opening his eyes, he did not see an animal but a person who freed his hands.

Brian sat up and put himself between the figure and Crystal. The entity spoke.

"You are free. I will not harm you. Go."

Their savior lumbered into the woods. Brian and Crystal jumped in his still-running truck and took off like a bat out of Hell.

CHAPTER 20

> Wednesday, December 24th
> Jack Aitken's Living Room, Bristow, VA
> 10:30 p.m.

Ding. Ding. Ding.

The soft chime of the grandfather clock broke the silence and caused Jack to put down his pen. After writing for nearly an hour straight, he flexed the fingers of his left hand and leaned back on the couch. The damage to his right hand had been extensive, and the ongoing rehabilitation forced Jack to learn to write left-handed. It had no positive impact; Jack's handwriting was as bad as ever. Rolling his shoulders, he heard an audible *c-r-a-c-k*, but neither a stiff neck nor a cramp in his hand was enough to get in his way. Not tonight, not on Christmas Eve. After all, this was *his night.*

For nearly forty years, Jack would wait for his family to go to bed on Christmas Eve, just like the boys and his sisters had done more than an hour ago. The house would fall silent, and the room would be dark except for the Christmas tree, whose twinkling lights would cast dancing shadows on the walls. Jack would bask in the glow of these lights and, in the quiet stillness, write personal, heartfelt Christmas cards to his loved ones.

The tradition started when he and Amanda began dating; he had performed it every Christmas since then and looked forward to the ritual with great anticipation. The atmosphere would calm his mind and allow him to reflect on the past year's events. It reminded him of the season's true meaning and helped him see how much his family meant to him. Then, he would put those thoughts down on a card he selected specifically for each recipient. In line with the hopeful tone of this night, he had even written one to George but saved Anne's for last.

Stretching his legs, Jack walked to the front door. Through the glass, he noticed a window box leaning to one side, probably due to the wind whose gusts blew the remaining brown leaves off the stems of the dead flowers, one by one. It was just another reminder of the significance of his hand injury, which had prevented him from doing his usual meticulous garden cleanup. He heard the wind pound on the glass and could feel the arctic cold sneak through the cracks around the door.

Powder-like snow flurries, which had started earlier in the evening, were now large, pentagonal projectiles blown sideways by the rising wind. The Christmas lights on the pine trees across the street illuminated the snow on their boughs in shades of red and green, and Jack realized that the black asphalt road in front of the house would soon disappear under a white blanket.

The beastly breeze caused Jack to fold his arms and rub them. He shoved his hands in his pockets and returned to the couch, happy to be inside. He sat down, and a stab of disappointment shot through him as he stared at Anne's blank Christmas card and fretted that the snow could prevent Anne from coming tomorrow.

He picked up the pen but struggled to make sense of all the thoughts running through his brain. It didn't help that an ornament given to Jack and Amanda on their first Christmas as a married couple caught his attention. It was a home with a front porch, and when the light in the picture window flashed, a couple kissing became illuminated.

"Nothing ever changes, does it?" Jack threw the pen down on the table in frustration. "I can't figure out what to say, and now the snowfall is getting heavier."

Rubbing his tired eyes, he murmured,

"We can't catch a break, can we? And it seems like despite all the feelings Anne and I seem to have for one another, we're not getting anywhere."

Shaking his head, he lamented, "We haven't got a prayer, have we?"

* * *

Simultaneously in Anne Bishop's Home
Ocean Isle Beach, NC

"*A white Christmas in the Mid-Atlantic region is possible this year. If you plan to travel, it would be a good idea to prepare for possible dicey road conditions...*"

Anne turned off the television, tossed the remote on the bed, and rubbed Daphne's ears. "No amount of bad weather will keep us home this year. Right, girl?"

The cocker spaniel dropped on the blanket. Rolling over on its back, the dog stared up at Anne with big brown eyes, begging for a tummy rub. Anne knew she needed to keep packing but could not help but comply with Daphne's demand. As Anne finished packing her things in an enormous piece of luggage, she hoped it would be a welcomed surprise for Jack and the boys to find out she intended to stay awhile. Her stomach fluttered, a sign that she felt a little nervous about meeting Jack's sisters.

Glancing at the nightstand beside her bed, it appeared empty without her badge, but she had given the committee plenty of time to find her replacement. It was time for her to get on with her life. Nose to nose with her dog, Anne whispered,

"Besides, I promised Jack I would be there, and it's time for a heart-to-heart talk about where we stand."

Daphne's warm, wet tongue ran up Anne's face.

"I know one thing." Anne kissed the top of Daphne's head. "You love me."

Anne zipped the suitcase shut and placed it on the floor. She stretched and yawned. Too tired to put the bag in the car, Anne decided to do it in the morning. What she really needed at that moment was a hot shower and then to get to bed. A long drive lay ahead.

In the kitchen, Anne's phone on the countertop vibrated several times. An illuminated text message appeared, but then the screen went dark. The pounding drops of water on the shower's tiled floor drowned out the phone's noise as Anne closed the bathroom door behind her.

* * *

At the Same Time

Knock. Knock. Knock.

Startled, Jack jumped up. It was kind of late for visitors, and he managed to bang his shin against the table. He blurted out, "OW!"

Rubbing the area, he muttered, "That's going to leave a heck of a bruise."

Limping slightly, he moved toward the front door. Jack could see the snow had begun to pile up, and a figure wearing a green down vest, dressed in dark blue pants and a matching turtle-neck shirt—the uniform of a delivery driver—stood on the rubber mat, holding a package. Jack flipped the porch light on and cautiously opened the door.

"May I help you?"

A young adult, perhaps in his late twenties or early thirties, with a neatly trimmed beard and wavy black hair covered in melting snowflakes, looked up and, with an accent, answered, "I am sorry to trouble you. It is very late, I know."

Holding the package in front of him, he continued, "The house next door is dark. It looks like no one is home, and I hate to leave this package out on the stoop since the box says it is perishable."

Jack read the side of the white box with orange and yellow circles and got excited. "Hey! Bilgore Groves! Every year, my grandparents sent us citrus fruit for Christmas from them! I would have thought they were out of business long ago."

Jack took the package. He knew they were not home after visiting with Zinnia and her family earlier in the evening. He informed the delivery person,

"They changed their mind and opted to go to midnight mass. I can take it for them." Jack leaned out the door, looking for a delivery truck. Skeptically, he asked, "So, where is your van?"

The man smiled and chuckled. "We're busy at this time of year and have two-person crews. We were in your subdivision earlier but missed delivering this package. My partner is down the road in another development and will swing by and pick me up."

Thrusting his hands in his vest pockets, the man turned and walked down the steps. Nearly ankle-deep in snow, he looked up the block, but the blizzard-like conditions made it almost impossible to see anything. Jack put the box of fruit on the floor and was about to shut the door, but stopped and yelled,

"Why don't you come and wait inside? It's too cold to stand out there."

"Are you sure?" the stranger asked as Jack ushered him back into the house.

"It is no problem. Sit in this chair, and you'll be able to see out the front door when the truck pulls up."

"Thank you, Jack." The grateful visitor rubbed his hands together.

Jack tried to place the man's accent while thinking, *Funny. I don't recall telling him my name.*

Drops of melted snow fell from the man's beard, soaking the carpet at his feet, and he ran his shirt sleeve across the top of his head to absorb the excess moisture from his hair.

"May I get you a towel?" Reaching out his hand, Jack introduced himself, "I'm Jack Aitken, by the way."

The stranger took Jack's hand in his.

"Gee, your hands are like ice," Jack declared. He also noticed they were the hands of a working man, heavily calloused.

"No, a towel won't be necessary," the man answered. "My name is Yosef."

"Yosef?" Jack asked.

The visitor nodded affirmatively, "It's Hebrew."

"I guess wishing you a happy Chanukah would be appropriate, then? Are you from Israel? Forgive me for being so forward, but I could not help but notice your accent."

Wearing a broad smile, Jack's guest admitted, "I am Jewish, but I celebrate many holidays and gladly accept your wishes for a merry Christmas."

"Yosef, may I offer you something to drink? I know you are probably still on the job, but perhaps a shot of brandy or something to warm you up?"

"Thank you for your hospitality, but no. I do not drink liquor."

"Well, that makes two of us," Jack replied jovially.

"It's kind of dark in here." Jack reached for a light switch, but Yosef said, "Please don't bother on my account." Looking around the room, he proclaimed, "It is perfect, just the way it is."

After a minute or two, Jack glanced out the window and reacted to what he saw outside. "They said there was a possibility of dusting, but I cannot recall seeing snow pile up this quickly. It is now up to your knees and shows no sign of stopping."

Sitting in a chair beside the Christmas tree, Yosef remarked, "This storm came up suddenly. It is freezing out there."

Turning back, Jack asked, "Do you need to contact the truck driver? I could step out of the room if you need to make a call or something."

Yosef pulled a bandana from his vest and patted his beard to dry it. Shaking his head negatively, he assured Jack, "No. I am sure he will be along shortly."

He began to examine Jack's Christmas tree. His blue eyes sparkled as he enjoyed the cornucopia of ornaments. "I've been admiring your decorations. Tell me, do you know the significance of some of these colors?"

Standing beside his guest, Jack replied curiously, "Come to think of it, I'm not sure that I do."

"Green stands for all the plants our creator has provided for our sustenance," Yosef stated.

Resting a round silver ornament in his palm, he said, "Silver and gold represent the rich blessings that we receive from God."

His tone turned more serious when he pointed at the tree skirt. "Red. This color stands for the blood of Christ shed to deliver us."

The duo stood in a moment of quiet reflection at the stranger's pronouncement. Then, pointing at the cards on the table, Yosef inquired, "I hope I am not intruding on something important?"

Jack removed his glasses and pulled a cloth from his pocket. He gently puffed, fogging each lens, and cleaned them before answering, "Oh no. I have been writing Christmas cards to my family. It is something that I do every year on Christmas Eve. This is my last one." Jack exhaled. "It is for someone who has grown to be quite important to me, but I have struggled to find the right words to convey how I feel about them."

Studying the nativity set displayed on top of Amanda's treasured cherry red piano, Yosef acknowledged, "A woman can do that to a man."

"And how," Jack agreed longingly.

Yosef went to touch the stable roof but stopped and asked, "May I?"

"Please," Jack answered proudly. "My father made that set."

Pursing his lips, apparently impressed, Yosef agreed, "Indeed. It is excellent work. Your father is a craftsman."

"Yes, he was." Jack acknowledged. "So was my grandfather."

"Forgive me, Jack. I am sorry for your losses."

"It's okay. Dad passed away about four years ago. He was eighty-nine."

"I was a carpenter once, Jack. It is good that you and your father had so many years together. The time I spent with my son on Earth was all too brief."

Yosef locked eyes with Jack. "Come, there is something you should see."

* * *

Wide-eyed and disoriented, Jack looked nervously around, attempting to get his bearings, and stuttered, "Wh-Where am I?"

To say he was no longer in his living room was a monumental understatement. He found himself standing on a sandy, gravel trail, like a roadbed, with the stone walls of what appeared to be an ancient city below him. A rocky, weathered outcropping whose slope rose into an imposing hill was a short distance away. A hot, gusty wind slapped Jack in the face, causing him to squint and put up his hand to block the sting of the grains of sand picked up by the rushes of air. Jack knelt and picked up a handful of light tan dirt along with small pebbles and stones, which he allowed to fall through his fingers before shaking the remaining soil from his palm.

"Where is everyone?" Jack asked out loud. It was eerily quiet and creepy. "What is this place?"

A voice, barely audible above the steady breeze, called out to him, "What are you doing?"

"Who said that?" Jack shouted. His question echoed several times, and then only the gusts remained.

"What are you doing, Jack?"

The same question, but louder. It seemed to be coming from the top of the hill above him. Keeping his eye on the summit, Jack began a slow, deliberate ascent on the narrow trail that led to the top. Afraid of heights, he pressed his body against the rock and mentally told himself not to look down.

"Ouch!" Jack looked at his thumb; droplets of blood fell into the sand. He licked the blood from his finger and examined the rock on which he had cut his hand.

"Limestone," Jack remarked. "I remember this from Earth Science class. I can even see the imprints of the shells from which it formed, but it doesn't crumble like typical limestone. There are only these jagged edges."

Glancing further up the path, Jack whispered, "What's that?" His eyes narrowed, perplexed by circular holes seemingly carved into the face of the escarpment.

Arriving at the spot, he peered into two horizontal pockets, each roughly a foot apart. The openings had an irregular shape, more oval than a circle, which meant to Jack that they were naturally occurring. The interior was dark, but the channels appeared to go deep into the hill. Two vertical holes with similar characteristics were beneath these gaps in the rockface.

The path was wide enough that Jack felt comfortable stepping back to get a different view of the unusual feature. His jaw fell open, and he began to say, "It looks like…."

The same voice he heard earlier finished Jack's sentence, "A skull."

Startled, Jack looked up but saw only an angry sky. Dark gray and black clouds gathered over him. A rumble of thunder rolled through the gathering storm and shook the ground under his feet. A blistering, wickedly serrated lightning bolt tore through the clouds and struck the earth above, showering Jack with bits of stone and dirt. Wispy seed heads from the grass that managed to grow in the cracks and crevices of the rocks violently whipped back and forth in the howling wind.

C-R-A-C-K!

Another ferocious flash of lightning struck the ground behind Jack, causing the pathway to slide down the hill to the valley below.

Jack glanced down fearfully. "I guess there is no going back."

Cautiously, his attention riveted on every step; Jack slowly scaled the rockface toward the top of the hill. At times, he almost crawled to avoid being blown away by the hurricane-like gusts. Nearing the summit, exhausted, Jack reached for a stone sticking out of the ground, but his injured hand could barely hold it. He lost his grip and began to fall. Flailing, trying to seize hold of something else, Jack closed his eyes. Fearing he was about to fall off the cliff, he felt someone grab his wrist.

A figure in a simple white cotton garment, wearing leather sandals, with a firm grip toughened by hard work, had hold of him. He pulled Jack to the top of the hill. The hem at the bottom of his rescuer's cloak waved in the breeze. On his hands and knees, catching his breath, Jack gasped,

"Thank you. You saved my life."

The clouds were so dark it appeared as if night had set in, but a large shadow still loomed over the stark landscape where Jack found himself. Still kneeling, he saw a thick, brown, heavily weathered, upright stake appearing to emerge from the ground before him. Fashioned from roughly hewn timber, it contained fissures and cracks running throughout. Streaks of coagulating blood dripped from the sides, puddling on the ground. Jack feared what he would see if he raised his eyes.

"I understand your trepidation." A shadow moved next to Jack, and he felt a hand on his shoulder. "Like you, I did not want to view his suffering."

Jack got to his feet and found himself facing a middle-aged man with a receding hairline and a graying goatee. He held a set of gold keys in his hand.

"I am the disciple they call Peter."

Jack trembled in the apostle's presence and opened his mouth but could not speak.

"You do not need to fear me, Jack. I am sharing my experiences with you so you might better understand what is happening to David and Louis."

Pointing at the empty, rugged wooden cross that creaked and shook in the wind, Peter said, "Victory over evil involves self-sacrifice. There is indeed no such thing as courage without first feeling fear. I understand your apprehension about your boys. I, too, was a prophet and faced crucifixion like our Savior."

Holding out his hands, the apostle added, "Look."

Peter showed Jack the open wounds on his palms where the Roman authorities hammered nails to hold him on his cross. Jack flinched, trying to contemplate the pain from such brutality.

"In your world, a Christmas tree symbolizes the birth of Jesus; this cross symbolizes his sacrifice that leads to our deliverance. It allows our wandering to cease and leads us to eternal paradise."

Peter's eyes were as blue as the ocean, and they met Jack's. "What happens Easter morning is the true gift. Christmas is meaningless without it." Pointing at the cross once more, he added, "The transformation in our relationship with God begins at the empty tomb, but our sins have to die here first."

The apostle placed his hand gently on Jack's shoulder and asked, caringly, "Do you understand?"

Jack's eyes lowered, and he softly answered, "Yes, I think I do. But why my children as the sacrifice? They are innocent."

Peter replied reassuringly, "That is precisely why it must be them, Jack."

Jack held his forehead between his thumb and forefinger with both hands and rubbed his temples. He continued wrestling with his children's fate despite the apostle's assurances. The silhouette from the stark and barren cross soared like a spire. It overshadowed everything.

Saint Peter could sense the conflict in Jack's mind and heart and said supportively, "I also know about doubt and denial, Jack. God will not abandon you or your children. I am esteemed despite my past failures."

Waving his hand, he suggested, "Perhaps I can show you the good that humankind, regardless of its flaws, may find even in the darkest moments and places."

* * *

Jack stood amongst a crowd of people, some wailing in uncontrollable torment. Several Roman soldiers knelt beside a white tunic, bickering with one another while throwing stones on the ground in front of them. Confirmation class taught him where he found himself, and Jack dared not look up for fear of witnessing Jesus's actual suffering on the empty cross he had seen only moments earlier.

Suddenly, a light streamed down through the dark clouds on a figure standing by the cross, looking up at Christ. Saint Peter pointed to the scene.

"Watch closely, Jack."

The view slowly came into focus until Jack could clearly see the face of a Roman Centurion. His jaw fell slack when he recognized him, and he whispered, "It's me again."

The deep lines in the man's forehead and face revealed that he was years older, but Jack saw his own reflection, just as he had when Gabriel had shown him a vision of the preparation for the slaughter of the innocents.

"Now listen," Peter encouraged.

A voice in a language Jack did not recognize called out, "*Eloi, Eloi lama sabachthani.*" Immediately after, there was an audible gasp like air slowly being let out of a tire, then Jack saw the Centurion's lips move and heard him say, "Truly, this man was the son of God."

* * *

Instantly, Jack was alone. Peter had disappeared, and the wind blew roughly through his hair, slicking it back and exposing his forehead. The same voice that had greeted him earlier asked him once more,

"What are you doing here, Jack?"

Jack called out, "Learning a lesson in faith."

"As you said earlier today," the voice replied, "we all have a little Scrooge in us, but that also means we have the chance at redemption. Just like that Roman soldier so long ago."

"I believe I understand the meaning of this vision," Jack said to no one.

The voice continued, "Putting it another way, sometimes it is better to buy when everyone else is selling. Lucifer and his minions seek to flip the script on the apocalypse. They believe they have already won, but we have a surprise."

"And that is?" Jack questioned.

"The Destroyer, the Four Horsemen, all of those who would be instruments of devastation will not bring ruin to the Earth. God intends to find another way to reconcile with his people and heal the world, not wipe it out."

Before Jack could speak, the voice said, "While humankind has managed to weaken itself slowly, many have never bowed low to idols and have remained faithful. God counts each hair on their head and will reward their steadfast belief in the face of the onslaught of those who would do Satan's bidding."

Suddenly, the wind abated, and bewildered, Jack feverishly searched around for the source of the voice, but there was none. Overcome by what he had witnessed, Jack fell to his knees and prayed,

"God, you tested Abraham, asking him to sacrifice Isaac, but you relented. I realize you are telling me I must accept what will happen to Louis and David."

Burying his face in his hands, Jack agonized, "But I don't know that I can do that."

* * *

"Jack."

Hearing his name, Jack pulled his hands away from his face and found himself staring at aquamarine-colored carpeting. He realized he was back home in his living room. Yosef stood over him, asking, "Can you hear me, Jack?"

With Yosef's assistance, Jack nodded, rose from the floor, and sat on the couch.

"What just happened?" Jack asked, but his visitor, sitting on the edge of the table before him, held his finger to his lips.

"Shh... I know you have questions."

Rubbing his hands anxiously, Yosef continued, "The first of which I am sure is whether that Roman solider, the one with your face, were you, perhaps in another lifetime?" His eyes widened as he asked Jack, "Am I correct?"

Like rapids in a river overflowing from the spring thaw, a flurry of thoughts ran through Jack's brain. This question being only one of many.

Yet, still in a state of turmoil from what he had just experienced, Jack merely answered, "Yes."

"It is a valid question, Jack," Yosef whispered. "Unfortunately, it is one for which I do not have a good answer. I know it is hard believing in all the words you have heard before. Faith. Hope. But all of these you must try to trust again."

Jack looked down and shook his head in disbelief. After a few moments, he said, "Joseph." Looking at Yosef with raised eyebrows, he added, "That is who you are, isn't it?"

Joseph smiled broadly and confirmed, "Perceptive of you, Jack. Yes, I am Jesus's earthly father."

"I thought as much." Jack inched forward and sat on the edge of the couch cushion. He said, "I mean no disrespect to you, God, or anyone else in this unfolding drama, but I am tired of pretending that my blessing of Louis and David's fate is a prerequisite or even necessary because we both know it isn't."

"That is fair enough, Jack," Joseph replied. "But, let me ask you a question then. Does it matter if you are that soldier or not?"

"It matters to me," Jack closed his eyes and answered with a heavy tone of anguish. "I don't want the sins of my fathers visited on my sons."

"Jack, don't you see?" Joseph clasped his hands together and pleaded. "Whether it is your lineage or not, the message is about redemption."

"Does that include my brother, George?" Jack laced his fingers together tightly and asked in desperation. "Is the message that no one is beyond being redeemed applicable to him?"

Joseph shifted and cleared his throat, uncomfortable with Jack's query. He exhaled and soberly responded, "I'm afraid your brother suffers from an illness that no doctor in Heaven or on Earth can cure. Sadly, not all who hear the call will repent."

Locking eyes with Jack, Joseph counseled, "You cannot free someone caged within themself."

Jack sprung from the couch, growling, "I can't accept that! God is supposed to be able to do anything, isn't he?"

Before Joseph could respond, Jack began ranting.

"Where is he, Joseph?" he snarled. "God's sitting on the sidelines while the world, like a sailboat without a rudder, steers ever closer to the rocks!"

Angrily, Jack thrust his fist into his hand. "Look at the deep divisions in the world today. Does he not see we are at one another's throats?"

Now wild-eyed, Jack angrily whispered, "The strength of hatred mocks everything about this holy season! There is no peace on Earth! There is no goodwill among men!"

"Jack, please," Joseph tried to calm him down, but Jack, gritting his teeth and trying not to wake his family, retorted,

"Why doesn't God save George from whatever fate awaits him?"

Beads of sweat rolled down Jack's forehead. He breathed heavily, spent from his tirade. Running his hand through his hair, he sheepishly admitted, "I know you are here to help me, Joseph. Seconds ago, I could not stop the torrent of angry words coming out of my mouth; now I don't know what to say."

Jack fell onto the couch, and Joseph tapped him on the knee several times.

"You are still quite the firebrand, aren't you? I saw wildfires raging in your eyes like when you were a younger man."

Joseph drew closer and whispered, "I was human like you once, Jack. I expressed my doubts and fears to God, too. Perhaps not as passionately as you, but I spoke my mind nonetheless."

Jack leaned forward and asked, "So where does this leave me?"

Pointing toward the ceiling, Joseph answered, "Jack, man sees the stars in the sky but does not always see the light. It all comes down to a choice."

"Choice?" Jack frowned. "I don't understand."

"The price of free will," Joseph responded. "Granting free will to humankind is God offering a part of himself that he cannot recover or regenerate, and that humankind cannot return or exchange."

Tilting his head slightly and looking Jack straight in the eye, Joseph added, "God will not intervene in ways you have requested or think that he should. The cost of original sin is the requirement of personal responsibility and accountability. God cannot just wipe that slate clean."

Joseph got up and paced around the room, saying, "Life is about choice, and having a choice means living with the consequences. Eating the wrong things leads to diabetes—overeating results in obesity. Smoking leads to cancer. You choose to get married or live alone. You buy this house or that one."

Jack rubbed his chin, feeling a growing bond between them, and listened intently to Joseph's rationalization.

Joseph continued, "What do we become if we lose the freedom to choose? Is becoming a zombie a desirable outcome? No! And I do not believe it is what God wants either."

Jack's eyes narrowed, and he inquired, "What do you mean by saying God does not want us to lose our freedom of choice?"

Joseph's eyes were ablaze like Jack's before, and he passionately asserted, "Our Father does not want robots! He is not looking for submission and blind obedience. He wants what both you and I want from our children. Affirmation and respect, freely given, not compelled."

Joseph sat down in front of Jack again and insisted, "God is not dead, nor does he sleep. When we repent and turn from sin, he rejoices in our choice! Change is coming, Jack. Louis and David are a part of that. God will open doors no one can ever shut. He understands what we are going through and promises to be with us through every trial in life. Your destiny is not shaped only by the economy, upbringing, or education. Our Heavenly Father influences your destiny, too."

Deep ridges emerged on Jack's forehead, and he asked skeptically, "How? How does God shape my destiny or that of any other person?"

"What did you always tell Amanda about your relationship?" Joseph asked. "Hmm?"

"That our destinies..." Jack went silent.

"That's right, Jack." Joseph nodded reassuringly. "God introduced the two of you for a reason. He needed two people to care for his prophets until they were ready to serve him and fulfill their purpose."

Skeptically, Jack challenged Joseph, "So we didn't fall in love out of our free will? How is that choice?"

Joseph wagged his finger and shook his head in disagreement. "I did not say that, Jack. What I said was he introduced the two of you. Your free will led you to love Amanda, just as it was hers to love you. It was what God hoped would happen as he saw something special in each of you that, when joined together, would be resilient. Your love, tempered like steel by the fires of life, prepared two of his most humble servants, Louis and David, to fulfill an extraordinary destiny."

Joseph paused and added, "Just like you and Amanda, God hoped Mary and I would prepare Jesus for his destiny. Being God, he knows what is best for us, but that does not mean we see the signs or listen to him whispering to us, suggesting what road to travel. He leaves the ultimate decision to each of us. Wise choices often take time to show results. You and Amanda made the right choices, which benefited your sons greatly."

"But there is a cost that went along with those choices," Jack insisted. "Our road might, in the end, turn out to be the right one. But it took a toll on both of us."

Jack bowed his head. "It may be that it cost Amanda her life."

Joseph went on, "A life she laid down willingly, Jack. You were there when she made that choice." Jack looked up instantly. "I know about that night. It took strength and courage on your part to honor it."

Joseph grabbed Jack's hands, saying, "You may not get to see the results of the good deeds you do now. Don't be afraid. Goodness will always prevail. God's word brings light to darkness and life where death once existed. Make him your choice, Jack."

CHAPTER 21

> *Wednesday, December 24th*
> *Tatiana's Room at Pergamon*
> *in the Present-Day Republic of Turkiye*
> *Around 10:00 p.m.*

Click.

With her door locked, Tatiana retrieved her pirated copy of the *Book of Demon History* from a bookshelf in her library. She opened it to where she had left off the night before and continued reading. Each word increasingly convinced her that the demon race, heavily influenced by Lucius, had lost its way and that his brother, Kazimir, offered a superior path. She read,

Humans have the potential to be a constructive resource.

"Not according to Lucius," Tatiana grumbled. Turning the page, another statement that Kazimir made caught her attention.

Demons should not harm or kill other demons.

Tatiana's eyes closed tightly, and she flinched while pressing on the right side of her midsection. In pain, she moaned, "Someone should have reminded Barbas before he beat me three weeks ago. My ribs are still sore."

After she rebuffed his advances, Barbas viciously assaulted her, but what hurt more was what occurred in the aftermath.

* * *

> **Three Weeks Earlier**
> **Bradford House, Culpeper, VA**

"You summoned me, Master?" Tatiana's slurred speech was barely audible as she gingerly knelt.

"Are all the team leaders for Lord Aitken's strike force assembled?" Lucius asked, ignoring her obvious discomfort and a conspicuous black eye.

"Yes, Master," she replied, wiping the drool rolling off her fat lip with the back of her hand.

"What happened to you?" George Aitken inquired, a tone of concern in his voice.

"Barbas demanded sex, and I refused him, my Lord."

George frowned and glanced at Lucius, saying, "What shall I do about this, Master?"

"Nothing," Lucius answered dismissively. Staring at his disciple, he added, "Lord Aitken, effective leadership requires that you not become tangled up emotionally when it comes to subordinates. You will find that paternalism is a useless emotion."

Lucius scowled at Tatiana and declared, "She must learn to handle her own affairs."

* * *

Closing the book, Tatiana could not help but smile, recalling that a few days later, Barbas showed up with bruises of his own, including a right eye so swollen that he could not see out of it. Barbas claimed that he had gotten into a fight in a bar in Culpeper and that his opponent looked worse, but rumors circulated that Lord Aitken had beaten Barbas within an inch of his life.

The tense circumstances at the Bradford House and demon protocol would not allow Tatiana to thank George Aitken publicly, so she did the one thing within her power to show her gratitude. Each day, the elixir he drank, which allowed Lucius to maintain control over his acolyte, was being altered and would eventually wean him from Lucius's dominance. Restoring Lord Aitken's free will was Tatiana's gift for his compassion.

* * *

Wednesday, December 24th
Apollyon's Necropolis
Around 10:00 p.m.

Knock. Knock. Knock.

Apollyon heard three taps on his door. Rising from the stone slab on which he rested and grabbing his battleaxe, he muttered, "Who could that be?"

He held the weapon tightly in his right hand as he opened the entrance to his chamber. He was surprised to see Princess Prosperine in the doorway. Dressed in an elegant, floor-length black dress with a stand-up collar, matching elbow-length gloves, and a veil-like cape, she held a bottle in her hands.

"May I come in?" she purred. "I thought a drink would be appropriate before tomorrow's trip to Heaven."

Bowing his head and lowering his eyes, Apollyon replied, "Yes, Princess. Please do."

Handing Apollyon the bottle, Prosperine strutted in and stated, "I understand you are a connoisseur of Hitian beverages. Where do you keep your glasses?"

The Destroyer's lips drew up in a broad smile as he admired the green, champagne-style bottle. It was unlike any in his collection, and he leaned his weapon against the wall as he appreciated it. Pointing to the corner of the room, he stated, "The glasses are against the wall." Looking at the princess, he asked, "Where did you get this? Hitian vodka is very rare."

"A woman has to have her secrets, Apollyon," she replied, holding two crystal glasses before her. "Lucius wanted to come and enjoy a taste with us but has been detained with other matters."

POP!

Apollyon pulled the cork from the bottle and poured generous amounts of the libation into each glass.

Prosperine held her glass up and declared, "A toast. To a successful meeting tomorrow. Whatever the outcome, may it be as you desire."

Hell's Guardian sipped the vodka, savoring it. Prosperine locked eyes with him and downed the contents with a mischievous grin. She slammed her glass on the stone table and slowly pulled the glove from her fingers, holding the tip between her jagged teeth.

Apollyon refilled her glass. "It is kind of you to come all this way, Princess. The vodka is magnificent! Smooth, and I can taste the hint of coconut from which Hitians once distilled it."

"I am glad you are enjoying it," Prosperine replied. Taking a seat, she crossed her legs and studied Apollyon's face for a moment before adding, "I thought you might be nervous, but I don't detect any anxiety at all."

Looking at the ornate urn on the table, she inquired, "Is this your gift for my..." Prosperine paused and continued with a hint of disdain in her voice, "Grandfather?"

The Destroyer nodded. "Yes, but I am not sure I will even need it. I believe God is summoning me to say that he is changing his mind."

Prosperine's lips puckered as if she had sucked on a lemon. Rubbing her chin with the talon of her index finger, she said skeptically, "I suppose you could be right. He has changed his mind in the past."

As Apollyon gulped the remainder of the vodka from his glass, he did not notice Prosperine reach out and run her claw-like fingernail across his wrist. Her light scratch did not draw blood but left a noticeable impression on the Destroyer's skin.

Leaning over, she hissed in his ear, "When they insist the matter is closed, you will deliver your gift of gold."

"Did you say something, Princess?" Apollyon asked.

"No," Prosperine smirked. "How about another drink?"

* * *

Walled Garden Outside Ancient Jerusalem

Make him your choice.

Joseph disappeared, but his words echoed in Jack's ears as he watched his living room begin to transform. The light blue carpet changed into a pea gravel path. His couch became a flower bed, with banana-yellow and sky-blue flowers, outlined with large rocks to separate it from the tiny tan and gray pebbles of the walkway. The Christmas tree in the corner spread out, and the ceiling disappeared, allowing other lofty evergreen trees to grow alongside it. Jack's eyes opened wide, amazed, as he searched and found that his house was gone.

The night became day, and Jack used his hand to shield his eyes from the blinding sun. Wandering through the garden, he lost himself in the beauty surrounding him. A gentle breeze carried the sweet fragrance of almond trees, whose white and pink blossoms fell to the ground and covered it like a blanket of snow. Buzzing bees chased one another from one red poppy flower to another, and larks raced from tree to tree, singing their extravagant songs as they went. Lebanon cedars, laden with brown seed cones, encircled the garden, some nearly 100 feet tall.

It was so serene until Jack reached the floral oasis's far side and found himself confronted by a steep rock formation that even a professional mountaineer would find challenging to climb. Small trees, somehow managing to root in the harsh conditions, dotted the rockface from the summit to the ground. There was one defining feature that was unmistakable. A rectangular hole, about the size of a doorway, was carved out of the stone. Sunlight flowed into the chamber, illuminating it like a spotlight with an eerie yellow glow, and a large, circular rock, like that of a tire from a massive John Deere construction vehicle, leaned against the mountain.

Jack gulped. "It's a tomb."

A familiar voice called, "Not just a tomb, Jack… it is *the empty tomb.*"

Joseph emerged from one of the garden paths, now dressed in a plain white tunic and open-toed leather sandals.

Stretching his arms wide, he said, "We have progressed beyond Christmas and crucifixion. It is beautiful, Jack. Isn't it?"

"Breathtaking is more like it," Jack replied, eyeing the crypt warily.

Joseph gently grabbed Jack's forearm, sensing his uneasiness and saying, "Death is nothing to fear. Even when we say goodbye, it is not forever."

Gesturing toward one of the pathways, Joseph requested, "Walk with me. Please."

As they slowly strolled, Joseph acknowledged, "I know you have other questions, Jack—one in particular. I thought it might be easier to talk here."

Joseph waved his open hand, saying, "Come, sit in the shade of these olive trees."

A cool breeze refreshed the two men, and after a few minutes, Jack asked, "What happened to you?"

Jack followed a leaf slowly falling to the ground and added, "I mean, there is so little about you in the Bible. I can see that you are kind; it would not have been unheard of to have Mary stoned for being pregnant, but you stood by her. Your presence at Jesus's birth bears witness to your steadfast love. I have always considered you an honorable, faithful servant to God. A responsible, virtuous man of character. I never saw anything scandalous or negative written about you, but you disappeared altogether."

Joseph turned red and answered, "Thank you, Jack, for all of that, but I had doubts, fears, and worries too."

Reaching into a pocket in his tunic, Joseph held out a worn wooden mallet and several crude iron nails. "I consider myself a man of wood and nails, a carpenter. A simple man."

"A quiet, unassuming person who cared for his family and protected them from harm," Jack reminded him. "You put the needs of Mary and your Earthly son before your own."

Jack paused and asked, "Why are you carrying a hammer and nails?"

Joseph stared at the open tomb in the distance. "They are a reminder that my son died a carpenter's death. The very instruments of my trade nailed my son to his cross."

Picking up a stone from the ground, Joseph tossed it onto the gravel path. "I understand how you feel about the danger your children are in. I understand fear and dread, just like you."

Locking eyes with Jack, Joseph continued, "By now, it may not come as a surprise, but you see, we have many things in common. I am the one person to have most closely walked in your shoes and know the path you must consider."

Glancing down, Joseph noticed Jack's injured hand. "How did you get that scar?"

Jack ran his finger on the mark, which resembled a railroad track due to all the stitches needed after surgery. He flexed his hand and answered, "I had my hand crushed by a monster known as a Strigoi."

"At the direction of Lucius Rofocale," Joseph interjected.

Jack removed his glasses and pretended to rub his eyes, but he was trying to hide his shock at Joseph's assertion. He asked, "How do you know that?"

"I know much more than that," Joseph asserted. "For instance, I understand that Lucius has tempted you twice, but you rejected his offers both times."

Pulling down his tunic, Joseph revealed a trench-like gash that stretched across his neck from ear to ear.

"You got away lucky, Jack. This mutilation was the price I paid when I rejected Lucius."

Pointing upward, he added, "He strung me up by my ankles from the tree we are sitting under and slashed my throat when I would not betray my son. I watched my blood pool beneath me, and he left me hanging here so Jesus would be the one to find me. It was supposed to be a message, a warning, but it did not have the effect that I believe Lucius intended."

Jack's jaw hung open in disbelief. He opened and shut his eyes several times and tried to speak but could not find the words.

Staring again at the open tomb, Joseph continued, "Lucius is a powerful adversary, Jack. You praised me for saving my family from Herod, but you have done the same. You underestimate your strength."

Looking back at Jack, Joseph persisted. "We are both providers, teachers, role models, and protectors. You asked what happened to me. I became a spirit, an advisor to my son. Only Jesus knew this, and we agreed he would not reveal it. This secret between a father and his son is why you read nothing about me after Jesus turns twelve."

Despite being stunned by Joseph's revelations, Jack noticed that the garden had gone quiet. The birds were gone, and along with them, their beautiful songs. No bees were buzzing, and the pleasant breeze was gone. Something told him that his time with Joseph was coming to its conclusion.

The Earthly father of Jesus rose from the grass, and Jack followed him where he did not want to go—the empty tomb. Jack peered in and found the crypt's interior was modest, with only a long rock slab along the wall for a body.

Jack stepped back from the entrance, and Joseph spoke. "All we hold dear about Christmas would cease to be relevant without the empty tomb on Easter morning."

Looking at Jack, he added, "Let us never forget that Christmas and Easter are linked, heart to heart." Joseph reached for Jack's hands and grabbed them tightly. "And hand to hand."

Joseph breathed deeply and exhaled. "Now, the question you asked during your shopping trip. While witnessing the nativity scene with Gabriel at the church, you wanted to know if Mary and I knew Jesus's destiny. In other words, like your children, did we know it was his destiny to die?"

"I realize what I am asking is very personal and likely painful," Jack softly replied. "But I need to know."

"You have a right to know," Joseph answered. "The short answer is yes, but we were unaware of the type of death he would face. I had never witnessed a crucifixion, so I had no idea of the suffering he would experience."

A tear rolled down Joseph's cheek. "I am glad that I did not know then what I know now."

Joseph tightly held Jack's upper arms and looked him straight in the eye. "I pray that you will not witness Louis or David's death. No mother or father should see such a thing."

Jack hesitated, then whispered, "Do you know how they will die?"

"No. I do not," Joseph swiftly replied. "I swear it. I would not lie to you."

Jack's eyes fell as he acknowledged, "I know that."

Pointing at the empty tomb, Joseph asserted, "This is why all of this must happen despite your doubts and fears. Jesus's birth brought God to all of us, and his resurrection brought humanity back to God. The paths we take now are essential. Whether we are ready or not, the future will come, but it is tricky and full of twists and turns. If humanity does not reconcile with God, they will be at the mercy of Lucifer and Lucius."

The sun, now a yellow, red, and orange mixture, was nearly below the horizon. Joseph kissed Jack on both cheeks, a kiss of peace, then said,

"Our time is almost at an end, and I have one more thing I want to tell you." Joseph paused, smiled, and said,

"Follow your instincts, Jack. Marry Anne. I lost my first wife and married Mary under unusual circumstances, but I never regretted it. Neither will you. If you do not take that risk, you will always wonder and never know the impact it could have. Anne already told you she is dedicating her life to protecting Louis and David. Such a gift, given out of the humblest love, should be reciprocated."

* * *

Wednesday, December 24th
Back in Jack Aitken's Living Room, Bristow, VA

In the blink of an eye, Jack found himself back home. It was silent except for the clicking of the swinging pendulum on the grandfather clock in the hallway. Jack looked outside and was startled.

"There is no snow on the ground." Jack looked back at the clock, and his eyes wavered several times in disbelief. "It is only 10:35 p.m. It's like I was gone for five minutes."

POW!

The blustery wind pounding on the panes of glass in the windows brought him fully back to reality. Jack parked himself in the chair where Joseph had sat earlier, removed his glasses, and rubbed his ear. The rough patch of cancerous skin cells was still there, reassuring Jack, in a way, that he was not losing his mind. Jack scratched his thigh and felt something in his pocket. Reaching in, he pulled out a hard, brown object and examined it. The texture was rough and pitted. His lips parted, opening his mouth ever so slightly, and he whispered,

"It's an almond. Like the ones in the garden." Jack beamed and held up the nut. "My God, it is all real. Every one of these visions is authentic."

Jack sat back in the chair and looked upward, amazed by all he had experienced. Then, he glanced around the room, still pondering his reservations about Louis and David's role as prophets. At the same time, he considered everything that Gabriel, Peter, and Joseph had shared with him. Each of them acknowledged his doubts while at the same time telling him not to be afraid. Despite their reassurances, Jack still struggled with the tug of war that had gone on in his heart, soul, and mind over the past four months since Sheriff Hill had revealed who David and Louis were to become.

A few minutes later, Jack murmured, "God, thank you for not pressuring me to accept this or threatening me if I didn't." Then Jack acknowledged, "I know I don't necessarily have a say in this. Still, after meeting with—what shall I call them, your delegates? I better understand your position."

"OUCH!" Jack cried. Absentmindedly, he had struck his right hand against the arm of the chair. Still seeing stars, Jack gently rubbed it and felt the scar that dominated his appendage like the San Andreas fault on a topographical map of California. It gave Jack pause, and he gnawed on his fingernail while reliving the confrontation with Lucius and the Strigoi a little more than four months earlier; the incident resulted in his life-altering injury.

Jack recalled his declaration to Lucius, *"I want my sons to live, and I want to be there to watch them grow up. I have grave concerns about what being a prophet for God means for their future."*

He cringed, hearing Lucius's giddy voice in his head. *"God can be so cruel."*

A dull ache seemed to rise in Jack's jaw, like how he felt after being beaten within an inch of his life. He even expected to look down and see the blood dripping from his lips to the floor.

Amanda's voice echoed in his head. *"You must believe, Jack."*

Jack heard Gabriel, Peter, and Joseph repeating, *"You must believe, Jack."*

Dredging up the smug look on Lucius's face made Jack's blood boil. He remembered him asking,

"Shall I draw up the papers?"

All the veins in Jack's body seemed to constrict simultaneously; he felt the heat of his anger rising from deep in his core. His righteous defiance filled the chamber when he uttered these words:

"My hopes for David and Louis are in God's hands, and I place their fate into those mighty hands."

A steely grin emerged across Jack's face at the memory of Lucius glaring at him with dagger eyes when he declared,

"Do with me what you will, but I will never submit to you or Satan!"

Grasping the significance of these remembrances, Jack rolled his eyes and admitted to himself, "I get the point, God. I need to put my money where my mouth is, so to speak."

Innocence. The word echoed through Jack's mind, but he wasn't only thinking about Louis and David now. He thought about the family next door. Earlier in the evening, when he stopped by to wish his neighbors a merry Christmas, the anticipation and joy in Zinnia and Liam's eyes were undeniable. Theirs was a childhood innocence, and it occurred to Jack that this goodness was partly what his sons' sacrifice would preserve.

Cautiously, still, with misgivings, Jack bowed his head and finally conceded to God, "Up until now, you have demonstrated the lengths you will go to protect David and Louis. Joseph trusted you. So will I."

Jack then saw the blank Christmas card he had started writing to Anne on the table across the room. He considered what Joseph had encouraged him to do and remembered one last detail about what occurred in the cave under the Antonescu house. What he tried to convince himself Anne had started to say before the golem arrived and saved their lives.

"Jack, I love..."

Glancing again outside, he realized there was no snow. *It won't prevent Anne from making it here tomorrow.*

Jack hurried to the couch, picked up a pen, and began to write.

Dear Anne,

It is a long-held tradition of mine to write personal Christmas cards to those closest to me.

Jack bit the pen cap as he struggled to find the right words.

I consider you to be one of that circle of people.

I must tell you what I am feeling deep inside of me. I once said to you that I would never fall in love again, but I can no longer continue to lie to myself. What started as a friendship has grown into something greater than I imagined.

Every word caused Jack's heart to beat faster.

Whenever I am troubled, the first person I reach out to is you. However, I feared I might risk our friendship if I expressed my feelings, particularly if you did not feel the same way. I have been scared for quite some time, but I am not afraid anymore. You made my heart come alive when I believed that was inconceivable.

There is no doubt in my mind that when I look into your eyes, I see a future that I never imagined would be possible for me. While I try to be strong for my sons, the truth is that I don't want to go it alone anymore. I never thought I would be laying my heart on the line this way, but every ounce of my being tells me that I need you and, more importantly...

Jack paused and took a deep breath. Then, he wrote:

I love you.

So, this leads me to a question I want to ask you...

CHAPTER 22

> *Christmas Morning*
> *Apollyon's Chamber in Hell*
> *Daybreak*

The sweet smell of lavender incense filled the compartment, and wisps of smoke emanated from the holes in the bronze censer on the table. Unlike the collectible bottles Apollyon was fond of, this censer appeared to be an ordinary object. Its spherical shape symbolized the Earth, from which the materials to make the icon originated, and it sat upon a conical base. The aroma was calming, as intended, but burning the incense served a dual purpose. When the smoke ceased and the scent was gone, Apollyon knew it was time to leave to see God.

Apollyon held his hand out, testing his nerves. Bulging veins crisscrossed the back of his extremity like a meandering river winding its way to the sea, and it shook like a leaf in the breeze. Despite having strength in biblical proportions, the thought of meeting God in his Heavenly palace was intimidating, even to the Destroyer. Unable to sleep, he polished the breastplate of his body armor all night until the light reflecting from it could rival a lightning bolt. The razor edge of his battleaxe was already sharp enough to split a hair, and the stiff leather manica and greaves, protection for his arms and legs, were covered by the finest gold mined by the damned souls of those who were misers in their mortal lives.

On the table was a bronze helmet adorned with a red plume made from the feathers of now-extinct animals. When Apollyon wore it, the pattern ran from side to side rather than from front to back. It was like no other helmet in creation, devoid of rivets or bolts, with a solid flange flowing from ear to ear, protecting the neck. Hitian artisans made the ceremonial headdress out of respect and to honor Apollyon's protection of their kingdom. A gathering in the presence of God seemed like the ideal occasion to wear such a uniquely crafted item.

A black silk cape that covered the entirety of the back of his massive torso completed the ensemble. Apollyon looked at himself in the mirror. He exhaled deeply, clamped his lips tightly together, and nodded, approving of what he saw. He stood up straight and tall, proud of the intimidating appearance he projected.

He raised his arms above his waist and held his hands apart, palms wide open in disbelief that God would even consider terminating his role in the looming apocalypse. He bragged out loud, "How could God not change his mind when he sees this?"

The room was quiet. Despite the soothing properties of the lavender and the self-assurance bordering on arrogance that Apollyon expressed to his reflection in the mirror, the air was full of tension. The Destroyer knew that his reason for being, his very identity, was at stake today. He carefully placed Lucius's urn inside the vest of his body armor.

The distinctive yet typical smell of sulfur once again permeated his room. Hell's Guardian got up from the slab of rock that he called a chair and entered the hallway. As he went down the corridor, he tried not to think about where he was heading. It wasn't hard to do. Even with his near-continuous scratching, he could not get any relief from the maddening itch on his wrist.

* * *

Christmas Morning
Simultaneously in Bristow, VA

S-W-I-S-H!

Jack sank his tenth free throw in a row. With cat-like reflexes, he grabbed the ball, quickly dashed the length of the basketball court, and scored a lay-up. Satisfied with his workout, he sat on a bench, took a long drink of water, and wrapped a towel around his sweaty neck.

Taking another drink, Jack leaned back, breathed deeply, and let the breath out, making a whistling noise as the air rushed across his chapped lips. He watched two squirrels burying acorns and closed his eyes to take in the beauty of the birdsongs. He could not help but reflect on all that had happened to him since Thanksgiving.

"What a difference four or five weeks can make." Reaching down to re-tie his sneakers, Jack added, "It wasn't such a happy Thanksgiving, but it is shaping up to be a merry Christmas!"

Jack felt an unfamiliar serenity. For the first time that he could recall, the warring factions of his soul, like the vision of World War I shown to him a few weeks earlier, were, if not at peace, at least abiding by a truce. The illumination of these visions had restored his faith to a level that had only existed before he angrily tossed his Bible into a desk drawer many years earlier.

Having been up before sunrise, Jack had earnestly, almost desperately, searched through that desk drawer. He finally found the Bible under a pile of papers. But Jack discovered something else... an egg. A yellow plastic egg that he and Amanda hid for an Easter egg hunt. Usually, there was a piece of candy or a quarter inside, but Jack pulled a piece of paper from his navy blue sweatshirt pocket and reread it.

Believe.

The paper had been in the egg. Jack carefully tucked it back in and zippered the pocket shut. There was no way Jack would lose it. He knew it would be in his wallet, along with pictures of Amanda and the boys, forever.

"Thank you for the gift, Joseph," Jack whispered, knowing who had placed it there. "I also wanted to thank you for your advice."

Jack's leg moved up and down nervously as he thought about Anne. Everything he wrote in her card last night was heartfelt, but he had not yet figured out what would happen next. He hoped for the opportunity to speak with Louis and David before he discussed marriage but opted to play things by ear. He pondered what to do but then smiled. For once, he had a problem he didn't mind having to solve.

DRIP. DRIP. DRIP.

Several raindrops fell on Jack's head as he gathered his things together and headed home.

Crossing Linton Hall Road, Jack almost drooled over the thought of eating a Bilgore Groves pink grapefruit. He recalled that each Christmas, he could smell the tart, but never bitter, aroma through the peel. Of course, Jack knew the box that Joseph had delivered the night before belonged to his next-door neighbors, but when he went downstairs earlier, the container was gone. Standing where he had left it, a quick Google search confirmed that the Bilgore family had sold the business back in 1986. Discovering the box was only a prop, part of the ruse allowing Joseph to meet him, caused Jack to frown in mock disappointment.

Almost home. The rain had been steady enough to saturate Jack's hair, and droplets began to run down his face. A few of them ran into his mouth.

"EW! I don't like the bitter taste!" Jack scrunched up his nose and spat out the raindrops.

Now soaking wet, he held out his hand to catch the falling rain. Jack noticed something unusual about what he collected in his palm. His eyebrow raised, and a worried look appeared as he studied the pool of water.

"It looks like blood."

* * *

Christmas Morning
Simultaneously in Pergamon

Lucius Rofocale's taloned foot rested on the marble wall of a portico overlooking the arid mountainside below. Pressing his index finger to his cheek, he stood wide-eyed. The black tar-like pools of his irises studied the horizon of the eastern sky. The arc of a crimson-red sun was rising. His tightly clenched jaw revealed the full extent of his determination to succeed where others, including himself, had previously failed. *Today*, he thought, *I will set Heaven on fire.*

For millennia, despite Lucifer's biting insults and dismissive attitude, he had methodically, with infinite patience, assembled the means to dispense demon justice to the so-called forces of righteousness. But, when he unexpectedly overheard an angel inform Apollyon that his role in the script of the apocalypse was changing, he knew the final piece of the plan had fallen into place. The question of how to deliver the master stroke, bringing the holy war to its conclusion, had been answered.

Now, after all the devious calculations and cunning planning, it had come down to this moment. Lucius's nostrils flared, thinking not only about the fate that awaited those in Heaven but exacting revenge on his current nemesis, Jack Aitken. His lips formed a smug grin at the notion. After finally witnessing the death of his great adversary, Mark Desmond, he now prepared to finish the job. Nice and slow. First, Jack Aitken would helplessly watch as Prosperine drained the life force from his sons, the *so-called* prophets. Then and only then would Jack experience his own death sentence.

Rubbing his clawed hands together gleefully, he boasted, "The finest part is that it will be at the hands of his brother! George Aitken will be my instrument of vengeance and settle all my affairs once and for all."

Fully afire, the blazing sun had risen, and gazing into it caused even Lucius to squint. He basked in the heat, but a nagging concern tugged at his confidence, and the uncertainty made him wonder if, despite the meticulous arrangements, things might still unravel. The one uncontrollable variable, the wild card hiding in the middle of the deck, was whether Apollyon still would play his part.

A rising wind failed to dissipate the rotten-egg sulfur smell surrounding Lucius. He heard his black robe flapping in the breeze like a flag snapping to attention as he stepped to the terrace and headed toward the monolithic entrance to Pergamon. The time was drawing near. The wait would be over, and he would soon know if Apollyon had performed his role.

* * *

Christmas Morning
Princess Prosperine's Chamber in Pergamon

THUD!

The body of a massive man struck the stone floor. The former football player had fought Prosperine, but she gained the upper hand and savored every suck.

"Humans taste better when they struggle!"

The Princess of Hell licked her lips. A plant-based diet was acceptable for an appetizer, but those who regularly ate meat, like this tasty treat, were divine! It was like eating wild game, tart yet rich when they fought back!

Prosperine barked to Tatiana, "Get this out of here and lock the door behind you. I am not to be disturbed. Is that clear?"

Tatiana bowed. "Yes, Princess!"

She quickly dragged the once muscular body of the athlete away.

Once the lock clicked, Prosperine retrieved a straw mat infused with oregano to spur prophetic visions and placed it on a diabase slab. The predominantly gray, rectangular block, made from an igneous rock formed deep in the Earth's mantle, contained specks of white and black. Prosperine had it polished to a smooth finish. Untying and removing a leather bag from her neck, she opened it and spread the contents, ground myrrh ashes, in a large circle around the mat.

Assuming a lotus position with her open hands balanced on her knees, Prosperine deeply inhaled the myrrh's vapors, which enhanced her meditative state and increased her psychic powers. Already fueled by the consumption of fluids from massive numbers of human bodies, her long, silky eyelashes fluttered, and the bewitching effect of the aromatics swiftly took hold. The princess's eyelids slowly began falling like autumn leaves gliding to the ground.

The rapidly descending veil of darkness signaled a trance-like state was imminent. Before she drifted away, Prosperine whispered, "Lucius's plan is masterful but not foolproof. I will ensure the pincer that he has skillfully positioned without detection, encircling Paradise, locks, and that our deliverer cannot change his mind."

Prosperine's body swayed uncontrollably, and as her chin fell to her chest, she muttered, "I will introduce humanity to the reality of Hell. Is this not why my father sent me?"

***

Christmas Morning
The Outskirts of Heaven

Arriving at his guard house adjacent to the gate to Hell, Apollyon discovered a free-standing wooden stairway without handrails. Kneeling, he ran his fingers across the smoothly sanded first step and inspected it closely, noting one distinct feature: no nails, screws, or fasteners of any kind.

Impressed, he rubbed his chin. "The work of a carpenter, a damn good one."

The staircase began to move as soon as he stood on the first step. Up to his knees in a white, cotton candy-like cloud, he gradually ascended to the heavens. It was like a ride on an escalator, and it took no effort on his part.

Starting in the troposphere, he passed over Mount Everest, the rooftop of the world, and continued climbing into the stratosphere. He reached the thermosphere, and the sky, which had been turquoise at the beginning, was now a Texas bluebonnet shade of dark blue. Soaring through the final layers of the atmosphere, he arrived in outer space. The darkness was like the blackest night but filled with dazzling stars that flashed like glitter.

Finally, the cloud stopped, and Apollyon saw a fortress of silver bricks and parapets with golden domes in the distance. Even from where he stood, he could see the perfect lines of the blocks confirming the artisan's expertise, and the structure sparkled brighter than any celestial body. Right or left, the walls went on, seemingly without end, their footings hidden by the same frosty white clouds that carried him there.

Before Apollyon was a winding, emerald-green road that steadily rose, ending at a gate. A chorus, singing praises to God, echoed around him. A chill ran down his spine, not inspired by fear but by awe. Tentatively, he stepped forward.

* * *

> **Christmas Morning**
> **The Bradford House, Culpeper, VA**

George Aitken gulped down the last of his morning elixir and slammed the glass on the desk blotter. The smell of bacon, something he would generally crave, hung in the air, but over the past several months, his appetite had diminished, and most foods no longer appealed to him. After the red rain that fell earlier, a promising omen, George wanted to be alone. Sequestering himself in the study, he was restless and walked unceasingly around the room.

"It is just nerves," he muttered, attempting to reassure himself. "I have left no stone unturned."

Glancing at the map on the opulent hardwood table, George began reviewing his plan's details again. He stopped himself. Waving his hands in frustration, he shouted,

"Enough!"

A hesitant voice from the guard outside the door asked, "Lord Aitken, are you alright?"

"Yes! Yes!" He stormed. "Go away!"

George loosened the collar on his black shirt, which strained to cover his bulging muscles, and flung himself angrily on the couch. Kicking off his steel-toed boots, he laid himself down, placing his neck on the armrest, using it as a pillow. The past few days, George had become increasingly irritable. He hated to admit it, but the recent nightmares that were vivid and painstakingly real caused his mood to be as dark as his clothing.

He knew some sleep would do him good. He wanted his might to be razor-sharp tonight. The fact remained, however, that he was too frightened to close his eyes. Each time he did, sleep only led to misery. George would wake in a cold sweat, screaming. Tiny as they were, for the first time since his death and return as Lucius's acolyte, hairline cracks in the wall of certainty that represented his ego were forming.

Closing his eyes again, he was determined to get some sleep. George tried to ignore the mental checklist in his brain and whispered, "Regardless of my dreams, what will happen today is for the best."

***

> **Christmas Morning
> The Gates of Heaven
> A Short Time Later**

Apollyon could not tell how long he had walked but finally saw Heaven's gates over the last hill. As they came into view, he paused to admire them. The vision was almost indescribable.

"Magnificent!" he marveled. "Beauty beyond anything I would have imagined."

Two stone columns with thin, vertical gold lines inset in their middle supported the golden gates. On top of each golden gate were bars shaped like an elaborate, 17th-century brass bed headboard. The middle section of the gates had six vertical bars whose ends on the top and bottom curved like a fiddlehead fern emerging in the spring. The curvature on the rod's top faced left and the bottom to the right. Finally, a singular horizontal rod bisected the middle of each gate. Two smaller bars, fashioned to appear like two fiddleheads facing one another, were fastened on the top and bottom of the rod.

Like a roof truss, a grand stone arch spanned the top of the gate, with one end fixed on top of each column. The centerpiece, a gold cross, stood like a spire in the middle of the archway. Light yellow, almost white, beams of light streamed through the gates, illuminating the area like a lighthouse beacon. To Apollyon's left was a wooden podium with a bearded figure, a caretaker, standing behind it. The gatekeeper rubbed his finger against his temple, and his eyebrows narrowed, causing deep channels in his forehead. It suggested he was concentrating and slightly perplexed at the same time.

Reaching the podium, the Destroyer towered over a man dressed in a white robe similar to that worn by monks. The rest of his attire was equally humble, with a braided rope for a belt and a brass key hanging prominently from it. The triumphant singing of the choir that had echoed so loudly while Apollyon was approaching the gate had quieted. He could not help but notice that he stood alone before the gatekeeper and had not seen another soul during his entire journey.

The man behind the podium eyed him warily. Apollyon removed his helmet and tucked it under his arm.

Trying to lighten the mood, he joked, "Traffic seems a little light this morning, don't you think?"

When the man did not respond, Apollyon thought of another way to reassure him. He lifted the key to Hell from his waist and presented it to the sentry.

"I presume you are the apostle they call Peter. I have heard of you. My name is Apollyon. I see your key; like you, I am a gatekeeper."

Startled, Heaven's gatekeeper's jaw went slack, and he recoiled at the sight of the unholy object. Quickly reaching into a compartment under the podium, he pulled out a box and held it open in front of Apollyon.

"You cannot bring that through the gates." Saint Peter blinked repeatedly. "Place it in the box, and I will keep it until you return."

Apollyon hesitated. He had never relinquished his key. He had never considered such a thing. Reluctantly, he complied. The apostle sealed the container and, holding it as far from himself as possible, placed it inside the podium.

"Please forgive the lack of a warm reception." Peter scratched the back of his neck. "The truth is that, well, there are parts of you that I should not permit inside the Kingdom."

Confused, Peter swallowed several times before stating, "What I mean is that parts of your body are not sanctified, and such impurity is not allowed in God's presence."

Shifting his helmet from left to right and holding it closer to Lucius's vessel hidden in his armor, Apollyon stared icily at Saint Peter and indignantly insisted, "I may be an abomination in your eyes, but I assure you I am not Frankenstein's monster."

Holding his hand out, Apollyon forcefully pointed to his wrist, asking, "Do you see any seams or stitches?"

Peter scratched his forehead and reached for the key tied to his waist. He inserted it into the keyhole, turned the key, and pushed the gates open.

"I meant no offense," Peter said. "You have prior authorization."

Pointing down the corridor, Heaven's sentry added, "Follow the passageway. It will take you to the throne room."

Apollyon bowed respectfully, then confidently crossed the threshold into Heaven.

*　*　*

> Christmas Morning
> National Earthquake Information Center,
> Boulder, Colorado

Glug. Glug. Glug.

Doctor Pamela Grey downed the last drops of her energy drink and threw the empty can in the recycle bin. She leaned back in the chair with her arms raised and reached for the ceiling. The long stretch felt good after so many hours seated in front of her laptop. Despite covering her mouth with her arm, Doctor Grey could not hide the gaping yawn on her face. The dark circles under her eyes betrayed the almost overwhelming fatigue that consumed her mind and body. She wearily shuffled through the pile of papers on her desk.

"Let me review these figures again. Maybe there is something I missed."

Shaking her head, Doctor Grey added, "Something that will convince the Directors that we need to go public with the findings."

Since her graduate student, Marty Pearson, had shown her the unusual seismograph readings nearly two weeks earlier, the duo's earnest efforts to convince the Center's Board of Directors to act on her research had been futile. Although she and Marty had worked nearly around the clock since then, her superior insisted further validation was required before they would publish the conclusions.

"I hope we aren't too late," the doctor thought as she gritted her teeth in frustration.

Her eyes glanced down at her watch, then opened wide when she saw the date.

"Christmas day?" The scientist rubbed her brow in disbelief. "It can't be, can it?"

Shooting a look at the lower right corner of her computer confirmed it. Suddenly, Marty burst into the room with something in his hand, shouting, "Pam, you need to see this!" The grad student nearly tripped over a chair leg as he bolted over to Doctor Grey's side and dropped a piece of paper on her keyboard.

"If they want validation of our research, I think this is it!"

Adrenaline rushed through her veins as she fumbled around her desk, looking for something.

"Pam," Marty tried to get her attention.

"I can't find my glasses, Marty!" she exclaimed.

Marty chuckled. "Uh, they are on top of your head, Pam."

"Talk about an absent-minded professor," Doctor Grey huffed, chastising herself. Pulling her glasses down to the bridge of her nose, she asked, "So what am I looking at?"

"This is a satellite photo of our target area from yesterday." Pointing at an irregular object in the picture, Marty insisted, "There is no mistaking what that is."

The scientists locked eyes, their mouths agape in shock.

"Oh my God." Doctor Grey could barely allow the words to fall from her lips. Removing her glasses to see the picture more clearly, she studied every detail before adding, "If I didn't know better, I would say I was looking at the San Andreas fault."

Marty nodded, and his face lost all expression. "It gets worse. The day before, this wasn't visible. I also rechecked the seismograph readings a few minutes ago."

Doctor Grey put the photo down and stared at Marty.

Sitting down, he continued, "The readings are off the charts."

Struggling to put the photo in an envelope, Doctor Grey's hands trembled as she dropped her research papers on the floor. Marty knelt to help pick them up, and Doctor Grey fumed, "Even after Barbados and Australia, the Board wouldn't listen."

The doctor rushed out of the room and hurried down the hallway, muttering, "They have to listen now!"

Marty called out behind her, "Merry Christmas, Doctor Grey." Picking up a few stray papers from the floor, he reflected silently,

Enjoy it while you can. I doubt it will be a happy New Year for any of us.

* * *

Christmas Morning
The Entrance to the Holy of Holies

Apollyon stood before a white veil spun from the finest linen and adorned with tassels around the edges. Embroidered in the cloth were shiny specks of gold, which reflected the radiance that had enveloped Apollyon like a spotlight ever since he walked through the gates. The curtain hid the entrance to a place he could not see. Earlier, only his hand shook, but now, despite his brawn and strength, his entire body was trembling. He just stood there, trying to discover the courage to find out what was on the other side of the veil.

The journey from the gates to where he stood now had been short, but along the way, Apollyon could not help but note the dichotomy between Heaven and Hell. The sweltering heat in Hell always caused Apollyon to sweat profusely. Wiping the dampness from his forehead with the back of his hand, he realized his nerves, not the temperature in Heaven, were causing him to perspire. Hell reeked of sulfur and brimstone; Heaven's scent was fresh and pleasing like the Hitian sea breezes from long ago.

Guarding Hell's gate, screams, cries of agony, and a low humming noise like a constantly running furnace filled his ears. What he heard now were not refrains of pain but hymns of praise. The joy in the choir voices surrounded him, and their infectious celebration stirred his emotions. It made him want to stay there forever.

WOOSH!

Suddenly, a mighty wind blew the veil violently in Apollyon's direction. It wrapped around his body and jolted him from his contemplation. The gusts calmed, and a voice, firm but not frightening, called out from the space beyond the curtain.

COME. Present yourself before me.

Apollyon gulped, but if he needed to spit, his dry mouth would not have permitted it. Tentatively, he pulled aside the veil.

* * *

"I-I am here, Lord," Apollyon responded, his usually booming voice quaking and barely audible.

As he stepped forward, the choir went silent, but a trumpet echoed around him. His feet felt heavy, like trying to walk through wet cement, but somehow, he took several steps into the room. His jaw dropped, and his eyes widened, awed by what he saw. A great throne made of a translucent mineral stood on a riser above him, surrounded by twenty-four similar but smaller seats. Upon the smaller thrones sat individuals dressed in white robes, the color of pure snow. Golden crowns hid their graying hair.

A rumble of thunder rolled through the room, startling Apollyon and causing him to look upward. The room had no ceiling, but cotton-like clouds rolled through the sky above. The sun's rays made it appear like day, but lightning bolts still blazed through the atmosphere. Glancing down, Apollyon saw the floor as a sea of glass leading to the ascendant seat of power, where the Son of God, in an ankle-length robe with a gold sash around his chest, sat above it all.

Jesus's hair was like wool, his beard a frosty white, and his eyes cherry-red balls of fire. His face was radiant, brighter than a star in the night sky, and he wore brass-colored sandals polished to a blinding sheen. Surrounding Jesus's throne, a halo as brilliant as a green emerald sparkled so intensely it caused Apollyon to lean sideways and turn his head away to shield his eyes. Saint Michael, wearing a silver suit of armor and holding a double-edged sword in his hand, stood by the Messiah's side.

All at once, the beautiful voices returned, exclaiming, "Holy, holy, holy is the Lord God almighty!"

Immediately, the twenty-four elders fell from their thrones and threw their crowns at Jesus's feet, professing, "Worthy are you, Lord, our God! All glory, laud, and honor to our redeemer King!"

Apollyon was awestruck by the spectacle and stood slack-jawed with nothing to say. It occurred to him that perhaps he should be kneeling too, but the singing ceased before he could decide what to do, and the same voice that had called to him earlier echoed in Apollyon's ears.

* * *

Remain standing. One should not kneel when facing judgment.

The room fell eerily silent, and Apollyon tentatively glanced around, scrutinizing the faces of those in attendance for a sign of what might be coming next. The voice continued,

I have summoned you here because of the faithful service you provided and to honor the purpose you have fulfilled.

Respectfully, Apollyon stood up straight with his helmet tucked under his arm. He could not tell if God was speaking out loud for all to hear or only in his mind. The Destroyer thought,

So, what I have heard is true. The Lord is not flesh but spirit.

Apollyon thrust his chin upward, proudly, accepting God's goodwill. But he noticed a stone-faced expression on Christ's face and the rigid cords bulging in Saint Michael's neck while his hand tightly gripped his sword.

"A warrior knows suspicion when he sees it," Apollyon whispered under his breath. He deliberately moved his hand away from the battleaxe attached to his waist.

They see me as a threat.

Jesus interjected, "As God in human form, the message of my ministry was one of peace, not war. Lucifer and his demons intend to change the script of the apocalypse, but so do we. They believe we are weak; that is the perception we want them to rely upon. What we are doing is calculated but not without risk. We want to hear from your lips that you are not a threat and would not make war on our Father."

Despite the fire in his eyes, Jesus gave Apollyon a cold stare, freezing him into silence. He resumed speaking very bluntly, "But as the angel we sent indicated, you are out, Apollyon. Your services are no longer required."

* * *

I have complete confidence in my son and advise him on such matters. The brutality and carnage you have wrought must end. It is a relic of the past and cannot be a part of our future.

Another long pause ensued before God resumed,

We must offer humanity another path to choose or risk them seeing us as no different than the evil we oppose.

The itch on his wrist was intolerable, but scratching it brought no relief. Still struggling with the burning impulse to scratch, Apollyon shook his head and pleaded, "I do not understand. Why am I out?"

Apollyon waited for a response, but after receiving no reply, he appealed directly to God and defended his past actions. "Have I not been a loyal servant? I have always done as you asked. What is to become of me? Perhaps there is still some way that I can be of assistance."

The duality of your responsibilities, serving Lucifer and myself, makes finding a role for you impossible.

Then, God delivered the decisive blow.

The carnage in Barbados confirms you lack the restraint needed to serve us.

The finality of God's words cut Apollyon like a knife. He now knew that a different outcome was out of the question. He felt their hostility, and his lip curled in anger. Apollyon rubbed his elbow across his armor, reassuring himself that the urn Lucius provided was still with him.

"It is just as Lucius predicted it would be," he grumbled.

Suddenly, out of nowhere, Apollyon caught a scent, turned up his nose, and sniffed the air. Perplexed, he murmured, "I've smelled that scent before, but that is impossible. It smells like Prosperine."

* * *

Still in her chamber in a semi-conscious state, Prosperine had monitored the conversation through the small scratch she inflicted on Apollyon's wrist. The veins in her neck pulsed as she sensed the Destroyer's wounded pride.

"You are not alone, Apollyon. I am with you," Prosperine whispered reassuringly. Moving in for the kill, she reminded him, "Remember, you still have a role to play for me."

* * *

Apollyon tapped his left ear. He was sure he heard Prosperine's voice telling him she was with him, but there was only silence. He struggled to focus and avoided eye contact, trying to hide his devastation. Bewildered and trying to maintain his dignity, the Destroyer said dutifully,

"I stand in the shadow of the wisdom of your judgment, my Lord."

"Then why have you disobeyed the Father?" Jesus asked pointedly. "Our message was clear, but instead of standing down, you stoked the fires of Hell and killed thousands."

You must answer for what happened in Barbados.

Apollyon lowered his eyes and stared at the floor, searching for the right words. So many voices were now in his head, and the accusations were flying.

Flustered and realizing there was no reason to hold back any longer, Apollyon assertively responded, "If you had not sent that Reaper to kill me, then what happened in Barbados would never have occurred."

Instantly, the chamber went silent. Turning to Saint Michael, Jesus inquired, "Do you know what Apollyon is referencing?"

Saint Michael shook his head. "No, my Lord. I know nothing about this."

Looking back at Apollyon, Jesus rubbed his chin in confusion and asked in a surprised voice, "A Reaper? What Reaper?"

Recalling the incident with the Reaper caused Apollyon to become frustrated and impatient with the proceedings. His eyes narrowed, and he petulantly snapped, "The Reaper that I had to kill!"

An audible gasp emanated from the twenty-four elders.

Saint Michael, his eyes ablaze, leaped from Christ's side and raised his sword to smite Apollyon, declaring,

"There is only one punishment for killing a Reaper!"

Instinctively, Apollyon reached for his weapon to defend himself.

WAIT! Michael, stay that sword!

God's command caused the Arch Angel to lower his weapon.

Someone else sent this Reaper. Apollyon was betrayed!

A rush of adrenaline caused Apollyon's heart to beat so quickly that he felt it might burst from his chest. Holding his battleaxe, prepared to defend himself, he tried to understand what God meant when he uttered the word betrayal. Shocked, the only thought that Apollyon could manage was one name that fell from his lips. "Lucius."

* * *

Upon hearing Lucius's name, Prosperine rolled her eyes, and her lips drew upward in a sly grin. She slipped her hand inside a pocket of her dress and simulated pulling something from it. She ordered Apollyon,

"It is time to deliver your gift to my grandfather. Take it out. Now!"

She sensed Apollyon hesitate, and her eyelids popped open. Her green eyes pulsated with an eerie glow as she demanded, "DO IT! DO IT NOW!"

Beads of sweat dripped from Apollyon's brow, and biting his lower lip fiercely, Apollyon tried to resist Prosperine. He wavered. Her grip on him was too formidable, and his hand trembled as he reached inside his armor. Apollyon gritted his teeth, fighting with all his being to regain control over his body. It was not to be. Unable to stop, he removed his hand from his armor.

His face was as white as a sheet, and Apollyon held the urn before him.

Prosperine was drained and felt like she might faint. The power drawing from her body to control the Destroyer was waning. She slapped her cheeks until they were the color of a ghost pepper to stay awake. Her nostrils flared, and her lips pulled back, baring her fangs.

Sneering, snarling, her snake-like tongue spitting, she screamed, "Tell God his granddaughter Prosperine says hello!"

"OPEN THE URN! DAMN YOU, OPEN IT!"

Exhausted from fighting Prosperine's orders, Apollyon's right eye began drooping, and though he was still upright, his knees buckled, and he began to stagger. His jaw fell open, and as he pulled the lid from the urn, he cried out, "Lord, please forgive me. Prosperine says hello."

A thunderous blast shook the chamber. The anguished cries of a millennia's worth of tormented souls, released from the urn and howling in collective agony, set off a shock wave that pulsed through the air and roared through the chamber. The unprecedented discharge of energy broke the steely bonds of Heaven and barreled downward like a runaway freight train toward Earth.

CHAPTER 23

Christmas Morning
Jack Aitken's Home, Bristow, VA

By the time Jack reached his driveway, the red rain had stopped. He coughed up another mass of saliva and spit it out, still trying to get the bitter taste of the raindrops from his mouth. The smell of burning wood from a neighbor's fireplace permeated the air and reminded him how much he loved the smell and feeling of a warm fire on Christmas morning. Preparing to join in the avarice of opening presents, Jack paused, and a chill ran through him as the sweat on his body cooled.

Without warning, he heard a loud rumble, like a short clap of thunder. Instinctively, Jack searched the sky, expecting to see a military aircraft from Quantico Marine Base breaking the sound barrier on a training flight. Instead, he saw an explosion, like fireworks on July 4th, except it was daytime.

Wide-eyed, he murmured, "What the hell is that?"

Wiping the raindrops from his glasses with the inside of his sweatshirt to gain a clearer view, he saw many sparks, like shooting stars, firing in all directions. His eyes opened and closed several times in disbelief as the sparks continued to fall, unlike a fireworks display that quickly burned out. A few seconds later, he started to say, "That was no—"

Before Jack could finish his sentence, he heard a whistling noise and found himself rolling around on the pavement, clutching his ears. The stinging feeling caused Jack to recall attending a rock concert at the Jones Beach Theater on Long Island as a teenager. It was an open-air venue, and despite sitting in the nosebleed section, his recollection was a ringing in his ears, so painful that he and Amanda left the show early. Now, he felt as if he were standing in front of a wall of speakers in the first row.

Jack staggered to his feet. Pulling his hands away from his ears, he looked at his palms, expecting to see blood. *At least my ears aren't bleeding. That means I didn't perforate my eardrum.*

Jack's eyes rolled back in his head as he struggled to overcome the dizziness brought on by the blast. He stooped over but could not tell if the ground was still shaking. The ringing in his ears reminded him of a derecho that hit the house on Christmas Eve several years ago. He stumbled toward the bluestone path that led around the corner of the garage to check for damage.

He noticed cracks in several windows and dents in the siding, and on the opposite side of the house, a few asphalt roof shingles lay in the grass. After kneeling to retrieve them, Jack noted that the wooziness persisted, and he was still trying to regain his balance. Somehow, he got to the porch and sat on the front step, rubbing his fingertips in his ears to try to ease the constant ringing.

"I guess I will have to call the insurance company." Pulling his fingers away, he added, "If this ringing in my ears doesn't subside, I will have to go to urgent care."

"DAD! Is the house okay?" Jack heard a muffled voice and looked over his shoulder. David and Louis stood in the doorway, with Emma and Michelle behind them.

Louis shouted, "We've been trying to get your attention."

Jack could tell his son was yelling, even though it didn't sound that way.

"What was that noise?" Emma asked, gazing warily toward the side of the house that bore the brunt of the gust. "It sounded like a freight train."

"Probably a derecho." Jack tried not to shout. The ringing in his ears began to ease somewhat. "They can have hurricane-force winds. It's happened here before."

Still tugging on his earlobe, Jack pointed upward and asked his sisters,

"Have either of you ever seen something like this?"

Michelle's jaw fell open slightly, mesmerized by the scene in the sky.

Emma's eyes narrowed as she concentrated on what she saw, and then, never taking her eyes away from the light show above her, she remarked, "It reminds me of the sparks that fly when someone welds two pieces of metal together. I have never seen something like that, or at least not during daytime."

Michelle agreed, "Me neither."

Jack sniffed the air. "I smell bacon."

"DAMN!" Emma dashed down the hallway to the kitchen, yelling, "I forgot all about it! I hope it doesn't burn, or the smoke detector will go off."

Reaching out for Louis, Jack joked, "Help your old man up, will you?"

"Let's have some breakfast," Michelle suggested. "That should make you feel a little better."

Stepping into the hall, Jack hung his vest on the knob of the upstairs handrail. The bacon smell made him remember Christmas when, as a kid, his father would make breakfast, and he and George would fight over the last piece of bacon. Jack lowered his head, wondering where George might be at that moment.

A loud gurgling noise emanated from his stomach, causing Jack to salivate. It distracted him from thinking about his brother and immediately reminded Jack that he was famished. Before closing the front door, he looked over his shoulder and saw sparks still shooting across the sky.

From the living room, David shouted, "Hey! Can we open presents now?" Jack just smiled and locked the door behind him.

* * *

> Christmas Morning
> A Short Time Later
> The Holy of Holies

"All are from the dust," Azrael, the Angel of Death, whispered as he rubbed his closely shaven brown beard and knelt at the entrance to the Holy of Holies. The hem of his black robe, the color of mourning, hovered over the ashes on the chamber floor. A faint metallic smell hung in the air. Undetectable to Heaven's residents, Azrael recognized it immediately. It was the aroma of cremation.

His silver skullcap protected him from debris launched by the explosion that continued to fall from the sky. On his last visit to Heaven, a choir sang carols of praise, but now, there was no singing, just the sound of a gust scattering dust in all directions. He glanced up at the tattered curtain that gently waved above him and shook his head, adding, "And to dust, all return."

Azrael's everyday responsibilities included overseeing reapers who shepherded the spirits of deceased humans to Heaven's gate for their final judgment. He had been investigating the recent disappearance of one of these soul harvesters when he received an urgent request to return home. Actual fatalities and physical death were unknown phenomena in Heaven until an hour ago. The stunned angels needed his knowledge and understanding of mortality to process what was happening. Azrael knew death only too well. He wore black out of respect for it and had passed that tradition on to humanity.

Lesser angels, those humans martyred for their faith and thus permitted into God's presence, surrounded Azrael, awaiting his instructions. The expression on his face, which was always solemn, wore a far more somber frown that underscored the gravity of the current situation. Unfortunately, thus far, the mission had been one of recovery and not rescue. The elders were dead, mostly vaporized and lying on the ground in ashes. Azrael leaned on his dark walnut staff to help him stand up. His hand brushed across the solid silver image of a phoenix on top.

He mourned, "I am afraid that no one is rising from the ashes today."

Azrael stepped inside and could not believe the destruction. Following a massive crack in the flooring, he stopped in front of the steps that led to Christ's throne. The floor was scorched, likely the spot where the bomber had stood, and the blast shattered the throne into shards of jagged rock. Two angels approached, carrying a twisted piece of metal, which they handed him.

"What is this?" Azrael questioned. Examining it, he avoided touching the razor-sharp, jagged edges but saw some of the ornate markings and concluded, "This is Saint Michael's armor, is it not?" The angels nodded in agreement.

Pessimistic, Azrael lowered his head and asked, "And the Arch Angel, himself?"

The sad faces confirmed his worst fear. Saint Michael was gone. Dead.

Azrael sighed, and a tear rolled down his cheek as he moaned, "Even this armor, fashioned from the strongest metal, could not protect him."

"Sir, come quickly!" a voice called from the riser above him. "We removed debris from the throne, and there is a body."

Locking eyes with Azrael, the rescuer pointed. "It is the Christ! I think he is still alive!"

Azrael raced to Christ's side. Laying his ear on Jesus's chest, a rare but sober smile emerged as he announced, "He is breathing!"

Azrael grabbed Christ's shoulders and shook him. There was no response, so he pulled up Jesus's eyelids. The fire in his eyes was dim and flickering.

"He is still warm but unconscious."

Wide-eyed, Azrael glanced around and inquired, "The Father! Is there any sign of the Father?"

"Father, can you hear me?" Azrael yelled, but his voice just echoed through the chamber.

Beads of sweat ran down Azrael's face as he realized the danger they were now in, and he frantically instructed the rescuers.

"The Father is gone! We must hurry! Pick up our Savior! Carefully!"

Quickly making eye contact with each angel, Azrael explained, "Without the Father and with Jesus incapacitated, we must go into exile. Soon, Lucifer will realize what happened, recognize his advantage, and attack Heaven to secure it. Without the Father and Christ, we are defenseless against his power."

Hastily, angels fashioned a stretcher and placed the comatose savior on it with the utmost care. They hurriedly evacuated Heaven but were unsure of where they were heading. Looking back, Azrael observed smoke still rising from the ruins of God's sacred sanctuary.

Furious at what he saw, the Angel of Death took his staff and, like an Olympic javelin gold medalist, heaved it toward Earth while he screamed, "Father, where are you?"

***

Christmas Day
Near Midday
Pergamon

All morning, Lucius had watched with bated breath, first for the explosion in the sky, but now he wished to see the last fragments resulting from the blast burn out in Earth's atmosphere. Tapping the talons of his hand on the rooftop ramparts, he patiently waited for the conclusion of the epic event he had orchestrated.

His lips drew up in a wicked grin, and Lucius boasted, "I wonder how Lucifer will reward me for this achievement."

"Don't you mean us, Lucius?" a loud voice answered him.

The reflection of the sunlight from Lucius's dark, leather-like skin usually blinded subordinates, but it had no impact on Prosperine. She arrogantly strutted across the plaza, her black hair waving in the breeze. The sound of her stiletto heels hitting the stone floor echoed all around.

"Princess, I did not see you there." Lucius bowed. He was concerned she had overheard him bragging. He bit his lip uneasily. "Forgive me if I sounded presumptuous."

"Think nothing of it." Prosperine smiled coyly and waved her hand, dismissing Lucius's concerns. "This is a day of glory, and we do make a rather good team, do we not?"

Prosperine explained her role in ensuring Apollyon would carry out their plan. Envious of her capabilities but realizing the value of her contributions, Lucius flashed the ghost of a smile and maintained,

"It is you who Lucifer should reward."

Prosperine yawned and rubbed the dark bags under her eyes. "Possession drains you, and it is nearly feeding time." She licked her lips as she considered her next meal. "Right now, my thirst is as intense as any desire to be rewarded by my father."

A demon guard appeared in the distance and hesitated, wary of approaching them. Lucius thundered,

"Come forward! I see you have something for us."

The guard fell to his knees. Lowering his eyes, he handed a scroll to Lucius and stuttered, "It—it—it's an urgent message from Lucifer."

"Dismissed!" Lucius brusquely sent the guard away. Holding up the scroll, wearing a quizzical smile, he suggested,

"Shall I open it, Princess?"

Prosperine studied her fingernails as she indifferently answered, "Certainly."

Lucius read the message out loud. Not unexpectedly, Lucifer, notoriously stingy with his praise, did not mention Lucius's contribution to today's triumph.

"You and Prosperine will join me tomorrow as I enter Heaven and take my rightful place on its throne. I have waited an eternity for this! Do not disappoint me by being late!"

Her lip curled, and Prosperine sneered, "I hope Heaven lives up to its reputation! We still have the extermination of humanity to plan for."

"I am sure it will, Princess," Lucius whispered. "I am sure it will."

Prosperine departed. Despite the breeze, the bitter smell of myrrh from her ritual, like burnt rubber, still hung around Lucius. He turned around just in time to see the final flare slowly smolder and extinguish in the atmosphere. The blood-red sky, filled with the debris ejected from Australia's volcano and the remnants of what had been Barbados, seemed a fitting backdrop to the morning's events.

Lucius continued admiring it, declaring, "The shot heard round the world. The start of our revolution!"

* * *

Noon on Christmas Day
Jack Aitken's Home
Bristow, VA

Reaching into a kitchen cabinet, Jack pulled out a white box with cursive blue lettering; it read, "Fishermen's Wharf." He opened the tinfoil-lined packet, tossed two small motion sickness pills in his mouth, and chased them down with a big gulp of water. Jack moaned as he blinked several times to stop the room from spinning or, if possible, slow it down. Tugging his ear, he remarked,

"I hate vertigo. At least the ringing is starting to abate."

Holding the top of a kitchen chair to steady his gait, Jack carefully entered the family room, but not before picking up a tan envelope from the table. After practically falling into a chair, he opened it. Removing his glasses, Jack held in front of him a certificate he found inside and declared,

"Michele, this is a great gift you and Em got the boys." Trying to read without squinting, which only exacerbated his vertigo, Jack continued, "Getting custom-fit golf clubs is just what they need."

Flexing his right hand, which was sore due to the changing weather patterns, he added, "Hopefully, I'll be able to grip a golf club again."

Pausing for a moment, he muttered, "Soon."

Emma put her book in her lap and happily replied with a proud grin, "It is always great to hit a home run with a gift! Their excitement made it worthwhile!"

Humming "Joy to the World," Michelle crinkled up the newspaper she was reading, tossed it on the coffee table, and chimed in, "Em, I could not have said it better!"

Flashing her brother a smile, Michelle chirped, "Wait and see. Keep up the rehab; you'll be as good as new!"

"I'd settle for eighty percent," Jack joked. He tried his phone, but there was no reception. His eyebrows lowered, and he stared at the garage door with a look of concern, which his sisters could not help but notice.

"Still not working, Jack?" Emma questioned. Jack nodded and answered, "Not yet. It makes me wish I had not given up the landline. Perhaps that would still be working. Anyway, I wanted to wish Josephine and the kids a merry Christmas."

"Or find out when Anne is supposed to get here!" Michelle's lips drew up in a playful grin. Her voice was unmistakably teasing when she inquired, "I could not help but notice a card still on the living room table. I don't suppose that it is for Anne, is it?"

"You are so bad, Michelle!" Emma lightheartedly chastised her sister and gave Jack a thumbs up, saying, "The card you gave me was beautiful, Jack."

"Thank you, Em!" Jack winked at his sister.

*　*　*

Jack shoved a handful of salted caramel popcorn in his mouth and continued reading his gardening magazine. Once finished, he placed it in the rack beside his chair and sniffed the air.

"That candle smells great, Em," Jack gushed. "The smell of pine is perfect for the season! It fills the entire room, and I can hear the sizzle too!"

"That makes me two for two on gifts today!" Emma bragged.

Using the remote, Michelle turned on the television. The picture was out of focus and rolling, the sound filled with periodic bursts of static.

Putting the remote down, she declared, "That static sounds like the snap and crackle from the fireplace."

Perplexed, Jack commented, "It has been like this all day. It reminds me of our childhood and that old black and white set during a thunder and lightning storm. I am surprised we even have any service at all."

Michelle chuckled in agreement. "Yeah, the one that had five channels!"

Suddenly, several beeps came from the television in rapid succession. It was the familiar signal of the emergency alert system.

"Shhh!" Emma interrupted them and pointed at the television.

"There is a news bulletin coming on."

This activation of the Emergency Alert System will be followed shortly by a statement from the President of the United States. Please stand by. This program interruption is not a test.

Similarly, three beeps sounded again, and the screen was black with only a header indicating to stand by for an address by the President.

Instinctively, Jack looked around for David and Louis. Earlier, they had been unable to mentally connect to their teachers about the Christmas message they were to deliver. Somehow, Jack managed to distract them by sending them downstairs to play a few new video games. At this moment, he knew that a Presidential address would only fuel their anxiety, regardless of the content. Nervously tapping his fingers on the coffee table, he told his sisters,

"Something like this is likely to freak the two of them out. David, in particular."

Quickly glancing behind him, he whispered, "If you see either of them enter the kitchen, please let me know. I will have to do something to shepherd them out of there until I know what is happening and what to do about it."

Michelle gave Jack a thumbs up. "I'm guessing these service interruptions are far more serious than we originally thought."

A monotone voice, struggling to cut through the static, began to speak, saying,

Ladies and gentlemen, the President of the United States.

The President began speaking in a steady but subdued tone.

My fellow citizens, I am speaking with you this afternoon about the impact of an event that occurred early this morning. Most of us likely believed that the loud boom, followed by the fiery display in the sky that we witnessed, impacted only our immediate area. I am sure by now that most of you realize that the effect is more widespread. Cellular and Internet communications became unavailable almost immediately after the incident.

The President paused for several seconds. Jack and his sisters leaned forward with their ears and eyes glued to the high-definition television, straining to hear every word while processing what they meant.

While caused by an entirely natural phenomenon, the sobering reality is that this rare occurrence has resulted in an unprecedented natural disaster, a global catastrophe. Truthfully, it is like nothing the world has been confronted with before.

Jack glanced at his sisters. Michelle picked the nail polish off her, something she always did when she was nervous. Emma was stone-faced, but her jaw was slack in disbelief at what they had just heard.

Our leading scientific minds have concluded that a massive solar flare, hidden from our telescopes and other highly technical instruments, erupted and released a burst of energy strong enough to destroy most, if not all, satellites orbiting the planet. Although the 1859 Carrington Event, a documented incident like what we are experiencing, produced a solar flare somewhat comparable to this morning's event, its impact was minimal when contrasted with the technological age in which we live.

Jack ran his fingers through his hair and scratched the back of his neck. Whether it was the pills he took or the sobering medicine that Jack believed was about to be delivered by the President, his vertigo seemed to subside instantly. Blasts of static came through the speakers, and the President resumed speaking once it stopped.

The force of this energy wave has resulted in a severe deterioration in communications, and many areas are experiencing problems with their electrical grid. Unfortunately, the consequences of this have been tragic, including auto-related fatalities due to the failure of traffic lights and a loss of power in hospitals, causing patients to expire in the operating room. Many buildings, homes, and businesses have sustained significant property damage. Unfortunately, while challenges such as those we now face usually bring out the best in people, there have been incidents of looting.

Looking upward, Jack wondered, *"Joseph, is this the beginning of the apocalypse? It sure seems like it."* He closed his eyes and prayed for a sign. Meanwhile, the President's address to the nation continued.

Several planes have fallen from the sky when their instruments failed, and the loss of GPS signals is causing difficulty in finding the wreckage. The truth is that at this moment, in many respects, we are blind to what is happening around us. Fortunately, the Christmas holiday has limited what could have been a cataclysmic loss of life as most Americans are at home or visiting with relatives.

I have been in touch with many, but not all, state governors. While some remain out of reach, as Commander-in-Chief, I have requested the mobilization of the National Guard and all first responders in their respective states. I am sanctioning the implementation of martial law to maintain law and order and ask that you remain in and around your homes for the immediate future. Unnecessary travel is discouraged and could be banned entirely depending upon the gravity of the situation in each locality. On a positive note, landlines appear generally unaffected by what has occurred. This means of communication is still available to us.

The reality is that the aftereffects of this extraordinary event will impact us all for some time, and it may be months—or, more likely, years—before we are back to any semblance of life as we knew it before this morning. Let me close by saying that Christmas is about hope. While this is a holiday like no other in our lifetime, years from now, after we overcome the challenges we now face, we will be able to answer the question with pride, "Where were you when the world changed on that Christmas morning?"

"Turn it off, Michelle," Jack requested. "I think that is all the news I can stomach right now."

Jack's thoughts returned to Anne as he appealed to a higher power, "God, embrace her in your protective arms, and please bring her here safe to me."

CHAPTER 24

> *Christmas Night Around 9 p.m.*
> *Jack Aitken's Home*
> *Bristow, VA*

"I'm cold!" Louis rubbed his hands together and pointed. "Look, you can see my breath!"

The sentence echoed through the empty streets of Bristow. The air was crisp, and the light breeze stung Jack's red nose as he paused at a crosswalk. Jack instinctively looked for a "Don't Walk" sign, but the screen was dark. Linton Hall Road was usually a busy thoroughfare, but the tree-lined street was eerily empty. It would have been impossible to see without the moonlight, as none of the streetlights worked either.

Being a civic-minded citizen, Jack had heeded the President's request and left the car in the garage. It appeared that many people had joined him in that decision and had done him one better; they stayed home. The trio had walked a little more than a mile to his in-laws' house to exchange gifts and have dessert with them. Crossing the street, they were making their way home. Coming and going, they had not seen another soul.

Reaching the sidewalk, David chastised his brother, "If you had worn gloves like me, you wouldn't be cold."

Louis groused, "Leave me alone, David."

"C'mon, guys, let's not fight." Jack encouraged his sons, "It's not much further."

Turning the corner toward home, Jack glanced behind him. He frowned and rubbed his chin. All he could hear were their footsteps, and while they had not seen anyone, he could not shake the feeling that someone was following them. Jack shrugged off his suspicion and quickened his pace.

Their white house with its black shutters came into view, and he was hopeful that Anne would have made it by then. His anticipation turned to disappointment as he realized her car was not there. Louis and David kicked a rock back and forth between them, lagging behind their father. Jack passed their mailbox with the name Aitken in black iron letters on top of it and headed up the driveway toward the garage.

BOOM!

Jack found himself face down on his concrete driveway for the second time that day. Unlike this morning, he did not feel a sense of vertigo, only an intense heat flash. Still on his stomach, Jack turned his face toward the warmth, and his eyes flickered several times. He was in shock. Where his home once stood was now a fiery crater. Shattered glass, splintered wood, and twisted pieces of aluminum siding were everywhere.

Glancing at Zinnia and Liam's house, he saw their tan vinyl siding melting into long strings, pooling on the ground like maple syrup poured over pancakes. The glass windows of the neighbor's home on the opposite side were all blown inward, and there was a gaping hole in the side of their garage. A broken gas main shot a pillar of fire into the air. Jack saw a figure emerging from the inferno in front of him. He hoped it was one of his sisters. It wasn't.

* * *

"Hello, Jack," George mockingly addressed his brother, then yanked him up by the collar of his jacket.

Their faces were inches apart as George affirmed, "I've been waiting a long time for this."

George tossed Jack like a rag doll across the yard. Jack felt a sharp pain in his back and realized he had landed on a jagged piece of siding. He reached for it, but his brother was standing over him before Jack could yank it out. With an icy stare, the elder twin grabbed a handful of the younger's salt-and-pepper hair and pulled him up. Then, George seized the shrapnel, causing Jack to wince in pain.

He twisted it, saying, "Isn't this what you always said I was good at, Jack? Putting the knife in and twisting it."

George's maniacal grin matched the intensity in his bloodshot eyes. He ripped the metal from Jack's back, causing his brother to gasp in agony. Jack retaliated, punching him in the head, but George held the bloody piece of metal in Jack's face and asserted, "It's easy to hurt others when you cannot feel the pain yourself! Let's consider us even now. You broke my ribs when we were in college. I just returned the favor."

* * *

Louis stood wide-eyed and slack-jawed, stunned by what he saw. David whispered to his brother, "I've got to help Dad!"

David rushed his uncle and, raising his right hand, slammed him in the back of the head. Seemingly unaffected by the blow, George dropped Jack and faced his nephew. He looked David in the eye and carefully approached him. David backpedaled as his uncle grabbed him by the arm.

"So, it seems that you are no longer protected, David. I promised I would come and take you away."

"I'm not going anywhere with you!" David shouted and tried to pull away from his uncle's grasp.

"Wait! Look!" George pointed in Louis's direction.

Louis struggled to escape one of George's demon team members, who had his hand over the young man's mouth. Louis's brown eyes were wide open, betraying his terror—two black Cadillacs with heavily tinted windows pulled to the curb. The chrome of their bumpers was so shiny the flames danced in the reflection. George shoved his nephew to the ground and waved to another team member.

He curtly ordered the demon, "Put him in the first car with his brother."

* * *

Clutching his side, Jack rolled away from a bubbling puddle of water on the ground next to him. The smell of rotten eggs was everywhere, and he realized what it meant.

The explosion broke the gas main leading from the street to the house.

On his hands and knees, Jack struggled to get to his feet. George knelt, pointed at the watch on his wrist, and taunted him,

"You always say that the longest ten minutes of your life was between when I was delivered and your subsequent birth. How have the last ten minutes felt?"

Using his index finger, George raised Jack's chin, locked eyes with his brother, and, with a dismissive sneer, insulted Jack,

"The truth is you have always been number two, Jack. Do you know what I mean? You are a worthless piece of shit, and I will rejoice when you are gone!"

Bruised and battered, the metallic taste of his own blood filled Jack's mouth. Spasms of pain ran through his body, and Jack asked George, "Why are you doing this?"

"It's really quite simple, Jack," George professed. "Do you remember our favorite movie, *The Godfather*?"

Jack, nearly out of breath, answered, "I remember."

"Good," George replied coolly. "And like Michael Corleone, I settle all family business today."

"Family business?" Jack asked, grimacing from the pain in his back.

George smoldered with resentment. It was difficult to discern between the smoke rising from the explosion and the wildfire smoldering in George's eyes.

"All my life, I have worn the chains of other people's expectations. Everybody wanted me to be what they wanted me to be."

His temper spiked. "Like Dad wanting me to be your protector!"

George's rage nearly consumed him, and he seethed, "Do you remember the pit, Jack?"

Bloody spit fell from Jack's lips. "We were twelve."

"YOU RAN!" George thundered.

"To get help," Jack countered.

"YOU LEFT ME THERE!" George viciously slapped his brother with the back of his hand, sending Jack rolling along the ground.

"All our life, I have been your personal bodyguard."

George brutally kicked his brother. Jack groaned, "I never asked—"

Wild-eyed with anger, George screamed, "THEY RAPED ME, JACK!"

* * *

Jack looked up and saw the suffering on George's face. Despite the savage beating, he still felt compassion for his brother and said breathlessly, "I'm so sorry, George. I didn't know."

Like a switch, George's demeanor went from blind rage to calmness. He collected himself and said, matter of fact, "The party's over, Jack. We, you and I, have reached a point of no return."

"Don't say that, George. It's never too late."

"There's the difference between you and me, Jack. You've always gambled on the good in me. This time, you've lost, and now, it's time to pay the cost."

"What are you saying?"

"Listen to this." George snapped his fingers, and a loud explosion, followed by a fiery cloud, came from the direction of Amanda's parents' home.

Jack willed himself to his feet and demanded, "What did you just do?"

George responded bluntly, "Killed Amanda's parents. Saved you the trouble of worrying about their interference in your life forever."

Before Jack could react, George shoved his fingers into Jack's wound. Jack's back arched in an excruciatingly painful contortion, and he gasped for air.

"Lynne. Our nieces and nephews." Waving his thumb over his shoulder toward the smoldering ruins of Jack's home, he went on, "Emma. Michelle. All dead."

Jack's mouth fell open in disbelief. His thoughts immediately went to...."

"Anne." It was as if George had read Jack's mind. "Blown up, too."

Jack's body slumped until he was left prone on the driveway. George whispered in his ear, "Checkmate, Jack! You lose. Once my Master finishes with you and your sons, I will have severed ties with my entire past, except for my own family, who I will dispose of in good time. You saw the fire in the sky this morning. The gathering storm has arrived, and you won't survive it."

George paused, adding, "As it has always been, Jack, I am the storm."

Jack glanced over his shoulder at the hole where his house once stood. A thought came to him that he never believed would have been possible. Jack begged God to allow him to find Saint Michael's sword so he could kill his brother. His mind raced from memory to memory of his loved ones. All of whom were now gone. Dead. He stared at the car holding his sons and could hear their pleas for his help and their fists pounding on the windows as they tried to find a way to escape. A picture of Anne's face, like a picture from his wallet, hung in his mind.

He gritted his teeth and ruefully acknowledged, "I should have left you for dead. You would be better off that way."

* * *

George pulled at his goatee, a vicious smile on his face. Jack's despair made his victory complete. Two demons mercilessly dragged Jack across the lawn and roughly shoved him into the back seat of the second car. George turned to bask in the flames rising from the pit that had once been his brother's house. His triumphant smirk quickly morphed into a surprised frown when he saw a hand emerge from inside the crater. He quickly reached the edge and saw his sister, Michelle, dangling over the inferno raging at the bottom of the hole.

George squatted like a baseball catcher and remarked, "Aren't you the fortunate one, Michelle?"

Michelle glanced upward. Blood ran down her temple, and black patches of charred skin hung from her face. Smoke from the burnt ends of her hair encircled her head. She fought to maintain her grip on the tree root she had managed to find. Astonished, she muttered,

"I must have a concussion. I can swear that looks like George."

"Ah, but it is me, Michelle," George replied. Glancing around, he remarked, "You are in a bit of trouble, aren't you?"

Michelle begged, "Give me your hand."

Her fingers began to slide, stripping the tree bark off the root, and her plea intensified. "I think I broke my arm. I can't hold on. Please!"

George grabbed Michelle's wrist, which stopped her from slipping further into the pit. A wave of relief washed over her.

"Thanks, George. Now pull me up."

Ignoring her request, George instead asked her a question.

"Speaking of breaks. Do you remember what the doctor said when I broke my arms simultaneously?"

Michelle's eyes narrowed as she replied in frustration, "I don't remember. Something about a clean break, I think."

"That's right!" George exclaimed. He leaned forward, and as he let go of his sister's wrist, he added, "That's what I am doing here. Making a clean break!"

Losing her grip, Michelle seemingly hung in mid-air before she began descending into the hellhole below. The look of terror on her face, bulging eyes, and flailing limbs desperately grabbing for something to hold had no impact on George other than to cause him to smile and wave goodbye as she screamed.

Then, George heard a moan emanating from the wreckage.

"Somebody, help me," Emma cried out. She asked, "Jack, are you there?"

George slowly walked in the direction of the voice.

Emma glanced up, and her eyes narrowed, puzzled by what she saw. She questioned, "George? Is it really you? Where have you been?"

George stood over his sister with a stare as cold as ice.

"What are you doing here, George?" Emma questioned. Then, she pleaded, "Brother, help me."

Tilting his head sideways, George unfeelingly answered, "Why? Do we know one another?"

Devastated by her brother's callous response, Emma took one last breath and succumbed to her massive injuries.

* * *

George stoically watched his sister expire. His thirst for killing sated for the moment; he opened the door on the passenger side of the first car and peered in on his nephews. Their eyes were wide open with fear. This reaction pleased George but simultaneously repulsed him. He ridiculed them, saying, "So much for God's prophets."

Louis sniffled as a tear ran down his cheek.

Enraged by what he perceived as weakness on his nephew's part, George scoffed, "Just like your father. No guts! You both sicken me!"

As the car pulled away, a few neighbors from down the street who were home for Christmas and witnessed George's assault on his brother stepped forward to confront the remaining demons sitting in the second vehicle.

One neighbor knocked on the window and demanded to know, "Where are they taking those kids?"

Still another stepped in front of the car, insisting, "You're not taking Jack anywhere!"

Wearing a vicious smile, the driver glanced at his sidekick in the front seat and floored the accelerator, running Jack's neighbor over. The tires burned rubber, and the car fishtailed as they drove away, both demons laughing.

Attending to their severely injured neighbor, the small group of good Samaritans took no notice of a piece of Jack's optimistic note to George or his Christmas card to Anne, dancing in the draft caused by the inferno. Nor did they see the edges catch fire and the phrase "I Love You" being slowly erased from both by the flames. Instantly, the remnants became charred embers that gradually floated to the ground.

CHAPTER 25

Christmas Night 9:30 p.m.
Back Seat of a Cadillac
Bristow, VA

"AAARH!"

Jack made a guttural sound in response to being tossed around the back seat during the demon driver's hasty getaway. The throbbing ache in his side taunted him as he gingerly crawled up from the floor. Surveying his surroundings, all Jack could see were tinted windows, so dark that there would be no way to know if it were daytime. Flexing his injured right hand and looking at his wrists, he wondered why he was not wearing handcuffs.

Still gritting his teeth from the pain, he muttered in frustration upon realizing his unexpected freedom of movement would do him no good.

"Now I see why George is so sure of himself and didn't bother to zip tie or restrain me. There are no handles on the damn doors."

A barrier with a pocket-sized peephole, only accessible from the front seat, prevented him from seeing his captors. The musky smell of sweat oozed from his shirt, which Jack pressed into his wounded torso to slow the bleeding and remain conscious. He knew he needed to stay focused and find a way out for Louis and David's sake.

He stared straight ahead as if he had laser vision like Superman and could burn a hole through the barrier and track the car carrying his sons. Images of his sisters', nephews', and nieces' faces flooded his mind. The cries he heard from outside the vehicle filled his ears, and he wondered which courageous neighbor died trying to protect him. Of course, there was Anne, too. Jack scratched the back of his neck and knew, deep in his heart and soul, things did not look good.

Jack closed his eyes, drove the heartbreaking visions from his brain, and cleared his head. Opening them, he spoke calmly,

"I'll cry later. First, I need to figure out where the hell they are taking us."

The car slowed down to make a right turn, which Jack surmised was onto Linton Hall Road. He pounded on the barrier with his fist, and the demon riding in the passenger seat opened the small window and peered in at Jack.

Laughing while thinking about running over Jack's neighbor, he pretended to be concerned. "Are you okay back there? I hope it isn't too bumpy of a ride."

Ignoring the sick reference to the person they had just run over, Jack challenged him, demanding, "Where are you taking us?"

Before the demon could answer, the driver slammed on the brakes, sending Jack flailing about the car and back to the floor again.

* * *

Just ahead, an ocean blue-colored car with lights flashing and the words *Prince William* County painted on its side emerged seemingly out of nowhere from a dirt road. Despite the dampness of the night, it kicked up a cloud of dust and stopped in front of the Cadillac, obstructing its way. As the dust settled, in the shadow of the headlights stood a tall, hulking figure dressed in a police uniform and wearing a broad-brimmed hat like Smokey the Bear. The officer drew his weapon and pointed it at the driver.

"Don't move!" He approached the car slowly and shouted, "Keep your hands on the wheel where I can see them!"

"Reverse!" the demon in the passenger seat shouted. "Throw her in reverse."

Instinctively glancing in the side-view mirror, the surprised driver responded, "I can't!"

A large, dark green SUV quickly pulled within inches of the Cadillac's bumper, boxing them in. The SUV door flew open, and a person not dressed in a uniform jumped out. The figure headed deliberately toward the passenger side of the Cadillac, aiming something in front of them at the window.

Rattled, the driver asked, "What do I do?"

Pulling a pistol from his coat pocket, the demon partner grinned, revealing a row of jagged, yellowed teeth with serrated edges like a great white shark, and boldly boasted, "These humans can't hurt me! Sit tight. I'll take care of it."

The door barely opened.

WOOSH!

Driven backward, the cocky associate slumped into his seat; his body fell on its left side. The demon's eyes were wide open, staring at the driver. His jaw hung slack, and several drops of blood fell onto his lips and spilled down the demon's chin. The tip of an arrow that pierced the dead demon's forehead emerged from the back of its head.

"Shit!" the driver shouted. Frantically pushing the body away, he heard a rapping on the window and an angry voice barking orders.

"Get out of the car slowly and get down on your knees with your hands behind your head!"

Tasting the reflux of his last meal, the driver slowly turned the handle on the door and pushed it open a crack.

The massive police officer, clutching his weapon tightly, angrily cautioned the demon, "I'm not going to tell you again. Get the hell out of the car, NOW!"

Holding his hands up, the driver exited the vehicle and sank to his knees as directed. The steely-eyed cop placed his pistol next to the demon's head.

"CLEAR!" the officer shouted out loud.

A light fog had begun to form, and out of the mist stepped a figure. The driver squinted, but then his eyes opened wide. Completely surprised, he recalled the deck of playing cards Lord Aitken had given the team in his pocket and slowly uttered, "It can't be you. You're supposed to be dead."

* * *

Jack heard someone say, "You're supposed to be dead," and the door opened. A strong yet feminine hand reached in, and a familiar voice told him,

"It's okay, Jack. You're safe now."

"Anne, is it really you?" he asked optimistically but moved too quickly, and stabbing pain in his side caused him to groan.

Anne leaned into the opening, and Jack's eyes lit up like a Christmas tree. He grabbed her hand tightly, and she helped pull him from the vehicle. They stared briefly at one another, each incredulous that the other was alive. Anne buried her face in Jack's chest. The intensity of the rain increased, pinging angrily on the car's roof as he embraced her. Steam rose after each drop that hit the hood of the running vehicles.

Breaking away, Anne anxiously asked, "Where are Louis and David?"

Jack took a deep breath, then answered, "George took them in a different car."

Anne's demeanor instantly altered. Her eyes glazed over, and her jaw tightened. She raised the crossbow she had been holding in her hand and, rushing forward, pointed it at the kneeling demon.

"Where is the other car heading?" Anne commanded. When she didn't get an immediate response, she pulled the trigger, and an arrow embedded deep in the demon's shoulder. He screamed in agony.

"I know that hurts. I soaked the arrows in holy oil. The next one is going to a different part of your anatomy."

Anne targeted the demon's groin area.

"Tell me what I want to know, or you'll be singing soprano."

"Okay. Okay," the driver stammered. Knowing he was likely to die one way or the other, he confessed,

"They are going to the Bradford House tonight and then plan to take the prophets to Pergamon."

"Thanks," Anne said glibly, then let the arrow fly right through the demon's head, killing him before he hit the ground with an audible thud.

"Ross, can you handle the cleanup?" Anne asked gruffly.

"Go, Captain. I will handle everything."

Anne slung the crossbow over her shoulder and, marching past Jack, asserted, "We'll get them back, Jack. Get in the car. We'll cut them off where Route 28 meets Route 29 outside Culpeper."

Jack opened the door. A damp odor filled his nasal passages. He thought, *"Smells like wet—"*

A long, red tongue licked him from his chin to his nose.

"Dog." Jack managed a smile despite the circumstances. "Hello, Daphne. I'm sure happy to see you!"

The cocker spaniel's nub of a tail rapidly wagged back and forth. Jack scratched her ears, then carefully pulled himself up into the SUV.

Anne reminded him, "Buckle up, Jack." She put the car in reverse and floored the accelerator. "We're about to hit warp speed!"

* * *

Simultaneously
Route 29 South Toward Culpeper

"Go faster!" George Aitken urged his driver to put the pedal to the metal as he gulped down the last of his daily elixir. He held the empty container in his hand, but before replacing the cap, he placed it under his nose and inhaled.

George scratched his cheek while his tongue rolled back and forth across his teeth. Then, shrugging, he tightened the cap and placed the flask in his coat pocket.

"I'm going as fast as I dare to, my Lord," the driver nervously responded, never taking his eyes away from the road. "The fog is getting thicker, and the highway is slick from the rain."

A stale, musty odor from the defroster caused George to open his window as a loud burst of static suddenly filled the car, causing the driver to flinch. He tightened his grip on the steering wheel as a voice came over the ham radio, *"India, Juliet, Two, Kilo, calling Zulu, X-Ray, Four, Quebec."*

George grabbed the handset and responded, "Zulu, X-Ray, Four, Quebec. I am receiving you, Barbas. Go ahead."

"Lord Aitken, I am reporting from the Bishop home blast site."

"It has taken you long enough," George curtly responded. "I heard from every other target hours ago."

George licked the blood from a small cut on his finger sustained during the beatdown on his brother. He heard a loud *C-R-A-C-K* in the background and asked, "What was that?"

Barbas answered, "The blast created a firestorm. The surrounding pine trees are ablaze, and branches are snapping off."

"I see." George reacted indifferently.

"We are still searching through the rubble for the body, my Lord," Barbas continued. After a lengthy, uncomfortable pause, he added, "Sir, the house is in splinters. There is barely anything left. It's possible we might not find—"

Frustrated, George cut Barbas off. "I don't want to hear Anne Bishop is dead," he shouted into the handset. "I want to see her dead. Find her body, Barbas!"

Angrily slapping the switch and turning off the radio, George listened to the wipers rubbing and squeaking across the windshield as the car barreled toward Culpeper. He glanced at his nephews, captive in the back of the vehicle. Their anxiety was apparent as Louis rocked back and forth in his seat, and David was talking to himself, uttering the same sentence repeatedly.

The cold wind shifted and started blowing the road spray into the car. George clicked the button to shut his window and turned away from the driver. He stared out into the darkness of the rainy night. The image of Emma, his sister, lying dead on the ground hung in his mind. A singular tear formed in his eye, fell onto his cheek and slowly inched down his face.

* * *

Simultaneously
Route 28 Toward Route 29

Anne's SUV skidded into the intersection where Linton Hall Road met Route 28. Despite the wet pavement, the tires smoked as she made a sharp right turn while maintaining a high rate of speed. The smell of burnt rubber filled the air as she floored the accelerator with no regard for the darkness of the road ahead.

"Something big has gone down, Jack," Anne claimed.

Gently pushing Daphne into the back seat, she confessed, "I'm not sure what, but it is more than just your brother's rampage."

Glancing down, she saw the blood oozing through Jack's shirt.

"We have to treat that wound." Anne slammed the cigarette lighter into its socket with the palm of her hand. "The only solution is to cauterize it. We need to stop the bleeding. When that pops out, you need to shove it into the wound, front and back."

Gazing at the console, Jack chuckled weakly, "I didn't think they had cigarette lighters in cars anymore."

"They don't," Anne replied. "This is a 2017 Toyota Sequoia. I bought it off the lot. It stopped being standard after that."

Anne fixed her eyes on the road while counseling Jack on what to do. "I won't lie. It will hurt like hell, but you need to push up and in the hole in your side while the lighter is glowing red."

Jack gulped as nervous beads of sweat formed on his brow. It felt like the lighter would never pop out. Jack tried distracting himself from what he was about to do by rifling through the glove compartment. He pulled out a blue ballpoint pen and asked, "Anne, how did you escape? George told me you were dead."

"Truthfully, I should be," Anne responded, pulling her cell phone from her pocket and handing it to Jack. "Turn it on, and you'll see what saved me."

Eyeing the cigarette lighter with uncertainty, Jack pressed the button on the phone, which, in the darkness of the vehicle, lit up with an eerie yellow glow. He read a text message:

Get out of the house now!

The lighter popped out, and the loud clicking noise startled Jack. He put Anne's phone down and took a deep breath before pulling the plug from the outlet in the dashboard. An odor like burnt toast filled Jack's nostrils, and the reddish-orange glow from the brass coils hinted at the heat emanating from it.

"Do the wound in your back first," Anne suggested. "You'll need to use your left hand, which is not your dominant side. Having a firm grip and keeping your hand steady is important. That is harder to maintain after you seal the first wound, and despite the injury, you will want to use your right hand for that."

Jack clamped his lips together firmly and looked at Anne through the corner of his left eye with shock and awe before replying, "You sound like you've done this before."

"Not exactly, Jack," Anne countered. "But something close to it. Pain will cause your hands to shake. Under those circumstances, it will be better if the second time is with your dominant hand."

"Okay, Anne. I get it."

Trying to divert his thoughts from the pain he knew would follow, Jack asked, "Who sent the text?"

Placing the pen between his teeth, without hesitation and before he could change his mind, Jack plunged the red-hot circular wires of the lighter into his back.

"*GRRR...*" Jack bit down on the plastic in his mouth, almost shattering the pen, and attempted to suppress a scream. The pain was blinding, and the sickeningly sweet smell of burnt flesh filled the vehicle.

"Good, Jack," Anne quickly looked down and reassured him. "Now, you have to do the front one."

Jack took several rapid breaths. His eyes rolled backward, and every pore in his body seemed to release sweat simultaneously. Beads of perspiration rolled down his back. Jack watched his trembling right-hand struggle to keep a grip on the lighter, but before it could cool down, he thrust it into his wound like someone might use an EpiPen. The lighter hit its mark, and a sound like pan-fried, sizzling steak radiated from his body.

The pen dropped from his lips, and through his gritted teeth, Jack reminded Anne, "You didn't answer my question."

Sensing they were near their destination, Anne's focus on their surroundings intensified. She responded to Jack without getting sidetracked, "I don't know. It is not a number that I am familiar with."

Reaching behind her, she patted her beloved dog on the head and managed a slight smile. "Fortunately, Daphne needed to go out, and I found it early this morning."

Anne paused, then added, "Along with something else that I will show you in a little while."

Jack handed Anne back her phone. His side was throbbing, but the bleeding had stopped.

"I don't understand it, Anne," Jack remarked while clutching the armrest as they approached a bend in the road. "Louis and David are no longer protected."

Anne saw a road sign she recognized, pointed, and declared, "Route 29. We're here."

She pulled the vehicle to the shoulder and locked eyes with Jack. "First, we get them back. Then we figure out what happened to their divine protection."

Jack nodded and heard a noise from the rear of the vehicle.

"What is that?" Jack asked.

"A surprise," Anne answered. "I'll show you. Come on; we must get a spike strip from the trunk."

* * *

As they approached the back of the car, the racket got louder. Anne hit a button on her key chain, and the trunk sprung open. Someone with duct tape over their mouth, trying to speak, with zip ties on their wrists and ankles, was lying there. Their eyes were wide open with fear, and beads of sweat fell from their forehead to the black carpeting below. Anne grabbed a pair of cut-resistant Kevlar work gloves and dragged out a long metal belt with sharp spikes attached to it.

Ignoring the trunk occupant, she explained, "Ross, the police officer who helped us, is a friend of mine. He was my driver with the Prince William County force. Ross is not JESU, but I trust him with my life."

The light from the trunk reflected on the metal strip as Anne examined it. "He got this tread shredder for me and will clean everything up back in Bristow."

"Who's this guy in the trunk?" Jack asked as he reached under the feet of Anne's prisoner and grabbed a hammer and spikes to secure the strip to the ground.

"That is one of George's henchmen," Anne grumbled as she unfastened the lock on the strip. The captive uttered a muffled scream as Anne slammed the trunk shut and started dragging the tread toward the highway.

The duo struggled with the weight of the strip. Anne gave Jack more details through her grunts and groans. "He is part of a team your brother sent to kill me. I had no time to interrogate him, so I took him for the ride."

Finally, they reached the other side of the highway and dropped the strip to the ground. Winded, they both leaned over, gasping for air. Anne finished catching her breath, and due to Jack's injuries, she hammered the spikes to secure the tread shredder. Returning to the car, Anne grabbed her crossbow and slung it over her shoulder, declaring,

"Once we get Louis and David back, we will head away from Bristow. I know a safe house in West Virginia. We can go there and get answers from the SOB in the trunk to the questions that we both have."

Anne found some underbrush to shield their presence. The night air was cold and damp. The smell of the wet grass under their feet was pervasive. She was all business, and while they waited, she told Jack what would happen next.

"The spikes puncture and flatten the tires." Grabbing Jack's shoulder, she cautioned, "If they are going at a high rate of speed, it could cause the car to flip. If that happens, we'll have to move even faster in case of a fire."

Waving her index finger, she reminded Jack, "Don't sacrifice good judgment for speed. We cannot let our guard down. Let's hope the fog and rain cause them to slow down."

Jack felt a knot in the pit of his stomach. Thinking about Louis and David made his mouth dry, but he hung on Anne's every instruction.

"We've entered the world of no mercy." Reaching into her coat, she pulled a pistol and clicked a bullet into the chamber. She handed it to Jack, telling him, "I soaked the shells in holy water. When you pull the trigger, go for the head."

The drops of rain that began to fall exploded like bursting bombs when they struck the back of her leather coat. Looking over Jack's shoulder, she scanned the highway for lights that would tell them a car was approaching. There was no sign of any yet. Checking Jack's wound one final time caused him to flinch, but she clasped her lips tightly together, satisfied that the procedure had been successful. She grabbed Jack's cheeks in her hands and held his head steady while she read his eyes.

"Leave George to me," she pleaded. "Despite everything he has done today, you still think he is redeemable, that you can somehow get through to him. This way of thinking is a blind spot that could get the boys killed."

Jack's eyes lowered, realizing that Anne was right, but she persisted,

"You're also in no physical condition to confront him. You said that the only other demon in the car is the driver. Get David and Louis to safety. I will deal with your brother."

Suddenly, two headlights became visible in the distance.

"It's showtime, Jack," Anne reminded him, bravely smiling. "We're going to get them back. Right now!"

Anne felt the adrenaline running through her body, a familiar sensation that her training, both with JESU and the police, had taught her to channel and use to her advantage. Her reflexes, perfectly tuned like a Steinway piano, were ready to spring into action at a moment's notice, and that moment of truth had arrived. Her focus was single-minded, to save Louis and David, but one other thought ran through her head:

God, I hope Jack will forgive me when I have to put George down!

* * *

Simultaneously
Route 29 South Nearing the 28/29 Intersection

Straining to see through the fog, George's driver updated him on their progress. "Lord Aitken, at this rate of speed, we should be at the barricade leading to the Bradford House in about thirty minutes."

George ordered, "Try reaching the car carrying my brother again. They haven't checked in yet." Rubbing his upper lip, he whispered, "Something doesn't feel right."

"Yes, my Lord." The driver reached for the handset and spoke into it, "Zulu, X-Ray, Four, Quebec to Charlie, Lima, Five, Victor. Do you copy, over?"

Like a freight train, the speeding jet-black Cadillac raced into the Route 28/29 interchange.

BOOM! BOOM!

Two loud noises in rapid succession were followed by the vehicle shaking violently. The car skidded sideways, and the driver turned the wheel back and forth in an attempt to regain control of the Cadillac while yelling,

"I think we ran over something!"

Checking the side-view mirror, the driver saw sparks flying from the road and shouted over the screeching as he jammed on the brake pedal.

"Sir, we've got a blowout of all four tires. We're riding on the rims!"

The car slowly came to a halt. George checked his nephews, who were frantically looking around, unharmed but visibly shaken by what was happening. He warned the two of them, "Do not move a muscle, either of you."

Barking at the driver, he commanded, "Do not give up the prophets, no matter what happens!"

The gray smoke from the smoldering tires merged with the fog, and George recognized a familiar voice calling from the mist.

"I want my sons back, now, you son of a bitch!"

Slowly opening his door, George leaned out and replied in the direction of his brother's voice, "You will have to come and get them, you pathetic piece of shit!"

"Let them go," a voice behind him ordered. "Or I will put an arrow through your fucking skull!"

George closed his eyes. Grinding his teeth, he angrily muttered, "Anne Bishop, I am surprised you are still alive."

"I'm full of all kinds of tricks," Anne tersely replied. "Now you and the driver get out of the car slowly, and I mean slowly, damn it."

Anne called out, "Jack, I have George in my sights. The driver is coming out now."

Jack closed his left eye and pointed the pistol at the driver's side door. The door opened, and as the driver stepped onto the road, a shot rang out, killing him instantly. He dropped to the ground in a heap.

"Okay, Anne," Jack yelled. "One demon down. Dead, just as we planned."

Jack moved forward as quickly as his body would allow him. He threw open the car door and peered inside. His sons, jaws slack and eyes wide open, sat in the back seat in shock.

Jack beckoned. "Louis. David. It's Dad. Come on out. You're safe now."

Neither of them moved.

Jack spoke firmly, "Boys, time to go. Move it!"

David bolted from the seat with Louis right behind him.

The smell of burnt rubber, coming from the smoldering remains of the shredded tires, was everywhere. George appeared from behind the car with his hands in the air. It had been raining for most of the evening, but the precipitation now included a mix of snow and sleet. The frozen raindrops bounced off George's shaved head and hung in his course goatee, forming icicles.

Anne held her crossbow high, ready to pull the trigger. George glanced down at the dead driver and saw his brother emerge from the darkness, pointing a pistol in his direction.

George remarked sarcastically, "I guess I was wrong about you, Jack." His lips drew up in a sick grin. "I did not think you had this in you!"

"How could you do it, George?" Jack screamed at him over the hiss of the burning rubber. "You killed Emma, Michelle, Lynne! You killed them all!"

"I did what was necessary, Jack." George's twisted smile remained. "Like you did just now."

Jack's hands shook, not from fear but in fury. He stood his ground but stayed beyond his brother's reach. Jack locked eyes with George and scornfully sneered,

"I don't care if we are twins. I am nothing like you!"

A tear rolled down Jack's face. Never taking his eyes off George, he pointed toward the Route 28 highway sign and shouted at Louis and David, "Anne's green SUV is over there. Daphne's in the car, and I want the two of you to go there and check on her. NOW!"

Neither son hesitated. They took off like lightning bolts, heading to Anne's car, and soon vanished into the darkness.

Jack heard the Arch Angel Gabriel's words in his head.

Lucifer is my brother. You have a brother, too, Jack. Tell me, would you kill him if he were a murderer? Would you put his head in the noose? Would you give the order to pull the trigger or flip the switch yourself?

Then, a single bark and the slam of car doors echoed through the night. With Louis and David out of view, Jack turned his full attention back to George and remarked, "Whoever or whatever you are won't change one fact; you won't give up. You'll never stop."

Jack's now icy stare countered George's depraved look.

"I can see it in your eyes."

Jack lowered his gun, and he told Anne,

"Do it. Anne, shoot him!"

Anne let her arrow fly before the echo of Jack's command disappeared. Shot through the eye, George collapsed like a ton of bricks. There was a loud thud and then silence.

Anne raced to Jack, and they embraced. Anne's hair, covered in snow, made her appear to have aged in a matter of minutes. On the other hand, Jack felt every bit of his nearly fifty years and then some. The adrenaline of the moment left him, and he leaned on Anne for support.

"Come on, Jack," Anne whispered. "Let's get you to the car and get out of here."

Jack exhaled, nodded, and whispered, "This isn't the first time you've saved us, Anne. Thank you for protecting Louis and David, just like you promised!"

As they walked from the intersection, they still could hear the sleet clicking on the remnants of the Cadillac. Jack turned to look over his shoulder one final time at his brother's lifeless body. He shook his head in disgust and despair.

Anne stopped him and ran her nearly frostbitten fingers down his cheek. The water vapor condensed in the air like a cloud as she tried to reassure him,

"That wasn't George anymore. That was a monster who took over your brother's body. You had to do it. He gave you no choice, Jack. He gave you no choice."

"Now I understand how Frankenstein felt about his monster." Jack wiped another tear from his eye. "I created this monster and, as a result, had to destroy it."

* * *

A Few Hours Later...

A coyote crossing Route 29 searching for a meal appeared in the darkness. Driven by hunger, the predator moved forward and sniffed George Aitken's lifeless body. Accidentally jarring the arrow with its snout seemed to cause the body to twitch, which caused the cautious animal to step back several feet. The rising smell of death, which drew the scavenger in, changed, and a different odor emanated from the corpse. The coyote whimpered, and even in the face of its growling stomach, the now overwhelming stench eventually drove the ravenous scavenger away.

CHAPTER 26

> *Friday, December 26th*
> *Abandoned Reymann Brewery Building, Wheeling, WV*
> *8:00 a.m.*

The gravel of the abandoned road crackled under the tires as Anne's SUV stopped, jarring Jack from his semi-conscious state. He sat up, stretched, and yawned while groggily asking, "What happened?"

Leaving the headlights on as it was still dark, Anne stared out the windshield, studying their surroundings. A breeze picked up a few brown leaves from a pile on the ground and pushed them across the hood of the car. She shoved a piece of chewing gum in her mouth and answered,

"You dozed off again outside Youngstown, Ohio, while I explained how the bomb scares were trial runs for all of yesterday's explosions."

Resuming her reconnaissance to confirm that George's henchmen did not follow them, she pulled a bottle of holy water from her jacket pocket and shook it while whispering, "While you slept, and using my powers of persuasion, our stowaway in the trunk confessed everything. Holy water may seem a simplistic weapon against evil, but it is quite effective."

Ever cautious, she finished checking the rear and side-view mirrors for anything suspicious and faced Jack. "George planned it all for months. Killing your family cemented his loyalty to Lucius."

She held Jack's hand as he took a deep breath and exhaled, processing what Anne had said.

Anne smiled gently. "I think I drove the 400 miles from Ocean Isle Beach in six hours. That must be some record."

Despite his grief, Jack reciprocated and smiled back. "I guess you forgot that 95 was the route you were on, not the speed limit sign."

He took another deep breath, looked out the window, and questioned, "So, where are we?"

"We're at an old JESU safehouse in Wheeling, West Virginia," Anne answered, while shutting the engine and headlights off. "It looks like it has not been used in decades."

Jack glanced behind him at his sons, leaning against one another, still asleep in the back seat. Guilt ran through his conscience as he recalled what he had told David and Louis last night. They were upset about the death of their aunts, and rather than console them, he had said, "Have one more good cry, but after this, no more tears."

Jack wondered if he had done the right thing and how he could strengthen his sons' coping skills in the coming days. As Anne had suggested, he also sensed something much more severe was occurring than George's attempt to kill all of them, but what? That was the question, for the moment, that remained unanswered.

Jack strained to see anything. Finally, through the darkness, his eyes were able to make out an imposing structure: a warehouse-style building with a red brick exterior. The sumac trees growing in the interior confirmed it had been abandoned years ago. The painted lettering on the outside wall was faded, yet the name *Reymann's Brewery* remained visible. The digital clock on the dashboard read 8 a.m. Jack frowned.

"It shouldn't be this dark at this time of the morning. I guess this is related to the explosion in Barbados or maybe the volcano in Australia. Regardless, it's eerie."

Looking at the missing and broken windows on the upper floors, he half-joked, "Could this building get any creepier? It looks like something from a slasher film."

Anne opened the glove compartment, pulling out a flashlight. She suggested, "Let's check the place out."

The pain in Jack's side caused him to wince as he stepped out of the vehicle. He gingerly shut the door, and Anne triggered the locks using a button on her keychain. The cold morning air sent a shiver down Jack's spine, fully waking him as they approached the building. Anne waved the flashlight from side to side, looking for anything unusual. Entering through a hole in the wall that had once had a door, they could hear water dripping from icicles on the rafters into puddles at their feet. Passing the light across the ceiling revealed a massive cavity that seemed to go up through the roof.

"It is rank in here!" Jack moaned as he curled up his nose and tried only to breathe through his mouth. "It smells like my lawn mower after I cut the wet grass in the summer, but I don't clean it thoroughly. It bakes in the garage, and due to the heat, what a stink! But this smells 100 times worse!"

Still fanning his nose, Jack looked up again. Worried, he queried Anne, "Are you sure this place is safe? It looks like it could collapse at any moment."

Anne's eyes finally adjusted to the darkness. She pointed to a corner with the flashlight and declared, "That way, Jack."

Stepping around debris on the floor, she explained, "This used to be a German brewery back at the turn of the last century. The roof is gone in other areas, but that corridor remains intact. They stored the finished beer there. I remember hearing about an office. We can set up the boys while we take our demon friend down the hall to the storage room for another talk."

* * *

Friday, December 26th
Linton Hall Road, Bristow, VA
At the same moment

FWEEET! FWEEET!

The reluctant police officer conducting traffic wrapped his cold, blue lips around his metal whistle and blew two shrill warnings. While holding his hand up, stopping traffic in one direction, he gestured to start it moving the opposite way.

Ross Martin, a more than thirty-year veteran of the Prince William County Police force, turned up the collar on his jacket against a frigid, beastly wind and jammed his hands in his pockets. He glanced at the forbidding sky and thought, *It seems terribly dark, even for this time of year.*

Still using his flashlight, Ross stepped under the yellow crime tape and headed toward the Black Cadillac parked in the right lane of Linton Hall Road. Fortunately, with the day after Christmas being a Friday, commuter traffic was light, but the ongoing crime scene investigation had forced the police to redirect traffic anyway.

Ross peered into the front seat through the open driver's side door. "Are we nearly finished here, doc?"

A tow truck pulled up behind the vehicle in anticipation of finally moving it. Tufts of ash blonde hair spilled out from under the ski cap worn by the coroner. She shivered as the cold wind blew down the back collar of her orange jumpsuit.

Looking up at Ross, she replied, "Yeah. Here come the guys with the body bags, now."

The flash of a camera caused Ross to squint. He scanned the car and noticed a partially opened plastic bag with white powder spilling out.

"What do you think?" Ross's eyes met the coroner's. "Looks like a drug deal that went bad."

The coroner nodded. "Looks like it." Carefully sweeping the powder into an evidence bag, she stated, "When I get back to the lab and test this, I'm betting it's heroin."

She stepped away from the passenger door and watched closely as her assistant slowly pulled the victim from the vehicle. The coroner examined a wound in the victim's face, and with a flick of her finger, the aide yanked the full-length zipper up and placed the cadaver pouch on a stretcher for transport.

Across her chin, she rubbed her yellow rubber-gloved hand and remarked, "Hell of a thing, though," Moving her finger in a circular motion, she added, "Seems like an unusual place for a drug deal gone bad."

Still too dark to see, Ross held the flashlight between his teeth and began writing on a notepad. Without stopping, he mumbled, "Bristow used to be a low-crime area, Doc. Things are changing, though, and not for the better."

Glancing at her watch, the coroner asked skeptically, "Ross, does it seem unusually dark to you?"

Replacing his notepad in his jacket pocket, he answered, "I thought it was me."

Ross watched as a funeral director loaded the body bag containing the second of the two dead men into a hearse and told the coroner.

"I'll get you my crime scene analysis by early next week." Then he inquired, "When do you think you'll finish the autopsy?"

"Tomorrow morning at the latest, Ross." The coroner clapped her hands to get the blood circulating in her fingers. "Without any identification, we'll have to put these guys on ice in the morgue to see if any family comes looking for them."

* * *

> **A Few Hours Later**
> **Prince William County Police Headquarters,**
> **Woodbridge, VA**

Tap! Tap! Tap!

Ross had nearly finished his crime scene report using his hunt-and-peck typing style. He reached for his roast beef sandwich and took a ravenous bite. Investigations were routine for someone who had been a police officer for so long. Thus, Ross had little trouble making last night's rescue scene look like a drug-related murder. Patting his jacket, he confirmed that the arrow-like bolts from Anne's crossbow were in his possession. Ross knew that the coroner would easily mistake the wounds for gunshots.

Only the most astute coroner would recognize the difference, and with the victims being John Does, he was sure this would go unnoticed. Ross glanced out the window, and while it had lightened up outside, it still seemed very dark. Raising the sub to his lips, Ross sank his teeth into the Italian bread and continued staring into the gray, overcast sky.

I hope Anne is okay, wherever she is right now.

Anne and Ross had been partners for years. As a good detective, he could sense that Anne had secrets, but he didn't care. She was a great cop and an even better friend. Anne had been there for him when Ross's marriage had gone belly up. She had covered for him more than once when he had drowned his sorrows in a case of beer and was too drunk to be on the job. He owed her, big time.

So, when she asked for his help with last night's rescue, he did not ask questions and had no guilt about covering up what had happened. Anne told him it was a life-or-death situation and that she couldn't tell him much more.

CRUNCH!

Ross bit into a dill pickle spear. His lips puckered from the sour taste. One of his fellow officers came over and dropped a piece of paper on his desk.

Ross asked, "What's this?"

"Look at the picture." The fellow officer chuckled. "After yesterday's explosion and losing all those satellites, we're back to 'wanted dead or alive' posters."

Ross picked up the paper and immediately recognized the face. He did his best to hide his reaction, but his heart began beating faster.

"Have you seen him around, Ross?"

Ross shook his head negatively and didn't say a word.

"They say his name is Jack Aitken. He is from Bristow."

"What do they want him for?" Ross asked, suspiciously.

Looking around the precinct, the colleague whispered, "His house blew up last night!"

Concerned, Ross frowned and probed for more information. "Why is there an APB on him?"

"Get this, Ross." The officer became animated, talking with his hands, and answered, "Calls were coming in today from all over the country, trying to track this Aitken guy down."

Ross's eyebrows narrowed, and rubbing his finger in his ear, he questioned, "Why?"

"There were simultaneous explosions everywhere, just like Aitken's house."

"That's weird," Ross conceded.

"It's weirder than that, Ross." The officer searched the room again before continuing, "His entire extended family is dead! It's like someone, maybe Jack Aitken himself, severed themselves from their family."

Ross's jaw dropped. "My God. That is unbelievable."

"Just keep an eye out for this guy, Ross," the officer cautioned as he walked away. "Be careful if you run into him. Who knows what he is capable of doing."

His co-worker was gone; Ross was dumbfounded. He muttered, "Jesus, what did I do, and what has Anne gotten herself into?"

Ross quickly hit the save button and e-mailed his report to his home computer to finish up later. Racing to his squad car, he thought, *I hope I can track Anne down before it's too late.*

* * *

Friday, December 26th
Under a Highway Overpass on Route 95 South
4:00 p.m.

Even at high noon that day, darkness had never entirely relinquished its grip. This unusual phenomenon allowed the night to descend quickly, and only the headlights of an occasional car or truck could pierce the dark veil enveloping the countryside. The highway overpass provided little protection from the heavy rain that had continuously fallen since daybreak. Still, the Strigoi, soaked to the bone, stood on the shoulder of I-95 with Route 40 above him, staring at the flashes of lightning illuminating the sky, waiting for the weather to pass.

As the raindrops fell from his sharply pointed nose, he understood that shapeshifting was proving to be a valuable capability. It allowed him to observe people up close, without being detected. Uncertain if it was his consumption of massive amounts of human blood in the past or something previously triggered in his primal brain, his knowledge of human behavior was growing exponentially. Now, disguised as a young man with jet-black hair, he meditated on the questions that dominated his thoughts.

Who am I? Where do I come from?

Glancing northward, he pondered where to head next when he noticed two lights flickering in the distance. The white beams drew closer, but a loud noise preceding their arrival was unmistakable; it was a tractor-trailer. Nearly blinded by the headlights, the Strigoi held his hand in front of his eyes as the truck pulled onto the shoulder and stopped before him. The window on the passenger side of the truck cab came down, and a face with a full beard popped into the opening.

Wearing a dingy baseball hat with the brim folded downward on both sides, the driver said,

"Helluva night to be stuck out here. Can I give you a lift somewhere?"

The Strigoi hesitated, unsure of precisely how to respond. After a few awkward seconds searching his growing vocabulary for something to say, he answered robotically,

"Okay."

Climbing into the seat, he added, "Thank you."

The trucker checked his mirrors and pulled the big rig back onto the highway. As he pushed the accelerator to get up to highway speed, he handed the Strigoi a towel to dry off.

"Name's Roy White."

Pointing toward the trailer behind them with his thumb, Roy stated,

"I'm delivering these heat pumps to Florida. It's been colder than normal down there."

The Strigoi nodded. Still unsure of what to say, he stared nervously out the window.

Roy White glanced at his new passenger and inquired, "You got a name, son?"

The Strigoi turned and answered, "Reid. Reid Bowman."

*　*　*

Friday, December 26th
Abandoned Reymann Brewery Building, Wheeling, WV
4:00 p.m.

"It's so dark outside," Louis Aitken announced while looking out a broken window at the pitch-black sky and swiping the flashlight app on his cell phone, which did not work.

Disappointed, he shoved the phone into his pocket and moaned, "My battery is dead."

"Mine too," David added. Staring at the outline of their parked car still visible in the alley below, he longingly said, "I wish I could go out to the car and charge it. I'm bored and want to play a game."

"Dad said no, David," Louis cautioned, as a big brother does to his kid brother. Glancing around, he moved closer to David, saying, "Don't leave me here alone. This place is scary."

A small fire flickered in a metal garbage can in a corner of the room. It was the only source of light or warmth. David dropped a piece of scrap wood they had gathered into the container; placing his hands closer, he tried to warm them.

"It is getting colder in here," he told Louis as he shivered. "But at least I don't have to listen to the banging from the trunk anymore."

Peeking down the corridor, David heard voices—his father and Anne and one he did not recognize. He could not understand the words but remembered the sound of a smack that echoed down the hall occasionally. A similar sound occurred when he punched his father in the head a few weeks ago.

"I miss talking to my friends," Louis loudly sighed. He rubbed away the tears from his eyes as he stared into the flames.

David agreed but whispered, "Yeah. I miss our teachers too. I haven't heard anything from Heaven, have you?"

"No," Louis responded, wiping his nose with his sleeve. "Not a word."

* * *

"AARH!"

The demon gnashed its teeth as Anne poured holy water on him again, raising painful boils and bloody blisters on his skin.

SMACK!

Anne slapped him across the face with the back of her hand. He could barely see her as one of his eyes had swollen shut. Jack Aitken stood, leaning against the wall with his arms folded. His face suggested he was content to let Anne torture him for information.

Defiantly, he told Anne, "I've told you everything I know, you bitch!"

SMACK! SMACK! SMACK!

His boldness brought immediate and painful retaliation.

Spitting blood on the floor, he taunted her, "You know, for a woman, you hit pretty hard."

Anne turned her back, and the demon heard two clicks. She reached into a case on the table.

"What's that in your hand?" the demon asked, as Anne turned around.

"This is a Mughal dagger." Anne presented it to the demon.

It had an elaborately carved handle made from green and white marbled jade, shaped like a horse head. The horse's bridle, fashioned from pure gold, glinted in the light of the fire from the oil drum next to them. The bottom of the handle had flowers on each side with petals made from red rubies. Etchings of the cross were at the top of the silver blade, which curved into a needle-like, visibly sharp point.

Anne continued, "It is a weapon made explicitly for the Mughal Emperor Babur, who ruled India in the 16th century."

She locked eyes with her captive, saying, "To kill the rakshasa."

"What the hell is a rakshasa?" the demon asked.

"It's Hindu." Anne ran the blade tip across the demon's cheek. Smoke filled the air, along with the smell of charred flesh, as he cried out in agony. She icily added, "For a malignant demon."

The echoes of the screams reverberated throughout the building as she added another long, matching, black scar to the demon's other cheek.

"Tell me how to break the spell and restore the prophet's protection," Anne demanded. "Or I will shove this in your eye!"

Her hand moved the blade forward slowly until the tip was millimeters from the demon's eyeball. The captive blinked several times but then grinned mockingly and began laughing in a deep, guttural tone.

* * *

Anne wiped the dagger blade clean and tossed the rag into the dying flames in the oil drum. Returning the dagger to its case, she declared unemotionally, "No person, or demon, could take that amount of pain. He would have told us."

She turned in Jack's direction and added, "He didn't know anything about Louis and David's loss of protection."

Anne noticed Jack's face had turned an ashen shade of white. Gently stroking Jack's shoulder, she asked, "Are you okay? You don't look so good."

Jack ran his fingers down his cheek. "I've seen entities these last few years that, even in my worst nightmare, I could never believe even existed." He flexed the fingers of his right hand, thinking about the Strigoi.

He bowed his head and scratched the back of his neck. "Hell, I've done things." Jack paused and locked eyes with Anne. "Killed things."

Shaking his head, he muttered, "The ability of people to do ugly, evil things to one another."

Jack sat on an old fermenting barrel and continued, "I thought I had seen it all but the eye . . . the eye. I didn't expect you to stick the blade through the demon's eye. I know you threatened to do it, but I did not think you would, you know, actually do it."

Anne's eyes cast downward as she replied, "I know it is hard to watch, but when you have dealt with demons and seen evil as I have, you understand that you do what is necessary."

Meeting Jack's gaze, she reiterated, "I will do whatever I have to do to protect Louis and David. Anything."

Jack nodded and embraced Anne, saying, "I know you will." Still hugging Anne, he asked, "So what do we do with him?"

Breaking their embrace, she pulled the demon's cell phone from her pocket and held it before her. She shoved the cell phone into the demon's mouth, saying, "Send a message. That's what we do."

* * *

Friday, December 26th
Ross Martin's Patrol Car in Front of Jack Aitken's House
8:00 p.m.

Ross slammed the door, turned the key in the ignition, and put the heater on full blast. Slipping on his gloves to warm his hands, he murmured with frustration, "I have been here for hours and gone through this lot from corner to corner, and I can't find one damn thing that tells me where Anne might have gone with this Aitken guy."

Just then, a call came over the radio.

"*Ross, this is dispatch. Are you there? Over?*"

"Dispatch, this is Martin. Go ahead."

"*I have an urgent message here saying you must call your sister.*"

Ross did not have a sister. He knew the message's meaning.

"Copy that, dispatch," Ross responded, like any other call. "I'll be 10-7 for a little while."

"Ross, I copy. We'll mark you unavailable."

Ross quickly turned off the squad car transmitter, grabbed his ham radio, and turned it to frequency 155.475. He shouted into the receiver, "Anne! It's Ross. Are you there?"

* * *

Ross watched the video on his ham radio receiver for the third time, still wide-eyed with disbelief.

Shaking his head, he asked skeptically, "Twins?" He sat back in his seat and admitted, "They definitely have a similar appearance. I give you that. You must agree that it seems more than coincidental."

"Ross, I promise you, I am not in danger," Anne answered, reassuringly.

"Jack and his brother were—" Anne caught herself and continued, "are identical twins."

"Anne, do you think this animal bite and subsequent rabies diagnosis caused his brother to have a mental breakdown or something?"

"I don't know, Ross," Anne replied. "But I needed to react quickly when I discovered what his brother was plotting. That's why I reached out but couldn't tell you anything. Jack is devastated by what happened. He has been through so much with losing his wife that I thought it best to get him away from the media. You know how they can be."

Ross acknowledged, "That I do, Anne. As long as you are okay, that is what is most important. I tied up everything here, so don't think twice about that."

"That was why I called Ross. I wanted to ensure that I didn't leave any landmines for you to step on. You're a great friend, and we both appreciate what you are doing."

"I'm just glad I remembered the super-secret code phrase about my sister calling," Ross said as he smiled. "It is a miracle that I never let anyone know I do not have a sister."

"I grew up an only child but always thought of you as my brother," Anne responded. "And I always will."

Anne saw Jack, Louis, and David emerge from the brewery and approach the car.

"Ross, I must go now. You take care of yourself, you hear?"

"10-4, Anne. You do the same. Stay out of trouble!"

Anne clicked off the radio and stared at the receiver in her hand. She sighed, realizing this might have been the last time she talked to Ross. Her training told her that avoiding further contact with him was the best way to ensure his safety. Moving forward, plausible deniability benefited them both.

* * *

Jack glanced at Louis and David sitting in the back seat of the SUV and ran his fingers through his salt-and-pepper hair. He hesitated and reluctantly asked, "Anne, are you sure we have to do this?"

Anne shoved her hands in her pocket to keep them warm and emphatically replied, "Absolutely! There is no way around it, Jack. We run the risk of being tracked if we don't."

"I'm not sure you realize what you are asking." Jack nervously pulled at the stubble on his chin. "This is going to be bad. Usually, I must manage the reaction of one of them. This decision risks sending both into a rage."

Snow flurries began to fall as Jack tried to figure out the best tactic to use for the circumstances they were in. It was nothing personal toward Anne, but he wished Amanda were there at that moment. She had a way of calming a stormy situation that Jack lacked. He knew there were no good options.

"Okay, we might as well pull the band-aid off," Jack moaned as the flakes began collecting on his head. "Let's talk to them separately and perhaps reduce the risk of their negative reactions feeding off one another."

Unenthusiastic, Jack's shoulders slumped as he walked toward the car.

* * *

"Dad's coming, David." Louis leaned forward, trying to read the expression on his father's face. Already anxious, Louis continued, in a higher-pitched voice, "He doesn't look happy."

"I hope we're not in trouble," David whispered, while squeaking his sneakers on the rubber car mat. His hands gripped together in tight fists like he was preparing for a fight. "I don't like it when he gets angry."

Louis sat back and began rocking as he was apt to do when trying to calm himself. He started pulling at the cuticles surrounding his fingernails, causing one to bleed. He was too nervous to feel the pain.

Jack opened the car door and tried to maintain an even tone of voice as he said, "David, I need to talk to you for a few minutes." He continued, peering in at Louis with a half-hearted smile, "Outside the car, okay?"

Slipping out of his seatbelt, David left the car without saying a word. Jack gently pushed the car door shut. He knew slamming it too hard would cause David to think Jack was angry, which would instantly agitate him. Jack led David in front of the vehicle, where Anne joined them.

Jack looked at Anne, hesitated, and then told his son,

"David, we need to take your phone," Jack let the news sink in for a moment and resumed speaking. "You may not know this, but your phone lets people track where we are going."

The young man glanced back at the car and his brother sitting in the back seat. He made no eye contact with his father when he softly asked, "So, I can't play any games?"

"You can play games, David," Anne interjected. "But not on the phone."

Anne pulled her phone from a pocket in her jacket and showed it to David, "I am getting rid of my phone too."

David's eyes followed Anne as she walked to the reservoir's edge next to the brewery and tossed the phone into the snow flurries.

S-P-L-A-S-H.

They heard the phone hit the deep water below. Following Anne's lead, Jack added, "I have to get rid of mine too."

Anne put up her hand to stop Jack and said, "We'll get rid of everyone's phone, but each in a different place."

Jack held his hand out, hoping David would turn his phone over without a fight. David wavered and then pulled out his phone. Seemingly ignoring his father, David handed it to Anne instead.

Surprised by David's reaction, Jack nodded approvingly at Anne. As David returned to the car, he whispered, "Impressive, Ms. Bishop. Very impressive indeed."

Having witnessed what happened, Louis bolted from the car and ran for the woods, screaming, "I'm not giving you my phone!"

Jack yelled, "Louis! Come back!" He took off after his son, shouting, "Anne, make sure David gets in the car. I'm going after Louis!"

Louis ran for a few minutes, then stopped to catch his breath. Looking back, he realized the snow was sticking to the ground, and his footsteps were easy to follow. Before he could start running again, his father caught up to him.

"Dad, please don't take my phone," Louis pleaded. "How will I keep in touch with my friends?"

A cloud of water vapor enveloped Jack as he replied, "Louis, I understand. I know, and I am sorry, but there is no other way."

Louis, grief-stricken, as if someone close to him had died, begged Jack with tears running down his cheeks, "I need my friends. Please don't take my friends away from me, Dad."

Jack rushed forward and embraced Louis, who collapsed in his father's arms. Inconsolable, Louis sobbed as Jack gently took the phone from his son's hand and dropped it in his pants pocket. Jack exhaled, and as Louis cried, he knew: *I just took my son's entire life away from him.*

* * *

> Friday, December 26th
> The Catacombs Under the Antonescu Home,
> Lake Waccamaw, NC
> 11:00 p.m.

The unusually severe thunderstorm for late December raging above Lake Waccamaw released a flash of lightning so intense that it illuminated the unseen cave entrance beneath the now-vacant Antonescu mansion. The ensuing clap of thunder shook the ground as a solitary figure stood at the opening, staring into the abyss. After seeing familiar landmarks along the highway, the Strigoi had Roy White drop him off and then headed straight for the lake.

The creature wondered,

It was strange that I did not feel the urge to kill and drink the blood of Roy White. Why?

Reid Bowman's doppelganger sniffed the air and caught a whiff of several familiar scents, one of which caused it to scowl in disgust. The ancient animal, sensing no danger, fearlessly entered the cave. Despite the chamber's darkness, the Strigoi saw everything, including the deep gouges in the mud from the struggle with the powerful entity that had unthinkably vanquished the Strigoi.

Flashbacks of the encounter caused it to flinch. It had a similar reaction earlier to seeing a yellow ribbon wrapped around a tree above a makeshift gravesite outside the Antonescu compound. The modest memorial was nestled in pine needles under a grove of trees. It was the site where the Strigoi had attacked and drained the blood of a young woman. These memories unsettled the beast.

The Strigoi could not understand why these things were bothering it. The brute searched for something, anything in the blackness of the cave to quiet its thoughts. A faint odor, undetectable to a human but not to an animal, filled its nostrils, the smell of burning. The beast dropped to its knees and groped blindly on the muddy floor of the cavern for its source.

Something crunched under his fingers. The Strigoi held the object up and studied it.

"Paper?" it commented, unsure where or when it had heard the word before.

The creature inhaled. The smell of the paper sparked something in its primitive brain. Inexplicably, it began examining the charred remnants and found a few letters it recognized.

"L-U-C . . ." The creature stopped, sneered, and then growled, "LUCIUS!"

Continuing the search, it came across a few more. "A-N-T-O-N . . . Antonescu." The word rolled off its tongue. The beast did not understand why, but at that moment, the image of a young woman with red hair appeared.

"Maricela!" The Strigoi blurted the word out, and a strange sensation came over it; the same feeling it had staring into the eyes of the last human it had killed—the body of the woman it had covered with a tarp to protect her from the rain.

It was not a good feeling, but the Reid Bowman imposter brushed it aside to look at one last piece of paper. It could still see the words *A-T-L-A-N-T-A and G-E-O-R-G-I-A* through the blackened edges.

"I've seen G-E-O-R-G-I-A before," the monster mumbled. "But where?"

Suddenly, the Strigoi's fiery red eyes opened wide. Ignoring the storm, the beast raced from the cave and, high-jumping the brick wall of the Antonescu compound like an Olympic athlete, headed toward the highway.

Its heart beating like a drum, the Strigoi reminded itself, *Look for a vehicle with a Georgia license plate.*

CHAPTER 27

> *Saturday, December 27th*
> *Ghawar Oil Field Eastern Province of Saudi Arabia*
> *Noon*

Oil field operator Tariq Shalhoub parked his pick-up truck next to well 666 and pulled the oil-stained, red bandana hanging around his neck above his nose. Like dead fish in a cannery, the smell emanating from oil that only hours earlier had laid deep in the Earth for millions of years hung everywhere. He grabbed his tablet, ready to record the daily output. Working for Saudi Aramco, the state-owned oil company, paid well, but keeping the 3,000+ wells running at total capacity was challenging. Tariq glanced at his watch and flicked it with his finger several times to make sure it was working correctly. Usually, when looking at the sky at this hour, he would wear sunglasses and still use his hand to shield his eyes, but not today.

Clad in blue overalls, nearly blackened by the oil they unceasingly brought to the surface, a five-person drilling team waved to Tariq, then got back to work operating their rig.

"Tariq!" He heard someone call his name over the noise of the equipment and turned around. A short, heavy-set man with a deeply tanned complexion, black hair, and a matching trimmed beard filled with grains of sand approached him.

"Farouk, how the hell are you?" Tariq smiled and firmly shook hands with Farouk Khouri, the rig supervisor, and his former boss.

"I am well, my old friend. It has been too long since you made your way out here, Tariq."

Farouk pointed at the sky and said, "If I did not know better, I would say it was 1991, and Saddam Hussain has blown up more oil wells."

"I cannot remember a sky so dark at midday," Tariq agreed. Patting Farouk on the shoulder, he asked, "Do you have the output figures for last week? I need to add them to my report and then take some samples to measure the quality of the oil."

"It's good to be in charge, eh?" Farouk joked. "Follow me. I have them in the office."

Suddenly, the ground shook, and the sand shifted under their feet. The men grabbed each other's arms for support. As quickly as the tremor started, it was over.

Unnerved by the sudden shaking, a wide-eyed Tariq checked around him for its source. Farouk scratched his temple with his calloused fingers and told his friend, "That is the third tremor already today ... And they are getting more intense. The company scientists insist that Saudi Arabia is not in an earthquake zone, but the last few weeks suggest otherwise. I should check the equipment to ensure there is no damage while you log in the figures."

* * *

An hour later, having logged the production figures, Tariq joined Farouk's team on the rig to take some crude oil samples. The loud, continuous noise from the drilling equipment and the whining from the pump jacks were deafening and made communication difficult. Periodically, a flash of fire would erupt overhead from the flare stacks, burning off natural gas, a byproduct of the drilling process.

"How are the production figures looking?" Farouk shouted over the machinery noise.

"Let me put it this way," Tariq answered with a smile. "Ghawar is in no danger of losing the title of the largest energy source on the planet."

Teasing his ex-boss, Tariq chuckled, "And, for once, your well is contributing its share!"

Tariq placed the test tubes filled with crude oil into a styrofoam container and yelled,

"You need to date and initial the seal, Farouk." Farouk nodded and went to grab the pen Tariq handed to him.

Without warning, a tremor, more potent than the earlier one, began rocking the oil derrick back and forth. Several crew members tightly gripped the infrastructure of the well and held on while Tariq found himself thrown to the ground. Loud popping noises, the bursting rivets that held the steel frame of the well together, caught Tariq's attention. He looked up in open-mouthed horror, unable to even scream, and instantly perished under the twisted metal of the oil derrick that came crashing down.

"NOOOO!" Farouk screamed as he saw Tariq disappear under the wreckage. The shaking and shifting sand prevented him from having any chance to help his friend.

Sticky, black oil was everywhere; it gushed out from the surrounding wells, coating everything, and caught fire when the flames from the flare stacks ignited it. It seemed like the air itself was on fire. Pipelines that carried crude away from the wells burst open, releasing a river of greasy, sulfuric-smelling fossil fuel, oozing over the desert.

BOOM! BOOM! BOOM!

Like an artillery barrage, explosions rocked the 3,200-square-mile oil field. The blast at well 666 sent Farouk hurtling through the air while killing his crew instantly.

C-R-U-N-C-H!

On his hands and knees, trying to shake the dizziness from a blow to his head, Farouk heard a slow rumble, like a thunderstorm, but beneath him. Fissures formed in the sand, and he crawled backward to avoid them. Gradually, a gash-like crack opened and consumed

Tariq's truck. Similar openings appeared as far as Farouk could see, and flames, like hellfire, erupted from the fractured earth.

It only lasted a minute or two, but the shaking felt like an eternity to Farouk. Still feeling the aftereffects, he stumbled to his feet.

"Jahannan," he whispered in Arabic. "I must be in Hell."

Firestorm. Conflagration. These words flashed through Farouk's mind as the flames devoured everything around him. At his feet, the scorched sand fused into a glass-like sheet. To the horizon, the fire flickered like a snake's forked tongue, and, looking upward, it appeared to reach into Heaven. A feeling of loneliness swept over him, despair like none he had experienced. Farouk thought *I am the sole survivor. No one could endure this.*

* * *

Saturday, December 27th
Abandoned Reymann Brewery Building, Wheeling, WV
5:00 p.m.

A gust of wind caused the weakened beams of the vacant structure to creak and groan as Jack headed to the entrance of the abandoned building. He raised his shirt and shined a flashlight on his torso, trying to gauge the healing of his wound. A sweet, musky odor filled the air. Jack could not tell if it was from the injured area or if he needed a shower. Fortunately, there was no drainage from the site, and it did not have an angry red color, so he knew there was no infection. The cigarette lighter had done its job.

He tucked his shirt back in and ran his sneakers through the brown snow that had collected where the door to the brewery used to be. It had snowed several inches the night before, but the color of the precipitation was like tree bark, not cotton balls. As unusual and even unnerving as the pigment of the snowfall was, Jack had more significant problems to face. After taking their phones and disposing of them earlier in the day, the brotherly love between David and Louis rapidly evaporated.

Louis began crying over losing his phone, but David, not wanting to hear about it any longer, had started viciously hitting his brother on the head. While not acceptable, this behavior had typically been David's way of reacting to Louis's moods. Usually, it blew over, but this time, Jack had to intervene to spare Louis a severe beating like the one he had sustained at David's hands weeks earlier. Physically separating the two of them had temporarily defused things, but it was not a solution to the problem.

Anne joined him, and, grabbing Jack's elbow, she asked, "What are you thinking about? It's David and Louis, isn't it?"

Jack stared into the gloomy forest surrounding the building, which seemed deep and mysterious, and answered, "Yes. I'm afraid you are getting a crash course in managing autistic behavior."

"I suppose that was going to happen sooner or later," Anne said reassuringly. "I will follow your lead, so let me know how to help."

"Tonight, we'll have David stay with you in the front seat," Jack reasoned. "I will plan to sleep in the back and try to talk to Louis without setting David off."

W-O-O-F!

Jack managed a smile as he glanced down and reassured Daphne, "Don't worry. You can sleep with us too."

He scratched Daphne's damp, floppy ears and sighed, thinking about David's reaction to Louis's understandable moping.

"I am sorry you have to witness this." Jack itched his forehead. "We—Amanda and I—always tried to prevent the family from seeing the boys this way. We were not embarrassed so much as we did not want anyone to see negative behavior and associate it with them. After all, they manage stress the only way they know how."

Jack's thoughts drifted back to his dead sisters. He felt tears welling in his eyes and paused to brush them away. Then, he added, "We always wanted the memories to be happy."

His voice trailed off. "I think we were pretty successful..."

Anne calmly encouraged him, "Jack, you should be proud of Louis and David. They are amazing young men, particularly considering the obstacles life has thrown at them." She sought to comfort Jack and asserted, "That is what I believe if you are concerned about what I might be thinking."

Jack closed his eyes and exhaled deeply. "Thanks. I needed to hear that."

* * *

A strong north wind made Anne shudder as they gathered more firewood. While the derelict building provided some shelter from the elements, with most of its roof gone, the dilapidated condition of the structure made it unwise to sleep in it. A chill ran down her spine, thinking about another long, cold night in the car with only the periodic running of the heater to keep frostbite at bay.

Anne whispered to Jack, "I know you realize this arrangement with the car won't work long term. I saw that the gas gauge was running low. As difficult as David and Louis's behavior is right now, their limited diet is another complication that will only escalate moving forward."

Loaded down with an armful of wood and trying to ignore his hunger, Jack agreed, "Yeah, rationing potato and nacho chips isn't a solution. Besides, all that salt makes me thirsty, and we are running low on water."

Heading back, Anne folded her arms to keep warm and lowered her eyebrows. This involuntary action was something she tended to do when thinking deeply. An idea entered her head—a place where they might go. But she quickly drove it from her mind and said instead,

"Let's focus on getting gas and food tomorrow. Then we'll figure out where to go and what to do next."

* * *

> Saturday, December 27th
> Grand Council Chamber, Justice Ecumenical Society United (JESU) World HQ, Vatican City
> Near Midnight

Wisps of smoke and the smell of incense filled the chamber where the JESU Grand Council was about to meet in an emergency session.

Chairman Popovic instructed, "Close the doors and leave us."

The guards left the room, and Popovic told the scribe, "This is an off-the-record discussion. You don't need to take notes. Is that understood?"

The recordkeeper nodded, put down his pen, and the chairman began to speak.

"After today's disaster in the Middle East, do we all agree that something beyond catastrophic is occurring?"

The only sound was the nervous tapping on the dais of the chairman's ceremonial ring. Without a single word uttered, the grave facial expressions of the Council members answered the chairman's question.

Rabbi Tannenbaum glanced at his peers and finally broke the silence. "I have asked for answers from our biblical and religious studies scholars, but thus far, they have been unable to shed any light on these events."

"So where does this leave us?" the alarmed chairman questioned.

"In the dark, I am afraid, Maximus," the rabbi regretfully responded. "While the Book of Revelation makes mention of an earthquake, the timing and location of recent events do not align with any apocalyptic texts."

Chairman Popovic turned to his right and asked, "Cardinal Borghese, do you have anything to add?"

The Catholic Council delegate cleared his throat. He sipped some water and responded, "At this moment, there are many frightened people around the world. As much as we want answers, we need to minister to their needs as well, as we did during the plagues of the Middle Ages."

"Thank you for that reminder, Francesco," the chairman acknowledged. "JESU's history has been one of service to humankind in its darkest moments, which is as important as the protection from evil we provide."

Knock. Knock. Knock.

"Come in," Popovic answered. Turning to the Council members, he said, "I have requested an update from Master Gyatso's IT team on the communications issues with our field staff."

A bald monk wearing bright orange and white Buddhist robes entered the chamber and stood at the dais next to Chairman Popovic. Bowing, the cleric said, "Greetings and salutations to you, Council members. Time is a precious commodity, so I will not waste it further. As you know, we remain incommunicado with the field agents. The destruction of satellite technology has seriously impacted our operations, but I am afraid I am the bearer of potentially even more troubling news."

Chairman Popovic frowned and guardedly asked, "What now?"

The monk folded his hands, almost prayer-like, and answered, "Sir, Master Gyatso believes we may be compromised and our systems hacked."

The Council chamber was abuzz with whispers. The chairman held up his hand, signaling his request for silence, and the holy man continued.

"He requests seventy-two hours to be certain of what has happened and will brief the Council personally on December 31st."

The chairman rose from his chair and solemnly stated,

"All subcommittee work will continue, and we will reconvene in three days. Meeting adjourned."

* * *

> Sunday, December 28th
> Route 76 Pennsylvania Turnpike, Sideling Hill Rest Area
> Late Afternoon

Jack pulled the SUV next to a gas pump and began exiting the vehicle to fill up the tank. An attendant approached him and said, "I'm sorry, sir, but I must do it manually. The automatic pumps are out of commission after the explosion the other day."

Anne poked her head out from the back seat and asked, "How long will that take?"

The attendant sighed and responded, "A while, ma'am."

Pointing toward a brick building with fellow travelers coming in and out like worker bees from a hive, Anne told Jack, "I'm going in to find a convenience store."

She handed him money to pay for the gas and inquired, "Is there anything in particular you want?"

"If they have a chicken nuggets meal for David, that would be great," Jack answered in a hopeful tone.

Anne gave Jack a thumbs up. "I'm on it. See you in a little while."

* * *

A half-hour later, the pungent smell of gasoline filled the air around the vehicle as the attendant continued to pump the gas by hand. A heavily armed National Guardsman passed by, and Jack pulled down his baseball cap to shield his face from view. He watched the numbers on the gas pump spinning higher and higher until they stopped at a total of $180. Jack opened and closed his eyes several times at the figure, shocked at the $8 per gallon price.

"What the hell happened that caused us to have eight-dollar gasoline?" Jack shook his head and wondered aloud. "Did we go to war with Iran or something?"

Returning with armfuls of groceries, Anne chimed in, startling Jack, "No, but the news isn't much better."

Jack grabbed two brown paper bags with some provisions from Anne and helped put them in the trunk. Extremely curious, he quickly asked,

"What happened?"

"A massive earthquake yesterday," Anne announced as she slammed the trunk shut and leaned against the SUV. "It destroyed the largest oil field and refinery in Saudi Arabia. The world instantly lost 25% of its oil supply, probably for good."

Anne gulped down some Tylenol for her headache and continued, "Our strategic oil reserves are at their lowest level in over thirty years. Overnight, the price went through the roof. The news ticker on the television inside indicated that the fires in Saudi oilfields are still burning."

"Jesus." Jack let out a deep breath. "I thought the large police presence at that plane crash site along the way was unusual, but this explains the National Guard being in full force here at the hospitality area."

"I don't think we need to be concerned about any APBs on you, Jack," Anne stated. "The government and law enforcement have a much bigger problem."

Jack declared, "Looting, food shortages, and supply chain issues are at the top of that list, I suppose."

Anne nodded. "Worse than that, I'm afraid. A full-blown panic is a real possibility."

* * *

The gas tank was finally full, and Anne moved the SUV to a parking lot near the picnic area. Jack reached between the seats from the rear and handed David a chicken nugget meal.

"It's not Chick-fil-A," David observed.

Jack replied, "I know, but it's the best we can do right now."

David began shoveling the salty waffle-cut fries into his mouth.

Jack observed, "I guess hunger is one way to solve picky eating."

Jack peered over at Louis, who sat in the back with his face to the wall. Still reeling from losing his phone and the lifeline to his social network, he had not spoken or eaten much in the past two days. Daphne had her head in Louis's lap, seemingly trying to comfort him. Louis gently stroked her gingersnap-colored fur.

Jack scratched the hair under his ball cap. Worried, he murmured, "On the other hand, if I don't get my hands on some macaroni and cheese for Louis, we might have a hunger strike on our hands."

Despite the cold, Jack and Anne sat down at a picnic table to converse out of the range of David and Louis's ears. The occasional woosh of the traffic from the interstate and the smell of diesel exhaust from the trucks were noticeable. Jack observed the two boys like a hawk, ready to break up another fight. Anne slid half a turkey sandwich to Jack as he sipped hot coffee from a recycled paper cup.

"Interestingly, you brought up Jesus before," Anne asserted. "In addition to the earthquake, the extreme cold over Christmas damaged or killed most of the citrus fruit crop in Arizona, Florida, and California."

Jack's eyes met Anne's as he responded with little emotion, "So, you're thinking all of this, from the tragedy in Barbados to the explosion on Christmas morning, and now a massive earthquake in a place where seismic activity is almost unheard of, is all connected?"

Between bites of her sandwich, Anne replied, "You disagree?"

"On the contrary." Jack grabbed a napkin and wiped a drop of mustard from his lips. "When Louis and David lost their connection with Heaven, I was concerned that something had happened. These incidents and their communication blackout are more evidence than is necessary to convince me that we have a serious problem."

Jack hesitated, then added, "It's got Lucius's fingerprints all over it."

"It may be worse than that." Anne thumped her chest several times with her fist and then continued,

"Sorry. I must have eaten too quickly. I've got a little indigestion. With everything going on with George and the upheaval in the aftermath of rescuing the boys, I haven't had a chance to tell you something the demon disclosed to me the first time I tortured him."

"Okay." Jack gulped. "What is it?"

Anne locked eyes with Jack. "You were wrong about Prosperine. She's no infant."

Almost on cue, a rush of wind blew through the picnic area, nearly bending the brown stems of the dead ornamental grass to the ground. Jack's red nose and rosy cheeks seemed to disappear instantly, replaced by a pale white complexion. Speechless, his jaw hung open, and only the sting of the cold wind on his face caused him to close it. The wind abated, and Anne continued,

"The daughter of the devil is a full-grown woman."

Jack shook his head back and forth in disbelief, finally offering up a rapid-fire series of questions.

"How can that be? Are you sure the demon wasn't messing with you? It's not possible."

"Demons indeed lie," Anne admitted. "But I'm confident that it is the truth."

Jack blinked several times and then rubbed his eyes. The deep seams in his forehead betrayed his uneasiness, if not outright fear.

Anne didn't sugarcoat her next disclosure because Jack needed to hear the whole truth.

"She feeds by sucking the life out of humans."

Before she could finish, Jack interrupted, "Like Maricela Antonescu. And let me guess. Louis and David are at the top of the menu."

"Unfortunately, yes," Anne confirmed in a firm tone. She reached into her purse and handed Jack a deck of playing cards. As he began to thumb through them, she studied the reaction on his face. "Do you remember our military discussing in the aftermath of the Iraq war how they were using a deck of playing cards to help identify and track down persons of interest, including Saddam?"

Jack nodded as he stopped to examine a picture he had recognized. It was his own.

Anne added, "This is your brother's version. Instructions are to take the boys alive and deliver them to Prosperine. These are her own words: 'I want to taste prophet.'"

* * *

Anne finished walking Daphne and checked on Louis and David. Both boys were asleep, so she returned to the picnic table. It was completely dark now, and Jack appeared not to have moved a muscle. The truth about Prosperine hit him hard and seemed to trouble him far more deeply than any of the other disastrous events of the last few days, almost as much as the death of his sisters and even his brother. Jack finished the last sip of his now ice-cold coffee and crushed the cup in his hand. Somehow, despite the rising wind, he managed to toss it in the garbage container on the first try.

"Good shot," Anne said, trying to lighten the mood slightly.

Jack smiled half-heartedly and responded, "You should have seen me in junior high. I was our sixth man, the first one off the bench.

That really frosted George. He always thought he was better. There are stories I could tell you...."

Holding up the deck of playing cards Anne gave him, Jack asked, "Is it okay if I keep these?"

"Sure," Anne responded. Curious, she inquired, "Why do you want them?"

Sidestepping her question, Jack stated, "I didn't recognize a lot of the people in the pictures."

"Most of them are high-level members of JESU," Anne answered. "I guess George had his sights set on them too."

Jack raised his arms above his head to stretch, and Anne cringed upon hearing several cracking noises from his shoulder joints. She probed, "Didn't that hurt?"

Jack answered, "It sounds worse than it feels. In the morning, I can give new meaning to the terms snap, crackle, and pop." Another blast of wind nearly blew his hat off, but Jack grabbed it and pulled it down tightly. "What do we do now, Anne? How do we protect Louis and David from Prosperine, Lucius, and the whole cast of demon characters?"

Reluctantly, Anne responded, "Jack, I think we need to stop running from one safe house to the next."

Grabbing Jack's hand, she rubbed his cold fingertips gently to warm them. Then she dropped a bombshell. "We need to go into hiding."

"Hiding?" Jack answered with a question. "What are you saying? Do you mean like Anne Frank hiding?"

Anne nodded. "Exactly."

Astonished and curious, Jack asked, "But where? Is there any place they will not be able to find us? And do we have a place that offers the kind of protection for the boys that is necessary?"

"I think I know a place, Jack. It's on Long Island, near where you and Mark Desmond grew up."

Anne spread a map from her jacket pocket on the picnic table. They held the edges down against the breeze, and there was just enough illumination from the solar-powered streetlight for Jack to follow her suggested plan.

"Just in case, we'll take rural roads to stay off anyone's radar screen until we get closer to Philadelphia."

Energized by Anne's suggestion and feeling hopeful, Jack leaped to his feet. "Let's do it! You can tell me about the rest on the way."

Jack sheepishly asked as they approached the car, "Do you mind driving? I don't like going over bridges."

CHAPTER 28

> *Tuesday, December 30th*
> *Plaza at Pergamon*
> *3:00 a.m.*

As the witching hour approached, heat lightning lit up the dark red skies above Pergamon like charcoal briquettes fanned by a blower in a fiery blacksmith forge. The smell of diesel exhaust emanated from the coal that burned in the ceremonial torches that lit the square. Standing stiffly at attention, demon legionnaires dressed all in black, ready for battle, filled the vast plaza as far as the eye could see. In great anticipation, they whispered to one another.

"Do you see them yet?"

A disturbance around the columns of the marble, Roman-style portico that led to Pergamon's inner sanctum signaled the arrival of the conquering heroes. Surrounded by an honor guard, Princess Prosperine, escorted by the evil mastermind, Lucius Rofocale, paraded across the amphitheater stage to thunderous applause.

The soldiers strained to glimpse the princess as she emerged from a stairwell dressed in ceremonial crimson vestments from head to toe. Her robe flapped in the steady wind running through the open court. Reaching a golden throne, Prosperine raised a blood-red diamond tiara high above her head, showing it to the legions, then affirmed her royal title by crowning herself. Joined by Lucius on the viewing stand, the demonic duo towered over the mass of armed forces below, who erupted in a prolonged ovation and shouted cheers of praise that shook the ground.

Underneath the VIP box stood a priest in a scarlet robe embroidered with yellow pentagrams on the sleeves, wearing a goat's head mask with prominent curled horns as a headdress. The thunder rolled as the priest stepped to a podium. An almost supernatural silence immediately settled over the mass of warriors, and the wind abated as the shaman began to speak.

"The presence or absence of leadership can determine the rise and fall of a civilization."

The acoustics of the venue were perfect and required no microphone. Facing Prosperine and Lucius, the cleric, arms upraised, paid tribute to their triumph.

"Along with our Lord Lucifer, behold the leaders who have delivered victory over God and his angels!"

More shouts of adoration rose from the legions, filling the plaza. The deafening roar echoed through the hills surrounding Pergamon as Prosperine and Lucius basked in the glory of their conquest. After ten minutes, the plaza fell quiet again after the princess and Lucius returned to their seats.

The priest resumed speaking and declared, "We pledge our loyalty to their leadership once more. We need nothing more!"

In unison, the armies of darkness raised their weapons in the air. Drowning out the thunder in the skies above, they affirmed,

"We swear our eternal allegiance and loyalty to our Father, Lucifer, his daughter, Princess Prosperine, and Lord Rofocale! Death to all who oppose them!"

Waving a hand in a gesture calling for silence, the priest continued.

"Commanded by our Princess and Lord Rofocale, we all share a common pride, being members of the legions of doom. They have revealed several truths to us: Nothing is possible unless one, and only one, will commands—a will obeyed from top to bottom; Our strength lies not in defense but in the quickness and brutality of our attack; The essential element of success is the constant and regular employment of violence against others!"

The malevolent minister gestured furiously, slamming fists repeatedly on the dais, declaring,

"But the application of force alone can never bring about the destruction of an ideal or prevent the propagation of it. One must be ready and able to ruthlessly exterminate the final upholders of that ideal and wipe out any tradition it may tend to leave behind!

"You and I have a rendezvous with destiny! The struggle for survival is about conquest. If demons are to live, then humans must die. In life, one is either a hammer or an anvil. Our race is to be a hammer!"

As the crowd roared, the priest pulled a deck of playing cards from inside the podium and demanded,

"You each have one of these. Take the cards out and look at them! These are our adversaries! Sear their faces in your mind! You will hunt and track them down like a jackal on the prowl in the darkness. For nearly 1,000 years, demons have waged war with our mortal enemy for the soul of humanity. Tomorrow, this war will end! We do not waste words any longer. We act! We will be hard, without mercy, and operate with the quickness and brutality our leaders exemplify!"

* * *

Standing before the stage, Tatiana was mesmerized and inspired by the speaker, but the moment she had really been waiting for had now arrived. Guards roughly shoved a hooded figure, bound in chains, onto the stage and into a position next to the priest. Tatiana pushed and elbowed her way to a spot right in front of the prisoner. She wanted to ensure that the first thing the captive saw when a guard removed the hood was her face.

* * *

Arms folded, the cleric waited for silence. A hush fell over the gathering. Silently, each demon wondered who was now on stage and what would happen next. The speaker loudly stated,

"The power and effectiveness of a good organization is even greater when discipline prevails. Obedience to the small details leads to greater results."

Removing the mask and headdress, the priest revealed his identity. Murmurs and low voices rushed through the plaza like wildfire.

"It can't be," a general standing next to Tatiana said to his lieutenant as he shook his head. "He's supposed to be dead."

The aide replied, "I know, but don't forget the rumor we heard. No one admitted to finding a corpse."

* * *

Tatiana eavesdropped on the conversation and smiled broadly. She knew the truth. After all, the ceremony had been personally planned and orchestrated by Lucius. While his ego relished the glory and adoration he received, the message about to be sent to the legions was equally important to him. Ruling by fear and intimidation was always Lucius's mantra, something Tatiana had come to understand. Still, the real secret, other than the priest's identity, was that Tatiana laid the groundwork for what was about to happen, and she had learned from the best.

* * *

Shockingly, George Aitken revealed himself to be the high priest. The actual consequence of Anne Bishop's arrow was not death, but a black patch covering his right eye socket.

He thundered at the demon legions. "I took command and expected obedience!"

His nostrils flared in anger at the hooded prisoner. Nearly foaming at the mouth, he pointed to his injured eye.

"This permanent souvenir of incompetence is what I received instead! Now, look upon the face of failure!"

George rushed over and ripped the hood from the prisoner's head, exposing Barbas, the lieutenant responsible for eliminating Anne Bishop. He locked his jaw as he warned Barbas, "I'm about to show you that life does not forgive weakness."

Bewildered, Barbas blinked several times to get his bearings. Finally realizing the peril, he pleaded, "Lord Aitken, let me exp—"

Before he could finish the sentence, George viciously slapped Barbas across the face, causing a split lip. Blood oozed down the demon's chin and dripped onto the stage.

George curtly answered, "Excuses won't compensate for the loss of my eyesight and, more importantly, the escape of my brother and the two prophets. You had one responsibility only, and that was to eliminate Anne Bishop. You failed!"

* * *

Down front, Tatiana somehow managed to restrain her glee. While George Aitken lectured the legions further about the danger of failure, she waved at Barbas, finally getting his attention. She pretended to dial a phone and mouthed at her tormentor, *"I texted Anne Bishop."*

Barbas's head dropped, signaling that he now knew that Tatiana had set him up. He also was aware that trying to convince anyone of her treachery would do no good. Realizing she got the best of him, he locked eyes with her one last time.

Grinning like the cat who ate the canary, she whispered to Barbas, "The best form of payback is…."

Tatiana paused and finished her sentence, "Revenge."

She blew a kiss goodbye in Barbas's direction and melted into the crowd.

***

George held an object in front of Barbas and asked him, "Do you know what this is?"

Knowing the fate that awaited him, Barbas did not bother to answer.

"Well, let me tell you." George paused, then said, "Better yet, let me show you!"

George savagely plunged the arrow Anne had shot him with into Barbas's eye, saying, "You know what they say in their good book: an eye for an eye."

Screaming in agony, Barbas fell to his knees as George twisted the crossbow bolt deeper into Barbas's socket.

"Get him up!" George screamed at the hesitant guards, who quickly picked Barbas up.

Dazed and blinded, Barbas could not recognize what George was now showing to the demon legions. He did hear Lucius's acolyte say, however, "Anne Bishop shoved this down the throat of one of Barbas's team members after she tortured him. She did it as a warning, and I will use it to warn all of you about the consequences of failing me!"

George deliberately approached Barbas, grabbed him firmly by the hair, and shouted, "Open wide!"

He then rammed the phone into the demon's mouth, shattering Barbas's teeth as he did so.

"Stand back," George told the guards, who dropped the traumatized, whimpering Barbas to the floor.

The blood vessels in George's remaining eye had burst from his maniacal ranting. Now a crazed soul walking around with blood in his eye, George shouted to the shocked demon army one last time.

"Bear witness to the price of failure!"

George pressed a button on the podium, which triggered the cell phone in Barbas's mouth. It rang once—

BOOM!

The explosion blew Barbas's head to bits. George wiped the shards of bone, pieces of brain, and flesh from his face. He asked the legions he now commanded, "Are there any questions?"

There were none—just a silence where someone might hear a pin drop or crickets chirping. Satisfied, George nodded and announced, "Good! Remember, failure is not an option!"

* * *

The sound of boots striking the ground reverberated as unit after unit of the demon army marched in lockstep, saluting Prosperine and Lucius before they departed to fulfill George Aitken's orders.

Lord Aitken knelt before his master and the princess. "I will see to directive one of this mission, my Lord, personally. Once fulfilled, and with the Princess's permission, I will make the goal of finding the prophets my only responsibility."

"Permission granted, Lord Aitken," Prosperine cooed. "I am so looking forward to meeting your nephews and your brother."

Prosperine paused and added, "This Anne Bishop seems an intriguing character, too. Turning her faith into fear and sucking her dry sounds enticing. Don't you agree, Lucius?"

"Yes, Princess," Lucius answered, then thinking about Mark Desmond, he cautioned, "But we may find that even a former JESU member can be a worthy adversary."

As Prosperine continued to revel in the review of her demon army, Lucius pulled George Aitken aside, saying,

"Well done, Lord Aitken. You sent the legions a message they will not soon forget."

Staring at George's face, Lucius could not help but see a resemblance to his brother, Kazimir.

"That eyepatch reminds me of someone I used to know." Lucius sneered and whispered, "Someone that I killed, actually."

"My Lord?" George asked, having not heard what Lucius said.

"Never mind." Lucius hesitated before continuing, "You will catch our enemy off guard. You know what I expect of you. Remember, no clemency or forbearance."

George bowed and replied, "Your counsel will ensure a victorious campaign. Your confidence in my ability to carry out this next phase of our operation is humbling. I promise that it will not be misplaced."

"Your handling of Barbas's failure validates my faith in you, Lord Aitken. The next time we meet, I expect it will be with news of our triumph."

"Master Lucius, I promise you a great victory tomorrow!"

***

> Tuesday, December 30th
> Queensboro Bridge
> 8:00 a.m.

"A snail can move faster than this!" Anne fumed as she impatiently tapped the steering wheel with her fingers. The SUV inched forward on the entrance ramp to the Queensboro Bridge.

"Welcome to New York City, Anne," Jack chuckled nervously, moving closer to the armrest between them to avoid looking down at the East River. "Wait until we reach 495 East, the Long Island Expressway. I guarantee it will not live up to its name."

"It has to be better than this!" she retorted.

Jack impishly grinned. "Spoken by someone who has never experienced driving on the longest parking lot in the world!"

HONK!

The vehicle ahead of them slammed its horn in a pointless attempt to make the traffic move faster.

"Damn!" Anne said, shaking her head, exasperated, before apologizing for her language. "Sorry, guys!"

Bark!

Scratching Daphne under her chin, Anne added, "Sorry to you too!"

Daphne hopped into the backseat and curled up in a ball between the boys. Louis whispered something to David that Jack could not hear. The brothers laughed, and a feeling of relief washed over their father. Finally, they appeared to be getting past the destruction of their cell phones. Jack exhaled.

The trip through Pennsylvania gave them plenty of time to work through the issue.

Anne had mapped out a route to avoid tolls and minimize the number of potential cameras that might catch their license plate number or faces. In a small town, she even found a thrift shop for them to buy new clothes. Rural roads in Pennsylvania eventually took them to the Newburgh-Beacon Bridge. Outside of Peekskill, New York, they caught Route 87 South and, ultimately, the FDR Drive. Even the Queensboro bridge had no toll heading toward Long Island.

I guess, once a cop, always a cop.

Jack wondered, *Or is it once a super-secret religious society member, always—*

"Dad, what's that?" David shouted, interrupting Jack's musing. He pointed out the window at a red tramway car slowly moving down its cables.

"That's a cable car," Jack answered. "It goes to Roosevelt Island."

Louis curiously asked, "A desert island?"

"Not quite." Jack smiled. "Nearly 10,000 people live down there."

* * *

Still crawling across the bridge, forty-five minutes later, caused the boys to pick up their Nintendo DS and headphones. This diversion gave Jack an opening he had been waiting for.

"I can't help feeling banished, Anne." Jack glanced over his shoulder at his sons. "Sort of like Moses being expelled from Egypt and driven into the wilderness. Why Lake Ronkonkoma? What I mean is, what makes it a good place to hide?"

"Decades ago," Anne responded, "Mark told me about an exorcism performed there in the 18th century."

"An exorcism?" Jack shifted uncomfortably in his seat.

Anne exhaled loudly, still frustrated by the traffic jam they found themselves in. She bit her lip and replied, "Mark described it as a complicated struggle. A legion of demons possessed a man. It took several days of almost non-stop prayer and recitation of the rite to break their hold on the man's soul."

Recalling the story caused Anne to stare out the windshield. The blare of a car horn nudged her back to the present as she allowed a car entering the highway to merge ahead.

Jack asked, "Doesn't that make it an unusual spot for a hiding place?"

"Let me put it this way," Anne responded. "The man's family was so grateful for his successful redemption that they agreed to become guardians. Sentinels, if you will. Mark said a secret annex was built in the home and stocked with enough food to feed four people for at least a year."

Jack commented, "After that experience, I understand why the family would agree to do it."

Jack looked down at the floor as he spoke. "Mark's legacy is complicated, isn't it? He performed far more virtuous acts than he gets credit for these days."

The car was now at a complete stop, and Anne mindlessly twisted her hair with a finger as she answered,

"He believed in preparing for the unexpected and the seemingly impossible."

Anne turned, and her eyes met Jack's.

"Mark warned me that there might come a time when going into hiding would be necessary to save the order."

Jack took her statement further. "Or save the world?"

"Uh-huh," Anne agreed. "He studied the apocalypse extensively."

Jack bit his nails nervously. "Something else just occurred to me. Who else knows about this place? With the world on the verge of chaos, someone else might get the same idea."

"Unlikely," Anne quickly answered. "Mark said he camped at Lake Ronkonkoma every summer. The home is isolated, and few people know about it."

Anne paused and gripped the steering wheel tightly before continuing.

"In fact, to most people, it appears as trees and mist. It is invisible, except to those who know the secret incantation that reveals its location."

Anne frowned. She removed her left hand from the steering wheel and shook it several times.

"I must be holding the wheel too tight, or perhaps it is all the driving I've been doing. My arm is sore."

She ruefully added, "Besides, with so much turnover at JESU, I'm the only one of Mark's protegees still alive who knows how to crack the code and break the spell."

* * *

> *Twelve Hours Later*
> *Outskirts of Lake Ronkonkoma*
> *8:00 p.m.*

Daphne stood in Jack's lap, looking out the window and fogging it with every breath. Sensing they were nearing their destination, she wagged her tail incessantly.

"In a few miles, take the next right," Jack directed as he scratched Daphne's back. "It will be Smithtown Boulevard."

"Got it," Anne acknowledged and said with a hint of relief, "Thanks for recommending an alternative route. I couldn't stand the Long Island Expressway any longer."

"You mean the highway to Hell!" Jack moaned. "It was shocking to see all those abandoned vehicles."

"Most of them ran out of gas and were just left there," Anne responded. "This gasoline shortage is going to be no joke."

Further reconciling himself to their decision, Jack murmured, "Another reason going into hiding could be a good idea."

Cracking open the window for some fresh air, Jack added, "I'm impressed that you had the money to pay for gas at these prices." He shook his head and moaned, "$12 a gallon and climbing. It's unbelievable."

"Well, they say everything is more expensive in New York," Anne joked. "Besides, my JESU training is kind of ingrained in me, if you know what I mean."

The cold air was invigorating, and Jack pointed to a road sign, saying, "If you grew up here, you don't notice the cost factor until you leave."

"I'm sure glad you know your way around here, Jack," Anne said as she took the right turn.

"George..." Jack paused and continued, "And I went to SUNY Stony Brook. We would drive around on Thursday night before we went home for the weekend. While we never stopped at Lake Ronkonkoma, we went through this area a few times. No one knew the backroads and hidden places better than he did."

Most of the streetlights were dark, and it was pitch black outside. Jack strained to read the road signs. He mumbled, "We just went through the Route 93 intersection. I am certain that Shore Road will be coming up shortly. I know it."

"Are we almost there, Dad?" David asked. "I need to go to the bathroom."

"Timing is everything," Jack grumbled softly before answering, "Almost. Hang in there."

* * *

"HERE!" Jack shouted. "TURN HERE!"

Anne quickly pulled the steering wheel down, and the car skidded onto an unfinished road.

"SHIT!" Anne called out as she pumped the brakes before they came to a complete stop.

Anne leaned into the back seat to check on Louis and David and asked, "Is everyone okay?"

Both boys nodded affirmatively. Jack rubbed his forehead and replied, "Just a bump on my head."

He looked down at Daphne, still in his lap, panting slightly but unharmed.

"She's okay, too."

Jack looked out the window and gestured. "There's a sign to the left, Anne. It says Lake Ronkonkoma County Park."

"We're almost there," Anne replied. "If what Mark told me is correct, this should be Shore Road. A driveway leading to a house near the lake is chained off. Let's follow the road and see."

The compacted sand road tracked along the shore of Lake Ronkonkoma for several miles. Anne slowly drove the SUV past several picnic areas, a fishing pier, and a playground before coming to a cul-de-sac.

"End of the road," Anne said. She pulled the vehicle around the circle and parked.

Jack unlocked the door and, once outside, handed Daphne's leash to Louis and cautioned, "Hold on to this tightly."

A dense fog hung around their knees, but as Anne spoke a Latin incantation, it seemed like the night mist simply parted as the Red Sea did for Moses.

"Jack, look." Anne pointed at two weathered concrete columns, which appeared as the fog retreated. A rusty, weathered chain groaned in the breeze, and despite the overgrown brush, a private drive on the other side was visible.

"Let's go." He gestured to David and Louis, who, with Daphne in tow, followed closely behind Anne and their father.

The air was cold, but a bead of sweat still ran down Jack's back. The leaves crunched under their shoes as they slowly walked up a gravel road that seemed to manifest itself with each step they took.

"We must be near the water," Jack whispered to Anne. "I can hear the water lapping up on the shore."

"Yeah, me too," Anne added, then she stopped. Pointing into the darkness, she guessed, "Look, Jack, in the distance, I think I see the outline of a house."

Deliberately, they moved forward. Suddenly, Jack's jaw fell open, and he gushed, "Look at that wraparound porch and the cedar shake shingles." He put his hands on his hips, admiring the home. "It's Victorian-era architecture for sure."

Surprised, Anne asked, "How do you know that?"

"I took a course in architecture in college," Jack replied. "I've always wanted to own a home like this."

The sweet scent of cherry pipe tobacco suddenly filled the air. Jack started to ask,

"Do you smell…"

G-R-O-W-L

"What is it, girl?" Anne heard Daphne signal a warning and reached for her gun.

A stick snapped, and a rough, gravelly voice emanated from the shadows, forcefully instructing Anne, "Take your hand out of your coat, miss. Do it slowly."

Anne complied, and then someone sternly told them, "All of you. Slowly put your hands up."

G-R-O-W-L

Daphne growled again. A click, the sound of a shell loading into a shotgun, echoed through the darkness.

"I won't tell you again," the same voice said, but in an even more strident tone. "Get your damn hands up!"

"JACK," Anne called out, grabbing her chest as she fell to her knees and slumped.

Jack dove to her side. Frantic, he asked the figure in the dark, "She needs help! We need to get her somewhere safe!"

A voice replied, "No such place exists anymore, son."

*　*　*

> Wednesday, December 31st
> Grand Council Chamber, Justice Ecumenical Society
> United (JESU) World HQ, Vatican City
> 9:00 p.m.

"Has anyone heard from Reverend Prince today?" Chairman Popovic asked aloud. He ran his fingers through his thinning hair, saying, "He told me he would attend tonight's briefing."

Holding up his phone, Rabbi Tannenbaum responded in frustration, "I have not seen Derek nor been able to communicate with any of my field contacts for the last twenty-four hours."

"I share your concerns, rabbi," Imam Kamil Mufti added. Perturbed, he forcefully exhaled. "I am also in the proverbial dark with my agents."

T-H-U-D!

Startled, Hindu Swami Aghamkar jumped from his chair at the sound of an object striking the table behind him.

"My God!" Cardinal Borghese shouted in horror. "It's the reverend!"

The corpse that had once been Reverend Derek Prince lay shattered on the floor. His blond hair, usually neatly combed, was matted with blood streaming from fresh wounds on his head. His eyes stared into space while several teeth dangled from the sockets of his dislocated jaw.

Rabbi Tannenbaum knelt beside the body, checking for a pulse. Realizing the reverend was dead, he feverishly searched the room for something to cover the body while anxiously asking,

"Who could have done this?"

Looking to the rafters of the Council chamber, Chairman Popovic demanded, "Guards! Search the place!"

C-R-A-S-H!

The heavy oak doors of the chamber became projectiles as they flew into the room, followed by another body cold-bloodedly tossed at the feet of Chairman Popovic. The overpowered guards, their lances held tightly across their throats, were steered into the room and roughly shoved to their knees. Dressed in black, from his eye patch to his shoes, George Aitken entered the room, a wicked smile on his lips, cynically announcing,

"I don't think that search is necessary."

Studying the picture on the card he held in the palm of his hand, he sneered as he addressed the chairman, "Father Maximus Popovic, I presume."

George snapped his fingers, and a swarm of demons quickly filled the chamber and detained each Council member. Struggling to free himself from several of his captors, the chairman angrily demanded,

"Identify yourself! Who are you?"

"I am Lucius Rofocale's disciple!" A wild-eyed George eagerly answered, "And I am here doing the Devil's work!"

The mere mention of Lucius's name caused the Council members to shoot concerned glances at one another. Pointing at the dead figure on the floor, George sarcastically stated,

"I found Master Gyatso for you, but I'm afraid he won't have much of a report to provide."

George pointed at his Lieutenants and ordered, "Confiscate their cellphones."

Defiantly, Chairman Popovic shouted, "That will do you no good! They are all encrypted with the most sophisticated security protocols."

George grinned and began to laugh. His evil cackle filled the chamber and then subsided as he mockingly asked,

"Like the computer security that prevented us from locating this secret chamber?"

Standing in the center of the room, George Aitken boldly proclaimed, "At this very moment, around the globe, your field agents are being eliminated. Not only did we hack your systems to find your sacred headquarters, but we have tracked the location of every operative in JESU!"

George's stride was full of swagger as he walked across the floor and got in the chairman's face. His bloodshot eye locked onto the chairman's, and he gleefully declared, "Right now, Satan is sitting on the throne of Heaven! In a matter of hours, no trace of JESU will remain. It will disappear—along with it, the last line of defense preventing the armies of darkness from marching over the face of the Earth!"

Catching his breath, George proudly asserted, "The game's finally over, chairman. Your side lost!"

George turned and headed for the exit. As he paraded out of the chamber like a victorious Roman general, he shouted out one last command.

"Bolt the doors. Then kill them! Kill them all!"

EPILOGUE

Two Weeks Later
Computer Room at Pergamon

The noise of hundreds of fanatic computer programmers busily tapping away on their laptops filled the room while code breakers, like an army of ants, worked to decipher and understand the steady volume of new information.

George Aitken scratched his forehead and asked, "How many phones have we decrypted so far?"

"About one hundred, Master," the Chief Technology Officer replied. "But we still have thousands yet to decode."

Summoning his demon team leaders, he questioned, "What is the status of the hunt for the remaining JESU agents?"

"Sir, we have captured every agent from the cards you provided except for your brother, nephews, and Anne Bishop."

A second demon lieutenant added, "We continue to pick up a few lower-level JESU operatives, but the four we just referenced have seemingly disappeared. We have not picked up their trail since they left an abandoned brewery in Pennsylvania."

George rubbed his tired eyes and rolled his stiff shoulders to stretch his muscles. Then, he demanded, "Turn up the heat on your interrogations and advise me of what you find out." Waving his hand, he said, "I have some other business to attend. Dismissed."

***

Descending from the final steps of the long, spiral staircase leading from the surface to the cave system under Pergamon, a blast of hot air struck George Aitken like a slap across the face. After the nearly one-hour trek, beads of sweat poured down his temples, and he used his shirt sleeve to wipe the perspiration from his brow. Finding the foreman he entrusted with his construction project, he inquired, "Are we nearing the end?"

The foreman stood at attention and answered, "Yes, Lord Aitken. When you give the order, we are ready."

"Very good," George responded enthusiastically, rubbing his palms together. "Let's get on with it."

George turned the corner and walked down a steadily narrowing, torch-lit corridor that opened into a room-size cavity. His wife, Josephine, and their three children were already in the space with chains around their ankles and wrists. The light from the torches reflected off the crystal embedded in the bits of granite littering the cavern floor, remnants of the drilling and digging that created the chamber. A sharp, acrid odor from the smoke of burnt rocks still hung in the air. With a hateful look, Josephine glared at George as he entered.

"I can't say it is good to see you again," she angrily uttered. "That eye patch suits you. I just wish that whatever caused your injury could have taken your damn head off entirely!"

George yawned. "Charming, Josephine. Such a lovely thing to say to your beloved husband."

"Beloved, my ass," Josephine scoffed before demanding, "Now let us go! I created the universal decryption software and everything else you asked for!"

"With all due respect," George replied sarcastically and examined his fingernails. "I think you are in no position to make demands of any kind."

"You promised, you bastard!" Josephine's chains rattled as she futilely struggled to free herself.

"I agreed to allow one of the children to be set free." George waved his hand to cool himself and relieve the oppressive heat in the chamber. He asked, "Have you made your choice?"

Josephine leaned in his direction, as far as her chains would allow, and gritted her teeth. The tangled, split ends of her unwashed blonde hair hung around her eyes as she acknowledged, "You know I can't do that!"

"Let Erin or Kate go!" their brother James cried out. His plea echoed down the corridor, and beads of spit hung in his beard as he told his father, "I will stay in their place!"

"No, James!" Erin cried out. "We need to stay together!"

Kate begged, "Daddy, please stop this!"

George ignored his daughters and stood in front of his son. Smirking, he replied, "How chivalrous of you, James."

Turning to Josephine, he cynically added, "I am sure your mother is very proud of you."

His arms outstretched like a preacher delivering a sermon, George smiled and said, "You heard me say I would let one of you go free."

A lengthy, uncomfortable moment of silence filled the chamber until George smugly finished, "I lied."

"I knew it!" Josephine screamed. "You heartless son of a bitch!"

George frowned and spitefully waved his finger in Josephine's face. "You didn't let me finish, dear."

Motioning to the guards, he said, "Unlock their chains. All of them."

In shock, Josephine shot her husband an amazed look. Stunned by his unexpected order, she hesitated before tearfully hugging her children for the first time in weeks. George stood stoically, watching the tender reunion. Finally, he turned to leave.

"Where are you going?" a surprised Josephine asked. "We're going with you. Aren't we?"

The two guards inserted themselves between George and his family. He lightheartedly called out to Josephine.

"On more than one occasion, I joked about our marriage being a life sentence with no chance for parole."

George locked eyes with his spouse. "Who knew I would be such a prophet?"

Bewildered, Josephine replied, "I don't understand. You just gave us our freedom."

"That's right," George replied. "Freedom to move around the chamber you are in."

Josephine skeptically asked, "So we are your prisoners again?"

"Not exactly." George licked the salty sweat from his lips before evasively answering, "You never stopped being my prisoners. Something inside me suggests I must have you and our children close by."

The guards slowly backed out of the chamber while a mason pushed a massive rock toward the entrance. The declining oxygen supply in the room caused the torches to flicker as the flames slowly began to diminish.

"Don't do this, George," Josephine pleaded, realizing his intent. "What about the children?"

George joked, "This way, we will all be together for eternity."

Just before the monolithic stone sealed the chamber, George heard screaming.

"NOOOO!"

Then, as the stone locked into place, the screaming abruptly stopped, and there was nothing but silence.

George stopped, closed his eyes, and murmured, "Ah. Peace and quiet, at last!"

* * *

Later the Same Day
Computer Room at Pergamon

George finished showing Lucius and Prosperine the computer operations center and stopped at a locked, gray, steel door. As he punched the code into the security system, Lucius commented, "This is quite the operation, Lord Aitken."

George pointed his finger around the room, saying, "Master, all this activity is channeled into what is behind this door and intended to lead to one outcome."

With a clicking sound and the release of pressurized air, the door unlocked and slowly began to open. Entering the room, George added,

"Here is the brain that will track down the remaining fugitives."

Prosperine brazenly asked, "You mean your brother and his sons, the prophets?"

"Yes, Princess," George responded. "We have severed the JESU leadership from its proverbial body. We have thoroughly interrogated and eliminated the members of the JESU Council, leaving four remaining high-profile targets."

The sparsely furnished, secured room had only a laptop on a small desk with a chair.

Surveying the space, Prosperine skeptically questioned, "This setup doesn't look very sophisticated compared to what is happening out there. How is this going to track down the prophets?"

George proudly pointed to the computer and answered, "This is a parting gift from my wife. I brought in a dark web hacker to ensure there were no backdoors or chances that she did something clever. It is known as artificial intelligence."

Prosperine glanced at Lucius and shrugged her shoulders.

Lucius asked, "What is artificial intelligence, exactly, Lord Aitken?"

"Master, we are taking all the information being obtained outside this office and feeding it into a database in this computer. The program on this laptop simulates a human brain, but it processes data at speeds far beyond that of a person. As it learns, it develops problem-solving capabilities."

Lucius scowled and asked, "Meaning?"

"I am giving the computer all the information on Anne Bishop we can gather, including aliases she used and the complete summary of her JESU training. I have already discovered she is 48 years old with a birth date of June 6th, 1975. She is an only child with a genius IQ of over 160."

Standing behind the laptop, George confidently affirmed, "Knowing her strengths, weaknesses, and decision-making tendencies will help us anticipate her next move."

George concluded his presentation with a mischievous smile and a gleeful sense of what would come: "If we use this information to locate Anne Bishop, we will find my brother and the prophets, too."

***

Oakland Cemetery, Atlanta, Georgia
Midnight

The misty, smoke-like fog crawled over the red brick walkways and around the ornate marble mausoleums of the cemetery. For several nights, the Strigoi had wandered the forty-eight acres of the graveyard searching for the Antonescu family crypt, and finally, it had located the tomb. As a supernatural entity, it could feel the paranormal energy that seemingly oozed from every grave as its fingers traced the edges of the large letter "A" carved into the sealed door of the burial chamber.

Left. Left. Left, right, left.

The sergeant of a regiment of ghost soldiers in gray uniforms called out a cadence, but the apparitions marched past him without a glance or hint that they recognized the Strigoi's presence. Another soldier, this time wearing a blue uniform with a rope tied around his neck, dangled from a tree limb, swinging in the breeze.

Returning its attention to the Antonescu tomb, the creature whispered, "Antonescu is familiar to me."

The Strigoi turned when a disembodied voice murmured, *"Family."*

A different voice said, *"Relative."*

The beast's eyes narrowed as its brain tried to understand the meaning of the words. It searched its surroundings, hoping to find something that might explain them. The Strigoi exhaled in frustration, releasing a cloud of water vapor that condensed in the cool night air. Looking down, the beast saw an urn in front of the crypt door, filled with fresh flowers. Inserted in the flowers was an object, and the Strigoi reached for it.

"Maricela," the monster muttered, recognizing the red-haired young woman in the photograph.

A gust, high up in the trees, stirred the leaves, and the Strigoi heard a whisper in the wind. Maricela's voice pleaded,

"Avenge me."

Staring at the picture, the Strigoi recalled looking into Maricela's deep blue eyes. The memory brought with it a certain serenity that was suddenly destroyed by a horrific vision. It saw Maricela's desiccated body and another woman standing over it.

Once more, the beast heard Maricela's voice. *"Prosperine."*

A series of flashbacks began running through the Strigoi's brain. The creature clutched its head and staggered back as it witnessed its birth. Then, the entity saw each victim's face and the fear as it took their lives. The Strigoi shook its head violently, trying to stop the pain of what it was experiencing, but it would not relent. It finally came to an end after the monster watched the rape of Maricela.

Leaning against the Antonescu crypt, the Strigoi panted as it tried to catch a breath. It inhaled deeply and admitted, "I understand now. I am an Antonescu."

Wiping the sweat from its brow, the beast vowed, "I created Prosperine. For you, Maricela, I will end her reign."

Clenching its fists, the Strigoi gritted its teeth and shouted angrily, "But you, Lucius. I will kill you for me!"

As its fists slowly opened, the beast stared and said, "It will take more than my brute strength to accomplish this."

After a few minutes, the Strigoi recovered, tucked Maricela's picture in the shirt pocket of the clothes it wore, and headed for the cemetery exit. Instinctively, the creature resumed its journey south.

ABOUT THE AUTHOR

John "J.D." Toepfer is the award-winning author of the riveting *Highway to Hell* series. Literary Titan describes it as *"suspenseful horror that gives readers bits of historical information, occult, and the supernatural, all combined into a thrilling read."* When he is not torturing his characters with unspeakable choices, J.D. often works in his other favorite medium, dirt. An avid gardener, many of J.D.'s best plot twists develop when his fingernails are filthy and the sweat is dripping from his brow.

STAY CONNECTED WITH JD TOEPFER

If you enjoyed this leg of the journey, there's more to explore! Dive deeper into the Highway to Hell Series by visiting our website and becoming part of our vibrant community on social media. Here's where you can join your fellow travelers:

Website: Sign up for our mailing list! Discover exclusive content, behind-the-scenes insights, and the latest updates at www.jdtoepfer.com

Author Pages: Follow J.D., check out upcoming works, and his full biography on—

Goodreads: https://www.goodreads.com/jdtoepfer

Amazon Author Central: https://www.amazon.com/author/j.d.toepfer

Social Media: Connect with us for engaging discussions and a chance to interact with JD Toepfer personally.

Facebook: search for *JD Toepfer, Author* [https://www.facebook.com/profile.php?id=100072007826901]

J.D. loves hearing from his readers and looks forward to sharing the ride! Remember, there are no stoplights or speed limits on the Highway to Hell!

Printed in Great Britain
by Amazon